KINGDOM OF LIES

KINGDOM OF LIES

OF LIES

by Lee Wood

ST. MARTIN'S MINOTAUR

New York ♒

This one is for "our kid," my little sister, Kathryn, of whom I could not be prouder.

www.minotaurbooks.com

Book design by Jonathan Bennett

Library of Congress Cataloging-in-Publication Data

Wood, N. Lee.
    Kingdom of lies / by N. Lee Wood.— 1st ed.
       p. cm.
    ISBN 0-312-34030-3
    EAN 978-0-312-34030-8
    1. Police—England—Leeds—Fiction.   2. College teachers—Crimes against—Fiction.
 3. Congresses and conventions—Fiction.   4. Women college teachers—Fiction.
 5. Americans—England—Fiction.   6. Leeds (England)—Fiction.   I. Title.

PR6073.O613K56 2005
823'.912—dc22

                                                                                2005045997

First Edition: November 2005

10 9 8 7 6 5 4 3 2 1

AUTHOR'S NOTE

While many of the places in this novel are genuine, with the exception of well-known historical and political figures, all characters are imaginary and any resemblance to real persons, living or dead, is coincidental and unintended. All events portrayed in the work, historical or current, are a product of the author's imagination and are completely, totally, and absolutely fictitious.

Well . . .

. . . most of it, anyway.

ACKNOWLEDGMENTS

I am grateful for the invaluable assistance of many people who generously gave of their time and expertise during the writing of this novel.

In West Yorkshire, my warmest thanks to Superintendent John Stewart, retired Superintendent John Moorhouse, Detective Chief Inspector Bob Browell, and Police Constable Phil Hall of Weetwood Police Station and to Police Constable Andy Wellbourne of Pudsey; Stephanie Dickenson of the International Medieval Congress at the University of Leeds; Dr. Stanley Ellis and the Yorkshire Dialect Society; Derek and Joan Green, Cowling; and the Yorkshire Dales Falconry and Conservation Centre in Settle. At Harewood House, I'd like to thank Piers Jackson, Jean Hunter, and former gardens manager David Walker, with a special thank-you to Trevor Nicholson, gardens manager. I'd also like to apologize to all the staff of Harewood House for dropping a dead body in the midst of their beautiful and gracious estate.

In Staffordshire, many thanks to Audrey and the late Michael Rogers, MRCVS, of Cheadle; the staff of Hanley Police Station, Stoke-on-Trent; Police Constable David Eivers, Tean; and Sarah Rogers Spruce, former WPC, Cheadle. A very special thank-you to Sergeant Simon Street, Staffordshire Police, for enthusiasm and guidance above and beyond the call of duty.

In London, I'd like to thank Chief Inspector Paul Morris, I.D. Officer Rosalyn Edholm, and Scene of Crime Officer Ashley Barrow of the Metropolitan Police; John and Judith Clute of Camden Town; Tania Rose and Marna Glyn of Charter 88; and Sherril Carter of the Royal Mews.

Thanks to Jill Kelsey and Sheila DeBellaigue of the Royal Archives, Windsor; Tony Chester, Kent; Angus Nurse, investigations coordinator for the Royal Society for the Protection of Birds, Bedfordshire; Dr. Jack Cohen of the University of Warwick, Coventry; Dr. Nickianne Moody of the Liverpool John Moores University; Mike Siddell, Askam-in-Furness, Cumbria; George Marley, clinical development manager, Northeast Ambulance Service, Newcastle; Dr. Elaine C. Block of Hunter College, New York; Kerstin Shirokow, Santa Barbara; Brother Yitzak and the monks of St. Gervais of Jerusalem in Paris; Val, Vince, and Oliver Morris, Paris; and Siony Foliente who put up with being my experimental "corpse."

Last, but far from least, I would like to single out retired chief inspector and former legal columnist for *Police Review* magazine, Ken Sloan of Stockport, Cheshire, and his wife, Gudrun, as well as Acting Sergeant Colin Waddington of Weetwood, Leeds, and his wife, Jill, for a very special thank-you.

They are indeed Britain's finest.

We commoners are too morally earnest for our own good. We think everything should have a function and a reason. This is why we need the monarchy. To remind us of the virtues of uselessness.

—Howard Jacobson, *The Independent,*
November 16, 2002

PART ONE

Leeds

PROLOGUE

THE LADY OF THE LAKE

Stars appeared briefly in the short summer night, vanishing as the dawn sky glowed rose pink. A stream flowed into the Harewood House estate's lake and out again over a feathery waterfall, water cascading down stone steps as it headed toward the river Wharfe. Past their season, bruised rhododendron flowers littered the ground like droplets of dried blood among the delicate blue campanula. A canopied launch moored near the dam rocked under weeping willows. The air was still with the promise of the day's heat to come.

An arm rose out of the lake, pale as a water lily, a woman's delicate hand opening expectantly. Her eyes stared from under the surface of the water as blond hair mixed with strands of algae swirled around her face. Tiny minnow sprat explored her mouth, lips open in a secret smile.

But nothing happened. Ducks left V-shaped trails, and flamingos ruffled their feathers irritably. A lone dragonfly lit on her fingertip to rub its jeweled eyes before darting away.

An hour later, the lady of the lake seemed to tire of waiting. Disappointed fingers curled around empty air before her hand sank back under the water. She drifted aimlessly away under a shroud of duckweed.

I

WEDNESDAY

Keen Dunliffe woke to one of those rare sweet Yorkshire mornings, light streaming in the window. He opened his eyes and looked out over fields heavily speckled with sheep. Sunlight between sullen clouds washed green pastures with variegated shadows. The Kestlemans' double-barreled chimney was barely visible behind hills divided by drystone walls.

Not quite awake, he buried his face into the pillow. A tractor grumbled in the distance, and a breeze off the moors carried the tang of new-mown grass. It was a perfectly lovely day and, somehow, Keen just knew he wasn't going to enjoy it.

Thomas purred, uncoiling from the foot of the bed to stretch, front legs stiff, arse jutting. The tabby yawned wide enough to expose freckles on the ridged inside of his mouth. Keen glanced at the bedside clock as it changed from 4:57 to 4:58.

"You don't fool me, cat," Keen muttered. "I don't care what it looks like, it's still the middle of the bloody night. Shurrup." The cat purred louder, glaring. Keen closed his eyes, ignoring him.

Undaunted, Thomas bumped his head under Keen's chin while kneading the duvet, digging one claw into Keen's neck.

"Ow! You little bugger . . ." Thomas thumped solidly to the floor. Keen groaned; no way he'd get back to sleep now.

Keen pulled on his worn robe and padded barefoot downstairs to put the kettle on. As it hissed, he took only a bottle of milk and a can of tinned cat food from the fridge, ignoring the bacon and brown eggs. Thomas's purr now an asthmatic rumble, he arched against Keen's legs as the man scraped the cat food into a dish and set it on the floor. The cat sniffed it reproachfully.

"It's better than I get, you ungrateful beast," Keen said sternly. His criticism was lost on the cat. He broke an egg over the congealed cat food. "Go ahead then, clog your arteries rotten with cholesterol, top yourself and see if I cry over your fat carcass."

The cat gobbled his breakfast as Keen bolted down a bowl of unsweetened muesli in chalky skim milk as if hurrying could keep him from tasting it. The kettle gurgled and snapped itself off.

When Laura took the Italian coffeemaker, Keen had stolen the mesh filter as much from practicality as petty revenge. He did his honest best to feel guilty, but smiled as he poured boiling water over the grounds to let the coffee trickle into a Pyrex measuring jug.

Laura had also taken all the china, fair enough since it had been her mother's. He poured his coffee into a chipped mug and topped it up with the last of the milk without adding, he was perversely proud of, artificial sweetener. He'd trimmed a little over two stone in the past year the hard way, one sugar lump at a time.

He set the rinsed milk bottle out on the steps before taking his coffee across the patio. His hillside lands adjoined with Derek's fields. He leaned against the stone wall, idly watching Derek's sheep wandering along endless tracks in the grass, bright eyes in their long-nosed skulls giving them the illusion of intelligence. Derek and his lads had sheared their flock two weeks ago and branded their stripped hides with green paint. Most had never felt rain on their backs before, and Keen had had a good laugh as they'd huddled under the trees in the summer downpour.

Thomas hopped onto the wall beside him. Rising mist drifted through Lindley Moor. A wagtail lit on the telephone pole in a splash of black and white feathers. In the quiet, a pair of large hares skipped through the pasture in a choreographed mating dance, twisting and turning and stopping every so often for a frantic three-second fuck before bounding off in perfect synchronous step. They vanished over the hillside, racing toward the Buckbothem farm where no doubt they would be fertile and multiply and the B6161 would soon blossom with furry splotches of half-grown bunny roadkill.

Keen had leased his rocky moorland years back to Derek and cleared the barn of rusty farm equipment, intending to convert it into a B and B. That had been Laura's idea, once the boys were in school, renting rooms to city tourists up on holiday in the "quaint" Yorkshire countryside. They'd both enjoyed DIY, he handling the carpentry and roofing and such, she the decorating. But renovation had ground to a halt the same time as the marriage.

He hadn't unlocked the barn in months, windows frosted with dust, lumber weathered gray. The farm was too big for one person. He'd meant to sell up after the divorce, but never seemed to find the time. Or so he told himself.

His father had left the land to Keen and the house to Keen's older sister. Janet wanted to sell it all off; her husband's video rental shop badly needed the cash. Then just a green police constable, Keen lived in section housing, virtually free rent with a sauna and a gym, color telly, money enough for endless pints with the lads. He'd been innocently callous and too busy to worry about the remote future of middle age. So he'd reluctantly agreed.

That was before Laura. Tough, practical, lovely Laura. Determined to escape the cramped Bradford council flats, she bought out Janet's half and haggled over price, indifferent to sentimentality. She'd hammered out a mortgage with the bank manager. Instead of letting him piss away his pay in the pub or buy a flash new car, she'd made Keen hoard his pennies and eat casseroles.

He'd been amazed as his overdraft cleared and his credit ballooned. They'd both cried the day he carried her over the farmhouse threshold.

On less than ten thousand pounds a year between his salary and hers as a part-time clerk in Harrogate, gas and electricity and water and insurance and council taxes and Inland Revenue left them near penniless. It hadn't mattered then. A few years on, he passed his exams and made sergeant, and she'd become full-time manager.

They'd gone through the worst of it, they had. The exhausting shift hours rotating through late turn, early turn, off the night shift at six in the morning and back to work at two had taken its toll on him, physically, mentally, sexually. They spent the one weekend a month they had in bed . . . sleeping. She'd had to do everything for the house, fighting the persistent rising damp, fixing burst pipes in the winter, everything. During a riot, he'd earned himself a bloody whack on the head along with a commendation he didn't want, while she tried to hide her worry and relief.

Never once did she suggest he leave the force. Never once was he tempted to go over the side with another woman. They were the envy of many whose own marriages crumbled under the pressure. He'd considered himself one lucky policeman.

Then, just when they had given up on ever having children, the twins had come along, sweet boys.

His throat went tight. He closed his eyes and pushed the ache away. It wasn't hard to do anymore. It only crept up on him whenever he was stupid enough to allow his mind to wander. He'd long since stopped trying to figure out what went wrong. He didn't know, likely would never know, and this blind spot depressed him like a flaw in himself he couldn't pin down, never mind ever heal. She was gone, the boys were gone, and that was that. The reasons didn't matter anymore.

Or so he told himself.

He sighed, and looked down at Thomas engrossed in raking his tongue through striped fur. Keen scratched the cat's ears, garnering him a faint glare and a pause in the cat's morning ritual.

He went upstairs to shower. Hot water beat him in the face as he inhaled steam. When his skin had flushed red, he turned off the hot water and waited for the well water to run up the pipes. The shock of cold made him suck in his breath. He'd give himself a heart attack that way, Laura had warned him, masochistic sod.

Standing naked in front of the mirror, he lathered his face and shaved, rinsing the razor in cold water because a senior officer had once told him the edge would last longer. He wondered if it was true, wondered if anyone had ever tested the theory, wondered how many other things people believed simply because someone in authority said it was so.

Only one clean uniform shirt left, he realized as he dressed. It was always a toss-up whether to drive out of his way to a cleaners, or wash and iron them himself. Laziness won. He stuffed his dirty laundry into a Morrisons carrier bag to drop off in Bramhope on his way home.

Keen stepped over Thomas basking on the front step, the cat's eyes shut and paws tucked under, and tossed his laundry into the backseat of the Vauxhall. "I want to see a row of dead mice lined up neat on that doorstep when I get home," he warned, "or you're out on your worthless ear, you hear me?" The cat yawned. Keen grinned, turned the car down the long gravel drive to the main road.

Driving the same route every day made him less aware of his surroundings. For instance, he thought, he hadn't actually read the signs on the roundabouts to work for years; they might have said THIS WAY TO THE KINGDOM OF OZ for all he knew. But should Leathley Methodist Church paint their gate blue, or BT remove the telephone box at the Poole crossroads, his antennae would quiver. The policeman's gut, a chafing sensation even when nothing *looks* wrong. There was just something about this day he knew he wasn't going to like.

Chapman stretched wearily as Keen walked into the office both shift sergeants shared, and filled him in on the night's events with few words in fewer minutes. Keen sorted through briefing folders and his in-basket before culling his memos into his two standard piles: "Do-It-Now" and "Ignore-Until-It-Goes-Away." The "Do-It-Now" pile was depressingly larger.

The clamor increased as officers filed into the parade room for the 6 A.M. roll call. His shift inspector met him at the door. Inside, PCs sprawled in chairs, chatting quietly and ignoring them both. The room shuffled to its collective feet when he and Inspector Ferguson arrived, and sat when their senior officers did, a courtesy both respectful and informal. Better to be respected than liked, but better to be both.

His notice scribbled on the whiteboard was still there: "Vehicles Used in Crime, check PNC and OIS which will most likely tell you who is using it." Someone else had emphasized the "OIS" with a wavy underlining. PC Ramsey glanced at him in chagrin. Keen remembered how stupid he'd felt his own first year in the Leeds City force, his previous main thrill as a young village bobby having been supervising the annual sheep dip. New computerized systems and regulations made the job even harder than ever to keep up.

Keen opened the folder beside him as the inspector started in without preamble, his cigarette-deepened voice casual. "3334."

"Sir."

"4359."

"Sir."

"4423."

Silence. Jenkins was late again. Keen made a note.

"4730."

"Sir."

"Welcome back, Paul."

"Glad to be back, sir."

Someone laughed. "Coo, what a poser! You'd still be off playing football with the kiddies, you would."

"Got that one right, love," Paul answered placidly.

Ferguson waited for the muted laughter to finish, then, "5289."

"Sir."

Roll call over, Ferguson leaned back, hands clasped across his stomach, as Keen began. "Right, first up: we still got that stolen yellow J reg Nissan knocking about. It was spotted last night over in Gledhow just after midnight, did another make-off at the Esso station. Same description: white male, twenty-five to thirty, wearing a red woolly hat. This time he was waving a pistol about. Presume armed and dangerous. Approach with caution, but let's get him, people." The PCs dutifully jotted down the registration plate number for the stolen car in their pocket notebooks. As a matter of habit, Keen memorized it.

"Next up, three more horses were slashed over at the Beckett riding school in the early morning."

"Shit," a PC murmured. "Not that game up again."

" 'Fraid so," Keen replied without looking up. He wondered himself what kind of sick bastard would knife such beautiful animals for no reason. "So keep an eye out round the area." He ticked his list. "Leeds University's got some sort of convention going on. Bodington and Weetwood Hall are both full up for the week, out-of-town professors bringing in fancy computers and the like, just the sort to attract unwanted attention from sneak-in thieves. Let's show a tad more diligence patrolling the area.

"All right, fourth and last, we got three people in custody on a robbery and kidnapping. Suspects are all on remand, but the witness is still being threatened. We'll want a DB10 alarm set up at his house." He selected a PC in the front row with a glance. "Go there, please."

He closed the metal-jacketed file. "That's it, lads and lasses, now bugger off on your constabulary duties."

Within minutes, the day shift had grabbed their gear and ambled away, leaving the hall eerily quiet. Ferguson vanished in search of a cup of coffee.

As Keen passed the Criminal Investigations Department's office, Edwards flashed a grin. Keen stopped and raised an eyebrow. "You're in a mite early," he said. El Cid didn't usually come in until eight.

"We're short-staffed again. Cassidy's off sick."

"What's his excuse this time, malaria?"

Edwards snorted. "Diphtheria, beriberi, some exotic disease or other he picked up over in Longleat Safari Park."

They both knew better; Cassidy was simply fed up with the job, and Keen anticipated yet another early "medical" retirement.

"You want a cup?" he offered.

"Sure. White, no sugar."

Glen Harper's office door was open, but the detective chief inspector hunched over his desk with the telephone jammed against his balding head and a finger stuffed into his opposite ear, deep in an intense conversation. Daheny walked in and Glen reacted to the sight of the day shift's desk sergeant by flinging a bound file out his open doorway. It hit the floor with a thud, startling them both.

"You busy, Keen?" Daheny said, picking up the file. Glen was still gabbling down the phone, nose three inches from the surface of his desk. Edwards had already slipped out the door.

"No."

"I got a PC not quite right happy at a sudden death calling in for supervision, can you go?"

"Where's Nigel?"

Daheny shrugged, indifferent. "On that arson inquiry for York."

"Okay. What's the problem?" He opened his locker and pulled out his nylon windcheater.

"Naked woman, drowned. Jogger found the body in the pond over at the Harewood House."

Keen paused with one arm through the sleeve of his jacket. "Any sign of a struggle?"

"Don't know, didn't say."

"Right, then. Get a doctor out to certify a Life Extinct."

In the Scene of Crimes Office, Dave Walsh squinted glumly at bits of broken glass strewn across his untidy desk, eyes puffy behind wire-rimmed glasses. His Mr. Coffee machine gurgled cheerfully, steaming Susan Huddleston's rubber tree plant. Dave's partner-in-crime was out.

"Got an iffy death at Harewood. Want a lift?"

"Sure." Dave rummaged in his desk for his Minolta and bags-and-tags. The prospect of a suspicious death perked him up considerably.

Harewood House belonged to George Lascelles, seventh Earl of Harewood and a first cousin to the queen. Keen didn't expect to meet him; the closest he'd ever come to his lordship was shaking hands as a lad with Jeremy Thorpe, the Liberal MP who'd married the earl's divorced first wife. Although the earl and his second countess lived at Harewood House, they ran their beautiful Georgian mansion as a business. Its bird garden and ornamental park, medieval church and ruins of the old castle, brought in enough tourist money to survive when other noble residences were donated to English Heritage in return for the family staying on as lodgers in their own homes. But whether or not the earl was in, discretion was needed to deter the tabloid press from bloating it into yet another juicy Royals scandal.

Keen drove through the gatekeeper's miniature Arc de Triomphe. At the ticket kiosk, he held up his wallet opened at his warrant card. The police car was sufficient, however, for the guard to wave them through without even a cursory look at the ID.

The public car park was empty, but Keen turned into a space marked STAFF ONLY at the front of the house and parked beside a lovingly polished Mercedes. Keen hefted the scene kit out of the boot as Dave draped the Minolta around his neck. Neither man spoke along the path behind the house's terraced garden toward the lake, but Dave grunted in amazement at a plant with enormous leaves like mutant rhubarb towering well over nine feet high.

The scene of the death was easy to spot from the bridge over the dam. PC Bealle had half a dozen members of the staff corralled under a large oak tree. Keen noted depressions in the grass of many curious feet trotting down to the lake like eager schoolkids before the police had arrived. Any traces of previous footprints had certainly been obliterated.

Bealle had answered the sudden death radio message. Now the young PC was green about the gills as he spoke with a gawky lad. The relief on his face as he spotted Keen was almost comical.

The body sprawled face up, bare legs streaked with algae, twigs and rotting leaves tangled in the blond hair. Dave growled his displeasure: Bealle had used his own jacket to cover the naked woman. The jacket was too short to be more than a misplaced gesture of chivalry. Keen made no comment as he studied the corpse.

Her face had been pretty. Now it was pasty blue, cyanotic. Her cheek was distorted, settled too long against a rock. One eye squinted out of a half-open lid and the other eye rolled white in the socket, true dead eyes, not the melodramatic pretense of an actor.

"Who found the body?" Keen asked.

"I did." The young man next to Bealle raised his hand. Dried mud speckled his green tracksuit, clashing with his ginger hair and abundant freckles. Perhaps eighteen years old, the boy grinned; to him, this was all as unreal as a television drama, not the tragic death of a human being.

"I'm here every morning 'bout eight-thirty for a jog round the lake afore work. I come right the way round there, see"—the boy pointed at the gravel footpath around a line of trees—"and I seen her floating in the pond."

"You pull her out?"

"Me? No, I went straight up the house to call 999."

"She were only a few feet out, facedown," Bealle said, his voice too crisp. "Mr. Westley showed me where he'd discovered the body and I went in to turn her over afore I pulled her out. No signs of life that I could determine." The PC was not trying to be funny.

Keen glanced at Bealle's muddy shoes and wet trousers, green stains around the knees.

"It were obvious she were dead already," Westley said peevishly. "I didn't want to be tampering with nothing."

"Of course, Mr. Westley, you did the right thing."

Dave squatted beside the body and lifted the jacket far enough for them both to examine the dead woman. Keen sniffed at the faint smell of decay. He was no forensic expert, but he guessed she'd been in the lake maybe ten, twelve hours. The lividity pattern of blood blurred under her skin from the shallow current rocking the body before the first gasses brought her up. Her goose-pimpled skin was unblemished but for a few pale marks where fish had nibbled at the dead flesh, palms and feet wrinkled as if she'd stayed in the shower too long.

White, fortyish. Small, five foot two at most, around seven stone. She'd been a beautiful woman in excellent physical shape, legs smooth and strong, hips trim, stomach flat. She had an even tan, bikini bottom outline but no top. Even naked, her body suggested elegance and wealth.

Keen noticed her pubic hair was dark, her blond hair expertly dyed. No stretch marks, small nipples on full breasts, no sign she'd ever gone through childbirth. No rings on her fingers, and no mark where one might be missing. Her nails were flawlessly polished, none broken. That much time in the water, it was unlikely they'd find any skin scrapings underneath where she might have defended herself. No visible antemortem injuries, no stab wounds, no cuts, bruises, or abrasions, no pressure marks around her neck, no obvious evidence of any kind she'd been attacked. Keen watched without comment until Dave had finished his in situ exam and dropped the jacket back over the body.

"Any idea who she is?" Keen addressed anyone in earshot. The small crowd murmured in consultation as Dave took samples from the lake, jotting down the temperature of the air and water in his notebook.

Bealle shook his head. "Mr. Westley also spotted women's clothing farther up the path there, 'bout five hundred yards. Posted a member of staff to keep an eye on it."

"I go by 'em, see," Mr. Westley added eagerly, "an' I think maybe some bloke's got his lass out in the bushes. Then I see this lady floating in the water and I think, hello, that's who's left their clothes."

"No handbag?"

The boy blinked. "Not that I seen."

A corpulent man in a rumpled suit headed down the slope, PC Kellett in his wake. The doctor's arms wound round as his shoes skidded on the dewy grass. He recovered and strode toward them. Stopping at the corpse's legs, he studied the body while pulling at a too tight collar around his stout neck. Two men in coveralls jockeyed a mortuary gurney along the gravel path, and looked at the officers questioningly. Keen shook his head; they'd have a wait before the body could be removed.

"Could we ask you to step back now, Mr. Westley?" Keen said.

"Oh. Right. Sure." The boy looked around, uncertainly.

"Bealle?" Keen nodded meaningfully toward the witnesses. The PC herded them farther away to take down their names, addresses, and whereabouts when the body was found.

"Mm-hm, mm-hm," the doctor muttered, then squatted to curl his fingertips around her wrist as if feeling for a pulse. "Mm-hm. She's blue, she's cold, and she's a mite stiff. Mm-hm. I'd say she's dead, all right." He lifted the jacket off the body to study her corpse just as Keen and Dave had done. "Mm-hm," he said again, and levered his bulk back upright. Bottle-bottom lenses magnified watery eyes. "She's also stark nekked." He handed Keen the PC's jacket.

"Mm-hm," Keen said, deadpan. "We'll notify Jimmy's for the postmortem."

Dave focused the Minolta, more concerned with his light meter and F-stop than his subject matter. He stepped around the body for a different angle, lips pursed as he took a final shot.

"Your call, skip," Dave said simply, waiting.

Keen's gut niggled. "Bring on the woodwind section," he said reluctantly.

As Kellett radioed for CID, Dave frowned at the jacket still in Keen's hand. He pressed a piece of cellotape several times to the inside of Bealle's jacket. When he'd finished, Keen signaled the PC over. "In a sudden death like this," Keen said to him quietly, "where there's even the slightest question she might have been raped, never put anything on the body. You could interfere with and possibly lose forensic evidence."

"Also makes for more bloody paperwork," Dave groused.

Bealle nodded earnestly. "Sorry, sir. I were meaning to screen the body from public view."

That came straight out of the training manual and, to be fair, there wasn't likely to be many fibers or foreign hair on a body that long in the water. Keen held out the PC's jacket. Bealle regarded it with barely suppressed revulsion. "Uh, Sarge . . . ? I don't think I quite want it anymore."

Barely out of his teens, Bealle had been on the force less than six months, a sweet-tempered, baby-faced probationer Keen doubted would last the course. He considered making it an issue; then tiredly draped the jacket over one arm. "We'll put in for another," Keen said, irritated by the lad's expression of absurd gratitude. "This can't be your first sudden death?"

"No, sir. I took a call last month on a ninety-year-old man dropped dead in his back garden. When I got there, the neighbors had him laid out so peaceful he looked like he could've woke up and walked away."

Edwards and four other DCs arrived along with an equal number of uniformed constables. As a frame tent was erected over the dead woman, Edwards directed the search corridor, POLICE tape strung from the oak to the gravel path. Dave rolled poly bags over the body's hands and feet and a larger one over her head. Fingerprints would have to wait until they'd taken the nail scrapings.

Keen turned to Edwards. "You mind giving Bealle a hand finishing up witness statements?"

"Right on it," the detective constable said cheerfully.

"Mr. Westley?"

The boy chatting with four middle-aged women jerked around, startled. "The lady's clothing?"

"Oh, right. It's this way . . ."

The lad fairly skipped with excitement. Dave followed while Keen scanned the ground, the footpath, the grass. No shoeprints pressed into the mud, no threads snagged on a branch, no safety deposit keys or cinema tickets dropped by accident. Life was rarely that convenient.

The woman's clothes lay meticulously folded on a bench sheltered by a gnarled willow. An older man in a beige uniform and shapeless hat squinted through his cigarette smoke as they approached.

"What do you think, Sergeant? You think maybe she killed herself?" Westley demanded eagerly.

Keen examined the bank at the water's edge. "Let's wait to see what the investigation turns up, shall we?" If this was where she'd gone in, there was no sign.

"Me, I can't see somebody taking off their clothes to commit suicide," Westley went on, not listening. "I mean, me mum would have a stroke they pulled me starkers out of a lake." Keen didn't answer. "We get skinny-dippers ever so often, when it's hot. Couples, usually. Not many want to go swimming on their own in the middle of the night . . ."

Dave ignored the boy, crouching by the bench to inspect the clothing. The older man flicked his ash into one cupped palm before smearing it against his soil-stained trouser leg.

"I didn't think about no handbag, just when you mentioned it. Maybe somebody done her and stole it—"

"Mr. Westley," Keen interrupted, "how old are you?"

"Twenty-three."

That surprised him, the boy's immaturity making him seem younger than Bealle. Keen kept his attention on the clothing. The white silk blouse was folded neatly on top of a red linen skirt and jacket, ornate gold buttons on the folded sleeves. The gold thread of a Crassfield & Robyns label glinted in the lining. The toe tips of satiny tights peeked out from underneath the skirt. Pumps with delicate heels were clean, no mud on the soles. Condensation rolled off the overhead leaves, tiny droplets beading the silk blouse. This was no tart's outfit.

"How long have you been with Harewood House?"

"Four months. Almost."

"You like gardening, do you?"

His tone was nonchalant but the boy wasn't stupid, only unsure of where Keen was leading. Dave glanced back over his shoulder, amused.

"*Landscaping*. Sure. I'm still at Askham Bryan Horticultural College, but I work part-time here. We did the main terrace and parterre restoration"—the lad waved a hand at clipped hedges and statuary decorating the fountains overlooking the lake—"twenty thousand box tree plants and forty-five thousand bedding plants. The grounds were designed by Capability Brown, you know."

Keen knew of Capability Brown, but waited for the lad to fill the silence himself. "My class also took third for a low-maintenance rock garden last year at the Harrogate Great Autumn Flower Show." Pride mixed with anxiety in his voice as he wondered what Keen wanted to hear.

The older man held his cigarette with thumb and forefinger. His fingers were blunt and ragged, knuckles scraped and nails stained with dirt. Honest hardworking farmer's hands like Keen's father had had.

"That's lovely. Really," Keen remarked casually. "Economy the way it is for the north, so many young people on the dole, no ambition, no job, no future." Westley caught his drift. "Thing like this, any employer would appreciate discretion. Shame to spoil your chances speculating on what might or might not have happened. Especially to the wrong sort likely to take things out of context, make it seem like you said something you didn't. Best you leave it to the experts, that's their job, right?"

"Yes, sir." The boy looked glum.

Keen ignored Dave's smirk. There wasn't an ice lolly's chance in hell the news of a nude woman found dead in the earl's fishpond would quietly fade into the back pages of the *Wharfedale & Airedale Observer.* Come the weekly Monday press office meeting, the police would do their best to play it down, give the choice bits away to the local journalists, let them deal with the out-of-town hyenas.

But he found himself looking at the tidy pile of clothes without really seeing them, his own gut nagging with misgivings. "Nobody's touched this?" Dave asked the older man.

"Nowt." The taciturn gardener took a last drag of his cigarette before stubbing it out on his boot heel, then tucked the butt into his trouser pocket.

"Constable said not to," Westley muttered sulkily.

Dave carefully slipped the plastic evidence bags around the clothing without touching them, separating each item. He used a pen to drop each shoe into its own bag. Getting decent fingerprints off the leather was a remote hope, Keen knew as well as Dave. Unless they came up with something more to suggest murder rather than accidental death, the clothing would be dried in paper bags to keep it from going moldy, then locked up in property store until she was identified and her next of kin claimed it.

"Done," Dave said, sealed evidence bags in one hand.

"Thank you for your help, gentlemen." Keen fished cards out of his wallet and handed one to each of them. "We'd appreciate your staying well back while we search the grounds, but if you think of anything else later on, please get in touch."

He trudged back toward the body tent, wet grass squeaking under his shoes. Edwards excused himself from a scowling Support Group officer Keen didn't recognize, and met him halfway.

"I only called for CID. Who the hell brought in the frigging muppets?" Keen demanded, annoyed.

Edwards shrugged. "Harper got a phone call."

Of course he had, Keen thought sourly. This was, after all, an earl's back garden. He just hoped it didn't turn into a circus. Still carrying Bealle's jacket, Keen watched the fingertip search as uniformed officers combed the ground.

Periodically, a bit of this or that was dropped into an evidence bag, but Keen was skeptical anything would be found.

The estate's garden manager arrived and Keen impressed on him the need for both as much information as his staff could give the police and as little as possible to the press. The manager understood completely.

"None of the family is here," the manager said, by which Keen understood he meant the Lascelles. "They're down in London. Lord Lascelles . . . that's the earl's son . . . he's producing a special *Inspector Morse* retrospective for the BBC."

Keen suppressed a smile, wondering how the viscount would appreciate the real thing manifesting itself in his own backyard.

"Any ideas how she got in at night?" Keen asked.

"Could be any number of ways, we're not a fortress here. Got a full-time constable handles security and there's CCTV cameras round the house, and on the gate by Stank. That's that little village on the estate's west end." Keen made a mental note to impound the videotapes. "But the grounds're too extensive. We've had the occasional poacher, but we're more interested in getting the public to come in, not keeping people out."

They watched the activity beside the lake. "Well, look on the bright side," the manager said gloomily, "gate sales'll double the whole of next month, no doubt." As his own radio cackled, the manager walked away.

The undertakers were finally allowed to remove the body when the search finished shortly after noon. Bealle kept the last few witnesses busy with questions as Edwards and Dave removed the tent and plastic sheeting. The two attendants lifted the corpse and tucked her into a body bag, her stiff-jointed arms flopping. Bealle turned yet another shade of green as pond water gushed from her mouth, thick froth bubbling inside the poly bag over her head. The body bounced like a disjointed doll on the gurney as it was wheeled up the grassy hill.

The excitement over, most of the spectators wandered off toward the house. Two middle-aged women argued over minor details while Bealle scribbled. Hidden birds in the trees mimicked their voices.

"Thank you, ladies," Bealle was saying in a tone one might use to get a garrulous relative off the phone. "This's all been right helpful." He smiled politely before following Keen back to the car park. Edwards waited, leaning against his car.

"Anything?"

"Nobody saw bloody owt," Edwards said. "Just that student."

"Think it's murder?" Bealle asked Edwards. Edwards glanced ruefully at Keen. Bealle hadn't been in the job long enough to know Keen had spent ten years in CID, eight more than Edwards.

"Her being naked is a bit peculiar," Edwards said. "But it's early days yet."

"Right, then." Keen tossed Bealle's jacket over his bag of dirty laundry in the back of his Vauxhall. Bealle pretended not to notice. "Give Dave a lift over to Wetherby, he needs to get this all catalogued and start on his situation reports," Keen said to Edwards. Dave would deliver the evidence to the forensic science labs to maintain his continuity as the exhibits officer, on the off chance the woman's death ended up in a trial. "I'll check the PNC, see if anything tallies with her physical description. When her prints come back, run them through Wakefield and give a Missing Persons over at Scotland Yard a bell."

"Okay, skip." Dave was scribbling his notes as Edwards drove away. Keen watched them go thoughtfully.

"Bealle . . ."

"Yes, sir?"

"If those are her shoes, they're too clean for her to have gotten here strolling in off the carriageway. Give a call in to Traffic, see if anybody logged in anything unusual in the area, cars parked where they shouldn't have been last night."

Bealle nodded and walked toward his car while speaking into his radio strapped to one shoulder. "4359 with a message over . . ."

The response was lost in a cackle of static.

At the corner traffic light, Keen spotted Moyra Lannes speeding toward the Harewood estate, the tenacious *Observer* reporter on the scent. He waved cheerily, earning only a scowl in return.

He stopped at a Chinese takeaway for stir-fried vegetables, mostly soya sauce and bean sprouts, and ate straight out of the carton with the same determination as he'd consumed his muesli. It took away the hunger but left him less than satisfied.

By the time Dave returned to the station, Keen had begun inquiries with officers on duty the night before, but come up with nothing. The rest of his afternoon was taken up with the paperwork, all painstakingly written out in his blocky handwriting. "The brief circumstances around this matter are as follows," he began his précis report, and continued in the same stilted police jargon, page after page of it, form after form. He paused only to look up the proper spelling for "indeterminate" in the battered dictionary he kept in the bottom drawer of his desk.

Then he made a call to St. James Hospital, another to the tech at Wetherby handling the postmortem samples, and yet another to divisional control officers on night duty, all without results. As if he hadn't enough to do, he filled out a 728 form for PC Bealle.

He briefed Saunderson for the 2 P.M. parade, but was busy elsewhere when the late turn section hit the streets. Graeme Davis, his chief inspector of operations, called him into his own tiny office. Outside the window, quarreling sparrows fluttered through unkempt foliage, Weetwood Station's contribution to encouraging wildlife. Although it wouldn't take any prizes at the Harrogate Great Autumn Flower Show, Keen preferred their own low-maintenance technique, rough birdhouses nailed to trees and wildflower seed strewn around lampposts to compete with the dandelions.

Davis had the *Yorkshire Post* spread across his desk, skimming headlines reading, BRADFORD COUNCIL ANNOUNCES HOUSING CLAMPDOWN and BRITISH GAS TO RENEW MAJOR MAIN LINES IN HORSFORTH.

"We're getting calls from the press on the Harewood incident," he said without looking up, jotting a note in a column margin.

"I saw Moyra this morning. She didn't stop to chat."

"Mm-hm," Davis responded, unfortunately sounding like the rotund doctor. "There's already been someone from the *Daily Mirror* snuffling about; the rest of the jackals can't be far behind."

"Will you be making an official statement?"

Davis turned the page and leaned on his elbows. "Just the usual 'we regretfully decline to comment on an ongoing investigation but we'll all be right thrilled to make details available to the press as soon as anything develops.'"

"Right."

"Nigel's peeved." This was said casually, while Davis still scanned the newsprint. Keen didn't respond. The call had been handled properly; if a uniform PC requested supervision, it was up to his shift sergeant to decide on CID or not. But that it had been Keen who had taken the call would do nothing but increase the personal friction between the two men. "You were there, what'd it look like to you?"

Keen shrugged. "Don't know. Suicide or accidental, I shouldn't be surprised. All depends on what Wetherby comes up with." Again, that nagging feeling tugged at him. Davis's concern was more prosaic; Mullard and a couple DCs would suffice for an accidental death, but if it became a murder inquiry, Davis would have to organize a larger team along with the budget it would entail.

"Wish she'd have picked a less ticklish spot," Davis said. "You started this one, you stay on it. Temporary CID for the follow-up." Startled, Keen stifled his reaction although Davis didn't look up. "How are we with that ram-running gang in Bramley?"

End of subject.

They discussed a few other cases before Davis glanced at him over his glasses. "Working late again tonight?" he asked mildly.

Keen kept his tone neutral. "No, sir."

"You going on the treasure hunt this weekend?"

His heart sank. He hadn't planned on it. "Might do."

"Be fun. See you there, then."

Keen slogged through the case files piled on his desk, fighting the losing battle against the sea of paper flowing through the station. The detectives' room remained quiet, the only other person being Terry Dales, the lone Crime Management Support Unit, ensconced in the corner computer desk he shared with Traffic's file manager, typing steadily.

Jasmine Farrell interrupted the calm around three, dashing in to root through her own files.

"Exciting case?" Keen asked her.

"Absolutely *fabulous*," Jazz said in a breathless rush. "Somebody's nicked a skip," and left with a quick laugh. "Cheers, love."

Half an hour later, Inspector Osborne dropped the 728 Sup 1 form in front of Keen, his fuzzy hair askew. "What's this for?"

Keen looked up in surprise. "PC Bealle is wanting a new jacket."

"*Obviously* he wants a new jacket. He's had his uniform less than six months. What's wrong with the old one?"

"Bad karma," Keen said laconically. Terry stopped typing to listen. When Osborne scowled, Keen added, "Bealle used it to cover the body of a dead woman he fished out of a lake this morning. Now, for some strange reason, it gives him the shudders."

Osborne raked his fingers through his hair, the result not any more tidy than before. "Oh," he said, defeated. "Oh, hell."

"There's nothing wrong with it. Have it dry-cleaned and switch with another station."

"They won't object to a little bad karma, I take it?"

"Dry cleaners can get out even stubborn karma these days," Keen said, unsmiling. "Special solvents."

"Hilarious, you are."

"Thank you, sir. Do my best."

"Bloody cutbacks." The inspector snatched the 728 off Keen's desk and left as Keen exchanged a wry look with Terry. The station stayed relatively quiet. Terry continued his rhythmical tap-tapping which Keen found oddly relaxing. The computer hiccupped.

"Oh, bugger," Terry muttered, not as soothed with silver-surfing the cybernetic waves of the Police National Computer system. He leaned back, kneading his neck. "You're working late, Keen. You for a cuppa?"

Keen checked his watch, surprised how much time had slipped away, now close to five. "No, thanks. Should be on my way, pick up something for tea."

Terry grinned as he pushed away from his computer. "You still eating that 'orrible rabbit food?"

Keen raised an eyebrow at Terry's expanding paunch. "You could do with a reduction of calories yourself, laddie. Do you wonders."

"And misery loves company," Terry paused in the doorway just long enough to quip.

"I should be so lucky," he said to himself, suddenly feeling lonely and tired. He retrieved his windcheater from his locker, shrugged it on, and left.

He bought broccoli and a package of boneless skinless (tasteless) chicken breasts at a Pakistani grocery in Adel. The chippie next door was off limits, but his mouth watered at the aroma of forbidden fishy delights. To get his mind off temptation, he mulled over the dead woman as he drove, instincts still uneasy as he parked in his farmhouse driveway. As he turned to pick up his groceries, the black and yellow cartoon character on the Morrisons carrier bag sneered at him from the backseat. He'd forgotten to drop off his shirts in Bramhope.

"Christ, what next?" he groused, slamming the Vauxhall's door. The answer appeared when he turned around. Hackwell, the dairyman, had exchanged his empty for a new bottle, now in shards in a large puddle of milk on the front steps. The suspected vandal was nowhere in sight.

"Bloody marvelous. Thank you ever so much, Thomas."

He swept up the mess and hoped the cat would show up for a damned good swat with the broom as well. Thomas didn't show even when Keen began cooking dinner, which only confirmed the cat's guilt. Although irritated by the broken milk bottle, Keen hoped the stupid animal hadn't run under someone's tires while fleeing from the wheels of justice.

He stuffed his dirty shirts into the washer, dumped in a cup of the green detergent (don't buy that blue brand, Laura had insisted, it's not ecologically friendly), and set the machine for boil. It huffed away cheerfully, giving off a warm tang of institutional clean.

Thomas was still out, doing whatever it was cats do. Keen left the back door open while he ate his dinner in front of the telly, something Laura had never tolerated, and watched the ITV news. While facts were scant, he marveled at the media's expertise in hinting at royal love nests and crimes of passion without actually *saying* a damned thing.

Between commercial breaks, he washed up his supper dishes and checked outside for Thomas. The washing machine had stopped, white shirts glued into a compact doughnut. He couldn't face the thought of ironing tonight.

The sky was still light as he flipped lethargically through the channels, settling on an old rerun of *Roseanne*. Not once did he even smile, the exaggerated laugh track incapable of tricking him into false amusement. How the Americans found such an obnoxious, shrill, obese woman so hysterically funny bewildered him.

Then, masochistic sod that he was, he watched a Woody Allen film he hadn't even liked the first time he'd seen it before he nodded off. The endless summer sun finally set, the sky dark when Thomas decided to announce his arrival by jumping on the sleeping man's stomach. Keen snorted and jerked upright with bleary incomprehension, then rubbed the cat between the ears in greeting before shoving him off onto the floor. Fumbling for the remote, he switched the yammering telly off, the sudden quiet heavy.

He shut the back door, locked up, and went to bed. Somewhere in the dark, a lamb cried for its mother, a melancholy sound. The humid breeze cooled the room as he fell asleep on his half of the bed, unable even after all this time to stretch out into Laura's half, and dreamed of a drowned woman's dead eyes.

I I

THURSDAY

His grandmother's antique clock on the lounge fireplace mantel bing'd out five o'clock, waking him. Thomas had already gone downstairs, waiting by his bowl impatiently. Keen slopped cat food into the bowl and left it on the back step, kicking the cat out of the house.

He choked down another bowl of muesli even more tasteless with tap water instead of skimmed milk, sipped his coffee, then dumped it, unable to drink it without milk *or* sugar.

The mashed doughnut of shirts had collapsed inside the machine, neat indentations in the wet cloth. He closed his eyes, then closed the washer door, hoping to sweet-talk Joanne Kestleman into doing his ironing for a few extra quid. He'd ring her from the station; even farmer's wives didn't rise at the crack of dawn anymore.

Fat raindrops cratered against the windscreen as he pulled into the station car park. Hunching his shoulders, he trotted for the back entrance to escape the deluge he knew was only moments away.

Jack Franklin had the front desk, on the phone as Keen waved hello. He waved back, reacting more to a gesture than the person making it, Keen knew.

The night had been quiet. No one had spotted the stolen Nissan, nor had there been any progress on the slashed horses. A drunk who'd bashed several cars in a Tesco car park with a shopping trolley was sleeping it off in custody, and a quartet of contrite students who had exposed themselves in a pub were waiting for their mums to collect them.

But nothing further on the dead woman. Once the early shift had gone, Keen settled behind his desk. Glen still hunched on his elbows, talking on the phone with a finger poked in his ear as if he'd never gone home. Edwards set Keen's coffee cup on his desk, a birthday gift from the twins, the red letters WORLD'S BEST DADDY scratched and faded.

"Mornin'," Edwards said, holding his own mug.

"Mornin'." Keen sipped his coffee and kept his reaction off his face. It had sugar in it.

Edwards tasted his own and grimaced. "I got yours."

"I've had my shots." They switched cups. Edwards's mug had a photo of a grinning monster with furry gremlin ears sticking out from under a New York City Police cap.

"'Member that nursing student whose Mazda got stolen by kids in local care? Otley's lads chased 'em clear to Rawdon before they rammed it into a lamppost?"

"Aye?"

"Leeds City Council's highway department is suing her. Claims she's liable for damages to their lamppost."

They snorted at the absurdity of life in general. But as Edwards loitered, Keen raised an eyebrow.

"You going on the treasure hunt this weekend?"

"Haven't decided yet."

"Need a partner?"

"You looking for one?"

Edwards grinned. "No, my wife's sister is up visiting from Wrexham. Babs says Cheryl don't go, we don't go."

Keen didn't much feel like a blind date. "I'll have to get back to you on it," he said.

"Right," Edwards said, and pulled a photograph out of his shirt pocket, the kind from a photo machine. "In case you change your mind."

"She takes a good likeness," Keen admitted.

Edwards's sister-in-law was a stunning redhead. He propped the picture against his basket overflowing with crime reports to be vetted. He gleaned a few to send to El Cid or to return to uniform officers for follow-ups, then ditched the no-hopers into a cardboard box to be fetched upstairs, filed, and forgotten.

He glanced at the photo occasionally before realizing his thoughts drifted more on a dead woman than Cheryl's model-gorgeous looks. He ignored it after that.

At eleven, he rang Joanne Kestleman, keeping his abject groveling down to a strict minimum. Then he phoned Wetherby, hoping a report back would give him a clue to the dead woman's identity. The tech had stepped out and would return his call later. He decided to buy an overpriced cheese and pickle sandwich and ate it in the canteen while gazing out the window at the adjoining university's athletic field.

The morning's thunderstorm had passed, steam rising from the grass in the afternoon heat. Normally, most students would be off on summer holiday, giving the police a welcome respite from the regular break-ins by local lads after student VCRs and stereos. But one week every year, a strange invasion of nine hundred academics arrived for an international conference on medieval history, overwhelming the usually tranquil village of Weetwood.

The conference was split between the Weetwood Hall, an elegant Georgian mansion, and Bodington Hall student dormitory, a jumble of drab modern buildings some fifteen minutes' walk away. Every hour on the hour, a horde of middle-aged professors ill-dressed for the humid English heat wave would trot from lecture to lecture, crushing underfoot chamomile flowers spattered in the grass like errant snowflakes as the outlandish parade wore a track in the field.

In the nick's car park, several young men and women in shorts and T-shirts also paused to watch professors scurrying like frenetic ants before resuming their own higher education, sweating and grunting through survival training against knife attacks, learning techniques in employing side-handled batons, and applying rigid Quickcuffs to a struggling suspect. Inside, in air-conditioned comfort, Keen chewed the last of his sandwich and went back downstairs.

Nigel Mullard stood by Keen's desk reading a case file. Keen had no doubt which one it was. He waited in the doorway behind the detective sergeant while Terry and DC Tom Flaxton pretended not to notice either of them. Mullard flipped to the last page and scanned it before tossing the file back onto Keen's desk. He turned around to meet Keen's eyes evenly. If the DS felt any chagrin, he hid it well.

"Anything I can do for you, Nigel?"

The detective's smile barely missed being a sneer. "Just keeping up with what's going on in my department, Sergeant." The emphasis on "my" was slight but discernible.

Keen didn't move out of his way as Mullard brushed past. The atmosphere lightened considerably in his wake. Keen picked up the file as Flaxton walked past, ostensibly on his way to refill his coffee mug.

"He's got no right . . ." Flaxton murmured.

"He's got every right." Keen dropped the file into his desk drawer. Flaxton flushed, but continued on toward the coffeemaker without further comment.

Half of every bobby's time seemed eaten up with paperwork. Two hours could easily be spent on a simple shoplifting arrest, a name written on separate forms thirty times. By half one, Keen signed his rank and number, and tossed another report into his out-bin. His phone buzzed.

Next. "Dunliffe."

"You're dealing with the sudden death at Harewood?" Franklin's voice said.

"That's right."

"Lady on line three. She's a professor at that conference thing going on next door. Says a friend of hers's gone missing."

"Thanks." He punched the blinking extension light. "This is Sergeant Dunliffe, can I help you?"

"Oh, hello," a woman with a strong American accent said. She sounded nervous. "I'm not sure what I'm supposed to do. I'm here at Leeds University for the medieval conference?" She paused. He heard the buzz of many conversations in the background.

"I'm familiar with the conference."

"It's about my friend, Chris. Dr. Christine Swinton." He scribbled the name down, glanced at his watch, and recorded the time, as well. "We came up from London and, um, we're sharing a room in a bed and breakfast together?" Her voice rose again, as if this were a question.

"Yes?"

That seemed to be the appropriate reaction. "She's been gone a couple days now, and I'm a little worried. I'm sorry to bother you because I know it's probably just me overreacting—"

"Excuse me, your name is?"

"Dr. Gillian Waltham. I'm from Portland, Oregon. That's in the United States."

"Right." Keen knew where Oregon was. He jotted down her name. "W-A-L . . . ?"

"T-H-A-M," she finished for him.

"Could you describe your friend?"

"Um . . . she's white. Forty-one. Short, a little over five feet tall. I'd guess she weighs around a hundred pounds. Blond hair, hazel eyes. Looks sort of like a miniature Meryl Streep."

Keen's skin prickled. "When was the last time you saw her, Mrs. . . . . Dr. Waltham?" He kept his tone even.

"Late Tuesday afternoon. I delivered my paper yesterday morning and she'd promised she'd be there." Keen heard the irritated hurt behind the concern. "But she didn't show up. I've asked around and no one has seen her today, either. The program book has a number for St. James Hospital, but when I called to see if something had happened to her, they suggested I call the police, ask you if there's maybe been a car accident . . . ?"

"Dr. Waltham, where are you at the moment?"

"Bodington Hall. It's one of those dormitories—"

"I know where it is. Can you find the Weetwood Police Station from Bodington Hall? We're in walking distance, left-hand side on Otley Road just before the intersection. Or I can come to pick you up."

"No, I'll walk. It's on our map." Her voice sounded tight and frightened.

"All right. It should take you about ten minutes. Ask at the front desk for Sergeant Dunliffe."

When he hung up, he handed Terry his notes. "See what you can pull up on a Dr. Christine Swinton in London, would you please?" In the SOCO office, Dave Walsh cradled a huge mug of tea.

"Those photos of the dead woman up at Harewood developed yet?"

"Yeah, somewhere," Dave said, and rummaged through a desk as littered as Keen's and handed Keen a thin envelope. "Here you go."

"I think we're about to ID our mystery lady."

He waited impatiently by the phone on his desk. When Franklin buzzed him, he started, already keyed up.

"Dunliffe. Yeah, on my way, thanks."

By the time he'd walked the short distance to the reception desk, he had his professional mask firmly applied. He opened the door and smiled at the woman waiting for him.

"Dr. Waltham?"

"Yes."

"I'm Sergeant Keen Dunliffe." He shook her hand. Her fingers were cold. "Would you like to come with me, please?"

She followed him to his empty office. Gesturing to a chair, he asked, "Can I get you a coffee or tea?"

"No, thank you." She sat with her battered briefcase on her lap, looking at him expectantly as he settled into the chair behind his desk.

She was pretty, late thirties, early forties, Keen guessed, slender and fair-skinned with freckles sprinkled across her nose. An unruly mass of dark hair had been twisted up into a loose chignon. A name tag hung lopsided on a South American embroidered waistcoat worn over a tailored cotton blouse. Although she wore a gray skirt and plain black pumps, he noted the similarity between her dress and the dead woman's clothing, conservative while too off-beat for the usual working woman. Academic chic.

He opened a file and clicked a pen. "Normally in cases of missing persons, Dr. Waltham, the law considers an adult free to go where she likes. We can't do much more than take a report, unless you know of any special circumstances like a history of mental illness, suicidal tendencies, an injury that might have caused some loss of memory . . . ?"

She shook her head. "Chris is in perfect health."

"You wouldn't have any reason to think she might be involved in any criminal activity?" He kept his voice neutral.

Light brown eyes studied him quizzically. "Of course not."

"Have you rung her husband or any relatives to see if she might have gone back to London, maybe on a family emergency?"

"She's not married, and it's not a close family."

"Where are you stopping?" When she looked at him blankly, he amended, "Your B and B?"

"Oh. Willow House on Foxglove Crescent."

He jotted notes as she spoke, not paying much attention to the report as his certainty grew. "Did she mention wanting to visit any particular place, or maybe taking a trip abroad?"

She sat straighter in the chair. "No. Detective—"

"Sergeant," he corrected her, "Dunliffe."

"Dunliffe, the only place Chris is supposed to be this week is at this conference, with me."

"You said you last saw her on Tuesday, about what time?"

"Late afternoon. We had lunch at the Stables Pub behind Weetwood Hall, then went to a couple of sessions. She said she was having dinner with someone else, but she'd be back around nine and we'd go out for drinks then."

"This other person, did she say where or who she planned to meet? A boyfriend, possibly?"

She looked vaguely annoyed. "No. It was strictly business."

"What sort of business?"

"Research for a book she's writing. History. Not medieval. I mean, she's also an historian, but her specialty is Georgian England." She paused to collect herself. "It's not my field, I don't know the details."

"And where were you, then?"

"I had dinner about seven with a colleague, Lena Baruch. Then I went back to the bed and breakfast around half past nine. I waited until eleven-thirty, then went to bed. But Chris never came back."

"When she left, did you see her drive off?"

"No."

"Do you know what kind of car she drives?"

"A red GTI. I don't know what year."

"What did you talk about, how did she seem? Nervous, depressed?"

"No. We just talked about . . . girlfriend stuff. Nothing important." She blushed, which Keen found disturbingly charming. "If she hadn't planned to come back last night, she'd have told me."

He laced his hands loosely on the report form. "Dr. Waltham, did you watch the news last night?"

Her face drained visibly. "No. I've been busy and there's no television in our bed and breakfast, anyway."

"I'd like you to look at a photograph. It may not be of your friend at all, but it will likely not be a pleasant experience for you all the same. Are you willing to do that?"

"Is Chris dead?" Her face was as rigid as a china doll's.

"We don't know anything yet. What we have is an unidentified lady who apparently drowned about the same time your friend went missing. Your description is similar to hers. Could you look at a photo and tell me whether or not this is your friend?"

She nodded, wordless. He selected one of the least shocking photographs, a close-up of the head with the nude body cropped out, and slid it across the desk. She stared at it for a long moment. "It's her."

"You can positively identify the woman in this photograph as Dr. Christine Swinton of London?"

"Yes." He allowed her time to absorb it; she was still too shocked for any reaction to have set in.

He made a notation on the back of the photograph and paper-clipped it into the file. "The facts aren't all in yet, Dr. Waltham," he said gently. "All I can tell you is that it appears to be an accidental drowning. I'm very sorry."

"I don't believe it," she said flatly. For a moment, he was puzzled whether she meant she didn't believe he was sorry, or couldn't believe her friend was dead. "Chris was an excellent swimmer. She loved the water. How could she drown? That makes no sense."

His instincts tingled. "Sometimes, and I'm not saying this is the case here, but accidents do happen, especially if that person has had a bit too much to drink."

She stared out the window, her hands inert on top of her briefcase. He caught himself looking for a wedding ring. Outside, trees still dripped from the morning's deluge as sparrows flitted from branch to branch. A pair of ring-neck doves pecked the ground in the underbrush.

"She wasn't an alcoholic, if that's what you're implying," she said, her words crisp, a teacher's voice.

"I wasn't implying anything, I'm only gathering facts." He changed the subject. "Would you know who the next of kin would be, who we should contact?"

"I guess her brother Max. He's in London. I don't know the number. If you can't get him, her mother's name is Verona Swinton."

He scribbled down the names, then regarded her, still immobile. "Dr. Waltham, would you like that cup of coffee now?"

She took a breath, as if to answer, then nodded.

"Milk?" Another nod. "Sugar?" A shake of the head. "I'll be two seconds."

On his way back from the canteen, he passed by the front desk. Still on the phone, Franklin held a palm over the mouthpiece and looked at Keen questioningly.

"Good call," Keen said. "We've got the ID, thanks."

Franklin smiled, and went back to his caller. Dr. Waltham sat in exactly the same position as when he left. She looked up at him, then at the coffee cup as if she had forgotten what she was doing there. Instead of sitting behind his desk, he took the chair beside her and watched her sip the coffee. He doubted she tasted a thing.

"Are you all right, Dr. Waltham?"

"I'm fine." Her strange apathy baffled him, as if she refused to give in to grief. He reached toward her arm to comfort her.

"Please don't touch me," she said quietly. He stopped and withdrew. "I don't mean to be rude. It's just that . . . I don't want to cry."

Her hand holding the coffee began to shake. She set the cup down carefully and folded her hands in her lap.

"You two drove up together from London?" he asked.

"Yes. But I don't know where her car is. I had to walk to the conference in the rain to give my paper and I was late." He heard the guilt behind the words, regretting her anger toward a woman who was already dead.

"I shouldn't worry, we'll find it." He paused. "Think you're up to showing me where you were staying?" She nodded, gazing off again out the window. "I'm just off to find a colleague then we'll go."

In the SOCO office, Dave Walsh was scribbling frantically on a towering stack of cards while his partner stood with her hands buried in an open filing cabinet drawer, a card clenched in her teeth.

"Yes?" Dave asked, and Keen knew what he meant.

"Positive ID. She were staying with one of the conference people at a B and B. Let's go check it over."

Dave ignored Susan's muffled whine of dismay as he grabbed his crime scene kit. When Keen introduced him to Dr. Waltham, she shook his hand and mumbled a bland courtesy with so little awareness Keen knew she wouldn't have been able to pull Dave out of an identification parade two minutes later.

Willow House was on Foxglove Crescent, a small cul-de-sac near the Meanwood Park Hospital, the small, two-story limestone-block building darkened by years of car exhaust. A decrepit Alsatian barked once from the back steps, then panted as if the effort had exhausted his last shred of energy. Ragged patches of winter coat still clung to his shedding pelt. His tail wagged slowly as they approached, stirring up a flurry of dog hair.

Dr. Waltham fumbled with her keys, but before she could unlock the door, it opened. A white-haired woman wiped her hands on a striped dishtowel.

"Oh . . . hello, Mrs. Birney."

"Is something the matter?" Mrs. Birney directed her question at the two men, one in police uniform.

"No," Dr. Waltham said. "My roommate's dead."

The elderly woman gasped. "Good Lord, what happened?"

"She drowned," Dr. Waltham replied tonelessly. "The police need to look at her stuff, if that's okay." Keen heard the brittle strain in her voice, and exchanged a look with Dave, wondering when she would break.

"It won't take long, Mrs. Birney," Keen said. "We'll do our best not to disturb your other guests."

"Never mind that, come in." She nudged the Alsatian barring the way with a gentle shove of her foot. "Move off, Ralph, y'awd beggar." The dog groaned, shifting his bulk onto rickety legs before limping down the steps.

Mrs. Birney fussed behind them up the stairs. Dr. Waltham unlocked the door at the top of the landing. It opened with a well-oiled click. "Oh, my," Mrs. Birney said disapprovingly.

For a moment, he thought the room had been burgled. Clothing, shoes, cosmetics, bottles, and toiletries had been strewn about, open suitcases overturned, loose notebook papers, catalogues, and books tumbling out of torn plastic bags. One bed was rumpled, duvet in a tangle, the other bed neatly made with a closed suitcase underneath it.

"Chris wasn't a neat freak," Dr. Waltham said indifferently, and sat down on the made bed. Dave glanced at him, shrugged, and began searching through the chaos of personal effects. Despite the clutter, it didn't take long. Christine Swinton had no drugs in the room, prescription or otherwise, no suicide notes, nothing that pointed to any tangible reason the woman might have died. Her handbag, like her car, was still missing.

Finished with sorting through the contents of her luggage, Dave went on to search the wardrobe. Dr. Waltham began to fold the dead woman's clothing and repack the suitcase. Keen watched her carefully. She faltered, a lace camisole in one hand, and jerked around with her back to the room. Keen took two steps to stand next to her without touching her. She looked up as tears finally spilled, clenching the camisole so tightly he thought she might rip it.

"Chris was my daughter's godmother. What am I going to tell Karen?" she whispered.

Very gently, he drew her into a hug. She buried her face into his shoulder, weeping. "Would you have someplace we could wait while Mr. Walsh finishes up here?" he asked Mrs. Birney.

"Breakfast room is downstairs," Mrs. Birney said briskly. Behind her rose-scented talcum powder and support hose, Keen sensed a hardheaded pragmatic Yorkshirewoman. With his arm around Dr. Waltham's shoulder, he followed Mrs. Birney.

They sat at one of a dozen small tables as Mrs. Birney disappeared into the kitchen to put the kettle on. Dr. Waltham blew her nose into a paper napkin, her eyes red. "Sorry," she muttered, embarrassed.

"No reason to be."

"I was staying with Chris in London," she said, and wiped her palm across her damp eyes. "I don't know how I'm going to get back, where I'm going to go. I don't know how to get in touch with her brother. She didn't even like him. I have no idea what I'm supposed to *do* now."

"Do you have any other friends at the conference?"

She nodded. "Lena. Dr. Lena Baruch. I work with her."

Mrs. Birney emerged with two cups of steaming tea. "There now," she said firmly, "I'm sure a nice cup of tea will do you good, love." She patted Dr. Waltham's hand before retreating back into the kitchen.

The traditional British cure-all, Keen thought, and watched Dr. Waltham sip dutifully to be polite before she set it back on the saucer. Probably only works if you're British. Dave peered around the breakfast room door. "Done," he announced.

"When you feel up to it, Dr. Waltham, I'd like to have a couple officers take you back to the conference, have you point out anyone she talked to, people who might have known her. I have a few things to clear up here, then I'll join you."

She nodded, but he doubted she was listening. Mrs. Birney showed them out, a tiny brass bell chiming as she shut the door behind them.

He sent Bealle and Jansen with the American to question anyone who might have seen the late Dr. Swinton while he returned to the station to brief the two o'clock shift sergeant. Before the next shift's parade had even finished, he'd slipped out the back way.

In a cobblestone square behind Weetwood Hall, the Stables Pub did its best to keep up with demand. Wooden tables overflowed with impatient academics waiting for food and beer while the harassed staff smiled desperately, sweltering in their smart navy and mauve uniforms.

Jansen interviewed a slim woman at a separate table who, judging by her bewildered expression, seemed to be having difficulty understanding what he was saying. Dr. Waltham sat across from a chubby man speaking with energetic intensity, unmindful of Keen's approach. Next to her, a plump woman in her mid-sixties with ash-white hair ate a plate of casserole.

"Zen I find a notation in za margin of an eleventh-zentury manuscript by a monk in Lienerberg who treated his pigs for the *exact* same problem," the chubby man was saying. "Zo I make a little experiment and sprinkle in some zpecial purple mealvorms, little tings viggling around." He gave an enthusiastic impression of a doomed mealworm snack, smacking his lips happily. "And my pigs *love* it. All zer shnout rashes just vent away . . ."

The plump woman paused with a fork of macaroni halfway to her mouth, and set it ruefully back on her plate.

"Hello," Dr. Waltham said wanly to Keen. "My colleagues, Lena Baruch and Karlheinz Schenkel." The man blinked at him through thick steel-rimmed glasses, his blond hair cut in a bowl style. With his blue eyes and pale lashes in a rosy-cheeked round face, he looked very much like an overgrown five-year-old.

"How nice to zee you again," Dr. Schenkel said blithely, oblivious to Keen's uniform. "I tink we met last year in Kalamazoo, *ja*? You remember, I gave a paper on pigs as anti-Semitic scapegoats in za Württemberg frescoes . . ."

"Karlheinz," Dr. Waltham said kindly as Lena Baruch shook her head. "He's a police officer investigating Chris's death."

"Sergeant Dunliffe. Pleasure to meet you." He sat next to Dr. Waltham and studied her pallid face. "How are you holding up?"

"Okay." She glanced in Jansen's direction. The PC was scribbling notes as the slim woman spoke and gestured in a manner that suggested English was not her first language. "There aren't many people I could point out. Nobody here really knew Chris except me."

"We've already spoken with that officer," Lena said, nodding toward Jansen. "None of us could tell him much, I'm afraid. I'd just met her. Jillie thought since Dr. Swinton had had a book published, she could give me some advice on my own."

"What sort of book?" Keen asked.

"Two, actually," Dr. Waltham said. "Her second just came out in Cambridge University's Georgian Historical Series. *George the Third and the Gordon Rebellion*. It's about the Catholic Relief Bill and the riots of seventeen eighty."

"But we didn't have much in common. I never read anything after fifteen sixty-two." At his look of incomprehension, Lena added, "The Council of Trent, you know," which clarified nothing.

Keen caught Dr. Waltham's smile before it vanished.

"But she was a good drezzer, *ja*, very nice . . ." Dr. Schenken murmured. Keen was amazed he noticed anything other than pigs. Jansen had finished his witness statement. As he joined them, he shook his head.

"Thank you all for your cooperation," Keen said, then to Dr. Waltham: "Don't worry about her car or notifying her brother, leave that with us." He retrieved his mechanical pencil and one of his official cards from his shirt pocket, writing his direct extension number on the back, and gave it to her. "If you need anything, please give me a ring."

She glanced at the card. "Cianan Dunliffe."

She'd pronounced it correctly. Surprised, he smiled. "Most people don't get it right first try."

She looked up at him, her eyes again distant. "It's old Gaelic. It means 'little ancient one.' Three Irish saints were named Cianan. I'm a medievalist, so I should know how to pronounce it."

He didn't quite know how to respond to that. He stood, gave her shoulder a consoling pat before he left with Jansen.

"'Little ancient one'?" Jansen teased, grinning.

"Learn something new every day, don't you?"

Jansen laughed. "Wonder what 'Kenneth' means?"

"It's Lithuanian for 'ugly idle git.'"

Although he knew he should have been heading home, Keen rang the tech at Wetherby's again, without success, then reread his case notes. Something about the woman's death bothered him, but nothing he could put his finger on. He was distantly aware of the brief swell of noise, the six o'clock evening relief change, then silence. Distracted, he glanced up at Graeme Davis leaning against the doorway, the CIO's arms crossed.

"Working late?" Davis asked noncommittally.

Damn. "Just finishing up, sir."

"Uh-huh." Davis shrugged his watch out of his sleeve to pointedly examine the time. "See you tomorrow, then," he said, and walked away.

At least Davis had the courtesy not to hover as Keen retrieved his windcheater from his locker. All the same, Keen had to fight his resentment. It had been well over two years since Laura had taken the boys and left him, and he'd buried himself in his work to compensate for the sudden, frighteningly empty hole in his life. He'd driven himself beyond his physical and emotional endurance, knew it even while he was doing it, unable to stop. He ran until he hit the wall.

It wasn't as if he'd had a nervous breakdown, he thought. In all his years on the force, he'd had only the one discipline offense on his record, *one,* damn it. He closed his locker and ignored the tattered photocopy taped to its neighbor. "You can always get another wife," it read. "In the CID you only get one chance."

Well, he'd had one of each and screwed them both up. But he was determined not to make the same mistakes twice. He would never end up some pathetic sniveler claiming disability and drowning his sorrows in a pint of lager. He'd handled it, and accepted the penalty as due and proper. Bumped back to uniform, he'd been grateful not to be suspended as well. Although he'd passed his inspector's exams and interviews, he accepted that single black mark as the likely reason he kept being passed over for promotion. But he didn't want to go on paying for it forever.

Turning the engine over, he let it warm up, taking comfort in the vibration of the car around him. Maybe he'd give Laura a ring, see if she'd let him talk with the boys and feel like a father again for a couple of minutes.

He drove home on mental autopilot, as oblivious to his surroundings as he was in the morning, his mood dark. The house's automatic light went on as he slammed the Vauxhall door.

Keen fumbled with his keys, got the front door opened and his own alarm shut off. He smiled wanly at the lovely sight of five freshly ironed uniform shirts hanging on the sunroom's curtain rod.

God bless you, Joanne Kestleman.

He tried several times to ring Laura, but the phone went unanswered, his unhappy mood deepening. He didn't feel like eating, pouring a few fingers of Laphroaig over a couple cubes of ice instead, and sat out on the porch alone to watch the sunset and the sheep in Derek's fields wend their way home. When the air chilled enough to send him back inside, he had another whiskey before he went to bed, the summer sky still light enough to make sleep difficult, turning restlessly for hours before he could finally drop off.

III

FRIDAY

A cat yowled. Keen dreamed he heard the sound, then woke with a painful jolt. He sat up too quickly, head light. Groaning, he looked at the clock. 6:38. He hadn't slept this late in years. A cat yowled.

Definitely Thomas, he recognized the little bugger's voice. His headache throbbed dully, his sinuses clogged. Slightly queasy, he pulled on his robe and gripped the railing as he walked stiffly down the stairs. He opened the back door and hung on to the doorknob to stay upright. The cat glared up at him reproachfully. His fur was wet, and the cat tracked muddy paws into the kitchen.

"Sorry 'bout that," he said contritely, as Thomas stalked indignantly to his bowl.

Keen didn't bother with a shower, just a quick swipe of his toothbrush to scrape the stale whiskey taste out of his mouth, and washed down the last two pills in the paracetamol bottle with the dregs of yesterday's coffee. He dressed quickly and closed the door, locking the cat into the house for the day. By the time he reached the end drive to his farmhouse, his headache had lessened. But between the painkillers on an empty stomach and the cold coffee, his gut now ached as well. He stopped at the gate to Derek Kestleman's property. He could just see the top of Derek's head on the other side of the hill, working on re-pairing the drystone wall.

His heels clanked on the steel cattle guard. Derek had heard him drive up, but only straightened once Keen got close enough to speak, pressing both fists against his back to stretch, his heavy short-handled hammer dangling from one fist. "Muh'nin'."

Derek Kestleman was a barrel-chested farmer with an equal amount of sheer muscle to beer gut, bandy legs, and broad shoulders. His sons were taller, slimmer copies of their father, all with the same round, weather-chapped face and generous grin. Derek would have made a wonderful criminal, in Keen's opinion; no judge could ever believe this man with the perpetual boyish smile capable of any wrongdoing.

Penny, the family's yellow Labrador, snuffled through the grass on arthritic legs while the sheep watched her with comical anxiety. She was far too ancient and overweight to be a threat, but the neurotic ewes stamped front feet in stiff-legged intimidation. The dog lifted her head to give a weary *huff,* more wheeze than bark, and the sheep scattered in alarm. The dog went back to smelling the flowers.

"Comin' along," Keen said, nodding toward the expanding wall.

"Aye, it is that. Goes faster with two." Derek mopped his sweating face on his sleeve. "E'en faster with three, if you've a mind."

Plumb string had been tied from stick to stick to curve around the lane. A long pile of dark rocks spilled along the edge, being worked without concrete into the traditional drystone wall. Each stone fit together with balance and precision, locking into the whole with every other stone, a skill preserved for centuries on the Yorkshire moors. Farther down the field, Byron, Derek's number two son, waved briefly, then easily tossed a cap-steean slab half his own weight on top of the stone wall before rocking it into position.

Keen had done his boyhood share of hammering bits off small packer stones to make them lock together perfectly, heaving the large through slabs onto the growing partition. It was backbreaking, knuckle-scraping, muscle-aching work, and Keen honestly would have welcomed the exercise.

"Another time," he said. He took a tenner from his wallet. "Gi' this to Joanne, tell her thanks."

Derek slipped the note into the pocket of his work shirt without false re-luctance. "Watched the news last night."

"Aye . . . ?"

"That yours?"

"Depends."

"Floater."

Keen nodded.

"Think it's murder?"

"Dunno yet."

Derek rubbed his nose. "Well, no rest for the wicked."

Keen grinned and nodded at the drystone wall. "Aye, you're right there," he said. He glanced at his watch. "Gotta be going."

"Ah'll sithee, then."

And that's what passed for extensive conversation in the Yorkshire country-side. He arrived ten minutes to the hour, not that anyone would make men-tion of it. Edwards dropped a file on his desk, accompanied by a cup of coffee.

"Thanks," Keen said gratefully, meaning the coffee.

"Cheryl's looking forward to meeting you this weekend." Keen winced. The price of the coffee was too high. "Found that red GTI. It's Christine Swinton's."

Keen leafed through the report forms. "Where?"

"Garth Moor Arms off Harrogate Road, near to Harewood House. One of the beat lads on last night popped in for a cuppa with their night shift recep-tionist." Keen exchanged an amused look with Edwards. "She's round twenty-five, fit, *very* tasty. Or so I hear."

"Hm."

"She asked him to do something about this red GTI hadn't moved in days, annoyed because it was in her spot. He ran a check and your interest report came up on the PNC. Bealle went out at seven to talk with the manageress. Room was let to a Mr. and Mrs. John Smith. Paid cash."

"Original."

"Manageress hadn't noticed anything out of the ordinary, and the maids said nobody'd been in it but the first night, no luggage left, nothing. Only luck we've had is the room wasn't let since."

Dave would go over the room meticulously, but the Garth Moor Arms was a first-class hotel. Any coital evidence left on the sheets would be long washed away, fingerprints wiped, rubbish already trucked off.

The GTI had the usual automotive kit: maps, tools of dubious utility, spare tire. But it also had an astonishing amount of bizarre junk, all dutifully itemized, including a broken model Fokker and an antique ice cream maker. Minus handcrank. Swinton had been as slovenly about her GTI as she was her B and B. But no handbag.

"Did she identify the victim?"

"Spot on."

"What about the man?"

"Never saw him."

Keen looked up. "Swinton registered alone?"

"Aye."

A clandestine rendezvous with a lover wasn't uncommon, fake names and cash payments typical. But in an upscale hotel, with a rich lady like Christine Swinton, perhaps her lover had reason to be more circumspect than the average bloke getting a leg over. Say he didn't show, would she have drowned herself over unrequited love?

"Coroner's report come back from Wetherby yet?"

"Not yet. Halifax's got two burnt to death up in Giro Heights, drug-related murder. Chapeltown's got a shot motorist, and Pudsey has a hit and run, seven-year-old kid on a bike killed."

Keen sighed. Even in death, Christine Swinton would have to wait in a queue like everyone else.

Edwards nodded at the report. "That's just the prelim. Only thing the tech could tell me is she tested positive for blood alcohol, but they haven't finished the drug screens. Met's notified the brother. He'll be up tomorrow round fivish to pick up the car and her personal effects."

"Okay, we'll leave it where it stands for the moment."

"Uh-huh." By his expression, Edwards's instinct was telling him something wasn't right with this case, too.

Keen was hungry, impatient for lunch. Shortly before twelve-thirty his phone buzzed. He grimaced, somehow knowing he'd go hungry again. "Dunliffe."

"This is Jillie Waltham," the American woman said, her words clipped in anger. He blinked in surprise, then remembered he'd given her his direct extension. Before he could ask what he could do for her, she said, "Someone's broken into my hotel room."

"Are they still there, Dr. Waltham?"

"Sticking around to find out seemed like major stupid, Detective," she said tersely. "I have no idea."

He didn't bother correcting her error this time. "Where are you now?" She and Mrs. Birney had fled to a neighbor's house. "Stay there, we'll have officers over in two minutes." He didn't wait for her answer, hitting the button to the shift sergeant. "Jack, we got a possible burglary in progress at twenty-four Foxglove Crescent. I'm on my way now." He hung up, and bolted out the door.

Kellett and Jansen had been contacted by radio, and were already at the guest house by the time Keen had picked up Mrs. Birney and Dr. Waltham. Both women were pale and tense, but calm.

Kellett kept one hand on his baton as he went around the back of the house while Jansen cautiously approached the front. "You and Mrs. Birney please stay here out of harm's way, all right?" Keen said, and followed Jansen.

The point of entry had been through the French windows up the fire escape, a small pane of glass smashed out, fragments spraying inward on the rug. A gentle breeze stirred the curtains.

"Careful of the glass," Keen said. Kellett nodded, searching the room cautiously. The room was even more of a shambles than the previous day, but whoever had broken in had gone. A quick survey of the house turned up no one else. Susan Huddleston arrived and began picking up bits of glass with tweezers, dusting for fingerprints.

Once again, Keen and Dr. Waltham sat in the breakfast room while Mrs. Birney busily brewed up another pot of therapeutic tea.

"I'd packed up Chris's things, thinking when you found her car her brother would take them," Dr. Waltham said without preamble.

"The car was found this morning," Keen said. "She'd let a room at the Garth Moor Arms Hotel. Do you know where that is?"

She shook her head, her brown eyes even darker with anger.

"It's near to Harewood House, not far from where her body was found." He paused. "She registered for two people, Mr. and Mrs. John Smith, paid in cash. Would you know why, or who the man was?"

She glanced away. "No."

"Maybe someone she met at the conference?"

"Definitely not."

"Any of her friends from London—"

She cut him off abruptly. "I don't know any of her friends in London. I hadn't seen Chris since college."

"Which is, what, fifteen years?"

Her fierceness dimmed. "Closer to twenty."

"So you don't really know if she were seeing anyone or not." She didn't answer. "Why would someone break into your room? What were they after?"

"I didn't wait around to see if anything was missing."

"Once our SOCO officer is finished, we'll have a look."

"Fine . . ." Dr. Waltham glanced toward the sound of a kettle whistling. "Are you going to want me to stay in Leeds, I mean, like for legal reasons?"

"I shouldn't think so, not unless we come up with a suspect you can identify. We'd appreciate knowing where you are while you're in Britain and we have your address in the United States if there's anything further."

She nodded, unhappy.

Mrs. Birney placed two cups of Earl Grey tea on the table and left with Jansen to give her statement in the little front foyer. The milk formed miniature hurricane clouds in his swirling tea. Kellett appeared in the doorway. "Susan's finished."

Keen followed the American woman upstairs, watching as she sorted through the belongings strewn about. Mrs. Birney frowned at the smudges of fingerprinting dust, but said nothing.

"Everything of mine seems to be here," Dr. Waltham said finally. "Passport, plane tickets, traveler's checks." She eyed the untidy heap on the bed opposite. "I couldn't tell you if there's anything of Chris's missing or not." Her eyes looked bruised with fatigue.

"If you find something is missing, give us a ring."

"Sure." She sat on the bed, not looking at anything. When it was clear she intended to stay there, Keen followed Kellett downstairs where Mrs. Birney waited.

"I apologize for the mess, Mrs. Birney."

"Nothing a little soap and water won't take care of." He heard the tight anger in her voice: anger with whoever had broken her window, anger with the SOCO officer for the black stains on her walls, and a deeper, more irrational anger at the disruption in her quiet, tidy life. She closed the door firmly, little brass bell tinkling with incongruous cheer.

The inevitable paperwork devoured the rest of his afternoon. He winced at the numerous misspellings in Bealle's reports, as well as the scant information. Bealle and Jansen had spoken to everyone at the medieval conference with even the remotest contact with the dead woman. No one noticed a thing, except for a very public quarrel she'd had with a Dr. Reece Wycombe over some obscure academic dispute, which Bealle had done his best to take down details of while obviously not understanding a single word of it.

Dave Walsh had returned from the Garth Moor Arms with, as expected, sod all. Most of the disparate fingerprints Susan found in Mrs. Birney's guest room would belong to the two women, layered one on top of any number of previous tenants to become one big unidentifiable blotch. But, interestingly enough, the doorknobs and brass handles on the armoire had been wiped clean, no fingerprints at all. Dave spent his afternoon piecing together the broken glass Susan had collected like a jigsaw puzzle. At three-thirty, he rang Keen's extension. "You might want a look at this."

Dave propped his chin on his fist as Keen studied the marks on the shattered glass, spray fixative permanently cementing it in place. Part of the distinctive pattern was smeared where whoever had stepped onto the glass had pivoted, but there was enough to leave a clear impression.

"That's not a shoeprint," Keen said finally.

"Nope."

"Then what the hell am I looking at?"

"A tire track."

"A tire track?" Keen looked up at Dave, baffled.

"A tire track. A sixty HR fourteen Uniroyal, to be precise."

"Dave, that's impossible. This were found inside a second-story bedroom." He held out a remote hope. "What did she have on the GTI?"

"Pirellis."

Damn. "How did it *get* there?"

"Buggered if I know. That's your job."

At four, Keen booked off. He had turned north onto Otley Road when he spotted Dr. Waltham walking along the footpath, hands in her jacket pockets, her head down. She looked utterly forlorn. He pulled over and rolled down his window. "Hello, there," he said. "Feeling any better?"

"Fine," she said automatically, then eyed him with an odd expression. "Well . . . not that great. The conference is nearly over, and Lena's left for Edinburgh. I don't know many people here, and anyway, the only thing anyone wants to talk about is Chris." She smiled wanly. "Or pigs." He smiled in return. "I don't want to go back to the B and B yet, so I'm just . . ."—she made a vague gesture—"walking around."

He nodded and paused. "Look, it's early but have you eaten yet?" It was an impulsive idea and he wasn't sure it was a good one, but it felt right. When she shook her head, he said, "If you wouldn't mind my stopping off home so I can change, I know a pub serves decent food."

She hesitated just long enough for him to be relieved she was about to decline, then surprised him. "Okay." She looked startled herself.

She got in. Neither spoke as he drove, the tension palpable, and he was already regretting his rash offer. "You live in Leeds?" she said finally, gazing out the window as they passed the cemetery.

He glanced at her, realizing she didn't know where she was. "No. I live up near Lindley Moor. It's a bit of a ways, if you'd rather not."

She smiled, a quick diffident expression not matching her eyes. "It's okay. Really." She said nothing more until they had passed Bramhope, then only looked at him curiously when he crossed the river the other side of Poole.

When he reached his turnoff at Leathley Grange, the road narrowing to a single lane through the fields, she said, "You live somewhat off the beaten path."

"It's where I grew up," he said. He slowed as they passed Mrs. Tillman walking her fat little Thelwell pony with ten-year-old Neomie perched on its bare back. They waved as he inched past, the pony shaking its head nervously. He waved back. No doubt Sandra Tillman would be on the phone to Joanne directly to find out who the strange woman with Keen might be. That was one drawback of country life, everybody lived in everybody else's pocket.

"Beautiful countryside."

He glanced at Dr. Waltham gazing out over the hills, more at ease.

"It's cold and windy in the winter, though." He wondered why he'd said it. Fast-moving shadows flowed across emerald and gold fields as the wind off the moors blew hazy clouds. The hills were dark with heather promising to explode into brilliant purple, every color of wildflower imaginable bobbed their heads along the sides of the road. Windswept trees hunched in the distance, and as Keen breathed in sharp air he thought, not for the first time either, there was nowhere else on earth he would have chosen to live.

"Oregon gets cold and windy in the winter, too," she said.

Then again, he thought ruefully, he hadn't seen that much of the rest of the world to know. "What's it like where you live?"

She smiled, quite a pretty lady when she relaxed. "Different. High mountains. Lots of trees, mostly firs and pines. Portland's west of the Cascades, near Mount Hood. In the winter, the wind down the Columbia Gorge can be a pain. One time after an ice storm, Karen and I snowshoed in to Multnomah Falls. Huge waterfall frozen solid, like a million tons of dripped white candle wax." She stopped, biting her lip as if embarrassed to be talking too much. "You ever been to the States?"

He smiled, knowing she had intentionally steered the conversation toward him. "No. Maybe someday."

His boys had wheedled about going to Disney World in Florida, something beyond his means. Tremayne hinted *he* would take the twins, and Keen was more grateful than he could admit when Laura threatened dire consequences if her live-in boyfriend so much as breathed a word. The lads could wait until they were old enough to appreciate such a trip . . . and for Keen to afford it, was the unspoken addendum.

He turned off the worn country road and down almost half a mile of gravel drive, pulled up in front of the house, and turned off the engine. In the quiet, he was suddenly ill at ease.

"Pretty house," she said. "And old."

"Not that old, only about two hundred years."

She laughed. "In America, that's prehistoric. You're renovating the barn?"

"We were," he said, then winced at his mistake. "I won't be a minute."

She got out of the car before he could come round, then followed him to the house. "Well, hello, you," Keen heard her say as he was turning off the alarm system. Thomas had stopped on the stairs to stare at her through the banister rails. She held her fingers a few inches from his nose, the cat sniffing warily. "What's his name?"

"Thomas."

She flashed him a grin. "Becket or More?"

"Neither."

"Aquinas? Dylan? Wolfe?"

"Just . . . Thomas. Like in 'tomcat.' Not too imaginative, is it?"

She chuckled, and scratched the cat's ears. His back arched, pushing his head into her hand and purring. "Well, it's better than 'kitty.' "

"If you don't mind him keeping you company, I'll be right back."

By the time he'd changed into jeans and a flannel shirt and come downstairs, she had Thomas cradled in her arms as she read the titles in his bookcase.

"Unconventional mix," she said, stroking the cat's head. Among his criminology textbooks and police law references, Home Office reports he'd never gotten around to tossing out along with back issues of *Police Review* and *British Journal of Criminology,* he also had collector's editions of Shakespeare and Oscar Wilde, Arthur Conan Doyle and Charles Dickens, his mother's poetry from Ireland and Wales, Robert Graves's histories and Ken Follett spy fiction, Minette Walters and P. D. James in dog-eared paperbacks, an *Encyclopaedia Britannica* Laura considered too out-of-date for the twins, an Italian-language Bible from God-knows-where, gardening books and bird guides, books on cars, books on antiques, books on fishing, children's bedtime stories for when the boys came to visit, his proper biographies side by side with Laura's trashy exposés, travel guides of all the places he thought he might want to visit someday but knew he'd likely never see. "You read a lot?"

"When I've got time. Don't much care for television."

She picked up the hinged, double-framed photographs on top of the bookcase. "Good-looking kids."

"My sons, Colin and Simon, fraternal twins. Colin's the towhead. They're nearly nine now. Live with their mother down in London." He hesitated and wondered why. "We're divorced." It felt odd to say.

"Me, too. I've got a daughter, Karen. She's nineteen. She's studying journalism at the University of Colorado." She smiled, fondling Thomas's ears. "Expose corruption, fight for justice. Save the world. More enthusiasm than common sense, I'm afraid. She was always more like Chris than me in some ways, the two of them spent hours on the phone arguing politics. Karen spent every summer here, she adored her aunt Chris . . ." Her voice cracked.

He wasn't good at small talk, and knew most people were uncomfortable with silence, a useful interrogation technique but not one he wanted at that moment. After an awkward silence, Keen asked, "You hungry?" He definitely was.

"Sure." She extricated herself from the cat's passionate embrace. "Goodbye, Thomas, nice to meet you."

Keen's hand bumped hers when they both reached to open the passenger door of the Vauxhall. She glanced at him with wide eyes, then waited for him to open her door. As he walked around the bonnet, he wondered how anyone could figure out the rules anymore, where the line was drawn between being a gentleman and a hopelessly sexist git. Thomas stared out the window reproachfully, his mouth open in a soundless yowl of protest as they drove away.

The White Rose pub overlooked the foaming waters of the weir at Lindley Bridge, the only building for miles tucked behind an ancient hedgerow and surrounded by fields of grazing sheep. Inside, several regulars nursed pints at the bar. Jersey and Alan paused in their game of darts to eye the woman with Keen.

"Nah, then," Lynette called out to him cheerfully. "Wheres'ta bin lately? Hennot seen you f' so long, ah almost didn't awn yer."

"Been a bit thronged lately," Keen replied, smiling. The publican's wife was at least seventy, fighting time kicking and screaming every inch of the way. Dyed yet another shade of auburn, her hair cascaded in tumbling curls.

"Has' ta, now? Looking nobbut dowly, t'as thin as a whippet moithered wi' runnin' about after t' criminal soart. Y'mun try ma new Black Forest wild cherry gateau, recipe's reet French ahten that *Gourmet* magazine." She pronounced it with the *t,* even though Keen knew she knew different.

"Champion, pet. We s'll have it at after, but just a shiver, mind. Me gaffers dahn on fat bobbies."

Lynette's husband appeared behind the pumps, Kyle's black hair silvered at the temples.

"What would you like to drink?" Keen asked her.

"I'm not that fond of beer, but I like cider."

"Strongbow ah'va tap or Woodpecker bi t' bah'lle," Kyle said.

Keen could see her translating Kyle's thick Yorkshire pronunciation into something closer to English. "Strongbow, please."

"Gi'us a gill a' Webster's," Keen said.

Holding both drinks, Keen steered her away from the curious and into the back room. A large fireplace held a single charred log, brass plates hung over the mantel with embossed scenes of fox hunting and duck shoots. Benches lined the walls, with three-legged stools on the opposite side of wood tables. He chose the corner by the window, waning daylight orange through squares of smoky bubbled glass.

Kyle left two plastic-bound menus unopened on the table. The fare hadn't changed in years, the menus more for show as the locals rarely bothered with them. Jersey and Alan were still throwing darts, heavy thunks and mock arguments, while Kyle shouted the orders at Lynette and ignored her bantering reply. Keen looked up from his menu at Dr. Waltham's bemused expression. "What?"

"Your accent's different."

"Excuse me?"

"When you're doing your policeman bit, you speak differently."

"I suppose I do." He shrugged. "Don't take much notice of it."

"It's not a criticism. I think Yorkshire accents are lovely."

"You do?" He didn't hear that one too often.

"Sometimes it's hard to understand what people are saying, and sometimes I think I'm not *supposed* to, but it's sort of musical. It's certainly not what I expected."

"What did you expect?" He took a long swallow from his beer.

"I guess I thought all English people sounded like Eliza Doolittle, or that weird food guy, Lloyd Grossman."

He almost choked. "Lloyd Grossman isn't English."

"I know."

"If it's any consolation, I were disappointed when I discovered most Americans don't sound like Andy Sipowitz. Being from the countryside, my accent might be a bit thicker than someone from the city. But if you think mine is rough, you should hear them from North Riding." He chuckled at her bewilderment. "It's from the original Danish. 'Riding' just means 'thirds.' There's West Riding, East Riding, and North Riding."

"I knew this was all Viking territory, but I'm not familiar with the actual morphology." She used the grammatical terminology casually, as if taking it for granted he would understand. Which, he realized, he did. "So there's no South Riding?"

He smiled. "We just call the leftover bits 'England.' " He swallowed several more gulps on his beer, stomach growling. "You gave a speech at this conference?"

"I delivered a paper . . . well, same thing, really."

"What about?"

" 'Eclecticism in Interpretive Comparisons of Alexander Nequam's *De Laudibus Divinae Sapientiae* and Adam of Balsham's *De Utensilibus ad Domun Regendam.*' "

"Ah," he said cautiously. "Interesting."

She laughed. "I think the word you're searching for is 'boring.' "

"No, I'm sure it's fascinating."

Kyle reappeared. "Wot'll you fowkes be etten tonight?"

"Could I have the fish with a salad instead of fries . . . ah, chips?" she asked. Kyle nodded, impassive.

"Same here," Keen said, and ignored Kyle's sideling glance more eloquent than any Yorkshire dialect. They both waited until Kyle had left. "You speak Latin?"

"Well enough for research, I suppose. My French is passable, but my German is awful. Some Spanish, Italian. That's about it, really."

Her tone was apologetic, which made him feel all the more intimidated. Keen looked at the foam in his half-empty glass, noting her own was still nearly full. "Had Latin in school, don't remember a bloody word of it. And the only French I know is likely to get me slapped." She laughed again, making him smile. "So what got you interested in medieval history?"

"I don't know," she said, her humor diminishing. He'd touched a nerve. "I guess I prefer things far enough in the past that they don't matter in the real world anymore." She looked away. "So. What made you decide to become a policeman?"

"Didn't want to be a farmer." He sipped his beer, slowing to match her pace. He was driving her back to Leeds tonight. One pint was the limit.

The strained silence was fortunately broken by the arrival of supper and Ronnie Norville. Ronnie was eighty-two and a fixture at the White Rose for half a century. His nose and cheeks were riddled with the fine lines of a habitual heavy drinker. Keen knew Ronnie was well on his way to being utterly pissed, but he carried himself with a stiff military bearing, leaning on his cane.

"Aren't ye g'n introduce me to y'r American lady friend?"

"Ronnie Norville," Keen said, but before he could introduce Dr. Waltham, she had her hand out.

"Gillian Waltham," she said firmly. "Just call me Jillie."

Ronnie held her hand prisoner with both his. "Fought with the Americans in World War Two, I did," he said gravely. "On the beaches of Normandy, D-Day. Brave lads, all." Finally, he allowed her to escape. "Fought in Belgium, Holland, e'en down in Morocco, right nasty war." And for the next hour, Ronnie regaled them with his favorite subject, his exploits as a young soldier freeing all Europe from the Nazi scourge near single-handed. Keen had heard it before, or at least several variations since Ronnie seemed incapable of telling the same story twice.

Keen was content to sit back and observe Jillie as she listened to Ronnie's legendary adventures with amusement, skepticism, and often, Keen suspected, total incomprehension. She was a good listener, chin cupped in her hand as she gave her full attention to Ronnie. Naturally, Ronnie hadn't had such a devoted audience in years. Not even Lynette placing two huge slices of chocolate cake in front of them could dislodge him, the man oblivious.

"That's the spirit we had in them days, aye, e'en the Falklands showed the world Britain was still a power to be reckoned with. Not like it is now with this shiftless namby-pamby lot in Parliament. The Iron Lady's gone, alas for this proud country of ours, I say."

"Who, Margaret Thatcher?"

Ronnie raised the dregs of his pint. "Greatest prime minister since Churchill," he proclaimed, drained the glass, and gave Keen a significant look. Keen signaled to Kyle standing at the bar wiping glasses, who pulled a fresh pint for the old soldier.

"God save our gracious queen," Ronnie declared exuberantly, and drained half his pint in one go.

"Gi' over, you," Kyle said. "Drink up. Your wife's waiting."

Ronnie's élan dulled, but he finished his pint and stood, amazingly stable on his feet. Bending over Jillie's hand, he mumbled, "Pleasure."

"He's a real character," Jillie said as he walked off with stiff care.

"He does liven the place up now and again."

Kyle placed two cups of coffee in front of them, pointedly overlooking the plates with half-eaten cake. Lynette would take it as an insult if they didn't finish.

"So what do *you* think of your prime minister?"

"I'm a loyal and dedicated member of the No Comment party," Keen said. "I try not to have too many opinions. They only tend to get me into trouble."

Jillie glanced down at her cake. "I can't possibly eat all this."

"I can't either. I'll pay the bill and take you back to Leeds."

When he came back to the table, she was gazing at her near empty glass of cider with a strange expression. He recognized it. *Fear.*

"I'm taking a train to London tomorrow. Would you know a hotel near the station?" She flushed. "Mrs. Birney is very sweet, and it's a lovely room, but . . . I can't stay there anymore. Especially after today."

"I understand," he said. He hesitated, about to make another impulsive offer he wasn't sure was a good one. "I have a spare bedroom," he said. He had more than one spare room these days. "And I can take you back to Leeds in the morning."

Her fleeting alarm startled him, before she reddened with embarrassment. "No, I couldn't," she said hastily. She hadn't been hinting, clearly distressed he might have thought she had. Or worried about what ulterior motives his offer might imply, he realized. "I don't want to put you out, you've already been so nice." She fumbled with her handbag. "I'm being stupid, really. Just drop me off at Mrs. Birney's, I'll be fine . . ."

He should have agreed, listened to her words and taken her back to Leeds. But he understood being afraid of being alone.

"Truth is, I wouldn't mind not having to drive out and back again tonight."

"Oh. I'm sorry." He wondered what for, and waited as she weighed his offer uncertainly. "You're sure it's no trouble?"

It was plenty of trouble. Not only wasn't he sure this didn't break police conduct standards, every gossip in a twenty-mile radius would be aware within the day he'd had a strange woman stay overnight. "Of course not."

It was dark enough to need headlights on the way back to the house; the distant pinpoints of lights of other farmhouses appeared and disappeared in the curves of the hills. They said nothing as he parked, the automatic lights coming on as he unlocked the front door. Thomas raced down the staircase, overjoyed to see her, tangling his body around her ankles. She scooped him up and held him upside down to scratch his belly. Amazingly, Thomas seemed delighted with this irreverent treatment.

"You're a friendly beastie," she said.

"Don't know why." Keen stood with his hands in his pockets, smiling. "He isn't usually. You must be good with animals."

She cradled the cat in one arm and scratched behind his ears. "We had a lot when I was kid, just about anything you could imagine: goats, donkeys, chickens, pigeons, chinchillas, llamas, Vietnamese potbellied pigs, the usual pound dogs, and stray cats. My uncle Homer built this incredible ant farm for my fifteenth birthday?" Again, her voice rose in that odd questioning sound that baffled him. "Great big thing, plate-glass boxes connected together with plastic tubing, millions of ants. It lasted until I went away to college." She ran out of words, suddenly breathless.

"Sounds brilliant." He didn't know what else to say. She held the cat as if to maintain the barrier between them. Her palpable distrust depressed him.

"It's still early. Would you like a cup of tea?"

"Too late for caffeine for me. Herbal?"

Not even his diet was *that* far into health food. "Sorry."

"I usually drink hot milk at night."

He grinned. "We seem to be having a problem with milk in this house lately. I might have some red wine around somewhere."

"Perfect."

He found a half-bottle of claret in a cupboard, unable to remember when he'd last had a glass of it. He pulled the cork and sniffed skeptically, hoping it hadn't gone to vinegar. It smelled acceptable enough, not that he could taste the difference between a hundred-pound Lafite-Rothschild and two-a-penny plonk.

Thomas was practically grinning with delight when he returned with the wine, purring audibly. Keen could see the vibration in his fur. "I called Karen last night to tell her Chris was dead," Jillie said to the cat. "She took it hard. I couldn't even tell her that much, just that Chris had an accident and drowned."

"At the moment, that's all we know, too."

"The news said she was drunk and went skinny-dipping in somebody's pond."

"We don't know how drunk she was yet."

She looked up, her eyes reddened. "Probably a lot," Jillie admitted, unhappy. "Chris wasn't much on moderation in anything. When we were in college, she loved to party, lots of politics, lots of pot and booze. We got arrested during a student antinuclear demonstration, I think. I never could keep all the causes straight. Chris was drunk and decided to dance naked in the fountain, *La Dolce Vita,* fountains to the people sort of thing. This cop tried to get her out, and grabbed her by the hair." Jillie grinned wryly. "You don't do that to Chris. She was small, but absolutely fearless. She punched him in the face and broke his nose, blood everywhere."

He looked down into his glass, the claret as dark as blood spilled against rain-slicked asphalt. Suddenly unable to drink it, he set it down.

"We got thrown in jail, where Chris demanded to call the British consulate and threatened to sue everybody in Boston." She had gone back to talking to the cat. "I was so drunk and so scared all I did was throw up all night. Some brave protester I turned out to be."

"What happened?"

She shrugged. "One of Chris's boyfriends bailed us out the next morning. We were kids, eighteen, nineteen. The judge just fined us for public disorder. My father was furious, said now I had a 'criminal record.' Uncle Homer thought the whole thing was hilarious." She drained her glass. "But life with Chris was always exciting."

"You and she were close." He made it neither a statement nor a question.

She knew exactly what he was doing. "We were then," she said bluntly. "She was my best friend. Maybe Chris was unconventional and didn't care about political correctness, but she wasn't a drunk, and she didn't deserve to die like she did."

"I didn't intend it to sound that way."

"I'm sorry," Jillie said, her indignation quickly deflated. "You're just doing your job."

"And I didn't intend it to sound that way, either." He smiled, trying to lessen the tension. "Look, we're both tired. I'll show you your room and let you settle in." He nodded toward the cat asleep in her lap. "You can even keep the teddy."

She stood, limp cat in her arms. "Mr. Dunliffe—"

"Keen."

"Keen. I apologize. You've been very kind, and I don't think I've even remembered to say thank you."

"Don't mention it." He showed her the downstairs guest room and lavatory. "Towels and extra pillows in the wardrobe. If Thomas is a bother, boot him out. I'm usually up by six, is that too early for you?"

"No, that's fine."

"Good night, then."

"Good night."

Before he locked the door for the night, Keen weighted an envelope on the window ledge with a rock, a note and a fiver inside for Hackwell, the dairyman. Upstairs, he went through his usual routine, brushed his teeth, took two fat Tylenols, undressed, and slid into his half of the bed. It felt odd to have a strange woman in the house. Propping the pillows behind him, he looked out into the utter blackness of the fields, and listened to the unfamiliar sounds below, water running, a soft voice murmuring to the cat, a door creaking shut.

He let his thoughts drift, then, as they bumped into painful memories, turned them toward the dead woman. He was unable to put the lively troublemaker Jillie described with the still blue face. He didn't believe in ghosts calling out for justice from beyond the grave.

But he did believe in policeman's instincts. And his instincts were still telling him something was definitely not right.

IV

SATURDAY

The tall pine cast blue shadows as Jillie struggled with her suitcases up the frozen walkway of her house, snow crunching underfoot. Mount Hood towered in the distance, as familiar as an old friend. Fat snowflakes spiraled lazily to the ground and Jillie wondered why she wasn't cold. The suitcases kept opening, clothes spilling out. To her relief, Karen opened the door, the warm light of the house at her back, smiling as she called out, "Maaaaa!"

The sound had been much too real to sustain the dream. Jillie's eyes shot open. She panted shallowly, rummaging through the fragments of dream logic before she remembered where she was.

She jerked upright as she heard it again, a forlorn, almost human cry. "Maaaaa!" She pushed a curtain aside to look out over the gentle swell of green hillside, winding fences of dark stone and flocks of white sheep cropping the grass. A lamb stood on sturdy black legs, neck thrust out and teeth bared as it protested, "Maaaaa!" It trotted toward its mother's nasal answer, ceaselessly whisking its tail.

Birdsong, high and trilling, mixed with clucks of chickens and honks of ducks. Some kind of farm machinery growled in the distance. Water sputtered through pipes, the house awake. A cat mewled, answered by a man's voice too low to make out anything more than his exasperation. The few stray hairs at the foot of her bed were the only evidence of Thomas's nighttime company.

She picked up her watch from beside the bed. 7:30. She dressed quickly in yesterday's clothes and ran her fingers through her thick curls in the vague hope she might look slightly less unkempt than a sheepdog.

She closed the bedroom door quietly and turned to find Keen Dunliffe in the hallway arch, coffee cup in one hand. "Good morning," he said, and nodded toward the kitchen behind him. "Coffee's hot."

She smiled nervously, not because of anything he had done, but because unfamiliar settings made her hyperaware, every smell and sound acute. "Sorry. I overslept."

"It's Saturday. Milk, no sugar, right?"

"Right." She was surprised. Even after eighteen years of marriage, Robert could never remember how she took her coffee.

She followed him into the kitchen where he poured her a cup of coffee out of a Pyrex measuring pitcher. Puzzled, she looked at the bottle of milk on the table, sides slicked with condensation. There hadn't been any milk last night. "They still do that? Deliver milk right to your doorstep?"

"A cherished British tradition. I suppose that makes me old-fashioned."

Her unease melted. "To quote my sophisticated college-educated daughter," she said and parodied Karen's mall-rat inflection, "that's rilly like, y'know, major *cool.*"

His smile broadened, the tanned skin around light blue eyes crinkling. He had a nice face, she decided, not handsome, but square and healthy. His dark hair was cut shorter than she liked, silver dusting his temples and an odd smudge of white behind one ear. He wore Levi's and a denim shirt, had strong shoulders and narrow hips with a touch of belly at his beltline. The casual clothes made him more likable and less aloof than he'd seemed in his uniform. Less . . . *conservative,* she thought.

The top half of the Dutch door was open, letting the breeze drift into the kitchen. Thomas appeared from around the counter, licking his chops. Keen nudged the cat with his shoe. "Through with your breakfast already, you greedy little bugger?" The cat ignored him. Keen glanced back at Jillie. "How about you? Hungry? I'm making eggs and bacon."

"Don't go to any trouble," she said hastily.

"No trouble. I indulge in a fry-up every Saturday. Something to look forward to after a week of eating livestock feed." He picked up a bag of granola as proof.

She smiled. "Okay. Thank you." She warmed her hands on the coffee mug, and made no offer to help; he knew where things were, she didn't. All she could do was get in the man's way.

Besides, it was a pleasure to watch him. He moved with rough grace, as choreographed as a dance. He spread strips of bacon out on a rack under the top broiler and set a stainless steel pan on the stove to heat. While it warmed, he popped slices of bread into a toaster, then lobbed a square of butter into the pan to sizzle.

He cracked the eggs into the hot pan one-handed, tossed the shells into a garbage sack under the sink, and grabbed a pair of tongs to turn the bacon over. Just as he flipped the eggs, the toast popped up with a ping. He had the timing down perfectly, plates on the table with the edges of the eggs lightly crisped, the bacon still hissing, and the butter melting over the toast. A jar of homemade black currant jam and a bottle of orange juice joined the coffee.

"You're good at this," she said.

"I am now. I had to learn how after my divorce. Could barely boil water for tea until I were over thirty. Surprised me, I actually enjoy doing it." He watched her as she took a bite. "What's the verdict, then?" He wasn't smiling, but Jillie was sure he was teasing her.

"Great. Even better since I didn't have to make it."

"You don't like to cook?"

"Not a lot. I've done it since I was nine years old, after my mother died.

My dad was a truck driver, so he wasn't home much. We went to live with his brother and I had to do pretty much everything, all the shopping and the housework. Same thing after I got married. Then all while I raised my daughter by myself and worked full time after my divorce. It gets old fast."

She saw the subtle shift, his eyes distant. He paid meticulous attention to his food and asked too casually, "What about Chris? Did she like to cook?"

She took a sharp breath, the sudden ache in her chest unexpected. He was nice, even sort of good-looking. But, she reminded herself, he was still a *cop*. "I don't think so. She made toast and tea for breakfast, and we always went out for meals."

"How much did you both drink at these meals?"

"No more than a bottle of wine between us," she said firmly. She didn't add she only had a single glass while Chris polished off the rest of the bottle herself. Her appetite was gone. "Still a policeman, aren't you, even out of uniform?"

He leaned back in his chair. "Sorry. I'm just trying to get a sense of the kind of person she was so I can better understand how and why she died."

Chagrined, she pushed the remains of her breakfast around her plate. "Okay, fair enough."

"This person she was meeting on Tuesday. Can you remember if it was a man or woman?"

That stopped her. "I don't know," she said finally. "I assumed it was a man, but I don't remember if she said that or not."

"Why would you assume it was a man, then?"

She frowned. Not because of his attitude; he had been relentlessly polite and considerate. But her own automatic assumption that anyone of importance would have been male irritated her. "I don't know, I just did."

"Do you remember what she was wearing?"

"A red skirt and jacket, white blouse. Red shoes." He kept waiting. "Um, panty hose. I don't know about underwear." She remembered something else. "A necklace."

He blinked. "What sort of necklace?"

"Thin chain with a gold pendant. I think it was a Greek letter."

"You're not sure?"

"I don't read Greek. It could have been Hebrew or Sanskrit for all I know," she said irritably. "I don't read those, either."

He ignored her pique. "Were it big enough to slip off over her head?"

"Like if she went swimming in a pond and lost it?" She shuddered. "Maybe."

"Would you recognize it if you saw it again?"

"Probably."

"What about her handbag, could you describe it?"

It was her turn to blink. "You don't have it?"

"No. It wasn't with her and it wasn't in her car and it wasn't in your B and B."

"It's about so big." She measured with her hands. "Brown leather, bronze hook clasp. Zipped back pocket."

"Any idea of what she carried in it?"

"The usual stuff, I guess. Lipstick, hairbrush. Pens, wallet, credit cards, money." She didn't mention Chris's ubiquitous small rolled plastic bag of marijuana with Zigzag rolling papers. As Keen tilted his head to look at her speculatively she felt her face flush. "Now that I've answered your questions, would you answer mine? You were there, weren't you?"

"Where she were found? Yes, I was there."

"So what do *you* think happened?"

His eyes were again meditative. "It's too soon to say," he said cautiously. "She might have gone to meet someone in secret at the Garth Moor Arms, since she registered under a false name. When he didn't show, she drank too much, went for a walk in the night and wandered into the grounds up at the Harewood House. Maybe she thought going for a swim might sober her up. It's likely just a tragic accident."

She wished she hadn't asked, and brushed a tear away angrily. She wasn't even sure who she was crying for, Chris or herself. When he covered her other hand with his, it took an effort to keep from pulling away, afraid of offending him. "I'm sorry if I've upset you," he said.

"That's okay. It's your job." She tried to smile, her face feeling rubbery. "Asking questions, I mean. Not upsetting people."

He smiled back. "I know what you meant. And it's not just my job. If it's any consolation, I don't think it was suicide. I think she were simply too drunk to know what she was doing. Why else would a lovely, bright woman get so pissed she would wander off alone in the middle of the night without so much as a towel, then leave all her nice clothes folded up on a bench to go swimming in a mucky fish pond?"

She froze, the hair rising on her arms. "Say that again," she whispered.

"About her being drunk?"

"No, about her clothes."

"She took them off and left them on a bench."

"Folded."

She watched it click, his eyes calculating. "Neatly," he confirmed, and stared at her. His palm still over her hand was warm.

"You saw our room at the B and B. Chris Swinton never folded a single piece of clothing in her life." She shivered. "She was *murdered*."

"Now hold on," Keen said sharply. "You don't know that, any number of things could have happened. Someone walking without knowing she were in the pond took the opportunity to sort through her clothes and nick her handbag."

"And folded her clothes for her as a courtesy? Rather a strange thing for a thief to do."

"I've seen stranger."

"What about someone breaking into our hotel room?"

"Do you know how many burglaries the Leeds police respond to every month? It could be pure coincidence."

"And how many burglaries where the thieves don't steal anything?"

"More than you'd expect," he insisted. "People hear glass breaking, and run up to see what's happening. They spook the intruder, he's out and gone before he can take anything."

Her certainty weakened. "But it *is* a pretty bizarre coincidence, isn't it?"

He began picking up the plates. "Doesn't prove it were murder."

They said nothing more as he washed the breakfast dishes. She collected the juice glasses and the coffee cups, bringing them to the sink. With a quick smile, he washed them as well, placing the wet dishes on the drain board to dry.

"It's going to be well on nine o'clock before I get you back to Leeds," he said, drying his hands on a towel. "You're sure you're up to going back to London today?"

"Yes," she said firmly. "I want to take the train as soon as I've checked out of Mrs. Birney's."

He hung the dishtowel over the sink faucet. "Where will you be staying in London?" That startled her. "If we need to contact you again."

"Oh. I was staying with Chris, but now I'm not sure."

"Max Swinton will be up around five tonight to collect her car. If you wait, he might give you a lift down—"

"No," she said, more sharply than she'd intended, and tried to soften it. "Just tell him I've gone back to Chris's place. I still have some of my things there, but I'll find a hotel as soon as I can, and leave her spare key when I go."

Keen nodded. "Will you be staying for the funeral, then?"

She inhaled sharply. "Oh, Jesus. The *funeral.*" She hadn't even thought of that. "Yes, of course. I should go, shouldn't I?"

"Well, let's get you back to Leeds, then, shall we?"

Although the silence was strained as he opened the passenger door for her, this time she managed to get in with more grace. He even closed it for her. Robert had never once done that. Feminist ideology or not, she secretly had to admit she liked it.

Thomas basked in the sun on a stone wall next to a pile of old lumber, paws tucked under his chest. The cat didn't open his eyes when they drove off, fickle beast. The car rolled and swayed over the ruts, gravel rasping as they drove to the main road.

She watched the scenery go by, not really seeing it. Country landscape gave way to buildings as they reached the city limits. "You know where the central train station is?" Keen asked.

"I figured a taxi should know how to get there." She winced, not meaning to have sounded so snide.

He didn't appear to have noticed, his attention on the road, hands casual on the steering wheel. "You'll want the one off City Square, behind Queen's Hotel. It's two hours to London, direct."

Driving by the police station, he passed Weetwood Hall. A few people still wandered around with congress badges and the coveted bright red program booklet clutched in their hands. When he pulled up to the curb by Mrs. Birney's house, he left the motor idling.

"Thank you for everything," she said. "I mean that, really."

"My pleasure." His expression was again neutral, none of the easy familiarity of the night before. "Dr. Waltham," he said, and that clinched it, "I know you'd rather believe someone killed your friend rather than accept she may have simply done something stupid." His light eyes were as cool and impersonal as stone. "We're none of us saints. But don't be turning this into something more dramatic than it is."

"And don't *you* write her off as an alcoholic slut until you've checked out everything else first," she said, indignant anger boiling up again.

He didn't seem to take offense. "I didn't plan to." He paused. "You're not a terribly good liar, you know."

Her face drained. "I beg your pardon?"

"Are you sure there's nothing else you haven't told me?"

"Like what?"

"Like what else might have been in her handbag?"

She gasped. The words had been spoken so blandly, he might have been asking her the time. She got out of the car and bent down, trying to keep her voice as indifferent as his own and failing. "I don't snoop through other people's purses any more than I want anyone snooping in mine. You're the detective. *You* figure it out."

She resisted the impulse to slam the door, and walked away. For a moment, she was terrified he would come after her, the car not moving behind her. Then to her relief, she heard him drive off.

Amused, Keen watched her walk stiffly into Mrs. Birney's guesthouse before he pulled away from the curb. He didn't drive to the station, instead kept on the ring road and headed north toward Harrogate.

Out of uniform, he paid his entry fee and pulled into the Harewood House car park already filling with tourists. Flags announcing a rally fluttered from tents in the vast fields. People ambled across clipped grass to ogle lovingly polished MG-TDs, TR-7s and Morgans, Austin-Healys and Aston Martins.

Keen crossed the dam in search of the bench under the oak. Laughter from the café mixed with children's squeals from the playground. The hardworking estate had little time between running conferences, rallies, dog shows, open-air theatre, musical concerts, even bungee jumping and paintball games, to deal with the annoyance of an inopportune death. The blue and white POLICE tape had already been cleared away.

He sat on the bench and gazed across the lake. A fine haze rose from the water. Ducks sunbathed on the opposite bank, mallards preening bright feathers, drab females nibbling the grass. A wary moorhen walked across water-lily leaves, guarding her numerous babies against pike perch, massive death which could rise from the murky depths to swallow a tiny ball of feathers in one gulp.

Keen had photographs of his grandmother in her volunteer nurse's uniform during the war when Harewood House had turned convalescent hospital for wounded soldiers, one of whom became her second husband. Keen's mother had played among the Regency and Chippendale furniture and Reynolds oil portraits with children brought up from London to escape the Blitz. She remembered their funny accents and haunted eyes, and how bravely everyone had taken the news when the viscount, off in faraway Europe with his Grenadier Guards, had been wounded and taken prisoner so like a heroic film star. Even with the savagery of the Nazis just across the water, the world his mother reminisced about misted over into a simpler, more innocent age.

And yet, until a few days ago, he'd never been to Harewood House. Never walked its parks with Laura. Never brought the lads to the bird garden on a weekend, he realized, and wondered why not. Surely his life hadn't always been that busy? All water under the bridge now.

The lake was deceptively peaceful, a breeze rippling reflected sunlight as his thoughts turned to the dead woman and his own reaction to her folded clothing. Could this be more than it looked like, an accidental drowning? More unsettling, did he *want* it to be?

Keen had been both a policeman and a detective long enough to know the average detective rarely came across a deliberately planned cold-blooded murder. But he hadn't gone into the job for the excitement. The prestige of CID was far more enjoyable than the actual work, which consisted mostly of tracking down dim-witted teenaged vandals, investigating bungled burglaries, arresting pathetic elderly shoplifters. What few murders came up were usually the result of too much booze and stupidity.

He'd convinced himself he didn't miss El Cid anymore. Let that bastard Mullard and his overinflated ego have at it. But he sat by the lake with growing uneasiness that he was overdue for a change in ways he wasn't sure he was ready for, that he'd allowed himself the comfort of treading water far too long.

Water. Water under the bridge . . .

Keen scooped up a handful of pebbles and walked to the edge of the pond. One by one, he tossed the pebbles into the water, examining their curved trajectory, the shallow plunk as they splashed. Feathery water plants swayed in the current. When he ran out of pebbles, he brushed the grit from his palms.

He followed the gravel walk along the lakeside that ended at vast open fields of sheep. No one would have walked into the estate from this direction.

He doubled back across the dam to a paved footpath just before the stables, and hiked down to a gate in the low wall demarcating the boundary of the Harewood estate. The tiny village of Stank wasn't more than a couple of stone farm buildings and a few houses with front gardens overflowing with flowers. From somewhere nearby, he heard a raucous wail he recognized from earliest childhood, the loud complaint of hundreds of sheep and their lambs penned in a barn waiting their turn to be sheared.

The footpath leading to the A659 was completely deserted. Bridle paths and country lanes riddled the rolling fields, all well traveled by hikers, horses, and bicycles. When he reached the junction, he collected discarded cigarette filters from the side of the road, ignoring candy wrappers and a dented Pepsi can. He retraced his path to the estate, and only had to step over the low white wall past the gate back into the gardens. It would have been easy enough for anyone to enter the grounds unseen from any number of places around the estate.

Standing on the dam bridge, he checked he was alone before flicking out one of the cigarette butts as far out over the water as he could. He studied the current as it floated. The butt washed up not far from where Chris Swinton's body had been found. Walking along the lakeside, he repeated his experiment. He threw the last butt near to the bench where the clothing had been left. The nicotine-stained filter spun slowly in the water. A sudden splash, a flick of a tail and the butt was gone. Keen was startled fish would eat cigarettes, and hoped the fish had spit it out.

He was certain Christine Swinton's handbag was in the water. Who would have thrown it into the pond and why, he didn't know, but he *knew* it was there. He wondered how he was going to talk Davis into paying for a diver to search the pond on more than just his hunch when he caught a whiff of tobacco and turned to spot the same gardener who had safeguarded the clothing watching him from the trees.

"Muh'nin," the man drawled.

Keen nodded. The workman fished a crumpled pack of cigarettes from his shirt, shook it, and proffered one to Keen. Keen shook his head, then eyed the canopied launch docked near the bridge thoughtfully. "You run that thing?"

The gardener exhaled smoke. "It's f' tourists, later on this afternoon."

"Mmm."

"What's in the water you're wanting?" The gardener smiled at his surprise.

"A woman's handbag."

"There be a reward f' findin' it?"

"Might be." That would be far cheaper and less complicated than going through the paperwork to request an underwater diving unit.

The gardener glanced at him shrewdly and chuckled. They stood in companionable silence as a trio of mandarin ducks cut intersecting vees in the water, their burnished orange and black feathers a bit too pretentious for a proper English countryside, in Keen's opinion. The ducks vanished under a cluster of the monstrous-sized leaves that had so astounded Dave.

"What *is* that?" Keen asked curiously.

"Gunnera manicata."

"In English?"

The gardener shrugged. "Only know the Latin." It seemed everyone knew more foreign languages than Keen. "I'll get agate m'work, then," the gardener said unhurriedly. "Got yer card if I find summat."

The gardener strolled off, and Keen expected he'd likely get a phone call the next day. He got back to Weetwood Station before noon. The station was quieter than the usual workday, making it difficult to think. Terry's computer was shrouded in its plastic cover. Glen's door was shut. Two PCs walked down the hallway, their conversation muted. Even the coffee urn by the window was silent. He rifled through files stockpiled on desks waiting for CID officers to return on Monday morning.

To his irritation, the coroner's report still had not come back. Keen frowned, tapping the end of his mechanical pencil on an open file. He dialed the coroner's office and let it ring, waiting patiently. Finally, it picked up.

"Lab," a man said, slightly out of breath.

"Sergeant Dunliffe from Weetwood Police Station. Would Dr. Penrose be around?"

"It's Saturday," the voice said, aggrieved. "Dr. Penrose doesn't come in on weekends."

"This is in regard to the woman's death at Harewood. I need to ask a few questions about the PM. You wouldn't have his home number handy, would you?"

There was a long pause before the man said cautiously, "We're not authorized to give out personal numbers for staff, sorry."

Ah. Journalists, Keen thought. "Look, if you want to verify this is official business, give me a ring back at Weetwood Police Station, Sergeant Keen Dunliffe."

There was an even longer pause. "I wouldn't have his number anyway," the man said, then: "But Dr. Penrose is in the book. Howard Penrose, on Morningside."

He hung up abruptly, leaving Keen puzzled. Odd anyone working for the coroner wouldn't know the doctor's home number. Directory inquiries confirmed Penrose was indeed listed.

A woman answered. "May I ask who's calling, please?" she demanded primly. He told her, and listened to footsteps and the tinny sounds of children laughing, a dog barking, and fumbling before a man's raspy voice said, "Hello?"

"Dr. Penrose? Sergeant Keen Dunliffe, Weetwood Station."

"What can I do for you, Sergeant?" The coroner's voice was warm, friendly.

"Sorry to bother you on a weekend, Doctor, but the PM report hasn't come back yet on the lady we found at Harewood House. Would you mind a couple quick questions about your postmortem exam?"

Strangely, Dr. Penrose gave him a similar pause and cautious reply as the technician at his laboratory. "Anything in particular?"

"Have you finished the toxicology screens yet? Did you find any particular substances, any specific drugs?"

Dr. Penrose cleared his throat. "We, ah . . . we still have . . . a few more details to clear up before I could give you anything of much use."

Keen actually stared at the handset before pressing it back to his ear. "Then could you give me any information on how much alcohol was in her blood system?"

"That . . . ah . . . would be included with the drug screens, Sergeant."

"How high was it, Doctor?" Keen said patiently.

"Pretty high."

"Numbers might be helpful."

"She was well within the legal definition of intoxication."

Keen massaged the bridge of his nose against the growing ache between his eyes. "Could you tell me the approximate time of death? Just roughly?" he asked, keeping his voice mild.

"That's . . . there are circumstantial . . . I have a few more test results I'd have to look over before I could pinpoint it exactly, but . . . roughly, I'd say between eight o'clock and midnight."

The estimate was so broad as to be worthless. "Am I mistaken in assuming it *is* you and not someone else who performed this autopsy?"

"Of course not." Penrose was now annoyed. "And my findings will all come out at the inquest, Sergeant."

"Which will be when?"

Keen listened to the long silence, making him wonder what the hell was going on. Whenever he had spoken with Dr. Penrose in the past, the man had always been cooperative, even gregarious. This sudden caution was baffling.

"Doctor, did you find anything unusual? Needle marks, bruises, abrasions, anything like that? Any illegal substances in her blood?"

"Obviously I wouldn't have those files with me at home, Sergeant, they would be at the lab." The doctor sounded petulant.

Keen leaned back, clicking the lead out of his mechanical pencil and pressing it back into the barrel. The coroner was a powerful official in his own right, and no sensible policeman would go out of his way to annoy him, certainly not a lowly sergeant. Keen wasn't feeling in a sensible mood.

"Dr. Penrose, why don't we consider this just a friendly informal conversation, nothing official. I would really appreciate it if you could give me just a *few* more details about your postmortem."

"I don't know what—"

"Contents of her stomach," Keen snapped. "To the best of your recollection, off the record, without benefit of your notes, could you give me some vague idea of the woman's last meal?"

Keen was over the line and he knew it. Then the doctor sighed. "Examination of her stomach and bowels indicated she had eaten an hour or so before her death," he said, resigned. "In my judgment, it appears she'd consumed salmon caviar, duck in an orange raspberry sauce, carrots, peas, some kind of apple pastry, and one hell of a lot of red wine. And that's *really* all I can tell you at the moment, Sergeant."

"Howie!" Keen heard the woman's annoyed voice in the background. "Damn it! You've left the dog dripping *all* over the carpet . . ."

Dr. Penrose said impatiently, "If that's all?"

Keen had pushed the coroner as far as he dared. "Thank you, Doctor, you've been right helpful." He hung up, resisting the petty urge to slam down the phone, and had the Yellow Pages open when he heard Reggie Logan's voice in the hall. "Hey, Reg?"

The uniformed PC appeared in the doorway of the CID office, Bealle peering over his shoulder. "Yeah, Sarge?"

"You two busy?"

"We're just processing an arrest, till snatch from a garage."

"You don't need Bealle for that. Get yourself a Yellow Pages," he said to the younger constable, "I've some phone work f'you, my son."

Keen wrote down the menu Penrose had given him while Bealle found another phone book. "That don't sound like a snack she whipped up herself," Keen said as the PC studied the list. "Let's start ringing up restaurants and check if this was on someone's menu Tuesday."

"Christ, boss," Bealle groaned. "Do you have any idea how many restaurants there *are* in Leeds?"

"No. Do you?" When Bealle shook his head, Keen said, "Let's find out, then, shall we? Also don't forget hotel restaurants and upmarket pubs. She had a car, so don't restrict yourself to the local area. Anything within West Yorkshire is possible." Bealle groaned again. "I'll take A to M, you do N to Zed."

There were more restaurants in Leeds than Keen had ever suspected, even after leaving out all the McDonald's and Pizza Huts and Indian and Chinese. It took time to explain the same thing over and over, waiting for receptionists to track down maître d's or head chefs who may or may not have been on that Tuesday evening.

By three o'clock, he'd had finished with the Fox and Hounds and was dialing the Furious Goose as Bealle, looking a bit dazed, talked to the chef at Sous le Nez.

"Yes on duck," Bealle said in a slow, distinct voice one would use for either a child or a foreigner. "No on orange sauce. No on peas. Okay, thank you very much." The PC hung up, sighed, and crossed out another number. He stared at the phone resentfully. "I'm starving. All this talk about food're doing is making me hungry."

"Dial," Keen growled, then politely, "Hello, could you tell me what was on your menu this past Tuesday?"

So it went for another hour. Keen was on hold when Bealle's face lit up like a child's on Christmas morning. "Canard is duck, right? And that were in an orange and . . . framboise . . . coulis?" Bealle struggled with the pronunciation gamely. "Salmon caviar, peas, that carrot thingie, and, uh . . . tarte tatin." He waved at Keen frantically. "And that were on Tuesday night's menu . . . ?" Keen hung up, not bothering to wait for his own call to return, and punched into Bealle's line.

". . . Tuesday specials," a woman's voice was saying.

"Would the staff from that evening be there this afternoon?" Keen asked.

She stumbled, jarred by the abrupt change of voices. "Well, everyone except Tony and Joey. Oh, and Tanya."

"And you are?"

"Patti Royds. I'm the weekend receptionist."

"Would you have a list of names, reservations made for Tuesday?"

"Yes," she said doubtfully, "but Tuesday's not a big night for us. Most people don't bother, we get a lot of walk-ins."

"Do you have the reservations handy?"

"Yes." He heard pages flipping. "Tuesdaaay . . . We had five. Landshaw, Scott, Marston. Bexley party of seven, that was a birthday celebration. And Nelson."

No Swinton, no Smiths. "Right, Miss Royds, there'll be a police officer there shortly, would you have everyone stay until we've had a chance to ask a few questions?"

Bealle had written down the address. "Good work, Malcomb," Keen said. His earlier irritation with the young PC was forgotten.

Bealle rubbed his head. "Thanks. I think I need an ear transplant. This un's about to fall off."

On the edge of the traditional Jewish district off Shadwell Lane, Ye Olde Oak Tree was a nineteenth-century house not quite grand enough to call itself a manor, surrounded by cut-rate shops, working-class pubs, and cheap office buildings. If there had ever been an old oak tree for its namesake, it no longer existed.

Inside, the restaurant's stained-glass windows blocked the view of its less elegant neighbors. Dark paneling and brass fittings reflected light from a fake coal fire warming the dining room full of white-swaddled tables and velvet-upholstered chairs. The restaurant was empty in the lull between lunch and supper.

Patti Royds looked like a college student, mousy hair pulled up from a narrow face making her eyes huge. He doubted she ever wore her unflattering black and white outfit for anything other than work. He smiled as he shook the hand she extended as rigid as a knife. It was cold and moist.

"I've had everybody wait in the staff room," she said, barely glancing at his warrant card before she led him toward the back.

A half-dozen people lounged on cheap plastic chairs. Most of the employees were smoking, watching him with flat wariness.

"I wasn't here Tuesday, I only work weekends and Wednesdays," Patti said, "but Roy was here, and Karen, and Hepza." She indicated each one as she named them. "Harry and Len were in the kitchen, so they wouldn't have seen any of the guests." The two older men dressed in white chef's outfits, unshaven and bored, sat apart with their noses wrinkled as if avoiding the cigarette smoke.

"I'm trying to find someone who remembers a woman who may have eaten here Tuesday. She had the duck in orange raspberry sauce, and she might have been with someone else."

The young man named Roy exchanged a startled glance with the other two women. "Sure. Man and a woman, came in around eight," he said. "Blond, nice looking for her age, if y'know what I mean. Red dress. Drank a lot."

"You served them?"

"No." Roy looked again at his companions. "That was Tanya's station. But she remembered them."

Keen was puzzled. "And she just happened to mention them?"

The three of them were staring, bewildered. "Well, sure. Yesterday," Roy said. "When the other blokes were in here asking questions." Keen felt ice sliver down his spine. "Tanya recognized the woman in the photograph. Couldn't really describe the man that well, though. Same age, brown hair, nothing special."

"Other blokes?" he said calmly. "You mean police officers?"

"Yeah, man," the olive-skinned girl called Hepza said. Her accent was softly foreign. He couldn't place it. "They came in after the lunch crowd, started asking if anyone had seen this blond chick. Weren't in uniform or nuthin', but they like showed us their IDs and a photo, and Tanya told 'em she'd seen her with some guy." She sneered at him. "Don't you people ever talk to each other?"

Apparently not, Keen thought. But it wouldn't have been Mullard, no matter how insolent the man might be.

"Of course," he said smoothly. "This is just a routine follow-up. Thank you all for your help. Miss Royds?" He steered her by the elbow out of the employee's lounge. Once they were out of earshot, he said, "I'd like to have Tanya's phone number and address, if you don't mind."

"But wouldn't the other officers have it?" she asked, her expression guileless.

"Just give it to me again, please."

Tanya North lived with her mother in the Gipton estates. He parked across from the shabby council house, ignoring the distrustful inspection of small boys with shaved heads as their unemployed older brothers loitered around defunct cars. Cardboard covered broken windows in the brick terrace house. Bin liners full of rubbish matched the shiny black paint of the railings. In the garden of an identical house next door, an elderly man watered a profusion of flowers. He glanced up with disinterest as Keen crossed the street, then shuffled into the safety of his own house.

The woman who answered the door reeked of gin. She didn't invite him inside. From what he could view of the interior, he didn't mind standing on the steps. Tanya wasn't at home, her mother said grudgingly. "She in trouble again?"

"Not at all," Keen assured her to her naked disappointment. "I'd like to ask her a few questions is all."

The mother leaned against the doorjamb, weighing him with narrowed eyes. She was at least succinct. They'd had a row shortly after Tanya had come home from work. The girl had left and her mother had no idea where she'd gone or when she'd be back. Nor did she much care.

"Thank you for your help, Mrs. North," he said politely. "Would you have Tanya give me ring as soon as she comes home?" He handed her a card. The woman took it without even glancing at it, smiled sourly as she slammed the door in his face.

Jillie left a guilt-sized tip, dragged both suitcases down the stairs, and apologized for the hundredth time to Mrs. Birney. Mrs. Birney smiled and waved as the taxi drove off, cordial and pleasant and clearly glad to see the last of her.

The smell of frying potatoes and a hundred people filled the City Train Station. Musical chimes were followed by an incomprehensible announcement over the loudspeaker distortion. But she managed to buy a cheap-fare ticket and follow the signs to the Leeds-to-London train.

Three porters ignored her as she struggled with her suitcases before a tall man in black leather, black fingernail polish, and black beads in his skinny braids of black hair helped her onto the train. She tried not to stare at the spiderweb tattoo across one eye and the rings piercing his ears, lips, nose, cheeks, and eyebrows. What nice teeth he had, was all she could think, so white and straight. She felt like an idiot.

The car was mostly empty, and Jillie chose a seat midway down by a window. The young man in black was with friends in another car, to her ashamed relief. A young couple sat down opposite her, a table between them, and exchanged brief smiles. The girl pulled a battered Ellis Peter's mystery novel from her bag while the boy ruffled the pages of a sports magazine. Jillie was grateful not to have to force polite conversation, and had just begun to relax when someone dropped a heavy purse onto the empty seat beside her like a bombshell.

"Well, *hello* there!" a cheerful American voice said. Jillie looked up at the woman blankly. She was on the far side of fifty, a spherical face on a spherical body. "I *thought* that was you. I was looking through the window, and I said to myself, my word, doesn't she look *just* like Jillie Waltham." The woman shoved a jumble of luggage and plastic shopping bags onto the overhead rack without pausing in her conversation. "So I got on, and sure enough, it *was* you and isn't it lucky this seat wasn't taken?" The woman levered her spherical buttocks into the seat beside Jillie, her purse upright on her rotund thighs, and smiled brightly.

The couple exchanged an amused glance. Jillie's stomach sank. They'd been introduced briefly and unenthusiastically by Lena, and she struggled for the woman's name before she remembered. "Dr. Rollins, how nice to see you again." Liar, she reproached herself silently.

"Honey, just call me Iffy, all my friends do, it's short for Iphigenia, isn't that the most *horrible* name? Gee, I'm not bothering you, am I?"

"Not at all . . ."

"That's fine then," Iffy Rollins said and smiled. The bright pink lipstick coating her mouth made her seem as huge and plastic as a Disneyland Seven Dwarfs costume. "Y'know, some people actually take student papers to grade while on vacation, can you *imagine*? But it's just awful to travel alone, isn't it? And we didn't get much of a chance to talk at *all* during the conference, so isn't it nice we get a couple hours just to sit and chat?"

"That would be lovely." *Liar, liar, pants on fire.*

"Yes," Iffy said, her smile growing predatory. "*Just* what I was thinking."

Jillie smiled back woodenly. For the next hour, she was trapped next to a window she couldn't even gaze out of at the green countryside rolling by. She punctuated Iffy's chatter with nothing more than "Really," or "How interesting," or "I couldn't possibly guess . . ." while wondering if her own eyes looked as glazed as those of the couple forced to listen to this incessant monologue.

"And frankly," Iffy was saying, "you'd think Camilla would *do* something about those teeth, *she* can certainly afford a decent dentist. But then I suppose they have so much in common, horses and organic gardening and all, looks aren't everything, are they?" She didn't wait for an answer, nor apparently did she expect one. "I mean, look at Fergie! She at least did something about her weight, and can you seriously tell me that hair doesn't come out of a bottle? Let's get *real* here!"

Jillie had gone from using actual words to polite noises to finally a sporadic toneless grunt, wondering whether the woman ever had to inhale, when they both squinted up at the tall shadow falling over their seat.

"Pardon me, ladies?" With the sun behind him, she couldn't make out his face under the thick shock of white hair, but Jillie would have welcomed the Boston Strangler. "I do apologize, but there does seem to have been some mistake."

"Whaddya mean, what *kinda* mistake?" Iffy said sharply.

"This seat is reserved, I'm afraid," he said, contrite, in a bass voice with a cultured English accent.

"Are you sure?" Iffy scowled. The couple across from them exchanged a puzzled look. "I thought booked seats were supposed to be marked." She turned to Jillie. "Did *you* reserve your seat?"

Before Jillie could answer, the white-haired man said smoothly, "Not in every case. Might I look at your ticket?"

Iffy ransacked her handbag before handing him her ticket distrustfully. Jillie refrained from checking her own, willing Iffy to have made a mistake.

He was quite tall, crouching slightly as if to keep from bumping his head on the roof overhead. After a moment, he handed back Iffy's ticket. "As I thought, this *is* my seat. You ladies were having such a lovely chat, I didn't want to interrupt. But unfortunately I've been, well, ejected myself at the last stop. There's a substantial fine, it's only fair to warn you, should the ticket guard catch you. I am sorry."

Iffy turned a peculiar shade of red, flustered. "Well, nobody said a *thing* to me about it. Where am I supposed to sit, are you *sure* you've got the right place . . . ?"

"Quite sure, so sorry. There is still plenty of space in smoking, I noticed."

"*Smoking!* I can't sit with smokers, breathing their dirty polluted air, I have *allergies,* I'll be *sick,* it's dangerous smoking on a train, it should be illegal, and if this were America, it certainly *would* be, y'know . . ."

"I do apologize, madam. If you'd like, I could ask the guard to explain it to you?" He straightened to look around as if attempting to catch a train conductor's eye.

"No, that won't be necessary," Iffy said hastily, the threat of a hefty penalty enough for her to heave her bulk onto her feet. She swayed with the moving train and glared at him poisonously before she shot a last sickly-sweet smile at Jillie. "I'm staying at this *darling* hotel right around the corner from Buckingham Palace if you'd like to get together . . . ?"

"I'm sorry, it's very kind, but I won't have the time," Jillie said quickly. When the woman looked skeptical, she added reluctantly, "My friend Chris Swinton?"

"Oh, yes, of course." Iffy had obviously forgotten about Chris's death, too wrapped up in her own private visions of the world to notice. She clutched the back of the chair, unwilling to give it up. "I'm at the Prince Regent, if you need someone to talk to, I've got *plenty* of shoulder to cry on." She laughed with bird-bright viciousness. "You must have dinner with me, you still have to *eat,* don't you?"

"I'll keep it in mind," Jillie promised vaguely.

Disappointed, Iffy's smile slid from her face, exposing the visceral loneliness raging underneath. Collecting her baggage, she walked down the aisle, head swinging ponderously from side to side in search of another seat. As the connecting doors between cars closed behind her, Jillie breathed a sigh of relief. She smiled with genuine gratitude at the man who sat down beside her. He returned it.

"This isn't a reserved seat, is it?"

"No, it's not," he confessed. "I was sitting behind you, and couldn't stand to listen to that rubbish another minute longer. Besides, you looked sorely in need of a chivalrous knight in shining armor." He proffered his hand. "Martin

Harding-Renwick, knight errant, slayer of dragons, and other noxious pests, at your service."

She laughed and shook it. His hand was large, firm, and warm, engulfing hers. Now with his face in the sunlight, she saw he was younger than she'd first thought, tall and lean, the white hair misleading. She guessed he was in his late forties.

"Jillie Waltham."

"Ah!" he said. "You wouldn't be the same Dr. Waltham as from the Leeds conference, by any chance?"

Her heart sank. "Yes, I am." Everybody from the medieval congress seemed to be on this damned train today. She steeled herself for the inevitable questions about Chris's death, resenting his now transparent ploy in ousting Iffy in order to pump her for the gossip.

"I didn't recognize you with your hair down, or I'd have rushed to your rescue sooner. Alexander Nequam and Adam of Balsham, wasn't it? Brilliant paper, by the way, I enjoyed it enormously."

"Thank you." She smiled, both genuinely pleased at the compliment while still wary of his motives. "Are you from Leeds University, Dr., um, Renwick . . . ?"

"It's plain Mister Harding-Renwick, I'm afraid. But please call me Martin. I'm not an academic, strictly speaking. I gave an ad-lib lecture on my company's genealogical software, 'Recent Developments in Computerized Multimedia Databases for Prosopography'? No?" It was said with faint hope but no disappointment.

"I'm sorry I missed it." She almost meant it.

"You didn't miss much. But I am glad I had the chance to meet you. You know . . ." He shifted closer to her with an intimacy she found more companionable than intrusive, to her own surprise. "I thought your correlation of Aristotle's influence on Adam's dialectic to Nequam's *De Contemptu Mundi* intriguing. I hope I'm not being presumptuous, but I wonder if you're aware of Andrew of St. Victor's work on the interpretation of original Hebrew texts in the Old Testament? I think if you look back at certain imagistic passages, particularly in his Samuel and Leviticus, Andrew could have had some influence on Nequam's choice of phraseology in his translations of the Aesop fables . . ."

The last of her misgivings melted, and for the next hour, Jillie was in medieval heaven, deep in the fast, animated conversation she had longed for when she decided to go to the Leeds conference in the first place. When green countryside gave way to old brick, glass, and concrete buildings, she scarcely noticed. Only as the train began slowing for arrival into King's Cross did she look around as if awaking from a dream. The couple across from them still had a glazed look about them.

"We're here already," Jillie said, regretfully. "So soon!"

Passengers retrieved overhead luggage and crowded the exits. When the doors wheezed open, Martin gallantly carried off Jillie's heavier luggage. The couple that had sat with them walked past behind her.

"Weren't that like bein' a' university, like, fascinatin' listenin' t'them two goin' on," the woman stage-whispered. Jillie pretended not to hear.

"Well, t'was better than that first'un blatherin' on about bugger all, but I still din' unnerstand a bleedin' word a'it," the man grunted. "I'll bet there's nuffink like that in *yer* silly book, now is there?" He thrust his chin at her tattered *Brother Caedfael* novel, his hands full.

"Sor'of, there is," she whispered back in protest. "But it *sounded* real innerestin'. Din' you fink it was innerestin'?"

"How should *I* know?" he complained. "Din' unnerstand any a'it. An' neever did you, you ain't been to no university, so don' be goin' on like you 'ave . . ."

They passed out of Jillie's hearing, still arguing heatedly as they disappeared into the milling crowd. Probably happy to finally talk themselves, she thought.

As she nervously looked around for Iffy, Martin went to snag a luggage cart. He insisted on escorting her to the taxi stand. While they waited, he handed her a gilt-edged card. "I'd love a chat with you again, Dr. Waltham, if you're in London long."

"Please call me Jillie." She glanced at his card. " 'Harding-Renwick Genealogical Research.' "

"It's a small operation, an office from home with a staff consisting of myself and a part-time secretary. But it pays the bills," he said ruefully. "Were your family from England?"

"My mother's parents were Scottish, and my dad's side is mostly German."

"Then you may yet be a descendant of Highland kings, perhaps a cousin of the glorious Stuarts. And German, we could check for any distant relatives of the queen's, any barons of Brunswick-Hesse or a landgrave of Luneberg-Wolfenbuttel, perhaps a minor but noble Countess von Glückensmeckleschwerinholsteinschloss." His wry humor made her laugh. "It's possible."

"But not very likely."

He shrugged expansively. "Fear not, fair lady, such minor oversights are easily amended. I have a wide selection of peerages on offer. Become the Marchioness Frizzlebottom of Snithering-in-the-Armoire for, say, a mere twelve thousand pounds?"

She laughed. "Marchioness of *what*?"

"That I made up, but I do sell real titles."

She was intrigued. "You're kidding. Does it come with land and a castle?"

"Of course not, nothing so sensible as real estate. But 'Lady Jillie' has such a nice ring to it, don't you think? I'm sure we could work up a suitably intimidating coat of arms embellished with those marvelous mantles and stately shields." His fingers sketched squiggles in the air.

"No, thanks," she said with a grin. "I'm happy being an ordinary American."

He tsked. "Nothing spoils a romance so quickly as a frivolous man," he said, "unless it's a practical woman."

"Isn't that Oscar Wilde?"

"Paraphrased."

She wondered if he was gay with a pang of regret, then dismissed the question as beneath either one of them. As Martin opened the taxi door for her, his expression became more serious. "I'd invite you to have dinner with me, but unfortunately I've another appointment. I understand you must be rather busy, but if there's anything I can do for you while you're in London, please give me a ring."

"Thank you, I will," she said warmly. Although he must have been aware of Chris's death, he hadn't once mentioned it, a courtesy she found oddly perceptive as well as gracious. As the taxi pulled away, she turned to wave through the back window. He raised his hand, the sun at his back and his expression lost in its shadow.

Thirty or so from the off-duty shifts had already converged on the pub by the time Keen arrived. He'd lost interest in treasure hunts after his divorce. Few of his friends had ever been other policemen, and after Laura left, he'd had fewer friends of any kind, preferring to retreat into solitude. He didn't want to be here now.

Brian Cormack handed out the list, Jasmine studying it with her partner, Andy Kellett. Her longtime partner—Stan, wasn't that his name?—must be pouring coffee at forty thousand feet over the Atlantic Ocean. How two people who rarely saw each other had remained together for nine years was a mystery for Keen.

Edwards arrived with his wife and sister-in-law, and his springer spaniel bounded out of the car. The dog barked excitedly, dancing around his legs.

"*Shut* it, Muffin!" Edwards shouted, and the dog slunk away to start up the routine around Babs's feet.

Keen smiled politely as Edwards steered his sister-in-law toward him. She was even lovelier than her photo; her flawless skin glowed, thick lashes framed huge green eyes, fiery red hair cascaded down her back. The photo hadn't shown off her trim figure and long, long legs.

"Keen Dunliffe, Cheryl Moseley."

"Nice to meet you," Keen said, and shook her hand.

"I'm so glad to meet you," Cheryl said in a breathless voice Keen suspected was practiced. "Bill's told me all about you."

"All lies, I swear," Keen said. Babs held the choke chain around the spaniel's neck while the dog sniffed Keen's heels, smelling God-knows-what on his shoes. Probably Thomas. Whatever it was, it excited him beyond his obedience school discipline and Keen's leg became the object of a passionate doggie embrace.

"Get off, you," Babs scolded, jerking the dog back. Cheryl started, then blushed. No one seemed to notice.

"May I have your attention, please!" Cormack shouted, waving a sheaf of paper. "We're about to start, so listen up!" As the laughter and buzz of conversation continued, Cormack's face turned crimson. "*Shut up* and *listen*, the lot of yuss!"

Once he'd gained their attention, more or less, Cormack went over the rules, which everyone ignored, before he selected umpires, Ferguson and Daheny. "All decisions are *final*," Cormack bellowed over the noise. "Their word is the *law* which you rabble will obey *unquestioningly!*"

Naturally, more time was wasted on ribald jokes before Edwards snagged a map and clue list.

"Time starts when you hit the road, but anyone back in less than two hours will be disqualified and banged up for speeding and reckless driving. This isn't the Paris–Dakkar rally and none of you is Nigel Mansell!"

"Oh, Lord," Edwards groaned. "Bet I know whose turn it were to make up the bloody clues."

Keen suspected he did as well. Rather than opting for nothing more challenging than "go north until you reach a pair of lazy bobbies hanging about a royal girlfriend" (which was, of course, the sleeping policemen to the car park of Nell Gwyn's freehouse), PC Alan Cooper would spend weeks devising cryptic clues with all the knobs on. Needless to say, this had not won him many friends.

Keen studied his clue sheet. "First clue. 'O, thereby hangs a tail, by many a wind-instrument that I know,'" he read aloud. "'The general so likes your music, that he desires you, for love's sake, to make no more noise with it. To hear music the general does not greatly care.'"

"What is it?" Babs said.

Edwards glowered. "It's bloody Shakespeare, is what it is."

Babs rolled her eyes. "I *know* it's bloody Shakespeare, Einstein. I meant, which play?" She snapped her fingers impatiently. "C'mon, Cheryl, you've done acting, you should know this . . ."

"*Macbeth?*" Cheryl tentatively offered.

"*Othello*," Keen said quietly. His teammates reacted with surprise, Cheryl blushing again. "Saw it last summer, Studio Theatre. My niece played Bianca."

His sister had had to drag him to the theatre, and he would have been more willing to have his fingernails pulled out before admitting he'd actually enjoyed it. He'd suspected the director had recycled a set for *West Side Story*, Othello in Royal Marine uniform and Desdemona in a poodle skirt, which, Keen assumed, made the production avant-garde. But he couldn't stop grinning as Othello energetically smothered the life out of Desdemona in the back seat of a '56 Chevy while Iago swaggered about like Fonzie, complete with pompadour and black leather jacket, and delivered lines peppered with "zounds" and "forsooth, I prithee, good sir" and "bless'd pudding!"

"Damned poncy clues," Edwards grumbled. Last time Cooper had made up the clue sheet, Edwards bitterly protested for a week; how the hell was any ordinary copper supposed to know that Dogberry were some poxy constable from *Much Ado About Nothing*? "Shakespeare. *Again,* fer fuck sake."

"D Team, your time starts . . . *now!*" Cormack bellowed. Keen checked his watch although they were still stuck on the first clue.

"Bastard," Edwards muttered. Keen was sure he meant Cooper, not Cormack.

"I don't get it," Cheryl complained.

"Likely isn't the theatre," Keen mused. "Too long ago, and I doubt Cooper would have seen it anyway." He thought for a moment and smiled. "Black Moor."

Edwards brightened. " 'Make no more noise, to hear music the general does not greatly care.' Remember that illegal rave in Black Moor last month? 'Orrible so-called music amped up loud enough so you couldn't hear yourself think. Got some overtime in on that one."

"Trespassers over on the rugby union grounds?"

"Let's go."

It was, as treasure hunts go, all right. The other half to the clue was taped to the flagpole, its scruffy wind sock (the "wind-instrument") hanging like a limp tail.

Edwards drove as Babs navigated, Keen and Cheryl in the back with the dog. Predictably, the Edwardses' mild bickering blossomed into an outright row within half an hour, making any conversation Keen might have struck up with Cheryl impossible. He tuned out the quarrel, exchanging polite smiles often enough to keep from offending her, and let his mind wander several miles north to the Harewood lake. Edwards became stuck on one-way streets twice and lost once, and by half-past seven pulled into the pub's car park, obviously not the first to return.

"Well, losers again," Edwards growled at his wife. "All *your* effin' fault, too, if you'd just've let me turn right on Stainbeck—"

"Oh, give it a rest, you silly bastard . . ."

The winners laughed as they were greeted with the traditional loud boos and flying crisp packets while Babs and Cheryl found seats at the back of the pub before the rest of the losers trickled in. As Keen went to get in the drinks, Edwards wandered toward the snooker tables.

Keen came back with halfs for the girls and a pint of Guinness for himself. As he studied the dark light through his pint glass he cleared his throat. "So. Cheryl." She looked at him expectantly, lovely eyes vacuous. The kind of eyes poets write of drowning in, Keen thought, then regretted it as his mind jumped to Chris Swinton's dead face. "What do you do in Wrexhall?" He didn't much care what she did, but it was a safe question.

"I'm a clerk in a medical supplies company," she said as briskly as if this had been a job interview. "Nothing as exciting as what you do, of course." He managed not to wince. "But I do a bit of modeling and I've acted in a telly commercial once, Jolly Giant toys? I was the stuffed penguin." To his surprise, he remembered it. There hadn't been much penguin to her outfit, as he recalled. "I'm hoping to go to acting school in London, that's what I'd like to do, act in the films."

He pretended not to notice as she slid closer to him, her body heat radiating perfume. Babs glanced around her sister's shoulder at Keen, one finely plucked eyebrow raised knowingly. As he picked up his pint in self-defense, he saw Glen Harper walk into the pub and shake a few hands. Spotting Keen, he discreetly signaled to him.

"Excuse me a moment, will you?"

"Sure." Cheryl's smile was electric.

He took a quick gulp from his pint before threading his way through the crowd. "Could I have a word, outside?" Harper said.

Keen ignored the curious glances and the sinking feeling, those innocuous words always the harbinger of unpleasant tidings as he trailed the detective chief inspector out into the deserted car park. Harper crossed to a Range Rover, the sides sprayed with mud. Mirrored windows concealed the interior and Keen followed Harper into the back seat.

Two men twisted around to stare at him. "Shut the door, please," one of them said. He was not a local.

Keen closed the door, observing the two men with interest as the Rover turned out of the lot onto the country road.

"Sergeant Keen Dunliffe," Harper introduced him. "Chief Superintendent Pete McCraig from the Met." Keen kept his surprise to himself as the man behind the wheel nodded a greeting in the mirror. "Justin Scudder." As Keen reached across the seat to shake the man's hand, Harper added, "Personal assistant to the home secretary." This time Keen wasn't as successful at hiding his astonishment. Scudder smiled, the gesture not friendly.

Nothing more was said until McCraig pulled the Range Rover into a gravel lay-by and parked beside a metallic-blue Jaguar with London registration plates.

"I understand you've been working the Swinton death?" Scudder said without preamble. He and McCraig had turned around, arms over the back of their seats.

"It's on my caseload," Keen said cautiously. "I haven't seen the pathologist's report from Wetherby yet, but she was apparently very drunk when she drowned."

"And stoned," McCraig said. "High levels of THC in her blood."

That neither surprised nor shocked him, and explained why Jillie Waltham was reluctant to tell him what else was in Chris Swinton's handbag. But it didn't tell him why he was in a Range Rover with two high-powered officials, wondering how they knew what was in the PM report before he did and what the bloody hell was going on.

"Inquest is Monday morning, we intend to keep it quick and simple," Mc-Craig said, while Scudder stared at Keen. "She definitely drowned, water in the lungs. No clear evidence she'd had sex before she died; coroner says it's possible, but any seminal fluid would have washed away after that much time in the water. Not much left to run a DNA analysis on."

"You've met the friend, Dr. Gillian Waltham," Scudder said.

"Yes. She identified the victim from a photograph. There was a break-in later at her B and B. Nothing taken."

Scudder leaned toward him. "What's your impression of Waltham?" In the closed vehicle, his voice seemed flattened, artificial.

"Intelligent, educated. Nice lady. I'd be very doubtful she'll prove a credible murder suspect."

"No one said anything about this being murder," Scudder snapped.

Keen gazed at him steadily before he answered. "I'm not meaning to be confrontational, sir. But I wouldn't be sitting in the middle of nowhere talking to you two particular gentlemen if this were a simple case of death by misadventure, now would I?" Outside, the setting sun broke through the clouds, an arc of light shimmering in the traces left by windscreen wipers.

Scudder and McCraig exchanged enigmatic glances before Scudder withdrew. McCraig chuckled. "Christine Swinton did drown. But not at Harewood. The water in her lungs didn't match the sample from the lake. Too clean. The pathologist found traces of soap in her bronchials, matching what they use at the Garth Moor Arms."

Which didn't surprise Keen as much as he thought it might.

"Also, the lividity pattern isn't right. Too much blood pooled in her legs like she'd been sitting up after she died, say in a car, before she ended up floating in the Harewood lake. She was drunk, but not to the point she would have been completely legless. However, she was stoned on more than cannabis; she'd ingested enough scopolamine to make the likelihood of her wandering onto Harewood in the dark under her own power rather slim."

"Scopolamine?"

McCraig nodded. "It's an anesthetic related to belladonna, mostly used in pediatric surgery. For some reason, it's popular with the trendy gay culture in the States along with poppers, amyl nitrite. It's not that common in Britain. Yet." Keen couldn't tell if McCraig had some drug expertise or simply boned up beforehand. None of this, Keen understood, would be forthcoming at Monday's inquest.

"How would you read that, Sergeant?" Scudder demanded.

"I wouldn't."

"Why not?"

"Because if I assumed the obvious, that it was a private party that got out of hand, she overdosed and drowned in a bathtub, and whoever was with her tried to cover it up, I'd be wrong."

"Why?"

Keen was tired of the game. "Because you're going to tell me I am, then you'll tell me the rest of it."

Harper exhaled, the barest hint of a laugh. Scudder glowered. "I'd heard you've had somewhat of an attitude problem."

Keen met his eyes evenly, an old anger stirring in his gut. "That is the correct word, sir. 'Had.'" He waited in the silence that followed.

Scudder leaned over the back of the seat. "This conversation is not happening, Dunliffe," he insisted, his voice lowered as if afraid of eavesdroppers. "Is that clear?"

"Yes, sir." Which explained why this conversation wasn't happening in the middle of a country lane lay-by instead of not happening at the station.

"Christine Swinton is the fourth person in the past seven months to be found dead on or near estates owned by the members of the royal family. A sixty-two-year-old man died of a heart attack in Paddington, practically on the doorstep of the Duke of Gloucester's architectural offices. A few weeks later, a twenty-three-year-old plumber took a header off a footbridge while fishing in Richmond Park near to where the Ogilvys maintain a house. Then last month, a fifty-year-old woman was found sitting on a bench in Kensington Gardens in a diabetic coma. The palace has expressed concern with the abnormally high number of deaths on their properties."

Keen couldn't help wondering what a normal rate might have been.

"On the surface, all died by natural enough causes, but the forensics people at Lambeth weren't happy with all the findings. Nor were the investigating officers. Little things just a bit off, nothing substantial. Nothing *provable*. Now the Swinton woman drowns in the Harewood lake with tap water in her lungs and scopolamine in her blood. We think these deaths might be related."

"Other than where they were found, any other connection?"

"None that we can see," Scudder said sourly. "But the Swinton case is special. For one thing, she's the daughter of the late James Witherstone Swinton."

Keen shrugged his ignorance.

"Former MP. Married to Verona Crassfield . . . of Crassfield and Robyns?" Keen knew the name. The Crassfield & Robyns chain of boutiques riddled half of England, chic clothes made in Asian sweatshops to sell at enormously inflated prices.

"Verona Robyns Crassfield married James Swinton, her father's solicitor, who turned a small family business into a major international firm inside ten years, then sold off the company shares just before the devaluation of the pound in sixty-seven, bought them all back at a pittance, made a fortune."

Smart or lucky? Keen wondered, while not failing to notice Scudder's insinuation of dishonesty.

"The wife's family were all solid Tories, but he ran for Labour, picking up a constituency in Oxfordshire. Surprised even himself, I expect, being elected MP. Never got beyond the back benches, and only lasted a single term. Then he joined the LibDems, did pro bono work for small companies against larger conglomerates. Most cases he lost, but it made him popular with a certain sort of people."

Keen had no doubt what sort of people Mr. Scudder was referring to; the council estates and Job Centres were filled with them.

"His loony left opinions didn't endear him to his wife." Scudder's mouth twisted, and Keen assumed it was supposed to be mirth. "Nor with the Crassfield and Robyns board of directors. His daughter took after his left-wing mentality as well."

It was one of those paradoxes in life, Keen was aware of; like most policemen, he came from working class and whenever he'd bothered to vote, again like most policemen, he'd naturally supported his own interests. But his faith in government, Tory or Labour, was minimal, and men like Scudder with his neatly knotted public school tie and his clubby Oxbridge prejudices were a good part of the reason why.

"You ever hear of Charter Eighty-eight?" Scudder asked.

"No."

"It's a citizen's group lobbying for a written constitution, mostly disgruntled socialists with nothing better to do than to organize meetings and grumble over their tea and scones." Scudder attempted a congenial smile and shouldn't have. "Christine Swinton did volunteer work for them. Unfortunately, these are the sort of gullible do-gooders easily infiltrated and exploited by hard-core terrorist elements."

"I didn't know the victim personally, sir, but I understood she was a talented historian," Keen said blandly. "I find it difficult imagining Dr. Christine Swinton as a brainwashed pawn for Hezbollah."

McCraig hid his smile behind his fist as he coughed.

Scudder didn't appear to appreciate Keen's sense of humor. "Not all terrorists are ignorant or unsophisticated. Those who cause the most damage are the clever, educated middle class who can blend into respectable society without being noticed. We believe all of these deaths to be politically motivated, and leaving the bodies on the doorstep of the royal family is sending a message, one causing grave distress to Buckingham Palace. Swinton may have been actively involved, or she may have been a dupe killed for having known too much. But we are certain she *was* involved in such a radical faction, that it is quite dangerous and must be stopped."

Apparently finished with his heated lecture, Scudder leaned back with an expression of grim satisfaction.

"Home Office has been asked by Her Majesty's Privy Council to set up an independent team to investigate the Swinton affair, but to do so quietly," McCraig said. He sounded bored compared to Scudder.

Keen wondered how much stock McCraig put into Scudder's conspiracy theory. He also wondered why Special Branch, or even MI5 for that matter, wasn't handling the case. Then, as he recalled the two men who had questioned the staff at Ye Olde Oak Tree, McCraig gave him the answer to why an ordinary Yorkshire police sergeant was conferring with a couple of high-ranking government officials.

"You've interviewed this Dr. Waltham twice now. She knew the victim well?"

"They were college roommates. Dr. Waltham's daughter was Swinton's godchild." Keen decided not to mention Jillie's arrest as a student protester.

"The time of death is a bit tricky. If she drowned in a bathtub, in hot water, the rate of decomposition would be different than had she drowned in a cold lake. Without knowing how long she was dead before she was put into the lake . . ." McCraig shook his head. "Based on the stomach contents, the coroner has concluded Swinton died between nine and ten Tuesday evening. According to your report, Waltham claims she walked back to the guesthouse alone before eleven. The landlady was out until near midnight, so she can't confirm Waltham's alibi."

Innocent people didn't think about establishing alibis, Keen well knew; it was the guilty who worried over such bothersome details.

"Americans love meddling in things that don't concern them," Scudder interjected. "Even if she's not directly involved, this Dr. Waltham could still know more than she thinks she does."

Somehow, Keen doubted it.

McCraig rubbed his chin pensively. "Since you've already established a connection on a professional basis, how difficult do you think it would be for you to get on personal terms with her?"

Keen hesitated, and glanced at Harper. "It's possible," he said reluctantly. "I took her to dinner last night." He stopped, heat rising on his face.

McCraig smiled. "Really."

"Nothing improper happened, sir. We went to a pub where we ate and talked."

"You talked to her about the case?" Scudder asked sharply.

"Of course I talked to her about the case," Keen said, embarrassment turning into irritation. "She's in a foreign country where her friend has just died, she were upset and alone. I didn't consider her a suspect at the time." Nor did he now.

"What else did you talk about?" Scudder demanded.

"World War Two. Foreign languages. Ant farms. Somebody named Alexander Nequam. I wouldn't bother," he added as Scudder reached for a pen inside his coat, "he's been dead a few centuries." This time it was Scudder turning red. "I'll put it all down in an appropriate report, if you like." Not smart to antagonize the man, Keen was kicking himself mentally, not smart at all.

"That won't be necessary," Scudder said stiffly. "Where is she now?"

"She took the train to London this morning."

Scudder looked alarmed. "Did she say where she'll be staying?"

"She's collecting her things from Christine Swinton's flat, but intends to get a hotel somewhere. I assume she'll be in touch with Max Swinton about the funeral."

"He picked up his sister's car this afternoon round five-thirty," Harper added.

"Find her. She's your assignment, Dunliffe. Get her to tell you everything she knows about Christine Swinton, any way you can." Scudder turned to McCraig. "I want him down in London first thing Monday, Pete."

"Kentish Town station is closest to the Swinton house," McCraig told him. "I'll liaise with them this afternoon."

"Right." Scudder glared at them before he got out of the Range Rover and slammed the door shut. He got in the blue Jaguar, gunned the engine, and vanished down the road, the Jag's screaming through the gears fading in the distance.

"We'll get you set up at Kentish Town," McCraig said. "Put a surveillance on for the funeral. If you don't find out where she's staying before then, let's make it a casual contact there. You'll be on official business, police condolences to the family."

"Exactly how close do you want me to try and get?"

McCraig knew what he was asking. Despite Scudder's zeal, the legal line between gathering information and acting as an agent provocateur was razor thin, capable of slicing a man to ribbons.

"Just do your best. At the moment, it's not *officially* a murder inquiry, so *officially*, she's not a suspect. Anything else you need?"

"I'd like to know who the two men were who questioned staff at the Oak Tree restaurant yesterday."

"Special Branch." Keen looked at him evenly, then at the DCI. Harper wouldn't meet his eye.

"I haven't been able to talk to Tanya North yet, either."

McCraig smiled thinly. "She's busy backpacking in the Pennines with her boyfriend. Her mother doesn't know because the boyfriend's black."

"I see." He watched a hawk hovering above waiting for field mice to emerge as the sky reddened, both out looking for an evening snack. "I rang the coroner yesterday, reluctant to give me much detail about his postmortem. I did manage to get him to tell me what the victim's last meal consisted of." He looked back. "Which your people already knew. Then myself and a constable wasted the better part of a day tracking down that restaurant," he said, his voice toneless.

"An oversight," McCraig said easily. "Won't happen again."

Keen nodded.

"Anything else?"

No, Keen thought he'd made his point.

"Good. We're settled, then." McCraig glanced at his watch. "It's a long drive to London, I should be going before it gets too late."

He drove Keen and Harper back to the pub. Harper ran his palm over his balding head as they both watched McCraig drive away.

"You knew," Keen said quietly once the Range Rover had gone. The pub door opened, three drunken policemen laughed and flailed their way into Andy Kellett's van. Andy, as their designated driver, flashed a completely sober grin at Keen.

"Yeah, I knew."

"When?"

"About two hour ago, and I weren't any more thrilled about it than you are. And I didn't know you were working your days off again, either."

Keen turned to face the DCI squarely. "Then you should also know I went back to Harewood House this morning." When Harper simply raised an eyebrow, he added, "My hunch is Swinton's handbag is in that lake. You might get a call in from one of the staff there who likely'll expect some compensation for his trouble."

"All right, sign a blank incidental expense form. If it turns up, we'll find the money from somewhere." He paused as Kellett drove past them, waving. "While you're at it, you might put in for that dinner you bought Dr. Waltham."

"Thanks all the same, no," Keen said, the embers of a slow anger still burning. "I was off duty and it were a personal matter."

"Not anymore, Keen. The Yank might be important, and she might not. But from now on, she's the *job*."

For a rash moment, Keen was tempted to tell Harper he wasn't CID anymore, to give the case over to Mullard and see how well he could charm the lady professor. He took a breath. "There's something else I somehow forgot to mention back there. Dr. Waltham also spent last night at my house. Nothing happened. She just didn't want to go back to her bed and breakfast alone after the break-in is all."

"Okay." Harper thought about it and shrugged. "Not a problem, might actually help." He waited. "Anything else might've have slipped your mind?"

"She told me straight-out she believes Christine Swinton were murdered." Which would be an odd thing to say if she *were* the killer, Keen didn't bother to point out. When Harper raised an eyebrow, he related that morning's conversation with Jillie in an indifferent monotone. After he'd finished, they stood quietly regarding the clouds rolling in. "She's not blind or stupid. It'll take more than the sight of my freshly pressed uniform to warm her up. She don't much care for the police."

"No?" Harper said far too innocently. A breeze rippled the grass and Keen shivered, wishing he hadn't left his jacket in the pub. "Why's that, then?"

"She and Swinton were arrested in the States during some college student protests." Harper seemed unsurprised. "Look, even when I was CID I didn't have much experience in undercover. If I start asking unusual questions, she's going to know something's up. She'll have a few of her own in return."

"Then lie," Harper said lightly. "Since she knows you're a police officer already, you won't be working undercover." Harper knew Keen well enough to sense his annoyance. "Play dumb policeman." He grinned maliciously. "You *do* remember how to play dumb policeman, don't you?"

Keen looked away across the fields. In the distance, tiny figures in white shorts kicked a football across cropped green grass. "Yes, sir," he said tonelessly.

Harper gave him a friendly slap on the back. "Don't worry. This crap'll sort itself out quick enough."

Keen rubbed his arms for warmth until Harper had driven away, before he headed back into the dark sanctuary of the pub. His eyes not yet adjusted, tables and people were blank silhouettes. "What'd the gaffer want with you?" he heard Edwards say. Keen turned. Edwards held a snooker cue in one hand. The pub door wheezed shut behind another batch of inebriated bobbies following a cabbie to his taxi.

"I'm off to London Monday."

"Oh, that's grand," Edwards said cynically. "What's in the big city they'll be needing a tyke like *you* for?"

"A funeral."

Edwards chortled. "S'long as it's not your own."

A solid crack of snooker balls and a muttered curse made Edwards look over his shoulder as Keen spotted Cheryl smiling provocatively in his direction. It only made his stomach tighten.

"The girls are waiting on you," Edwards said, his attention on the game. "I'll be just one more minute . . ."

Keen pasted on his best smile and walked back to where his date chatted with her sister, the springer spaniel panting between them, wet tongue lolling.

"We were wondering where you'd got to," Babs said cheerfully. "Bill's abandoned me, alas, another snooker widow left to water me beer with tears."

He didn't sit down. "I'm sorry, I have to leave. Police business."

Cheryl's bright smile dimmed perceptibly. "On a *Saturday*?"

As he struggled to find a plausible excuse, wondering how adept he was going to be at lying to Jillie Waltham, Babs rescued him.

"I did warn you," she said to Cheryl with a wry wink for Keen, "that's what they're all bloody like. Try being *married* to one, love. You live half your life watching telly alone and the other half watching him snore while trying to keep the kids quiet." Cheryl's pout seemed another sensual expression Keen suspected she practiced in a bathroom mirror.

"Sorry, really, maybe another time . . ." he blurted before he could escape. Once outside, he took a deep breath and wiped his hand across the back of his sweating neck, not realizing until then how suffocated he'd felt. He started making up a few lies in advance to practice as he got into the Vauxhall and drove away.

PART TWO

London

V

MONDAY

By the time Keen arrived at the Kentish Town Station, it was already mid-afternoon. Anemic clouds did little to filter the scorching sun. He showed his warrant card to the officer on duty at the police car park. The man pointed, dark circles of sweat under his shirtsleeves.

"Find a space back there," he said lethargically.

Keen parked the Vauxhall between two panda cars. His civilian shirt stuck to his skin as he buttoned up his collar and clipped on his tie.

Although officers were coming and going through a side door, Keen headed for the front entrance of the mustard-yellow brick building with PO-LICE in black letters on the white glass globe of an antique lamppost. The door into reception was locked. He looked through the heavy plate glass of the waiting room at the desk officer talking to a young black man with sunglasses and a red, green, and black knit Rasta cap. He could hear nothing, the room soundproofed. When he caught her eye, he smiled. She returned it briefly, a sign she was aware of his presence, then turned her attention back to the agitated man.

The waiting room was grim enough, plastic chairs in institutional drab, grainy photographs of criminals wanted on Crimestoppers. A Zero Tolerance poster against domestic violence had been defaced, beard and glasses crudely sketched onto a smiling young man in a pub. "He gave her flowers, chocolates, and multiple bruisings," the print read. Someone had scrawled "And then went back on duty" underneath. That this was in the public waiting room of a police station bothered him. The fact that it hadn't been removed bothered him more.

The black man jabbed a finger repeatedly as he emphasized his inaudible remarks. Bored, Keen gazed out the window, watching a portly man struggle with an old lawnmower as he cut the yellowed grass of St. Patrick's Catholic Primary School. Keen idly wondered where his own sons were at that moment.

He heard the buzzer, and turned to see the WPC at the desk motioning for him to come through. The angry man had gone. He went in, the reception door closing behind him with a solid thunk.

"Afternoon," the desk officer said. "What can I do for you?" She was slender, with frizzy hair in a neat French braid. At a desk in the corner behind her, a uniformed sergeant ignored them both.

He opened his wallet to his warrant card. "I'm Sergeant Keen Dunliffe out of Weetwood Station, Leeds. Somebody's expecting me."

She squinted as she considered. "Riiiight . . . That would be Phil Reaves. He's around somewhere, I'll just give him a bing-bong."

She pressed the button on a squawk box, and after two attempts to contact him through his radio met with static silence, she punched another number. "Anybody there know where Phil is?"

Through the babble of voices, one asked, "Phil who?"

"Detective Sergeant Philip Reaves," she replied, unfazed. "Is he back there?"

"Nobody here but us chickens." Keen heard raucous laughter.

The desk officer rolled her eyes at the lame humor. "Got an officer here needs to see him."

More white noise before another voice said, "Be there in two shakes."

Keen thanked her and stepped back to wait. She disappeared with RSPCA officers come to collect a stray dog caught by a beat bobby after it had bitten a child. A skeletally thin woman in dirty jeans and sweatshirt came in, agitated. Sighing, the sergeant in the corner stood up and sauntered over to deal with the skinny woman.

"But I don't *want* him back at my place," she insisted. Her hands trembled as she mauled an unlit cigarette, flecks of tobacco trickling out. The sergeant was a muscular black man with a placid smile and tired eyes. He leaned against the counter, talking to her with easy familiarity.

"I understand," he said patiently. "You still doing the hard stuff, Dotty?"

She shook lank hair from her eyes to glare. Her shakes got worse. "Not in months." She shoved her sleeves up defiantly. "I got meself straight and I don't want him back messing up me life, you hear me?"

The desk officer returned with a WPC leashed to an enormous hound weighing nearly as much as she did. The desk officer held open the front door where two RSPCA officers waited by a van. The dog towed the struggling WPC along, happy tongue lolling even through the leather muzzle. He whimpered, tail wagging him clear to the shoulders, pathetically eager to please and unaware he wasn't likely to live out the day. The WPC smiled briefly at Keen as the monster dragged her out.

Keen checked his watch, wondering if he was being intentionally left kicking his heels, when the door to the inside of the station finally opened. "Hi. You Dunliffe? Sorry to make you wait."

He didn't seem apologetic in the least. Detective Sergeant Phil Reaves was an energetic man in his thirties, with an athletic build middle age had yet to soften. He wore his dark hair brushed back in a styled cut. He shook Keen's hand with a touch more force than necessary, a friendly challenge, blue eyes bright in a tanned face. Keen wondered if he got it naturally or went to one of those salons. "The DCI's expecting us."

Keen followed him past open doorways of rooms stacked floor to ceiling with cardboard file boxes. Corkboards along the hallways fluttered with pinned notices. Cabinets and racks overflowed from cramped offices into the narrow halls, officers squeezing past each other.

They went up a stairway to a room noisy with clerks typing. On one wall, a gigantic blowup of a man's face wearing a police cap had been posted. He gazed down, wise and respectable, the very image of a dedicated London bobby. THIS MAN IS NOT A POLICE OFFICER! had been printed in bold letters underneath, alerting those real but possibly less photogenic coppers of a dangerous con artist.

Reaves paused as a uniformed sergeant and three PCs stood around the suspect card file cabinet dominating the room, no space anywhere for the late turn parade to sit. The sergeant juggled her clipboard as constables wrote in their pocket notebooks.

"Suspect gave his name as Fitch, but that's likely an alias . . ." One of the PCs peeked over her shoulder. She arched an eyebrow as he looked up innocently.

"Just seein' how it's spelt, Sarge."

"F-I-T-C-H," she spelled out. The PCs suppressed grins as they scribbled. "Rhymes with 'bitch.' You need that again, Constable?"

"Nope. Thanks, Sarge."

Without comment, Keen followed Reaves to another office as compact and paper stuffed as the rest. The close air reeked of stale cigarette smoke. His DCI sat behind a desk far too large for the room, but not large enough for the paperwork heaped on it. Behind him, a map of the Kentish Town police territory was pinned to the wall, red lines dividing it into three sections. Colored pins had been stuck into it, whatever voodoo they signified not readily apparent to Keen.

The detective chief inspector looked up as Reaves knocked on the jamb of the open door. "Come in and shut the door," he said bluntly.

The two sergeants sat on metal folding chairs. "I'm Charles Galton." The DCI was ruddy cheeked with a mouth that didn't seem to smile too often. His eyebrows and lashes along with what was left of his hair were a nearly invisible blond, making his cold eyes even starker. "You Keen Dunliffe?"

"Yes, sir."

Keen suspected Galton maintained his scowl of impersonal dislike for everyone. "You settled into the section housing yet?"

"Not yet, I just got here."

Galton grunted, picking up a pack of Marlboros. While the DCI lit a cigarette, Keen glanced at Reaves. The sergeant sat stiffly, his face stoic. Galton inhaled a long drag, then leaned back. "Reaves'll get you settled in once we're finished," he said, smoke wafting out with his words. "I assume you've been briefed up there." The way Galton said "up there" left nothing to doubt about his opinion of the north.

"Yes, sir." It wouldn't pay to be affronted. "Mr. Scudder from Home Office outlined the situation."

Galton puffed disinterestedly. "I want this operation kept small. The less people on it, the less chance of someone screwing up. If you need something, go through Reaves or me, no one else."

"Understood."

Galton opened a file on his desk, squinting through the smoke. "We're still waiting for the Yard to send what information they've got. We've put what we have so far on inquiries of the deceased's address in Primrose Hill with the general case background sent down from Leeds. Look it over here. Nothing leaves this station."

He shoved a thick folder across the desk and waited as Keen scanned the files. There was little in it he didn't already know. Christine Swinton's neighbors seemed to know little about her, a surprisingly private person despite her political activity and several arrests. He expected Special Branch's "Registry" would hold more information gleaned from "reports after meetings," agents infiltrated into political groups to spy on millions of key people, from MPs and businessmen to socialist workers and activists, regardless of any criminal activities. Innocence didn't count with Special Branch.

"Inquest finished this morning at ten. Officially, it's been ruled an accidental death." Galton looked at Keen, eyes glacial. "I'm told you're acquainted with one of the primary witnesses?" Witness, not suspect.

"Yes, sir. Dr. Gillian Waltham, the American friend of the deceased."

"The brother wasn't keen on us searching his sister's house." Galton's lips twitched with what might have been humor, but gone so quickly it was hard to tell. "Worried we'd nick the silverware. He got a solicitor, so we got a warrant from Clerkenwell. The place is a complete tip. A lot of unusual rubbish, but nothing incriminating. We're still waiting for the expert to finish examining her computer." He took another drag on his cigarette. "The funeral is tomorrow, eleven-thirty. The family has a private mausoleum in the West Brompton cemetery. Reaves will lead the surveillance team for idents of everyone who attends."

"I'll meet up with Jillie Waltham there," Keen said. "Conveying police condolences to the family."

"Good. I don't think it's necessary to impress upon you the delicate nature of this case."

"No, sir." Or whose arse it would be should he balls it up.

The phone rang. Galton picked it up and punched the hold button without saying a word into it. "Anything else you need at the moment?"

"I'd like to see the files on the other deaths Mr. Scudder mentioned."

Galton eyed Reaves. "We'll get that sorted for you." It was a dismissal. As they stood up, he put the phone to his ear and stabbed the blinking light. "Galton."

"He's not so bad," Reaves said once they were out of earshot. "I've worked with worse. Where's your car?"

"In the station car park."

"I'll get you a permit. You got any luggage?"

"In the car."

Reaves led him to the back exit. Keen retrieved his suitcase from the boot of the Vauxhall, and followed Reaves into the section housing across the car park, a seven-story apartment building. Masculine laughter and the solid clunk of snooker balls echoed along the hallway.

"Sidney!" Reaves rapped on the glass window of a tiny corner cubicle. A uniformed sergeant looked up from his paperback. "Got a man needs a room."

Sidney smiled good-naturedly, his teeth crooked. He leisurely selected a key from a rack. "No problem." As he unlocked the lift and they rose to the fifth floor, Sidney explained in a strong Welsh accent that the top two floors were restricted for women, showers and toilets were community, one at each end. Two canteens downstairs, a television room, and a full gymnasium and weight room in the basement were Keen so inclined. He was, but doubted he'd have time to take advantage of it.

The lift opened onto an unexceptional corridor. Sidney jiggled the key into a lock, and let Reaves and Keen in before him. "It's basically your bedsit-type thing here," Sidney said as Keen set his suitcase on the narrow bed. "Not much for lux." Sidney handed him the key, and left.

The furniture was cheap pressboard built-ins, but the room was clean and the window had an intriguing view across London. Through brown smog smeared between high-rise buildings, the pale silhouette of Canary Wharf jutted from the horizon, the blinking light on the pyramid-capped tower barely visible. Westminster and Tower Bridge spread majestically across the Thames. The view when he looked down was quite different: trash-strewn rooftops, brick walls graffitied, old lawn furniture and rusting toys abandoned in empty weed-choked lots.

"Care for a pint?" Reaves offered.

Keen didn't like London, never had. But he was tired and thirsty. "Sure."

Outside, the muggy heat hit him with near physical force. "Hope you don't mind walking. I'd take the car, but it's a bastard to park around here."

"Don't mind a bit," Keen said. As they walked along the pavement toward Kentish Town Road, Keen unclipped his tie and jammed it into his trouser pocket. The sweat under his armpits itched.

"This your first time in London?"

Keen shook his head. Laura and the boys had an apartment near to where Sherlock Holmes was famed to have lived. Laura liked the area, and found the foreign tourists clutching guidebooks as they searched for a fictional address among the pubs of Baker Street enormously funny.

"I'm London born and bred, Barking actually, but I love Camden best," Reaves was saying. "You get every sort coming here, hippie students and yuppie toffs, New Age tourists, Greeks, Italians, blacks, Asians. You can find anything you want, legal and otherwise. Every kind of food you can think of. I know a place off Chalk Farm where you can get kosher Chinese pizza." He grinned at Keen's perplexed look. "With or without mango chutney. You'll never be bored here."

The Chester Arms was a corner freehouse with peeling paint and unhealthy geraniums slumped in baskets outside. Inside, the pub was dark and smoky. Half a dozen men hunkered on stools, strong shoulders and short haircuts marking them as off-duty bobbies. A couple others were scattered around the tables, some with lady friends, most simply engaged in the timeless ritual of knocking back a few pints with the lads.

"I'll get the drinks in, what'll you fancy?"

"Webster's, if they have it."

Keen smelled frying onions and potatoes, knew that half the varnish on the pub's dark wood paneling was decades' worth of congealed grease. In the back room, he could just see the bottom half of a man leaning over as he aggressively played pins, his rear end jerking in rhythm with his cursing. Thankfully, no piped music played.

Reaves set down two pints of beer, foam sliding over the rims. "No Webster's. McEwans's. On me."

Keen didn't decline, letting the cold liquid wet his dry throat. It was sweeter than he liked, his taste spoiled by good Yorkshire breweries.

"Busy station?" Keen asked as he set his beer down.

Reaves laughed. "Does the pope shit in the woods?" He took a long drink of his own beer. "Kentish Town has at least seventeen thousand known criminals walking about, and those are just the ones we've got files on. The Met's domestic-violence units dealt with sixteen hundred incidents this year alone, and that's *down* from last year. We get something in the region of two thousand handbag snatches during market times. King's Cross is the Mecca for tarts. You get girls working from ten o'clock in the evening till ten the next morning, back out at two o'clock until eight, eighteen hours a day, seven days a week, because they're all junkies supporting a two-hundred-fifty-pound-a-day habit."

Reaves spoke in a fast, clipped London accent, half smiling as he reeled off his facts, ticking points on his fingers. He clearly enjoyed his job, regardless of the grim realities he recited.

"You get twelve-year-old call boys working for ten quid a pop. Ages 'em fast. My wife works over at St. Mary's, shocking what she sees. Once they're too old, they'll handbag-snatch, they'll burgle, whatever it takes to get the money. Lots of youth crime, vehicle crime, criminal damage and assaults and fights, you name it. We got gang warfare around Euston Square, overcrowded high-rise flats a few blocks from here getting worse every day. Young people out roaming the streets, no jobs, dealing drugs, basically taking over the estate, the residents too frightened to deal with it."

Keen nursed his beer and kept his mouth shut. Reaves shifted hands to itemize his next list of facts. "Now to handle all this, we got fifteen officers for the whole division, two stations, this one on Holmes, and one at Albany

Street. Two officers on the desk takes you down to thirteen. Two more officers for control, that's eleven. You know how it works. If it's busy in the custody, we'll need a jailer, now you're down to ten. Then somebody's gone to court and you're down to nine. For the *whole area*. Nine officers against seventeen thousand bad guys. So, yeah, I'd say it's a busy old place." He leaned back, satisfied.

Keen grunted ambiguously, studying Phil Reaves. The younger man seemed unable to sit still, his foot tapping with nervous energy, fiddling with a signet ring on his little finger.

"Suppose it makes a change for you? Me, I couldn't imagine working up on a northern force," Reaves said. "Can't stand boredom." He grinned, white teeth even.

Despite Reaves's attempt to impress him with the busy life of the big city, his not-so-subtle innuendo about Keen's country mouse existence, Keen also knew on a force the size of the London Metropolitan Police, detective sergeants were ten a penny. Not only was Keen ten years older, he'd served more years in CID than Reaves's entire career in the job, a large disparity between their actual status. He also knew how many Met officers put in for a transfer every year, anxious to escape to safer and saner provincial forces. Or simply burned out and resigned altogether, the gaps filled by less and less experienced kids.

So he chose to ignore it. "What can you tell me about Primrose Hill?" he said, changing the subject.

Reaves shrugged. "Not a lot. I went to one of their Neighborhood Watch meetings once, all middle-class socialists, y'know, the 'trendy left.' Fed us caviar on toast, fancy French cheeses, pricey wine. It's an old-fashioned village mentality up there, very compact, very insulated, people like to wander out and have coffee on the footway if it's a nice day, look at the view and pretend they're really somewhere else. They're the sort who like to say, oh, yes, we're all good socialists, we *care* about deprived areas and all that, but it's a hell of a lot easier when you live in a posh million-pound Victorian flat." Keen heard the tinge of envy behind the sarcasm.

"Like Christine Swinton."

"More like her daddy, the late great James Witherstone Swinton. You know much about him?"

"Used to be an MP," was his only comment.

"One term," Reaves said derisively. "Made brilliant speeches, but leaned too far toward the screaming loony left, which was probably why he wasn't reelected."

"And his daughter?"

Reaves considered for a moment as he savored his beer. "She'd had a handful of arrests for things like chaining herself to a chemical factory with those wankers from Greenpeace. Lying down on railroad tracks protesting lamb exports." He snorted his amusement. "Just for being a general nuisance, basically, but hardly what I'd consider a hard-core extremist. Last arrest was a few years ago, trespassing with those 'The Land Is Ours' nutters marching all over some lordship's country property in Oxfordshire. Not a peep from her since."

"What about this Charter Eighty-eight?"

"They're not doing anything illegal, so far as I'm aware. She dropped them round about the same time she dropped 'The Land Is Ours' and the rest of that lot."

"Any idea why?"

Reaves shrugged, but his eyes were shrewd. "Her daddy died."

Keen waited for an explanation. When it wasn't forthcoming, he asked, "What do you know about her friends, neighbors?"

"She didn't seem to have many friends," he admitted. "The only one who knows much about her is the next-door neighbor, something Selwick . . . no, Selkirk. Linda Selkirk, I think is her name. It's in the witness reports. She runs the local Charter Eighty-eight meetings. Her husband has aspirations of running for political office, so he's mates with the home beat bobby supervising their Bonfire Night, the biggest in London, probably. It's quite famous, you've likely heard of it."

Keen shrugged, unimpressed. "We have Guy Fawkes Day in Leeds, too."

"That's right," Reaves said slyly, "a Yorkshireman, wasn't he?"

And too bloody bad he'd failed to blow up Parliament, Keen thought silently, if he could've taken the rest of London with him. Keen didn't rise to the bait. After a moment, Reaves let it go.

Three boisterous men jostled into the pub, laughing a shade too loudly. They were mid-twenties, with muscular physiques earned from hours spent lifting weights. It wasn't hard to spot off-duty lads, but these swaggering bobbies were particularly obvious, out looking for trouble for the fun of it. Keen scanned the room, observing how others were reacting. Most, he noted, gave them a wide berth, particularly one woman who looked vaguely familiar sitting by herself at the bar.

Reaves eyed the three briefly before he scooted his chair to turn his back to them. "So. I've heard rumors round the station you've made a name for yourself up there in Leeds," Reaves said, the effort to make conversation strained.

"Me?" Keen stared at him, a flutter of dread in his gut. He bought a few moments by drinking his beer. "You must be talking about the Great Slurry Snatch."

Reaves looked incredulous. "The *what* snatch?"

"Slurry. Liquid shit. Farmers store it in tanks to ferment before they spread it over their fields. It's what gives that unmistakable perfume to fresh country air."

"This is a joke, right?"

Keen maintained his deadpan expression. "Dead serious business to farmers. Somebody rolled up a fleet of tankers while the farmer were on holiday and drained the lot. Poor sod was going to have to sell off his cattle, couldn't afford the extra fodder, not enough decent grass in the field to support them, terrible loss."

Reaves's eyes narrowed, unsure if he was being had or not. "How much did they take?"

"Fifty thousand gallons." Keen sipped his beer, watching Reaves trying to compute the logistics of stealing fifty thousand gallons of liquefied shit. "Not the first time, either. There's a whole gang of slurry thieves up far north, Scotland's been having a right time of it. Their National Farmer's Union notified us so we had an idea of their MO and what to look for when it started happening around our area."

"Rotten manure?" Reaves said, still unable to grasp the idea.

"We took tire-track castings, and got the tracking dogs. Sniffed them out." Reaves glanced at him suspiciously. Keen didn't smile. "Seems each batch of slurry has its own bacterial mix, sort of like a DNA fingerprint."

Keen noticed as one of the three recent arrivals behind Reaves turned his attention on the lone woman at the bar. "Why don't you mind your own business, Williams?" Keen heard her say, her face stony.

"We matched a set of tires while Wetherby forensics compared remains in the tankers, came up with an exact match." Keen kept on talking. "Broke up a gang taking down several million pounds a year selling illicit slurry."

Reaves was barely listening to him now, the noise level in the pub dropping as others watched the storm brewing at the bar.

"I'm just thinking of you, sweetheart," the sandy-haired man was saying. Just a good-natured lad out for a little fun was his expression. "You're better off behind a desk rather than out there on your feet."

"That's a load of crap," she retorted. She was slight and flushed with anger. If she wasn't so angry, Keen thought, she'd have a nice smile. Then he recognized her as the WPC with the huge dog.

Reaves pretended to ignore the exchange behind him, the quarrel growing louder. "Sorry, darlin', but women's bodies aren't built for our kind of wear and tear. Can't argue with medical proof."

Keen sipped his own pint, wary. Others around the pub, mostly men, were listening to the argument with disgust or amusement, the rest assuming a cautious mask of indifference.

"Bullshit," the WPC said. "There's not one shred of evidence . . ."

The blond man shrugged. "Believe what you like, Bernadette." His voice caressed the woman's name, and Keen knew by his tone the woman hated being called Bernadette. "Women aren't as strong as men, never will be, that's a fact of life. You take the same money, you best be able to do the same job as a bloke, and I can't see it, not physically. Shouldn't be on the sharp end, y'know? No insult intended, darlin' . . ."

"Oh, it's not, is it?"

Another man beside him murmured uncomfortably, "Williams, leave off—"

"But if you really want to be 'one of the boys' . . ."

The woman's flush deepened. "Oh, that's rich. Why don't you come out and call me a slag plonk right to my face instead of whispering behind my back . . ."

"Hey, I didn't say that." Williams put up his hands in mock surrender, his grin even wider. "*You* did."

Keen's stomach tensed with an unpleasant feeling of déjà vu, certain the woman was about to throw her beer in Williams's face. The pub was eerily hushed. Then she slammed the glass back onto the bar and walked away. She passed them, glaring straight ahead, her stride stiff.

"C'mon, Bernie," Reaves called, his voice placating, but low. "Ignore him . . ."

The woman either ignored him or was too angry to hear. She banged the door open and left the pub. The noise switched back on as if nothing had happened.

Keen observed the officers thoughtfully, noting who was still grinning, gauging how much was simply rictus from embarrassment rather than agreement with Williams's hostility. Reaves's energy level had dropped a notch as he ran a finger idly down the side of his pint glass, clear streaks in the condensation, then nodded his head sideways, indicating Williams. "He's just ticked off because Bernie won't let him climb into her tights, that's what it's really about."

Keen shrugged. "Happens."

Williams ordered another pint from the barmaid who served him without a glance or smile, ignoring his vulgar jokes. Laughing as he turned with his fresh pint in hand, Williams glared at Keen, sullen challenge in his eye like a ram in must spoiling for a fight. Keen looked away.

"Besides, he's Islington, not Kentish Town," Reaves added. Keen wasn't sure how that made any significant distinction.

As if he had overheard, Williams pushed off from the bar, walking over to lean on the table and stare at Keen. Reaves shifted in his seat restlessly.

"You know what me old da used to say?" Williams said to no one in particular. "If a woman can't stand the heat, she should get back in the kitchen." He laughed at his own joke, seemingly unaware he was alone in his mirth. He sat down uninvited and leaned into Keen's face. "Right?"

Keen said nothing, looking back blandly.

"Williams," Reaves said quietly, "the man's a visitor, show a little courtesy."

"Where you from, then, out-of-town guest?"

"Leeds," Keen said reluctantly.

Williams made a production of sucking in his breath and shivering. "Oooo. Practically the North Pole." He cracked up in another peal of laughter, his sidekicks chiming in as sincerely as a canned laugh track. Keen realized the man was not as drunk as he pretended to be, just drunk enough to excuse his belligerence, looking for a target. Reaves leaned back as if resigned, removing himself from the hostilities.

"You ever work the mean streets with a Double-yoo Pee See?" Williams said.

"Sure. Many times. But I got my own theory," Keen said, thickening his country Yorkshire accent.

"Do tell."

"Well, it's exactly like *you* said, biology."

Williams grinned inanely, while Reaves cradled his pint and watched.

"Biology?" Williams prompted.

"Female biology. The maternal instinct to protect their young, they're born with it. It's like wolves. See, in women this urge gets all mixed with who they see as part of their family, they'll stop at nothing if they think one of their own is in danger. Can't help themselves, that's just their nature. Mother picks up a two-ton car with one hand to pull her child out from underneath. She don't bother to stop and think that might be impossible, she just goes and does it."

Keen paused, knowing Williams was not the only one listening.

"We got this five-foot-five WPC tackled a huge bloke used to play for Newcastle United," he went on. "Mean bastard he were, seventeen stone, take five men to hold him down. Her partner nicks him for car theft and gets a crowbar in the face. He's down, blood everywhere, the bloke legs it. She takes one look at her partner and goes absolute bugfuck. Chases the bastard down, jumps on his back and like about to rip his head off." He smiled ruefully. "Actually puts him in hospital. Then he goes and files a complaint he's been unduly thumped by the police. Like to ha'seen the look on the magistrate's face when this tiny WPC showed up in court, all apologetic and sorrowful."

A few of his audience laughed, but Keen noted Reaves was not smiling. Williams appeared bewildered. Oh, well, in for a penny.

"Then there's the other side of the coin."

"Which is?"

"Same reason I'd take on a man in a fight afore a woman. They're vicious, do anything. Go for your eyes, your balls. If you're not part of the group they're going to protect, they start looking at you like *you're* the threat, you'd best grow eyes in the back of your head." He finished the last of his beer, white foam webbing the inside. "They're not like lads, take a bit of fun and forget it. They got long memories, never forgive the least little hurt. You ask any man in here with an ex-wife."

"Got *that* bloody right," someone said, aggrieved. More laughter, some of it even feminine. The fire was out of Williams's eyes.

Keen stood up. "Be right back," he said and headed for the loo. He took his time about it. When he came out, Williams had rejoined his buddies at the bar. He was still laughing but his expression was uncertain. Reaves leaned against the wall next to the toilets with his hands in his pockets, waiting for him.

"All due respect, Dunliffe," he said quietly, "anybody ever tell you you're full of shit?"

"Sure. My ex-wife. But she's prettier than you when she says it."

Reaves's eyes narrowed. "You honestly believe that load of decomposed slurry you were just handing Williams?"

"Not a lot, no. Women're like anybody else, there's good ones and bad ones. Only difference is they have to try harder than us to prove they're the good ones, is all. Not that your friend there is likely to pay much mind to what some tyke Yorkshireman really thinks, now is he?" He'd dropped the farcical "ee by gum" accent.

Reaves smiled grudgingly, then glanced over toward Williams. "Nah. Some people never do grow up."

Keen rubbed at the heat headache lodged around his eyes. "Look, I've taken up enough of your time. I've been on my arse all day, like to walk around, work the kinks out before we go to this funeral tomorrow."

Reaves didn't object. "I'll see you tomorrow, round when? Eight-thirty?"

"Fine."

"I'll have something for you by then from the beat officer one way or the other on the Swinton woman."

"Good. Appreciate your help."

Reaves chuckled. "It's what they pay me for."

Keen didn't know if he would ever trust Reaves, never mind like him, but he'd survived the ritual; they'd butted thick-skulled heads like two adolescent bucks, testing each other before getting down to serious business. He watched the younger man saunter out of the pub, remembering when his body had been as sound without the workouts, his waist as narrow without diets. Remembered when he'd carried himself with the same benign cockiness, before time had kicked the stuffing out of his ego.

When he left the pub, the stifling heat quickly sucked the energy from him as he wandered the streets with other people sharing the late afternoon sun. Walking along Chalk Farm Road until he had reached the bridge over Camden Locks, he leaned over the water to watch the street theatre below.

Trendy artistic types, anorexic bodies encased in black leather, strolled self-importantly along the quay, hands weaving patterns in the air as they lectured one another. A woman with bright orange hair and green lipstick wearing zebra-print leggings skated by on Rollerblades. The canal reflected huge white letters on a red brick converted warehouse declaring itself Dingwell's Free House. Arcades strung with lightbulbs pulsed with a subsonic drumbeat of heavy rock music, laughter, and the clink of tableware. He was not part of this world, as alien here as the man in the moon, and already as homesick.

He found a pay phone near the Camden Town tube station, a slick Plexiglas bubble over a chrome telephone where the only privacy afforded was because the streets were too noisy for anyone to eavesdrop. He dropped fifty pence in, and jammed the handset against his ear to block out the howl of rap music blaring from a boom box. A small crowd of black rappers nodded belligerently to its militant beat as a blue and white police car sped by, lights flashing, siren wailing. Other than one rapper who thrust a lackadaisical middle finger after it, no one showed the slightest interest. The phone rang twice before Laura picked up.

"Hi. It's me. I'm in London." He listened more to the tone of her voice than her words. "No, I'm here on a job. Laura . . ." He found the words almost physically painful. "I know it's not the access schedule. But would you mind if I dropped by and saw the lads for a few minutes? I won't stay long." He hoped to God he didn't sound like he was begging.

His arm resting against the phone, he pressed his face into the cradle of his elbow, eyes closed, the receiver crushed against his ear. "No. Yes, I know. Okay, I won't. Okay. Yeah, cheers, love," he said, all in the same monotone, his pulse shuddering in his throat. He hung up gently, and took a deep breath. Then he straightened, grinning with relief, and headed for the tube.

Although Max Swinton had phoned to assure her she was welcome to stay in the house at least until after the funeral, Jillie spent Sunday calling the airline to change her return ticket, then searched for a hotel in the London phone book, gasping at the prices quoted before giving up and going to bed. Monday morning, she slept late and woke hungry. Already, London broiled, heat shimmering in the dry dust and sour belch of car exhaust. Walking along Primrose Hill, she found a pub serving a "Genuine Traditional English Breakfast."

Nearly everything came fried, fried tomatoes with fried eggs, fried bacon, and even fried toast. Something the color of bitter chocolate but meaty had been panfried crispy along with fried sausages which were filled more with vaguely pork-flavored bread than meat. The only thing not fried were baked beans.

Sweating and uncomfortably full, she loitered window-shopping before the heat drove her back to Chris's empty house. Inside, the utter silence unnerved her. Jillie fiddled with Chris's high-tech stereo until she found a station playing jazz interspersed with commercials for obscure products being pitched in elegant English accents. She cranked up the music to banish the quiet from even the remotest corners of the house, and lay on the couch with her eyes closed, trying to relax. The funk bass line throbbed at the pit of her already queasy stomach. Later, when it was cooler, she'd go out again in search of an affordable B and B, if London had such a thing.

Loud as the music was, Jillie still jumped when the doorbell rang, her nerves frayed. Peeking through the front-door spyhole, she saw the distorted fish-eyed figure of a woman, and opened the door reluctantly.

The woman smiled. "Hello, I'm Lynne Selkirk. You must be Jillie, Chris's friend from America. I've met your daughter, Karen, isn't it?"

"Yes, hello."

"I live next door. Chris asked me to collect her mail while she was away, then I heard what happened. Drowned. I still can't believe it." Lynne tsked with sympathy. "And here I am worrying about her mail. How are you holding up?"

Jillie nodded. "I'm okay, thanks," she said, then, "When did you find out Chris had drowned?"

"Friday, when the police came by to ask my husband and me a few questions. Not much we could tell them. It's all routine, I suppose. For them, anyway."

"Oh." She stared blankly as Lynne Selkirk wiped her face shiny with perspiration, then she belatedly asked, "Would you like to come in?"

"I was going to invite you over to mine for a drink, if you'd prefer."

Jillie wanted nothing better than to escape Chris's empty, cluttered house. "Let me turn off the stereo."

Like Chris, Lynne Selkirk lived in a three-story terrace house overlooking Chalcot Square. Her brickwork had been painted a pastel Mediterranean blue, window shutters gleaming white. Ivy had engulfed the porch columns and hanging baskets of blue and white petunias gave off their musty sweet perfume. A terra-cotta strawberry pot by the door was already burdened with ripening fruit.

Inside, the rooms were shaped eerily identical to Chris's, although the furnishings couldn't have been more different. A pale blue and gold Chinese carpet dominated the sitting room, the few chairs and antique cupboards in immaculate condition. A large ficus balanced out a dumb cane in glazed stoneware pots. Oil paintings hung on the walls, most of them still lifes and country landscapes, bland but tasteful, to Jillie's untrained eye. As Jillie sat down on the sofa an exact match to the blue in the carpet, Lynne said, "Tea or a soda?"

"Definitely a Coke."

As Lynne puttered in her kitchen, Jillie inspected the contents of an oak bookcase, rows of well-worn leather-bound books, ribbed spines and faded gilt lettering. She twisted her head to make out titles like *British Democracy at the Crossroads,* and *Constitutional Change and the Future of Britain,* and *Crisis and Reform in Twentieth Century Monarchies.* She straightened guiltily as Lynne returned with a tray with two tall glasses filled with more ice than soda, lemon wedges on the rims.

"Look all you like," she said as she handed Jillie a glass. The melting ice in the tepid cola gave it an odd hot-cold sensation. "I'm the local group representative for Charter Eighty-eight, maybe Chris mentioned us?"

"A little," Jillie admitted cautiously. "You're trying to get a British constitution like the United States has, isn't that it?"

"Not exactly." She sat on the sofa, crossing one leg over the other. "We have a constitution. Ours is just unwritten." Her eyes twinkled at Jillie's bewilderment.

"If it's unwritten . . . how do you know what it says?"

"We don't. We make it up as we go along, the 'we' in this case being whichever government happens to be in power."

"Ah." Jillie tried to appear less puzzled. "But what about the Magna Carta?"

"And here I thought you were another historian?" The woman's cheerfulness took any sting out of her words. "That was written for the nobility, to establish sovereignty of Parliament over the crown. It never had anything to do with rights for us peasants." She grimaced. "I'm sorry. This probably doesn't interest you, and I know we ought to be talking about poor Chris . . ."

"No, it does interest me," Jillie said hastily. She didn't want to talk about poor Chris, grateful for the opportunity to discuss anything less emotionally hazardous.

"All right," Lynne said wryly, as if she understood Jillie's evasion. "Most people haven't the vaguest idea what the British constitution *is*; they've left that up to the lawyers and politicians. But that's the problem; politicians and lawyers are usually more concerned with maintaining their own power than in protecting civil rights, a sure recipe for corruption."

"So does Charter Eighty-eight want something more like an American-style government?"

"Oh, God forbid," Lynne said quickly. "We don't want an American-style *anything,* just a democratic constitution will do quite nicely, thank you." Lynne studied Jillie over her cola. "Are you *sure* I'm not boring you?"

Jillie smiled. "No. I can see why Chris got involved with it."

"Actually, I think Chris rather looked down on us middle-class bourgeois pretending to be radicals," Lynne said, regret in her voice. "She had a gift for fiery rhetoric, although she tended to frighten a lot of people off with it."

"But you were still good friends?" It bothered her to have to ask; she had no idea who any of Chris's friends were.

It bothered her more when Lynne hesitated. "I'd like to think so. I didn't know her that well, I didn't even know who her father was until after he died! We argued a lot at the meetings, which she enjoyed, if that's any criterion for a friendship. Ted—that's my husband—and I didn't really get to know her until we'd gone on a protest over in Farnham. There were about fifty of us who'd all been arrested . . ."

Jillie laughed. At Lynne's puzzled reaction, she explained, "I think all of Chris's friends were required to have spent time in jail with her."

Lynne grinned. "I see, another fellow convict! She could be great fun, such a bundle of energy from such a tiny woman." Lynne sobered. "So it was sad to see the change in her . . . after her father died. She'd always been a bit, I don't know, not exactly secretive but . . . kept herself to herself, I suppose. Ted called her the Greta Garbo of Primrose Hill. Sometimes we'd go months without seeing her. The few times we tried to invite her round for dinner or drinks, she always had some excuse. Ted thought she might be trying to hide a drinking problem."

Jillie's stomach tightened, half wanting to deny the accusation out of loyalty, half fearful it was true.

Lynne shrugged. "I think Chris just got on people's nerves, the way she could bang on with preaching republicanism and abolishing the monarchy. She seemed to think all that was necessary was to start chopping off heads." Lynne smiled impishly, unaware of Jillie's distress. "Starting with the queen and not stopping until we'd beheaded the entire House of Commons just for good measure. She could be entertainingly bloodthirsty if not terribly realistic. 'Down with the ruling classes, throw all the gentry out on their asses.'"

Jillie smiled, but she could hear Chris's voice in Lynne's parody, her caricature too close to the reality for comfort.

"Chris did have a thing about the royal family." Jillie thought of Iffy Rollins with distaste. "My interest in English politics and royal families are more eleventh and twelfth century, I'm afraid." She had no more interest in the royal family gossip than she had in *National Enquirer* tales of three-headed Elvis space aliens and crystal-worshiping movie stars on macrobiotic diets. It depressed rather than amused her how many people enjoyed being willfully stupid.

Lynne shrugged eloquently. "It does sell a lot of newspapers, all those conspiracy theories about Diana's death, will Charles marry again, what Harry is smoking at university. But frankly, the royal family is irrelevant. The question isn't whether a constitution can survive within a monarchy, but whether the monarchy will be able to continue to exist *without* it."

She stopped in chagrin. "Do listen to *me* bang on. Bad habit, I'm afraid. My husband is running for a seat on the City Council, and I'm beginning to sound more and more like him these days."

"Actually, you sound like Chris." Jillie returned her smile. "I miss her."

Lynne's eyes suddenly reddened, and although her smile remained in place, she pressed her fingers against her mouth. "So do I," she said finally. "I wish I could tell you more about Chris instead of blathering on about a lot of silly politics."

Jillie cleared her throat, again close to tears.

"We have a charter meeting scheduled here for tomorrow evening and thought to cancel it. But on such short notice we decided it was better to have it as a remembrance for Chris." Lynne brushed fingertips under her eyes. "The funeral is tomorrow, did you know?"

"Yes. I talked to her brother yesterday."

"You know Max and Celia, then?"

"No, I've only talked to Max on the phone. I'll meet them at the funeral."

"You're in for a treat, dear. Amazing how Verona Swinton could arrange the funeral on such short notice, like she keeps the Church of England on retainer for just such emergencies."

After an uneasy silence, Lynne glanced at her watch. "Anyway, my daughter will be home from playgroup soon. Ashley's five. You're welcome to dinner tonight, around half sixish? Nothing fancy, it would just be the three of us. Ted is off at a seminar in Brighton until the end of the week." She grinned, the impishness back. "He's getting in a bit of practice for his political campaign. You know, kissing everyone's baby but his own."

Gratitude washed over her; she was more relieved than she could have imagined. "I'd be delighted, thank you."

Jillie scurried back into Chris's house to escape the ferocious heat. She checked her watch, computing the time difference between London and Oregon, longing to hear Karen's voice. Her daughter would still be asleep at this hour. She decided a cool bath might help her relax. As she soaked to escape the heat, she closed her eyes and let her mind drift. To her surprise, she found herself thinking about Keen Dunliffe rather than Chris or even her daughter.

Now at a safe distance, she could admit that under different circumstances . . . *much* different circumstances! . . . she might like to have gotten to know him better. Memory fragments projected like mental snapshots: his smile as he pulled his car over and impulsively offered to take her to dinner, his gruff affection toward his cat, the morning light silhouetting him in the hallway arch, coffee cup in one hand.

Don't confuse kindness with desire, she warned herself. Instead, the memory of when her hand had met his as they both reached for his car door kindled a quiver in her stomach, a warmth that tingled clear down to her knees. She allowed herself that pleasant quickening, admitting it was a curious, bittersweet relief to discover not all her sexual interests had been extinguished, then smiled ruefully. Too bad they had met only because Chris had died. Too bad they had argued and parted in anger. Too bad he was so far away in Yorkshire.

Too bad he was a cop.

At least she wouldn't have to worry about any inconvenient romances on this trip, she thought, *thank God*. She was safe. She leaned her head back, sighed, and sank down into the wonderfully cooling water.

Half an hour after he'd left Camden Town, Keen rang the doorbell of the flat on Dorset. He heard the sound of small running feet. "It's Daddy! Daddy!" The boys' piping voices were muffled through the closed door. His smile faded as it opened and he saw it was not Laura, but her fiancé with the poncy name, Gavin Tremayne. The boys bounced excitedly around Gavin's legs. "Daddy! Daddy! Daddy!" They were really too big now to pick up, but Keen bent down to catch them as they launched themselves at him.

"Laura's expecting me."

"I know." Gavin made no effort to hide his displeasure. "She's upstairs on the phone, finishing up work." He ran a hand over his scalp, rearranging the thinning strands while eyeing Keen's still abundant hair with undisguised resentment.

"Daddy! Daddy! Daddy!" The twins were turning it into a gleeful chant as they climbed up his torso. He hefted both boys onto his hips, their arms garroting his neck, small booted feet kicking his thighs.

"May I come in?" Keen asked, his arms full.

Gavin scowled, then turned to let him in. The boys slid to the floor, but kept Keen's hands trapped in theirs. In the lounge, the television played cartoons with the sound turned off. Badly animated robots jerked across an equally defective background, spraying bullets and spurting fire in a mass orgy of cartoon destruction. Gavin snatched up the remote control, and the robots vanished without a trace.

"Laura says you're joining us for dinner?"

Keen nodded, ignoring the man's hostility. He was thoroughly tired of angry people. "I'm sorry if I've put you to any trouble."

"It'll stretch. I hope you're not expecting anything too fancy."

"It's Monday," Laura's voice said. "He'll be wanting his beans on toast."

Keen turned, genuinely happy to see her. She smiled back, faint lines etched into the echo of her youth. She covered the gray in her hair with diligent care, and although the once lean body had succumbed to too many hours behind a desk, he liked the softness the extra weight gave her. Her green eyes took him in appraisingly. "Then again, he's into celery and rice cakes these days. Christ, Keen, but you're looking fit!"

Before Keen could react, Gavin wrapped his arm around her waist possessively. Keen exchanged a rueful glance with Laura that said far more than words could. "You too, love."

She extricated herself skillfully from Gavin's grasp, pecked the glaring man on the cheek, and said, "Colin, Simon, please set an extra place for your father?"

The twins abandoned him, careening into the kitchen to argue at the top of their lungs over tableware. Keen caught a glimpse of a napkin fluttering like a flag as the boys shot toward the dining table, carrying fragile glasses and porcelain.

"They can be quite a handful," Keen said, trying to be sociable with Gavin.

"Especially when something gets them keyed up like an unexpected visit from Daddy. It's going to be hell settling them into bed tonight, thank you very much."

Keen decided he loathed the man, smiled pleasantly, and shut up.

Dinner, which Keen remembered Laura used to refer to as "tea," was roast chicken with new potatoes and string beans. He did his best to make appreciative noises over the wine (Gavin's the expert, Laura said, earning herself a wan smile from both men) and engage in small talk.

"Colin's decided he's not going to be a fireman anymore, he wants to be a paramedic like Josh on *Casualty*," Laura said, smiling.

"Yeww." Simon grimaced. "It's disgusting! We saw this one show, and this man were riding a horse—"

"*Was* riding a horse . . ." Laura corrected softly, and avoided Keen's glance.

"*Was* riding a horse that got scared by this tractor and jumped over a fence so he fell off and the horse *kicked* him right in the head, bang, like that, and there was blood and *brains* coming out—"

"Not at the table, Simon," Gavin scolded. Keen felt a pang of jealousy. These were *his* boys.

"I don't want to be a paramedic anymore, anyway," Colin announced. "They don't make very much money. I'm gonna be one of those people who look at stars. They have all these fancy instruments and they get to go live in space stations and look at the planets for alien thingies. I'm going to be an astronaut!" He waved his fork for emphasis, a string bean flying off into orbit.

"Well, *I'm* gonna be a policeman like Daddy!" Simon declared.

Not to be outdone, Colin quickly said, "Well, I'm gonna be an astronaut *and* a policeman! I'm gonna be the first policeman on Mars!"

Giggles. Gavin looked up from his plate tightly. "Astronauts, firemen, paramedics, police. That's more exciting than being a pen pusher, isn't it?" Maybe the boys couldn't hear the acid, but Keen looked back at him, expressionless. "Not many kids around saying, 'I'm going to be an investment banker when I grow up.'"

"Gavin, please," Laura said quietly. Keen recognized that soft voice, had lived with the woman for eighteen years and knew exactly what it meant. He studied his silverware, also knowing how he should have responded all those years, remembering how he had. He was curious to see if Gavin was any smarter than he'd been. Apparently not, as Gavin, having less experience with Laura, chose to ignore it.

"Not much glamour in working nine to five to pay the bills. Kids grow up admiring people who can't even make it through college but think wearing police uniforms magically turns them into superheroes."

The twins were wide-eyed, wondering what the hostility was all about. Keen noted the hard set of Laura's jaw, and knew, not without some satisfaction, Gavin wouldn't have a pleasant night of it later.

"It's the telly," Keen said, trying to keep his voice casual while wondering why he bothered. "Fiction. Actors pretending. *Casualty, The Bill, NYPD Blue,* none of it's real. There's not much glamour in my job, either. Most police work isn't much different than yours, Gavin, there's an awful lot of paperwork and pen-pushing—"

"Spare me your sympathy," Gavin snapped. Keen had been right. It hadn't been worth the trouble. "I'm not talking about television. I'm talking about the real world, the one this family has to live in. Uniformed thugs beating the piss out of ordinary citizens, lying in court and covering up for each other, all in the name of law and order, no better than criminals the lot—"

"Gavin!" It came out in an angry hiss. The boys jumped, their eyes round. "Simon, Colin, you may be excused. Please go play in your room." The twins didn't even make a nominal protest as they fled. Once they were out of the room, Laura glared. "Damn it, Gavin. Do you have to pick a fight every time he comes?"

"That's lovely." Gavin tossed his napkin down with theatrical pique. "That's *just* lovely, take his side against me, won't you."

"Listen, you," Keen said, his own anger surfacing, "I don't care what your opinion of the police might be, idiotic as it is, but I'll be damned if I'll sit by while my boys listen to you slag off their father—"

"Keen." It was that voice, and it took all his self-control to back away, old habits hard to break.

"I didn't invite him," Gavin complained. "He has regular access rights, for chrissake. I live here, too, Laura, and it's not that much to ask after a hard day to come home and not be expected to play congenial host for your flipping ex." To Gavin, Keen no longer existed, only an annoyance to be gotten rid of.

Keen took a deep breath before he pushed back his chair. "He's right, Laura. I shouldn't have barged in on you and upset the children's routine." Gavin glared, unsure whether he was being insulted or not. "If you don't mind, I'll go say good night to the lads and be on my way."

The low muttering of their quarrel followed him as he climbed the stairs toward the boys' room. He knocked before opening the door a crack to see them sitting on the floor, playing with toy cars across a rug printed with striped roadways twisting through a greenbelt. A maze of blocks and toy houses and books and Lego pieces had been arranged into a sprawling toy town on its surface. "May I come in?"

"Sure. You can have the police car, Daddy," Simon offered magnanimously.

"Cannot! That's *my* car!" Colin protested, then reddened. "But you can have it if you want, Daddy."

Keen closed the door, shutting out the quarrel below, then settled cross-legged onto the floor, wincing at still sore muscles. "No, I'll just watch you lads."

The boys played ram raiders on their hands and knees, driving toy cars into Lego shops and knocking over cardboard houses while bickering over the spoils and supplying a variety of sound effects themselves. "Daddy?" Simon said eventually.

"What?"

"Gavin doesn't like you very much, does he?"

The twins stopped playing, both looking at him while he considered his answer. It was so hard to walk this tightrope. "I suppose not, Simon. But you don't like everybody you know at school, do you? Sometimes it's the same for grown-ups, it's hard to get along together."

"Is he mad at you because you're a policeman?" Colin asked.

"No, of course not," Keen lied. Lying seemed to be getting easier. "I think Gavin just wants you to like him, too."

"I hate Gavin," Colin said stubbornly. "He's mean. If I were a policeman I could kick him in the teeth, and nobody could make me do anything I didn't want to do, like clean up my room and eat yucky parsnips, and I'd make him go away."

"That's not what policemen do, Colin. I don't get to kick anyone in the teeth or do whatever I want. My job is to help people and catch the bad guys."

"That's not what Gavin says," Simon declared.

Keen fought down a flash of anger, wishing he *could* throttle the living day-light out of Gavin. "Well, he's wrong. Maybe he only says those things because his feelings are hurt you want to be a policeman like me, and not an investment banker like him."

Colin thought about it, his eyebrows pushed together under his fringe of fine hair. "Does Gavin make more money than you, Daddy?"

Quite bloody likely, Keen thought sourly, wondering where his son's sudden preoccupation with money came from, but he said, "I don't right know, Colin. It would be rude to ask, now, wouldn't it?"

Simon frowned as Colin said, "But what does a vessment banker *do*?"

"It's an important job," Keen said seriously, although he couldn't admit he had only the vaguest notion of what Gavin did for a living. "Gavin helps people look after their money. I'm sure he'd be happy to explain it to you if you asked him."

"Would your feelings be hurt if I want to be a vessment banker instead of a policeman?"

"No. If you want to be a 'vessment' banker or a policeman or an astronaut or anything else when you grow up, I'll always be proud of you."

"Daddy?" Simon's voice was timid. "Gavin and Mummy are getting married. He gave her a ring and everything."

"I know," he said gently, hoping the hurt didn't show.

"Doesn't Mummy love you anymore?"

"Yes, I'm sure she does. But she loves Gavin more."

"Why can't you make Gavin leave and come live here with us?"

"Come here," Keen said, holding out his arms. Immediately, they clambered over their toy village, houses and cars and shops trampled underfoot, and nestled into his embrace. "Look, you two, we've gone over all this before. Mummy would be very angry with me if I tried to make Gavin leave. And we can't all of us live in the same house. Four men? We'd drive her crazy." He tickled Simon and Colin, forcing a giggle from them. "You don't want me to come live in London. What would I do with the house, hm? And Thomas and all the sheep? They wouldn't like living in the city. Can you imagine what Mummy would say, all those sheep in her garden?" He didn't have to tickle them this time to get the giggles. "You don't know how lucky you are, you've got two houses, one bedroom for you with Mummy and one with me."

"And one for Thomas," Simon insisted.

"And one for Thomas," Keen agreed.

"And one for the sheep!" Colin squealed.

"No, I think we'll keep the sheep outside for now." He glanced at his watch. "It's getting late, lads, so if you want to say goodbye before I go, it's wees and teeth, go to it." He hugged them both tightly before they peeled off their clothes and pulled on garish Teenage Mutant Hero Turtle pajamas. They scrambled into the bathroom to squabble over toothbrushes, and were busily spraying the mirror and each other with toothpaste when the door opened. He looked up, still seated cross-legged on the floor, at Laura.

"They're getting ready for bed."

She sighed at the bathroom door. "I usually have to argue for an hour to get them into bed. Mean old mum."

It took fifteen minutes more to get the boys settled down and into their beds. "Daddy? Are you going to come this weekend?"

His access rights only gave him one weekend a month. He glanced at Laura before he said cautiously, "I can't promise anything, Colin. I might have to work." The twins were crestfallen. "But I'll come the weekend after that, absolutely positively definitely certain."

Two weeks seemed an eternity when you're eight. Or a divorced father.

"We'll see," Laura said as she tucked the covers under Colin's chin. She turned, the look in her eye as much a promise as her words. "Daddy has to go now."

"Bye-bye, Daddy!"

"Bye-bye, Daddy!"

"I said it first!"

"Did not!"

"Did too!"

"Go to sleep, both of you!"

"See you soon, lads."

Laura closed the door, and stood next to Keen, their heads bent together as they listened to the muffled sound of eight-year-olds skirmishing. Laura smiled and raised a finger to her mouth, then tiptoed away. Keen followed her downstairs. The lounge was empty.

"Fancy a cup of tea before you go?"

"Where's Gavin got to?"

"Down to the pub for a good sulk, I expect. He won't be back for at least an hour."

"Wouldn't mind a cuppa, then, thanks."

He sat on the settee as Laura fussed in the kitchen, putting the kettle on. "What's this case you're working on?" she said when she returned, more to make conversation than curiosity.

"Special assignment. Can't go into it much."

"All right." She wouldn't pry, never had. "If you're still in London come Saturday and have some free time, I'm sure we could work something out. It doesn't always have to be by the book, you know."

He caught himself staring at the diamond ring on Laura's finger, the stone appallingly large, then looked down at his own blunt hands. "I appreciate that. But I weren't lying to them, Laura. I might have to work. It's really what I'm here for."

"I know it is."

She got up as the kettle whistled. Alone, he rubbed where the wedding band had encircled his finger for eighteen years, gone now, but the naked sensation still strange. He thought about Christine Swinton, no mark on her dead fingers, and Jillie Waltham's barren hands. A piece of jewelry did not a marriage make. Laura returned with two teacups. He recognized her mother's china, the familiar blue morning glories jarringly out of place. He had drunk from this very cup at least a thousand times, the gilt rim tarnished with decades of mouths and washing up.

"Thanks, love." He sipped, knowing it would be exactly as he liked, milky with a hint of sugar. "I apologize for tonight—" he started.

"Oh, shut it," she said tiredly. "Gavin can be a complete arse sometimes."

"Why are you marrying him, then?"

She sighed, half a laugh, half a sob. "He's not generally like he was tonight. He's good with the boys and he can be great fun, really he can. It's just that he's so jealous of you."

"Don't see why," he said quietly, knowing he was stepping into dangerous territory. "He's getting everything I ever wanted. A lovely wife. Two beautiful children." Her look stopped him.

"I'm in no mood for your pity-poor-me act tonight," she said, her face as immovable as stone. "It's good, but it's still an act."

He studied the patterns the milk made in his tea. "Not all of it."

"No," she agreed. "But it doesn't solve anything."

"I miss my family. And I still love you, Laura." His voice was devoid of any emotion, simply a statement of fact. He didn't look at her in the prolonged silence.

"I still love you, too," she said eventually. He listened carefully, hearing both truth and finality in her voice. Only then did he look up, seeing the woman he'd known almost half his lifetime and knowing she had always been a stranger to him.

He nodded. "Boys doing well in school, are they?"

She relaxed visibly, back onto safe ground. "Fine. Simon's having some problems in maths, but that's mostly bruised ego because Colin is such a whiz. I keep trying to find something he's better at than his brother, but so far that's only getting into trouble."

He smiled. They talked awhile about the school, Laura carefully steering away from the question of cost.

Laura knew what she wanted; she wanted her children to escape the council housing and the privation she grew up with, the economic limitations of the north, would do anything to make sure they had it, if it took working two jobs and marrying a balding, petulant investment banker. Her children would grow up to speak with proper grammar in the right accent, know the right friends, have the right schools on their CVs, have every advantage money could buy. A quality education cost money, a lot of money that Keen did not have. His sons would be neither firemen nor policemen when they grew up, no matter what they fantasized as eight-year-old boys.

When it came down to Laura's choosing between her husband and her sons, Keen had never stood a ghost of a chance. He wondered what Gavin wanted from Laura and whether or not he found it in her.

They kept to the safe subjects, she asking after the Kestlemans, he telling her a few funny anecdotes from the nick, balancing the fine circumspect line along the pain. Keen glanced at his watch markedly. "I ought to be going. Better if I'm not around when Gavin gets back."

She smiled, that twisting half-smile that had always made her seem like she was laughing at a private joke, the familiarity an ache in his chest. "I suppose so."

She walked him to the door, hand on the knob as he retrieved his jacket from the coatrack. "Keen . . ." She hesitated. "I'm not one of those women who use their children as a weapon against their ex-husbands."

"I never thought you would be."

"What I'm saying . . ." She bit her upper lip. "What I'm saying is they are your sons, Keen. I want you to see them as often as you can. Screw Gavin, all right?"

"No, thank you, love. I'll leave that ghastly chore to you."

She tsked at his pale attempt at humor. "Whenever you are in London, please call. The boys need their father, too. They need *you*."

He traced two fingertips along her chin, then drew her in against his chest. When she hugged him back tightly, he had to blink and swallow hard. He pressed his cheek against her hair, and inhaled the sharp scent of hairspray and the softer musk underneath. When she drew back, he was surprised to see her own eyes were wet.

"You're still a sappy old tyke, you are," she said softly. And for a moment, she lost her carefully practiced Received Pronunciation, the Yorkshire lass he'd once loved again in his arms.

"Yeah, I know." He kissed her lips, a chaste pressing of flesh, then released her. "Try not to get the boys' hopes up about this weekend. I do want to see them, but—"

"The job."

"Right. But I'll try."

"Right. Cheers, love."

"Cheers."

The sky had deepened to an electric indigo, the residual heat still oppressive. He turned on the pavement to give her a quick wave, seeing only her silhouette framed in the doorway, the square of light behind her. She waved back briefly, then shut the door.

V I

TUESDAY

Keen woke well before the alarm, still tired. Dream fragments left their emotional fingerprints, heavy with a vague frustrated anger. His travel clock read 6:43. Sunlight spackled through the curtain's weave and voices mumbled in the hallway. Outside, the symphony of traffic congestion had begun. He groaned as he rolled over to stare up at acoustic ceiling tiles. A water stain had left a faint line like the faded map of some ancient continent, ominously impenetrable.

The alarm clock rang.

After he'd showered and shaved in the community toilets, he trooped back to his room in his old robe, barefoot and hair dripping. He'd brought his one suit, the all-purpose dark wool suitable for funerals, weddings, and interviews, and dressed while gazing out over the surly streets of a London now stripped of her night glamour.

His hair was still damp when he crossed the car park, asphalt already radiating heat, feeling alien and uneasy in civvies as he entered the station, surrounded by unfamiliar uniformed officers. He nodded to the female desk officer who smiled back warmly, recognizing him, which meant more to him than it did to her, he was sure.

He found Phil Reaves in the CID office, desks packed cheek by jowl and piled high with paper. Even with the sunshine through the windows, the lights were on, washing everyone's face a sallow blue. One fluorescent tube flickered in terminal spasms. Reaves stood with his arms crossed and shoulders hunched as he spoke with a seated heavyset detective. Both men's body language shouted of aggressiveness. As Keen weaved his way through the desks, Phil broke off his discussion.

"Mornin'," Keen said.

Phil merely nodded. The CID inspector flicked him a disinterested glance. He was overweight and pushing fifty, with chronic discontent settling over his features until they'd adhered into a permanent mask. "I don't *care* what the friggin' regs say," he said, ignoring Keen. "Next time, you will *ask* me first. Is that clear, Sergeant?"

"I see your point, sir," Phil said. Keen noticed it was neither an agreement nor an apology. The inspector grunted, mollified, then began shuffling files, dismissing them both. Phil jerked his head to one side, and Keen followed him out the door. Phil muttered obscenities under his breath, and Keen decided not to ask him about it.

Entering yet another tiny, paper-jammed office, Phil opened a desk drawer and took out a small tape recorder sealed with a paper label marked "Metropolitan Police, Master Tape." He plugged the jack of a long microphone cable into the recorder, and handed the lot to Keen.

"What's this for?" Keen objected.

"What do you think?" Phil snapped. "Microphone clips inside your shirt, out of sight. Just keep your jacket on. You've only got forty-five minutes of tape, don't waste it. Don't break the seal on the machine, or the whole thing'll be inadmissible."

Keen said nothing, shoving the tape recorder into his pocket. Phil picked three files and held them out one by one to Keen.

"John Wortley, white male, sixty-two, married, no children. No police record. Retired butcher, lived in Streatham, died of cardiac arrest on December fifth last year. His wife said he'd been on heart medication. His body was discovered in Paddington, looked like he'd felt the attack coming on and sat down in a stairwell. No one spotted him until it was too late. Wife had no idea what he was doing there." Phil recited the information in a clipped, impersonal voice as Keen scanned the file, the initial report, subsequent witness interviews, coroner's autopsy report ruling. "He was also a Mason," Phil added, "but not high up, and CID can't come up with any link."

"Mmm." There probably was none. "What about Special Branch's Registry, anything in that?"

Phil scowled. "That's been slow in coming, claiming the usual bureaucratic balls-up." He slapped another file into Keen's palm. "Daniel Barrow, white male, born in Cape Town, single, twenty-three. Apprentice plumber lived out in Pindsmere, small village between Surrey and Hampshire. Died of head injuries after falling off a footbridge in Richmond Park where he'd apparently been fishing illegally. Blood alcohol was much higher than the empty lager bottles in his tackle could account for. Traces of THC in his blood, did a hair analysis. He was a regular cannabis user."

He pointed to a notation. "Also found benzoylecgonine," he said, pronouncing the chemical name carefully, but not slowly. "That's a byproduct of cocaine, shows up about two hours after it breaks down in the system, lasts about twelve hours. Pathologist said it was unusually pure. No police arrest record other than a speeding fine four years ago. Lived with his girlfriend; she says he was a heavy drinker, but he didn't do coke and it wasn't like him to bunk off without telling her. She didn't even know he liked fishing. Didn't catch any fish that day, by the way."

"The two men ever meet? At a pub, maybe? Plumber come to fix a leaky faucet in John Wortley's flat?"

"Nope. CID couldn't make a single connection." Phil handed him the last file. "Alice Guiscoigne, white female, fifty-two, widowed. One son. Mrs. Guiscoigne lived with her son in Maida Hill. She was under a doctor's care for diabetes, had an insulin kit in her handbag with a used syringe and an empty vial, apparently overdid the injection. No one found the kit until after it was too late. Sad, really. She sat in Kensington Gardens with hundreds of people walking by for hours. Someone finally called an ambulance, but she was pronounced dead on arrival, never regained consciousness." He pointed his chin at the files in Keen's hands. "Same as the first two, no link at all."

Keen skimmed the interview with her son. "Not much here," he remarked. He handed the file to Phil and watched him scan through the report.

"Skimpy," Phil admitted. "Doesn't seem as someone took their time about it, does it?"

"We might think about redoing the interview," Keen suggested.

Phil looked up, his expression one of amused hostility. "Not 'we,' white man. You're only here to keep our lady professor happy. Anything else is our nick's responsibility." He tossed the files back onto his desk.

Keen stared at him, perplexed by the undercurrent of animosity.

A constable leaned into the doorway. "Ergo says the surveillance carrier is in transport ready to go whenever you are, Sarge."

"Righto." He turned to Keen. "We have to be there early for the setup. You taking your car to the funeral?" It wasn't an offer of a lift, Keen understood.

"Hadn't planned on it." Keen kept his voice neutral. "Don't like London traffic. Tube's fine."

"Shall we, Sergeant?" Keen followed Phil out into the hall, the younger man's spine stiff.

Brushing past several uniformed bobbies in the stairwell, Phil banged open the door leading out to the car park. Keen squinted in the harsh sunlight. A wilted-looking PC in civvies leaned against the surveillance carrier, a dusty nondescript white van with one-way smoked windows, doing his best to stay in its meager shade.

Phil stepped in front of Keen to block his way. "Slurry, huh? Great story, very funny," he said hostilely. "Except the whisper's gone round that you've got a real attitude problem, working with you has put some unusual wear and tear on your former colleagues. Not quite so funny." He waited for an explanation.

Keen's heart skipped a beat, but he met Phil's glower evenly and said nothing.

Phil's eyes narrowed more in anger than from the strong sunlight. "Suit yourself, mate. But I'm not Williams. Don't start in playing mind-fuck games with me, you got that?"

"Look, all I want is to get the job done and go home. Can we drop this now?"

After a moment, Phil looked away, his mouth working as if trying to dislodge a particularly annoying seed stuck in a molar. "Yeah," he said finally. "Just so's you know where we both stand."

Keen had known exactly where he'd stood for the past two years. "I see your point," he said, unsmiling.

Phil glanced at him sharply, but his pique visibly diminished. "You'd have to change at Embankment for the District line."

"I'm familiar with the London Underground."

"Personally, I can't stand the Tube," Phil said. "Something about the smell. Care for a lift?"

"Wouldn't say no."

As they walked toward the van, Keen caught Phil studying him slyly, the humorous glint back in his eye. He suspected Phil Reaves was one of those men who were fundamentally incapable of holding a grudge for long, his own cheeky humor too irrepressible. "Just tell me one thing. The Great Slurry Snatch, that was for real?"

Keen nodded. "It was for real, and it was my nick."

Phil snorted, amused. "Not my planet, Leeds."

Jillie arrived for the funeral in a wool skirt and heavy sweater, the only black clothing she'd brought. Sweating and clutching a small bouquet of flowers, she was pleased to see such a surprisingly large number of cars slowly following the hearse into the West Brompton cemetery, happy Chris had been so popular.

But as people began filling the rows of folding chairs on the lawn, Jillie realized most of the mourners were well over seventy, murmuring and patting the hand of Chris's mother. Verona Swinton wore black silk and lace that would have looked suitable on Queen Victoria. The heavily pregnant woman next to her seemed more bored than grieving. The man standing over them must be Max, Jillie thought, trying to find a resemblance between Chris and this pale basset hound of a man. A little girl next to him clasped her tiny hands encased in white gloves neatly in front of her as if she'd been trained, dark eyes huge in her too still face.

At the grave, Jillie laid her cellophane-wrapped carnations beside the grandiose wreath and studied the mahogany coffin, gleaming brass handles and hinges. Unable to picture Chris lying inside, her throat ached suddenly.

"Excuse me, aren't you Dr. Waltham?"

She quickly wiped her eyes, and looked up. A horse-faced man stood hunched awkwardly, partly due to the large cast on one leg, Jillie surmised. She swallowed a few times before she could say, "Yes?"

"I'm Dr. Reece Wycombe." He shook her hand, his palm clammy. She resisted the urge to wipe her hand on her skirt as Dr. Wycombe cleared his throat. "I worked with Chris on her books."

"I know, she told me."

His expression made it clear he was worried exactly what Chris had told Jillie.

"Chris and I had our differences, sometimes rather heated ones, but I had the greatest respect for her." He smiled self-deprecatingly. "She had a first-class mind. Her death is truly a tragic loss."

He didn't seem like such a bad guy. "It is." She glanced around. "And I'm glad at least *one* of her colleagues showed up."

Dr. Wycombe smiled without humor, his lips a bruised color. "You haven't met the mother yet, I take it." It wasn't a question. He grimaced, shifting his weight off the foot with the cast. "Dr. Waltham . . ." he said uneasily, patting a handkerchief against his forehead. Jillie was certain it wasn't just from the sweltering heat. "I edited both Chris's previous books, and her work was excellent if erratic. But her new book I felt needed extensive editorial restructuring before I could include it in the series. I should point out mine was not the only opinion. I'm only one of several editors for the Georgian Historical Studies series. Her opinion differed. It happens."

"It wasn't finished anyway."

He glanced at her uneasily, his rubbery mouth working. "You've read it?"

"Not yet. I'd like to, would you have a copy?"

"Unfortunately, no. I returned her manuscript."

"So why was it so controversial?"

"'Controversial'?" He tsked. "Chris could be overly melodramatic. Her rough draft was remarkable, even brilliant." He smiled unconvincingly. "I might even carry on, write something of my own based on her research, as a memorial to her work. But even in a 'squishy' science like history, no matter how entertaining a theory might be, one must substantiate it with reliable evidence. She hadn't, it was that simple."

Dr. Wycombe wet his lips, his tongue startlingly pale. "But I understand you're staying on in Chris's house?" He sounded as petulant as a child, his tone almost angry. "I've always helped Chris in her research, introduced her to useful contacts and lent her quite a bit of source material. She borrowed a rather valuable book of mine. It's irreplaceable, so I'd like to have it back, if you wouldn't mind."

She blinked in surprise. "I'm sorry, that has nothing to do with me. You'd have to ask her brother about it."

After a moment, Dr. Wycombe turned away and stalked off, his walking cast thumping the ground. Jillie watched him retreat, then joined the gathering around the mother, waiting for an appropriate moment to extend her condolences.

"Max Swinton?" she said to the sad-faced man. "We spoke on the phone."

"Ah," he said, extending a hand. "You must be Jillie Walthill, Chris's American friend."

She was about to correct him, then felt awkward under the circumstances. "I'm very sorry about Chris."

"Yes, terrible tragedy." He glanced over at the large woman in black trying to catch his attention. "My sister was too young, so talented, a great waste . . . Mother . . . ?"

Verona Swinton's features were obscured under the black lace. Even sitting, she was an imposing figure, not with grandmotherly softness, but monolithic, all steel and barbed wire.

"This is Jillie Walthill."

Jillie extended her hand. "I'm Chris's friend from America, Mrs. Swinton."

"I remember you," the woman said coldly. Jillie knew by her grating tone what the woman really meant was she remembered the roommate Chris had been arrested with so many years ago. "You took my daughter to this silly conference in Leeds . . . where she drowned, drunk in a fishpond," Verona Swinton said crisply, without a trace of grief. Beside her, the pregnant woman grimaced with distaste.

"Max, for God's *sake*," she muttered, and rolled her eyes toward the four-year-old girl listening quietly.

He bent down over the girl. "Why don't you go look at the pretty flowers, sweetheart," Max whispered. She glanced at him, enormous eyes lovely with thick lashes, then walked obediently over to an immense wreath, more interested in the cavernous hole in the ground than the floral display. Max pretended not to notice, sweating and smiling relentlessly.

"My poor, misguided Christine," Verona Swinton continued. She dabbed her eyes under the lace with a neatly folded handkerchief. When she withdrew it, it was still creased into a meticulous point, not even dampened. "I prayed she would find someone suitable and marry, settle down and have children. But she was always a disappointment, I daresay. Do you have any children, dear?"

"My daughter, Karen," Jillie said mechanically, as if watching this horrible scene from a far remove.

"Only the one? No sons? Pity. Better than having no children at all, I suppose. If the good Lord had to take one of my children, I must find it in my heart to be grateful it wasn't Max. Not with a wife and family who depend on him."

Speechless, Jillie was unable to answer.

"I suppose it's a blessing Christine left no one behind." She sighed, a great exhalation of breath fluttering the black lace.

"Chris was my daughter's godmother," Jillie murmured.

"Was she?" Verona Swinton said irritably. "Hardly *real* family, is it? And you're divorced as well, I hear. Such a shame. Maintaining moral values is so crucial in good families these days." There was a slight but unmistakable emphasis on the word "good." Mrs. Swinton patted the pregnant woman's hand proudly. "I do wish Christine could have lived to have seen her nephew." She looked back at Jillie. "Your own daughter . . . Carol, was it . . . ? She's in good health, one hopes?"

"Perfect." The word came out clipped.

"How nice. Perhaps you too may have a grandson someday."

Jillie had thought Chris's depiction of her mother was an exaggerated joke.

Now, struggling to quell her indignation at this appalling woman, she realized Chris may have understated it.

"I've told Mrs. Walthill she's welcome to stay in the house for a couple of days, Mother," Max said. His voice sounded strained. "She can keep an eye on things until we can sort something out." Max avoided the pregnant woman's glare of outrage.

"How kind," Verona Swinton said, glowering through the haze of black lace. "Celia, darling, why don't you pop over when you're feeling up to it?" Celia either couldn't or didn't bother to hide the rapacious gleam in her eye. "Christine had many of the family heirlooms, and the house itself is valuable property. Godchildren are not legal heirs, as I'm sure you understand, don't you, dear? Everything belongs to Max now. *Everything.* I'd hate to see anything go missing while you were there."

Jillie felt the blood drain from her face, speechless. "Oh, Mother," Max muttered through clenched teeth. His hands fluttered like dying butterflies. "Mrs. Walthill, let me help you find a seat, shall I?" He led her away as Celia glared poisonously after them.

The little girl furtively nudged the dirt spilled out from under the blanket of AstroTurf, watching it trickle into the grave.

"Jewel!" Celia snapped. The child jumped, then faced her mother with a strangely blank expression. "Stop fiddling about with those damned flowers before you get your new dress dirty . . ."

"I'm dreadfully sorry, Mrs. Walthill," Max said, steering her toward the back row of chairs nervously. "I wish I could say it's just stress. Truth is, my mother's old-fashioned ideas would put the most backward of wogs to shame."

"Waltham," Jillie said softly.

"Beg your pardon?"

You could, she thought, but you're not likely to get it. "My name is Jillie Waltham. *Dr.* Waltham, not Walthill."

"Ah, Dr. Waltham, so sorry. Look . . ." He held her forearm, glancing anxiously toward his mother and wife, and lowered his voice. "I realize all this has left you at loose ends, so please stay as long as you need—"

"No, thank you. Your mother just called me a thief, in case you didn't hear it. I'll be out this afternoon," Jillie said, still trembling with anger. "I hope you can trust me not to rip off the family silver."

Max patted the air appeasingly. "Dr. Waltham . . . May I call you Jillie? Jillie, I do apologize. I'm returning tonight to Brussels on important business I've already had to interrupt because of the funeral. It's only for another week, I have a return flight Thursday night." Sweat beaded on his forehead. "So you see, I *need* someone in the house. Burglars, you see. They read the obituaries, break in while the house is left empty. I couldn't have Celia over there, not in her condition."

She was astounded by his tactlessness. "So why don't you just hire a security guard?" As he laughed feebly, she realized why. Security guards cost money, money his mother controlled with an iron fist, while Jillie could do the job for free.

"Please accept my apologies. You would be doing me a favor, and in return, you'd save on a hotel." He tried an ingratiating smile that made his hangdog face look even more sickly. "Only until this weekend?"

"All right," Jillie said, curbing her resentment. And it was true she could ill afford what would have been a huge hotel bill. "But just until the weekend."

She allowed him to seat her as mourners milled about on their collective arthritic legs. For a brief moment, she noticed a plump, short-haired woman staring intently at her. Thinking it was someone she should recognize, she groped for a name. A friend of Chris's from the conference in Leeds? A group of elderly men hobbled in front of her, and when they had passed, the woman had disappeared. Instead, she spotted Lynne Selkirk waving at her.

To Jillie's amazement, Lynne wore a shocking-pink dress with a rainbow silk scarf draped over her shoulders. Sharp-heeled shoes sank into the soft ground, forcing her to walk like some ungainly flamingo, so comical Jillie almost laughed in spite of herself. As Lynne passed somber mourners, they glared disapprovingly.

"Damn, damn, damn," Lynne muttered and plopped down beside Jillie. "I feel such a tart trying to balance on these heels. Wouldn't Chris love it if I made a spectacle of myself, pitching headlong into her grave?"

Jillie giggled. "You'd scandalize the whole family."

"And wouldn't *that* be frightful?" Lynne said acidly. "I take it you've met the bereaved mother?"

"I've offered my condolences," Jillie said with what she hoped was equally dry irony.

At eleven-thirty exactly, Verona Swinton lifted her veil to glance meaningfully at her watch. The vicar, in a long white surplice and red embroidered pallium, stepped up to the podium and opened an oversized Bible at the first of many pagemarks, stared at the text over the top of his glasses, waiting for silence.

" 'Wherefore, as by one man sin entered into the world, and death by sin, and so death passed unto all men for that all have sinned . . .' " he began in a sepulchral voice, words rolling out like polished marbles, more sound effect than substance. " 'As it is appointed unto men once to die, but after this the judgment . . .' "

Light glinting off his glasses hid his eyes like a mask of blank coins. Jillie wondered who had chosen the selection of biblical verses, rambling diatribes against sin inevitably resulting in death, usually painful and lingering.

" 'Until thou return unto the ground, for out of it wast thou taken, for dust thou art, and unto dust shalt thou return . . .' "

The silence deadening, the vicar tucked fingers into yet another bookmark. " 'And death and hell were cast into the lake of fire. This is the second death, and whosoever was not found written in the book of life was cast into the lake of fire . . .' "

A few blown noses punctuated the sermon, but Jillie suspected it was hay fever, too many hothouse flowers. Chris must be spinning in that gleaming mahogany and bronze coffin.

" 'That as sin hath reigned unto death, even so might grace reign through righteousness unto eternal life by Jesus Christ, Our Lord, amen.' " He shut the Bible with a thump and looked up.

"Amen," the gathering echoed dutifully.

"Amen," Jillie breathed, thankful for the end of this macabre service.

And that, apparently, was that. The flock of senior citizens murmured formulaic regrets to Chris's mother before meandering toward the parking lot. Two workmen began stacking chairs while two others leaned against a white van, waiting for the crowd to clear out before the coffin could be lowered and the grave filled in.

"That," Lynne said, "was utterly dreadful. Don't forget the meeting tonight; we'll try to have a proper Irish wake for Chris."

"Chris wasn't Irish."

Jillie admired Lynne's droll smile. "Quite all right. Her funeral wasn't Christian. Canapés and straight scotch, eight o'clock?"

Lynne wobbled away across the grass, cursing under her breath. Jillie was wondering what she should do next when someone touched her arm. She looked up at Keen Dunliffe dressed in a plain dark suit and tie.

"Hello, again."

"Hi," she said, startled. "What are *you* doing here?"

"Public relations. Leeds Police felt someone should extend our condolences to the Swinton family. I had a couple weeks' holiday due and planned on coming down to see my sons. So I got volunteered." He glanced past her to Verona Swinton kissing cheeks with the last of the well-wishers. "Are you by yourself?"

"Yes."

"You look as if you could do with a drink. After I've paid my official respects, buy you a pint?"

She was surprised by the offer; they hadn't parted on the best of terms. "I'd like that." She grimaced in Verona Swinton's direction. "I've already paid mine, if you don't mind."

"Wait a couple minutes for me? I'll be right back."

She watched as he patted Mrs. Swinton's hand and shook Max's before squatting in front of the little girl Celia held prisoner by one hand. He said something that made the child smile before she glanced up at her mother, her smile flickering away like a candle blown out in a cold wind. Poor little thing, Jillie thought sadly.

When Keen returned, all he said was, "Charming family." They walked out of the cemetery and turned up Old Brompton Road. Within a few blocks past the exhibition center, the character of the neighborhood changed, old buildings gentrified instead of decaying. Here, she noticed, were plenty of small hotels and bed and breakfasts, already making plans.

Keen chose a pub busy with the lunch crowd, although it was hardly more than a small room made even smaller by the huge circular bar in the middle. They sat down on rickety chairs around a table made of a discarded telephone cable spool. "Strongbow?" he asked.

"Yes, please. The small size."

His face creased in a grin. "Right. The small size."

She studied the chalkboard over the bar until he returned with amber cider in one hand, dark brown beer in the larger glass. "What's bubble and squeak?"

He glanced at the chalkboard. "Mashed potatoes and vegetables, usually spinach, fried up together."

"Why's it called bubble and squeak?"

He shrugged. "Don't right know, really."

"I don't even want to ask what spotted dick is."

"Actually, it's not bad as puddings go. Are you hungry?"

"A little. Would they have any regular food?"

He was having trouble keeping a straight face, and she wondered what he found so funny. "Regular food?"

"Something with normal names. I'm not brave enough to order anything called bangers and mushy peas, or toad in the hole."

"Oh, you mean like buffalo wings and Hawaiian pizza. Pineapple and bits of half-raw bacon. The single most disgusting thing I've ever tasted in my life."

"It's ham."

"Here we call it 'bacon.' "

"Here, cookies are biscuits and biscuits are crackers, French fries are chips and chips are crisps—"

"*There,* football is soccer and soccer is unheard of, you get lavatory and laboratory confused, and if a decent Englishman asks an American for a rubber, he's likely to have his face slapped—"

"*You* drive on the wrong side of the road and you dress your cars up with boots and bonnets—"

"While American cars all have trunks and hoods like blinded elephants."

She laughed. "I've never had so much trouble speaking English in my life!"

"That's because you *don't* speak English, you speak American." He was still grinning. "Feel better now you've got that out of your system?"

She nodded. "Much. Thank you."

"Good." He sipped his beer as his pale eyes appraised her. "You have a nice smile," he said when he put the glass down. "Glad to see you've found it again."

His warm familiarity under other circumstances she might have found flattering, even reassuring. Instead, it somehow rang false. She tensed, wary and not sure why. "I haven't had much to smile about. So how long are you in London for?"

"Don't know. All depends on how much time my ex will allow me to spend with my boys, really."

"If you're here on vacation, who's working on Chris's case?"

He leaned back, still relaxed although he seemed less self-confident. "I'm not the only police officer in Leeds."

"So there still *is* a murder investigation?"

"The coroner ruled her death as accidental. The only case still open is the break-in. That doesn't mean the police won't follow up all evidence we have, but we're not investigating a *murder*."

"But what if I could help?" she said carefully.

He watched her with a blank expression. His mouth opened as if to say something, then closed. Finally, he said colorlessly, "Help how?"

"I'm staying at Chris's house. Her brother's asked me to house-sit until the end of the week. He's in Brussels until Thursday and worried about burglars."

"If he's that worried, then you shouldn't stay there," he said flatly.

"I know." She leaned over the table on her elbows. "But I think she was murdered. I also think that break-in wasn't a coincidence." She couldn't contain her excitement. "What if there's something in her house that could tell us why?"

"The police already searched Chris Swinton's house, they've gone over it thoroughly. There's nothing there."

"That *you* found," she said with more confidence than she felt.

"Jillie—"

"Listen a minute! Chris was a political activist." When he didn't answer, she pressed on. "She was also an historical researcher, like me. She told me she was working on something so controversial Reece Wycombe refused to publish it. What if the two things are connected?"

"Do you know what it was? This research of hers?"

Jillie shook her head. "All she'd say is that it was the sort of thing that if she couldn't get a respectable academic press to publish it, she knew the tabloids would. I might be able to figure out what it was. Without me, would you even know what you were looking for?"

He stared at her for a long moment, then drained his glass. "Fancy another?" he said brusquely.

She glanced at her half-full glass of cider in surprise and shook her head. He scraped his chair back noisily on the wooden floor and headed toward the bar. When he returned, he set his beer on the table, frowning as he looked at her.

"Listen to me, Jillie. You're an academic, and I'm sure a very good one. But you're not trained as a detective. *If* someone did break into your room looking for something and didn't find it, they might try Chris Swinton's house next. Personally, I don't believe whatever research your friend was doing could be serious enough to get anyone killed over. But if you *do* know something about what she was involved in that might have to do with her death, then tell the police and let us handle it."

"I don't know anything *specific* yet . . ." Jillie protested.

"Then stay out of it. Don't go looking for clues that aren't there and clutching at straws. If Chris did die in an accident, you'd be wasting police time on a wild-goose chase. Wasting police time is a chargeable offense in this country and you could well find yourself in more trouble than you bargained for. So *please,* let us do our job and don't play Miss Marple, all right?"

He wasn't being impolite, seemingly genuine in his concern, but her face flushed. "Nancy Drew," she snapped.

"What?"

"I'm American, not British, as we've already established." Before he could interrupt, she said hotly, "I don't care what you tell me it looks like, Detective, I *know* Chris was murdered. She was my friend, and you're not going to stop me from trying to find out who and why."

She felt childishly triumphant, but surprised to find no anger in his face.

"Right, then," he said impassively. "Let's start, shall we? Where were you between the hours of ten and midnight on Tuesday last?"

Her jaw dropped. "I told you. I had dinner with Lena Baruch, then walked to Mrs. Birney's around nine-thirty. I was in bed by eleven-thirty."

"Did anyone see you after you left Weetwood Hall, did you talk to anyone on your way back to the guesthouse?"

"No . . ."

"Mrs. Birney didn't see you come in?"

"No. What *is* this? I'm not a suspect!"

"So you have no alibi during the time Christine Swinton died."

"*Alibi?* You can't be serious? *I'm* the one who reported her missing," Jillie said, astonished. "*I'm* the one who identified her."

"You could be cleverly shifting suspicion from yourself."

"If I were so clever, wouldn't I have come up with a better alibi for the time? If I were the killer, do you think I'd be badgering you for an investigation? Why would *I* have killed Chris?"

He stared at his beer, as if reading something there. "I don't think *anyone* has. What I'm trying to make you understand is that to prove murder, you need motive and method as well as suspects. So let's begin with you. Are you sure there's nothing else you haven't told me? Any arrests on other charges you weren't convicted of?"

"What the hell are you talking about? Parking tickets? Overdue library books, *what* other charges?"

"Possession of illegal substances? Cannabis, for example?"

She felt her face drain. "You found her purse," she blurted.

He raised an eyebrow. "Not yet. I merely made the assumption that some-one arrested for student protests could have been charged with smoking marijuana, as well. Are you saying there were something in Christine Swinton's handbag you neglected to mention before?"

She tried to stand but his hand against her arm forced her back into her chair. "You tricked me," she snapped, her jaw clenched so tightly her teeth hurt. "You rotten . . . *jerk.*"

"I'm not trying to trick you. I'm no brilliant solicitor, but once you're in the witness box, that's exactly the sort of trap some lawyer a great deal more clever than I am will use to tear you apart. Are you so certain Chris Swinton were murdered you're willing to go through that?"

She glared at the table, her indignation dissipating. "Yes," she said, the word forced out in a whisper. "I have to." Tracing the bubbles racing up her glass, she evaded his eyes. "Because Chris was everything I'm not, idealistic and wild and passionate. She knew some things are more important than being polite and safe. Like doing the right thing in spite of being scared because it's the *right thing.* Because being safe is a fairy tale." She wasn't sure who she was trying to explain it to, him or herself. "Because if you don't, you end up being someone you despise."

He sighed. "This isn't my patch, Jillie." At her incomprehension, he said, "I don't have any authority in London. I'm only down on holiday to visit my lads."

"Fine. So, Detective Dunliffe, are you going to help me or not?"

He shook his head, not in negation but disbelief. "On one condition."

"What's that?"

"You stop calling me Detective Dunliffe. I'm not a detective and I'd prefer you just called me Keen."

Jillie found herself smiling, liking this man in spite of herself. "Deal."

"And if there *is* something in that house, you let me handle it. For your own safety."

"That's two conditions."

Keen snorted, his eyes crinkled in a silent laugh. "Damned stubborn woman. Now, do you want lunch or not?"

"*. . . not a murder inquiry . . .*"

Phil listened with his head bent over the tape machine, grinning as if this were all a joke. Although it was anything but, Phil would never have admitted it. Certainly not to this sour-faced, Northern uniform-carrier Galton had foisted off on him. He had better things to do than chase figments of some Home Office Colonel Blimp's imagination while the real cases he'd spent months working on were parceled out.

After witnessing and signing the forms, Phil had broken the seal on Keen's tape recorder to extract the master tape. As they listened, another working duplicate was being made, punctuated every ten seconds with an electronic voice.

On tape, Keen's strong Yorkshire accent and Jillie Waltham's nasally American one seemed amplified, neither of them pleasant, in Phil's opinion.

"What if I could help?"

"You've pulled, mate!" Phil crowed. "Hope you got a condom isn't past its bonk-by date." He enjoyed the twitch in Keen's jaw, that stony impassiveness showing cracks.

"Nineteen minutes, forty seconds," the robot voice whispered.

". . . worried about burglars."

". . . you shouldn't stay there . . ."

He looked up at Keen in disbelief. "You tried to talk her out of it?" He shook his head pityingly. "Galton'll love you for that."

". . . went over it thoroughly. There's nothing there," his tape-recorded voice was saying.

"Without me, would you even know what you were looking for?"

Phil's eyes widened. "Wow." He stifled a laugh.

"Twenty-one minutes, ten seconds."

"Fancy another?"

Recorded footsteps, tinny music, faint laughter, the buzz of discordant voices and the clink of glasses. Then a sharp click and the sound abruptly ceased, only the hiss of blank tape.

"That's it?" He glanced at Keen, puzzled. "What happened?"

"I'm not accustomed to all this fancy high-tech gear you lot have in the Met," Keen said with an innocence Phil knew was as artificial as his own skepticism. "Must've knocked it against the bar, turned it off accidentally."

Phil studied him. "All right, so what happened after that?" He wouldn't challenge the man; it wasn't worth the effort.

"She asked me to help her and I agreed."

"Just like that?"

"Good as." He shoved the now empty recorder toward Phil. "In any case, I'm done with this."

"Why?"

To his surprise, Keen said sharply, "Because this whole thing is a waste of time, she doesn't know owt. Scudder's a bloody paranoiac. Swinton was just another fuzzy Hampstead Heath liberal, and Waltham is a history teacher, not some yobbo anarchist. We're chasing fairies."

"How about this so-called highly controversial book? You don't think there's anything to that?" This time Phil didn't try to hide his sarcasm.

Keen snorted with equal contempt. "You trace whoever Swinton was with that night, and we're going to find a couple of idiots who drank too much and took too many drugs for their own good and one of them ended up drowned in a bathtub. If it were just another prostitute, nobody would give a damn. But because a rich activist got herself dumped in some poncy lake, well, then *obviously* it's got to be this huge political conspiracy, dunnit?"

"It's not our call," Phil said, amused. "We're supposed to keep Home Office happy, and you're not telling them what they want to hear." Phil wanted to tell them what they wanted to hear, and as quickly as possible, so he could get back to doing real police work.

"I don't give a damn what Home Office wants to hear. She's not a snout and I'm not her handler."

"Too bad. I was hoping to pick up some pointers on how you sexy Yorkshiremen pull the birds." Phil pouted in mock dismay.

"Shurrup, Reaves, you're startin' to annoy me. Seduction wasn't part of my job description, and I'm no bloody good at it, anyway."

"Not her type, are you? What *is* her type, then?" Phil flexed his arm, fist to his forehead in a bodybuilder pose. "Younger men, maybe?"

Keen scowled. "*Not* policemen."

Phil dropped his pose. "And here I'd always thought women couldn't resist a man in uniform."

"If Galton doesn't like my methods, I'd as soon go home, if it's all the same to him," he said as Phil ejected the cassette and sealed it with a paper label.

Phil wrote the date, tape, and exhibit reference on the label before jotting down both their call numbers. "Don't get your hopes up, Dunliffe. He's not likely to let either of us off that easy."

"So while I was out wasting the Met's money on drink, what did you do all day to make yourself useful?"

Phil handed Keen a fat envelope of photographs from his desk, before unfolding two pages of computer printout. "Had these developed while we ran number plates through the PNC. Did a match of names to cars, for the most part."

He watched Keen flip through the photographs, scanning the faces, most of them elderly and sour. Phil smiled as he paused at one of Keen and Jillie standing in profile, sunlight glinting around her hair. It was as pretty as a magazine ad. Phil leaned toward him, his head twisting to look at the picture.

"She's a bit of all right, isn't she? Took these shots meself. Canon 25Z with a four-hundred-millimeter zoom. Problem with telephoto, see, is the maximum aperture is so small; f8 on a fast shutter speed and it's a bastard not to underexpose the shot, especially through one-way glass. Personally, I find a narrow depth of field gives a flattened perspective, rather flattering for portrait shots, don't you think?"

Keen gazed back at him steadily. "You finished now?"

Phil chortled and sat back, yawning openly as Keen sorted through the rest. "Y'got names for all the faces?"

"Not all. Mostly friends of the mother, society people, in the papers a lot." Keen held one up to him. "James and Colette Preston. She's on the committee for the Kensington Ladies' Lawn Bowling Society. Got herself an OBE last year for invaluable service to the usual good causes," Phil said with amused derision, "consisting mainly of donating large amounts of *Mister* Preston's money. He's a retired solicitor, still keeps an office on Wellington."

Keen flipped through several more before Phil stopped him. "And that handsome bloke is Dr. Giles Roxbury. *Very* posh Harley Street obstetrician. Divorced four times, lady on his arm is his model-of-the-month."

Keen stopped at another, turned it over. The back was blank. He held it up. "Who's this?"

Phil looked at the stocky round-faced woman with hair clipped bluntly at her chin. She stood apart from the crowd, hunched with hands in the pockets of her slacks as if cold. He shrugged.

"Don't know. She didn't talk with anyone at the funeral. Way she's dressed, she's probably just a nosy passerby."

Keen paused again as he shuffled photographs, this time at one of a couple in conversation; a tall, morose man with a walking cast on his left foot and a middle-aged blonde Phil remembered the entire surveillance team laughing at as she negotiated the soft ground in sharp heels. "Dr. Reece Wycombe, professor of history at Kings College, Cambridge. Woman is Lynne Selkirk, Chris Swinton's neighbor. Possibly the only friends of hers other than your girlfriend who bothered to show up."

Keen stared at the photograph of Wycombe and Selkirk long enough for Phil to ask curiously, "Something?"

"No." But he didn't discard the photo.

"We've interviewed the Selkirks, but they couldn't tell us much. No previous connection between Wycombe and Selkirk, likely this was their first meeting."

Of the forty-odd people attending the funeral, Phil had put names to faces of ninety percent of them.

"Felix Schaefer," Phil said when Keen came to the last of the photographs. The man was mid-thirties, thin shouldered but well dressed. The camera had caught him glancing at his watch with an expression of bored distaste. "Chris Swinton's solicitor, no connection with Preston. She apparently didn't trust her daddy's friends."

"Quick work." Keen handed the photographs back to Phil. "Good job."

"Gorblimey. An actual compliment?" Phil said in mock astonishment. "Careful, it might go to me head."

"I'll bear that in mind," Keen said tersely.

Phil stretched, his joints popping, and looked at the clock. If he left now, he could collect Yvonne from the child-minder before he picked up his wife from hospital. About the only good thing come out of this silly case was more free time to spend with his family. "Well, I'm off. What're you doing the rest of the day?"

"Spending the evening in the Swinton house sorting through rubbish and eating takeaway, I'd expect," Keen said distantly.

"Sounds like a laugh. See you tomorrow, then."

* * *

She should have been looking for clues, Jillie thought, wondering if she would even recognize a clue if she saw one. Instead, she did what she'd always done whenever she was upset. She turned the stereo up and cleaned house.

The kitchen was first on the agenda. Chris had been a slob, but not necessarily a filthy slob. She loaded the dishwasher and set the machine going, the increasing noise comforting. The sound of normal life. She tidied drawers crammed with tableware and wadded-up napkins, rearranged cans and packages in the pantry, wiped down counters, washed windows, scoured the stove.

Chris didn't appear to have been much of a cook, nothing much in the refrigerator beyond leftover Chinese takeout cartons, a rancid cube of butter, a pot of yogurt capped with green fuzz, drying cheese, and three eggs, one cracked. She tossed the takeout, yogurt, cheese, and broken egg into a garbage can lined with a three-week-old *Guardian*, but kept several bags of designer coffees. At least she could make coffee in the morning, although the milk had long curdled.

A two-inch shell of ice encrusted the freezer. She wondered at her surprise to the evidence of police presence; impressions left in the frost where packages of TV dinners had been extracted, then stuffed back in at random. She threw out meat ruined by freezer burn. The frozen TV dinners followed, their sell-by dates long expired. She had nearly finished when she slam-dunked what she was certain was a package of ground mammoth. It split open a box of antiquated Birds-Eye chicken dinner, exposing the edge of a spiral-bound notebook inside.

Cold shards of ice melted on her hands as she peeled open the torn package. A small, green notebook had been sealed in a Ziploc bag before being entombed in thick frost. She chipped away at the miniature glacier with a butter knife to dislodge the icebound notebook.

She handled the damp pages gingerly, the paper still cool, each covered with scribbled notes, margins decorated with restless doodles and sketches, the ink blurred slightly. Jillie recognized Chris's nearly indecipherable handwriting from years of trans-Atlantic Christmas cards. She was able to discern some of the cryptic writing.

"Mem. o/t Crts and Cabs of G III, Rch Bknghm, see 34–67, x-ref c Rd Dltn, pg 776, BrtL, bollocks!" Jillie made out, and smiled, understanding about half of the notation. "G III" she knew had to be George the Third. She scanned the rest of the pages, picking out "Ldy An Hmltn, Auth. Rec. o/t Crt," and "J. Ltft, herbrm coll. Ernst, Dk Cmbrld, Wm Edwd, RL ff 29882" with the "RL" circled in red ink and surrounded with exclamation points. On another page, Chris had written "Wtrclrs on vellum (RL 30917) same lot Jan/55 M. S. Merian"—or maybe it was Harriet, Jillie wasn't sure—"see lf/hd cnr JH, x-ref c RA Add 19/5040." The "RA" had been decorated with a happy face in the margin.

It might as well have been labeled CLUE. The police hadn't turned up the notebook, even after searching the freezer. Jillie did a victory dance around the kitchen. Hah! Touchdown and score for our team, Detective—excuse me—*Mr.* Dunliffe!

She knew with time she could decipher much of Chris's references. Her own research often resulted in scrawling intelligible to few people other than herself. But the cryptic diagrams and charts Jillie could only guess at. Whatever Chris had written, it was either valuable enough or she was neurotic enough to have hidden it.

She set aside the notebook and started in on the kitchen cabinets with renewed energy. She filled another plastic garbage sack with trash before standing on a kitchen chair to sort through a shelf of cookbooks, dusty and neglected.

The police had obviously inspected these as well, finger streaks on the dusty bindings where they had been handled and replaced in haphazard stacks. As Jillie reorganized them, she admired some of the titles, suspecting Chris hadn't bought them for their recipes; a handbook by the Military Survival Press on *1001 Healthy Field Recipes for Dog, Cat, and Lizard,* another entitled *The American White Trash Cookbook,* one on Tibetan Ghost Festival cookery, and several cookbooks in French, including Alexandre Dumas's huge and heavy classic, *Le Grand Dictionnaire de Cuisine.* Dusting it off, she replaced it on the shelf as the front doorbell rang.

She glanced at her watch, slightly after five o'clock, surprised at how quickly the time had gone. Lynne's Charter 88 meeting was in less than two hours. Keen Dunliffe smiled as she opened the door.

"Hullo. Found any clues yet?"

"Matter of fact . . ." Suddenly giddy, she said, "Come up, and let me show you my freezer," in a bad Mae West parody.

As they sat together on the dead woman's settee, Jillie held the small notebook on her lap, and impatiently brushed stray hair from her eyes before running a finger along the cramped handwriting. " 'Brt L' I'm sure means the British Library. Something like 'Memoirs of the Courts and Cabinets of George the Third' by Richard Somebody, maybe Buckingham, pages thirty-four to sixty-seven."

"I'll take your word for it."

He followed her finger as she said, "This is a reference to work by another Richard Somebody starting with *D,* but I'm not sure what 'bollocks' refers to."

He realized she wasn't joking. "It means she likely didn't agree with him," he said without a smile.

"Oh." She was still reading, unaware of the humor.

"Any idea why she would keep this in her freezer?"

"Probably for the same reason I would. It's a cheap safe. I keep my passport and important papers in my freezer because if the house burns down, it's the last place to go." She looked at him with ill-disguised eagerness. "So is this notebook enough evidence that something suspicious was going on?"

"I shouldn't think so." He sat back, rubbing at the stiffness in his neck. "A notebook full of unreadable scribbles hidden in a freezer might prove Chris was a nutter, but not that she were murdered." Her face fell with disappointment. "How long do you think it'll take you to figure out what all this means?"

She flipped through the notebook. "A few days maybe." She closed it and held it in both hands possessively. "I'll go over to the British Library and start first thing tomorrow morning."

"Why don't you make some notes to start? I'll be taking that with me to photocopy, just to be sure we don't lose anything."

He stood up, his leg suddenly chill without her warmth against it. "And while you're doing that, I'll have a look round."

He left her to scribble frantically and wandered through the house. Galton had understated it, Keen thought. Christine Swinton's house seemed more like a warehouse for a museum of absurdities. Swinton had left plenty behind, but none of it gave him any feeling of the woman it had belonged to; he was far more aware of the presence of previous searchers. Despite all the exotic and often grotesque possessions, the house was oddly impersonal. Instead of reflecting her personality, it seemed like so much clutter gleaned from jumble sales and souvenir shops.

The police had taken her computer and files, her address book, any letters or papers they could find. Keen had read the inventory, puzzled by how few personal letters she'd kept. Most of her post was bills or notices of university seminars. And all recent, which indicated that while she saved just about every other odd bit of rubbish, she had deliberately discarded her old correspondence. A rather unsentimental habit for someone who hoarded cuddly toys.

Spotting a box of photo albums on the landing, he opened one at random. Instead of photographs, the album held garishly bright cards, the sort he could find in phone booths all over London. "Submissive Schoolgirl Seeks Strong Studs." "Dominique Is the Name, and Pain Is the Game." He grunted to himself in surprise.

"They're sex ads," Jillie offered from below, which surprised him more. She leaned against the stair railing, smiling.

As he flipped pages, he said, "Did Chris ever talk to you about her sex life?"

Jillie laughed. "She wasn't moonlighting, if that's what you're thinking. Chris was a collector. So's my daughter. Chris got her into it when Karen was here a couple of summers ago. It's a popular hobby with women. Sort of like how boys collect baseball cards or comic books."

"You don't mind your daughter collecting these?"

"I wasn't too thrilled about it when she was sixteen, no. I'd rather hoped Chris would expose her to English culture, not English sleaze."

He didn't comment, setting the album back where he'd found it.

"Look," Jillie said, "it's almost seven-thirty. Lynne Selkirk is . . . was Chris's next-door neighbor. She's invited some of Chris's friends over tonight for a sort of Irish wake. Maybe you'd like to come?"

He kept his expression neutral. "I would, but only as a friend, not as your private detective."

To his surprise, her face suddenly flamed a deep red. "That's fine. I won't mention a thing. I have to change . . ." He wondered what he'd said wrong as she brushed quickly past him up the stairs.

When she came down, she wore a bright dress snug to the waist that suited her figure. She'd pinned her hair up, stray wisps around her face. The color on her cheeks was still high, and he noted the hint of mascara and lipstick. When she smiled at him shyly, he wasn't sure whether to be flattered or disgusted with his success.

"Fritchie should be aggressively recruiting more from the working class." The thin man in the thick glasses gestured vehemently with his wine glass, wine sloshing. "Still too many from the golf and horsey set."

Jillie sipped her own wine and tried to remain invisible in a roomful of strangers arguing about issues she could barely follow.

"Come on, Melvin, she's done pretty well in spite of the damage Dobson did," the woman beside him countered, a heavy-set brunette in an Indian-print skirt. Unfortunately, the material was too sheer, the unflattering outline of her panties and knee-high stockings visible.

"So why is it three-fourths of quangos are still white, male, middle-aged, and middle-class?" a strikingly tall woman with iron-gray hair said. Jillie wondered what a quango was, thinking it sounded like some exotic Australian fruit. "What about ethnic minorities? Where are all the disabled? You've only thirty-eight percent women, and only three percent of them earn more than fifty thousand a year . . ."

Jillie drifted past another heated argument. "That White Paper doesn't reflect the realpolitik of religious representation in this country whatsoever. Just what makes an Anglican bishop any more qualified to sit in the House of Lords than someone who could be elected by the people . . ."

"It's not a question of republicanism versus a monarchy, we're *supposed* to be nonparty political," a frizzy-haired woman perched on the sofa arm was saying. She glared through half-glasses as a man seated next to her laughed, a mulish honk. "But we should be concerned by the Royal Prerogative and misuse of residual monarchical powers by the prime minister—"

"Particularly this one," the honking man snorted.

"He's no different than the last lot," another man interjected, red faced and sweating with alcohol, heat, or emotion, Jillie couldn't tell. "But the people of this country must not be cheated out of *real* political change, *again* . . ."

Lynne paused on her way from the kitchen with a bottle of wine in one hand and Gordon's gin in the other. She murmured, "Sorry, not exactly a proper Irish wake, I'm afraid." She gestured with her eyes toward Keen at the other end of the room. "And your friend doesn't seem to be enjoying himself much, either."

Of the more than thirty people attending Chris's "wake," Keen was the sole person wearing a suit jacket and tie. She winced. He *looked* like a cop as he circulated from one group to the next, holding a glass of whiskey heavily laden with ice that he had barely sipped from all evening, listening politely and saying nothing.

"Where did you meet him?"

"In Leeds," Jillie said, cautiously.

"At your medieval congress?"

"Well, sort of." She hoped Lynne didn't ask what he did. *Oh, he works for the government . . . wait, that wouldn't go over well here . . . let's see, he's a . . . civil servant . . . damn, that's no better . . .*

Lynne chuckled as she topped up Jillie's glass. "He's rather cute, if you could get him out of that awful tie. I haven't seen anything so hideous since the seventies." She left to refurnish her guests with alcohol.

"Lynne tells me you're the American friend of Chris Swinton's?" Jillie turned. The woman's translucent pale skin and fine blond hair blunt cut at her shoulders lent her an air of theatrical fragility. "Jillie . . . ?"

"Waltham."

"Molly Sutton." They shook hands, Molly's cool and firm. "I'm sorry about Chris." She didn't seem upset.

"Were you a friend of hers?"

"We'd met. Chris didn't come to many meetings. Lynne's one of the few who could get along with her." Molly glanced around. "Which is why this might seem a rather heartless sort of memorial. But"—she raised her glass— "here's to Chris."

Jillie clinked wine glasses with Molly and sipped judiciously. She'd already had two glasses of wine and her head felt light. Molly smiled as Keen moved to include himself into their conversation.

"Molly Sutton, Keen Dunliffe," Jillie introduced him, then added, "He's a friend of mine. From Leeds."

"Well, Mr. Dunliffe, what do you think of our little organization?"

"It's been educational."

Molly laughed, a light tinkle of amusement. "But have we converted you?"

"I try to keep an open mind," Keen said.

"As I suppose should we all," she responded with one raised eyebrow, smiling shrewdly. Jillie was certain she knew exactly what Keen was. Molly's glance refocused past him. "Andrew!" she called out, then explained quickly, "He's from the *Economist,* I've been trying for ages to talk to him. Would you excuse me . . . ?" She threaded through the crowd toward a man who had just entered, wearing black leather trousers and jacket and holding a motorcycle helmet under one arm.

Jillie stood with Keen in exile from the strangers gesturing passionately as they argued. She glanced up at him wryly. "Are we having fun yet?"

"Absolutely," he responded, then said in an accent she couldn't identify, "And what is your opinion, Dr. Waltham, on abolishing the BBC-TV license fees under Article Ten of the European Human Rights Convention protecting free speech?"

"Huh? What's a TV license?" She shook her head. "I feel like Alice at the Mad Hatter's tea party."

"It doesn't seem too many here even knew Chris."

"Guess not." She studied his tie. The wide off-green fabric did appear suspiciously shiny. "Where *did* you get that tie?"

Startled, he looked down. "Present from my sister. I've had it for years."

"I think all your ice has melted by now."

He set down his whiskey-tinted glass of water. "Would you like to go?"

"Very much."

He steered her toward the front door where Lynne Selkirk hoisted a bottle in both hands as apology for not shaking Keen's goodbye, and kissed Jillie on one cheek. "Do come again, Mr. Dunliffe," she said brightly. "I'd be happy to mail you some literature about the charter, give you an address for our group in Leeds . . . ?"

"I'll think on it," was all he said.

They said nothing on the short walk back to Chris's house. "Would you like to come in?" Jillie said once she'd unlocked the door. "I could make some tea . . . ?"

He decided it wasn't a proposition, but a desire not to be left alone in the dead woman's house.

"That'd be lovely."

He didn't really want any tea this time of night, but sat in the cluttered lounge listening to her rattle about in the strange kitchen. She emerged holding two mugs with tea bag strings dangling from them. It was weak with too much milk. He sipped it and suppressed his reaction: the milk was canned condensed, sickly sweet.

"Thanks for coming," she said. "I hope you weren't too bored."

"My pleasure." He cradled the mug in both hands, no room on the end tables to set it down. "Jillie, I'd prefer you didn't stay here on your own. I could sleep on the settee—"

"I appreciate the offer, but no, thanks," she said tightly. He knew he'd just superseded any anxiety she had of being alone with his premature offer. She amended quickly, "No offense intended . . ."

"None taken. I should be going." He drained the cup and looked around futilely for a place to leave it.

"Set it on the floor, I'll get it later."

He took out his wallet and gave her one of his Weetwood cards with a London telephone number on the back. "Just in case. If there's any problem, *anything,* you can ring me at this number. It's for the Kentish Town Police Station."

She looked at him askance. "What do they do, put you up in a spare jail cell?"

"No, in the section housing." He smiled at her mystification. "It's like a college dormitory for police."

She grimaced. "Worse than jail, then." The humor faded quickly. "I plan to go to the British Library as soon as they open, and I'll probably be there all day."

He knew what she was saying. "I'll see you tomorrow. Dinner?"

"Okay. But Dutch."

He didn't argue. "Meet you around what . . . five-thirty?"

"At the library."

"Fine. Cheers."

She smiled. "Cheers."

Keen waited until she had locked the doors before walking down the steps. As he reached the pavement, he spotted the red flare of a cigarette in the darkened window of a house under renovation directly across the park. He frowned, then walked toward Regent's Park Road.

He didn't bother to acknowledge two brawny men in a car parked around the curve of a sham tower on the corner. Squeezed into the small car, arms crossed and shoulders hunched under a worn leather jacket, the passenger chewed openmouthed on a wad of gum and flicked him an insolent glance as Keen walked past.

Then he turned the corner, and the street life changed. Music and drink and happy people spilled out of brightly lit pubs. He considered getting in a pint before deciding he wasn't in the mood, no solace in pretending to be part of a crowd of strangers.

Half an hour later, he was back at the Kentish Town Station housing. Three tired WPCs silently shared the elevator up with him, and smiled with polite indifference when he got off on his own floor.

London at night was beautiful, jeweled strands of traffic, the beacon over Canary Wharf flashing with stately vanity. An occasional murmur of voices and footsteps passed by his door, a soothing distant ocean of toilets flushed. Unused to the white noise of the city, he tossed restlessly in a strange bed far from home.

* * *

Brng-brng. Brng-brng. Jillie awakened abruptly from a dreamless sleep. Even the telephone ring in Britain seemed somehow anachronistic, as if she'd never quite believed all those trendy foreign films.

Brng-brng.

Her travel clock said three in the morning. She supposed it could be Karen, or more likely Uncle Homer getting the time zones wrong. She wasted several more seconds fumbling for a light switch before she raced down the stairs.

"Hello?" she said breathlessly.

For a moment, she thought she was hearing the hiss of long-distance lines, waiting for her voice to bounce off the satellite or travel by cable under the Atlantic. Then she realized it was someone's breathing, heavy and harsh.

"Hello?" she repeated, this time more sharply, a thread of fear prickling the hair on her neck.

"I can give you what you want, bitch, I know how you like it . . ." the whispering voice said, thick with menace.

She stood paralyzed with dread, then slammed the phone down. She turned on every light in the house before dragging a blanket off the bed and huddling on the couch wishing now she hadn't rejected Keen's offer. But she wasn't a wimpy little girl who needed a man to rush to her rescue, she could handle it. With her arms clamped around her knees, she wasn't aware when she dozed off.

Close to dawn, the phone rang again. She shrieked awake, then gingerly picked up the phone and said cautiously, "Hello?"

A puzzled male voice said, "Who is this?"

From years of indoctrinating her daughter never to give out her name on the phone, Jillie automatically said in her teacher's voice, "Who are you calling, please?"

"Where's Chris?"

"Who's calling, please?"

The voice changed instantly to a raw viciousness. "Listen, bitch, you tell that lazy cunt to get 'er fat arse on the phone *now*—"

It was the same man. She hung up. Seconds later, it rang, insistent. Then silence. She jumped as it rang again. Bursting into tears, she snatched it up and screamed, "Stop it! Leave me alone!"

The line was so silent she thought he must have gone. "Listen . . . what I said before, I'm a little drunk, I didn't mean it," he said finally, childish bewilderment in his tone. "Please just tell Chris all I want is to talk to 'er—"

"No, *you* listen," Jillie said, her voice shaking. "If you call again, I'll call the police. I mean it," Jillie said, sounding pathetic and weak even to herself.

"Don't hang up on me," he warned, his tone again ominous. "Don't you bloody *dare* hang up on me, *you fucking bitch, do you hear me*—"

As if it had scalded her, she slammed the phone down. Within seconds it rang again. She picked it up and hung up without answering, then took it off the hook. Sleep was impossible. Terrified whoever it was might turn up if he became too frustrated, she frantically pulled on her jeans and shirt, tennis shoes and a jacket.

The phone was making a distraught wailing sound. She ignored it and grabbed her purse. Outside, the sky was pale gray, streets quiet. A few windows were lit, those early-morning risers readying for the day. She pulled out Keen's card, all her self-assurance exposed as an idiotic pretense now . . .

No. She *couldn't* call him, couldn't admit she was wrong. Besides, it was just a phone call, a silly, obscene phone call, and she well knew how little the police could do about that.

No, she wouldn't be bullied into cowardice. She'd wait and tell him about the call in a sensible, calm adult manner. More people were out, sleepy women huddled at bus stops, people driving by on their way to work. In a few more hours, she could escape into the security of the British Library and surround herself with people and books and sanity.

VII

WEDNESDAY

The canteen was nearly deserted; Keen sat alone at one table while another had been staked out by four lads from Traffic telling jokes and laughing raucously. Keen sipped coffee and flipped through his photocopied pages. Those cryptic notes written in pencil hadn't reproduced well, which didn't help making out anything.

"Why is arresting a Paki like listening to an outboard motor?" one of the PCs behind him asked his mates. Keen turned a page. "Because they're always going, 'but-but-but-but-but-but . . . *sir!*'" The four guffawed loudly.

Keen didn't even smile, not so much because he disapproved of racist humor, but he'd heard it before and hadn't thought it funny the first time round. He did smile, however, when he heard a sharp breath and a murmured warning, "Button it, Calder," and assumed that the nick's superintendent had walked in. He looked up in surprise as Phil sat down across from him.

"Mornin'," Phil said with a grin.

"Mornin'." Keen glanced over his shoulder as the four bobbies quickly vanished out the canteen door, then back at Phil curiously.

Phil gave no sign he'd heard their conversation, simply nodding at the photocopies. "Studying for your OSPRE exams in your spare time?"

Keen leaned back and swirled what was left in his coffee cup. "Don't usually make you take it twice once you've passed," he said laconically, and enjoyed Phil's reaction. He'd notice soon enough how long it was taking Keen to get his promotion to inspector, which cut down on his satisfaction. Keen pushed the photocopies across the table. "Our lady professor found something that your lot managed to overlook."

Phil shuffled the copies. "Where?" he said tersely.

"In the freezer."

"We searched the freezer." Phil looked up, unsmiling. The suggestion it was planted went unspoken.

"She'd sealed it inside a TV dinner."

Phil grunted, reluctant. He turned another page. "What *is* this shite, anyway? Looks like Greek to me."

"Latin and French, actually. Research the dead woman were working on. Jillie's at the British Library tracing some of it."

Phil visibly lost interest in the photocopies. "Oh, 'Jillie' is, is she?" he said cynically. "What's she hoping to find in this, anyway?"

The brief pleasure Keen had sparring with him had already evaporated. "Something Chris Swinton could have been killed over."

Disdainfully, Phil snorted. "Now who are you trying to fool? Wasn't it you said no one's going to have snuffed it over a lot of egghead research? If it *is* anything, it'll be the political angle," he declared firmly and flipped another page. "So fill me in on last night's seditionist meeting. Hear any good treason?"

"Sorry, no. Frankly, some of it was rather sensible."

"Oh, dear. That's *not* what Mr. Scudder wants to hear, is it?"

"I'm not being paid to lie to the man."

Phil flashed him a quick, ruthless grin. "Wrong again. That's exactly what you're being paid to do."

Keen kept his tone bland. "I'm being paid to keep an eye on Dr. Waltham. Of course, if she makes a couple of your fearless CID lads outside the house as easily as I did, she might start asking awkward questions. Might as well have had a marked patrol car out there last night."

Phil snorted, unimpressed. "I'll pass the word on."

Keen suppressed a sigh, already tired of Phil's hostile humor. He handed over his notes with more than twenty names of people he'd met at Lynne Selkirk's. "You might check to see if any of these names rings a bell." He pointed to a name he'd ticked. "This un's a journalist for the *Economist*. I can tell you that much."

Phil barely glanced at it before stuffing the list into his shirt pocket. His indifference annoyed Keen. "I've got a couple hours free. Give you a hand with witness statements, if you like."

Phil balanced his chair on its back legs. "Nah, thanks all the same, pal. We might be barely competent to handle it on our own. Besides, a few people from the funeral know you're a copper. You being out of uniform, they might get the mistaken impression you're CID. Don't want to give anyone the wrong idea, do we?"

Keen's stomach soured. "Please yourself."

"All you need worry about is keeping a smile on your lady friend. And if you can't enjoy it, try to relax, lie back, and think of England."

"What the hell is it with you?" Keen asked quietly, suppressed anger stirring. "Why do you keep trying to get my back up?"

Phil righted his chair with a solid thunk, his eyes hard. "Because I don't like working with anyone I can't trust. What exactly *did* happen to your last partner?"

For a moment, the undertow of a deep fury he'd thought buried paralyzed Keen. "I don't owe you, or anyone else, an explanation." He stood up and walked away without another word. His rage passed quickly enough, but left him feeling oddly hollow. There was no place for him here, and nowhere else to go.

His sons were still at tennis lessons or riding school or whatever it was Tremayne was paying for this week, and with Jillie cloistered away in the library, he was restless and bored. At noon, he borrowed a clerk's desk while she was at lunch to use her telephone. Its Metropolitan Police ER shield and crown had been taped over with a cruder hand-drawn logo: ROBIN'S BATPHONE.

He rang in to Weetwood to have Dave fax him a copy of that odd-shaped tire track found in the break-in. Then he reread the case files. The Guiscoigne interview was pathetic, only the most basic details. Despite Reaves's warning, he dialed Guiscoigne's number. As it rang unanswered, a shadow fell across the desk. He looked up at the glowering uniformed female officer. Bernie. Sighing, he hung up and waited.

"I heard about that load of crap you gave Williams, Sergeant," she said acidly. "I'm not some delicate little lassie who needs to have you big strong men come rushing to my defense."

"I apologize if I've caused you any embarrassment."

She glanced around the room stiffly, her face quivering. "But it was . . . I also wanted to say . . ." She stopped.

"You're welcome," Keen said quietly. She flushed, but her expression softened. He held out his hand. "Keen Dunliffe."

Her grip was deliberately too strong. "Bernie Pearson." He'd been right; she had a lovely smile. "Maybe I'll see you round the nick?"

"Hope so."

"Anyway. Cheers, then."

"Cheers." He watched her leave, then read case files until Robin reclaimed her batdesk.

At a little before five-thirty, Keen checked his watch against the clock on the square tower of the British Library and went inside to escape the oppressive heat. He waited for Jillie by the tower of ancient books at the top of the stairs, and studied the bust of George the Third in his laurel leaves, the mad king slack-jawed even in marble. When she hadn't appeared by six, he went in search of her.

He found her in one of the reading rooms, up to her nose in books. She didn't look up as he slid into the empty chair next to her and cupped his chin in his palm.

Her hair falling across her shoulder, she scribbled furiously for several moments before she was aware of someone next to her. She glanced up, startled, as he tapped his watch pointedly. "Five-thirty?"

She gasped, looking at her own watch. It was quarter after six. "Oh, my god, I just completely lost track of the time." The woman across from them glared poisonously. Jillie shot her a smile of quick apology that was not accepted. "How did you get in here?" she whispered. "The reading rooms are restricted to academic researchers. I didn't know you had a British Library card."

"I don't. But I *do* have a warrant card."

"Warrant card?"

"Police ID. Don't leave home without it."

"Oh."

"*Shhhhh!*" the woman opposite hissed, unimpressed.

Jillie carried the books she'd reserved for the next day to the issue desk. As she filled in her slips, Keen glanced around idly, spotting a young woman yawning over a single book. Their eyes met before she closed the book with a faint smile.

Outside in the stifling heat, street hawkers jostled for the limited space, hustling identical postcards and key chains and art posters and T-shirts and fridge magnets. Euston Road was crowded, St. Pancras and King's Cross stations busy with rush-hour commuters. He held open the door of a Pizza Hut for her.

"You can eat pizza on your diet?" she said dubiously.

"They've got a decent salad bar."

"You're a masochist, you know that?"

"So I've been told."

True to his word, he ordered the salad plate while Jillie headed for the all-you-can-gobble pizza slices. He watched her start up an animated conversation with the couple choosing their gooey slices, then chat with the dignified woman behind the counter dressed in the hideous red uniform and silly hat.

Americans, he mused; so unself-conscious, familiar to the point of ridiculous. Unaware of the subtexts going on right under their noses, the venerable traditions of British class snobbery a mystery to them. It was all too easy to laugh at it, he knew, while secretly envying them.

Sunlight shimmered in her hair as she turned to smile at him. His groin unexpectedly stirred, and he quickly unfolded a paper serviette over his lap. He had to be a masochist to enjoy being around the things he could never have. He was just your ordinary working-class cop, while she spoke six languages and had a Ph.D. And an arrest record, he reminded himself as she sat down, the mouthwatering perfume of pizza enveloping him. And an American passport and a family and a life of her own thousands of miles away.

"You okay?" she asked with concern.

"What? Yes, of course. Why?"

"You look like you've got indigestion."

He nodded at her pizza. "Mind you, *that* will give you heartburn."

"Forget it. You can't make *me* feel guilty." She took an enthusiastic bite.

He pretended to ignore it. "Find anything exciting at the library?"

"Okay, so how much do you know about George the Third?" She took another bite, wrapping delicate threads of cheese around a finger.

He stabbed a cherry tomato through the heart. "I saw the film. He was mad, his son was twit, and he lost the American colonies. What else is there?"

"He wasn't mad, he had a disease called porphyria. Anyway, that's not important. He was a Hanover, and they only got the throne when the last Stuart, Queen Anne, died. The closest Stuart heir is Catholic, the Jacobites and Bonnie Prince Charlie and all those guys, right? The Act of Settlement bars them from succession. So instead it goes to her maternal third cousin, who was the elector of Hanover, this little chunk of Germany about the size of, I don't know, Vermont, maybe? A whole lot smaller than England, that's for sure."

Keen was following, just barely. He hadn't been a bad student in school, nor a particularly good one, either, leaving with adequate O levels. He'd floundered through enough kings and battle sites on school exams to keep his father from clipping him one about the ear. But he found long-dead nobility even more tedious than living ones.

She chewed another bite of pizza quickly and swallowed, eager.

"The Hanovers weren't popular. They didn't even speak English until our George, and he was the first even to be *born* in England. He was sort of like this naïve ethical schmuck who hung out with the stableboys and walked around Windsor by himself talking to people in the streets."

"Not to mention pine trees."

Jillie laughed. "That's later, and it was oak."

Even with subjects he did enjoy, he'd struggled to earn his certificates in criminal law and AFR fingerprint databases. He wouldn't have had time to study for his inspector's exam if Laura hadn't done all the shopping and laundry and cooking and kept the boys quiet, things he'd once taken for granted. But if he had hopes of further promotion, he knew he'd need a higher degree, a prospect that clenched his gut into a tight knot. *If* he were ever promoted to inspector, he thought ruefully.

"Now," Jillie said, "in seventeen sixty, when he was twenty-two, he succeeded his grandfather because his own father had already died when George was thirteen. The next year, his mother, Princess Augusta, arranged his marriage to Charlotte of Mecklenburg-Strelitz—"

"How do you do that?"

"Do what?"

"You've been in the library one day. How can you rattle off names and dates that fast without even looking at notes?"

"*You* teach college kids history they're not really interested in year after year, and you'll figure it out," she said, lips shiny with oil. He had to resist the urge to reach over and wipe off a spot of pizza sauce on the corner of her mouth. "Back to George, who's making a fool of himself chasing Lady Sarah Lennox. But no way his mother will let him marry *her*. Too English. So Mom scouts around Europe for the perfect princess and finds Charlotte. She's young, respectably middle-class, and ugly as a mud fence. And German. Horace Walpole . . . you know who he was, don't you?"

"Yes," Keen said dryly. "I know who he was."

The monotone lectures of his own comprehensive schoolteachers were nothing like her lively enthusiasm as she spoke about a long-dead king with cheerful irreverence, as if George the Third had been an amusingly eccentric neighbor. He wondered if he'd been a better student had he had more teachers like her.

She wiped the smudge away with the bright red serviette and nibbled pizza crust serenely. He snapped the spine of a carrot stick and decapitated a mushroom.

"He wrote her duchy was so small, you had to have a magnifying glass to find it on the map. So Mom ships over poor Charlotte and marries her off to George. He bought Buckingham Palace as a wedding present, did you know that? Except then, it was just this ordinary brick house out in the 'burbs . . ."

She propped up another slice sagging under the weight of cheese and pepperoni slices. Another cherry tomato met with a violent end.

"This is all very interesting, but what's it got to do with Chris's research?"

"Right, sorry. One of Chris's notes referred to one their kids, Ernest, Duke of Cumberland. And a William Edward. I don't know who William Edward is; George's son was William *Henry*. I thought maybe she meant 'Edward William,' but the other son is Edward Augustus. So I spent most of today looking up what I could find on Ernest, hoping maybe William Edward would be his illegitimate son or something."

She licked her fingers before pulling a small spiral notebook from her handbag, riffing through her own scribbled notes.

"Ernest Augustus, sixth son of George the Third, born seventeen seventy-one. Served in Flanders against France, wounded in the Battle of Tournai, lost his left eye and about half his face. Made duke of Cumberland in seventeen ninety-nine. A right-wing Tory heavily involved in politics. King William died in eighteen thirty-seven, and his brother Edward's daughter, Victoria, became Queen of England but *not* of Hanover because Salic Law denied women the right of succession. So *she* starts up the Royal House of Saxe-Coburg-Gotha, which is now Windsor, while Ugly Uncle Ernie became king of Hanover instead."

"This is giving me a headache." He wasn't joking.

Jillie had abandoned her pizza, the last slice cooling on her plate. He glared at it, then impaled his shriveled lettuce leaves vindictively. "We're getting to the interesting parts," she said, oblivious to his animosity toward innocent vegetables. "In May of eighteen ten, Ernest comes back to Saint James's Palace after a concert and goes to bed around midnight. About three in the morning, he's woken up by somebody in the dark tapping him on the head with a saber. He grabs it by the blade, cuts his hand, and starts screaming for help. The duke had two valets, one of them named Neale, who comes charging into the room with a poker. But there wasn't anybody there except the prince, who was buck naked with a bump on his head and a few minor cuts on his rear end."

This hadn't been in any of the school textbooks he'd been required to study. He found his curiosity sparked in spite of himself.

"Ernest is running around yelling, 'Where's Sellis?' That's his other valet. So they bust down the door to Sellis's bedroom to find *him* lying dead on the floor with no pants on and his throat cut. Blood all over the place and the window open. And nobody ever finds out who attacked the duke." She grinned. "Guess what the official verdict on Sellis was."

That seemed a daft question. "Murder?"

"Suicide." She laughed at his surprise. "Ernest was having an affair with *Mrs.* Sellis, who had a bastard child by him. Not our William Edward, though. Also, Sellis was Corsican, like Napoleon, and he was Roman Catholic. Ernest hated Catholics. And to top it off, Sellis tried to blackmail Ernest for making homosexual advances, which better explains those scratches on Ernest's bare butt. In any case, these two guys were involved in a really sick relationship."

In some ways, he thought, their interests weren't so different. While she searched for clues in old books and his police inquiries used forensics and footwork, they were both after answers to murder. Hers just happened to be a bit out of date.

"So the duke murdered Sellis?"

"Oh, definitely. Then he tried to make it look like a bungled burglary. Everybody knew it, but what can you do? The court decided Sellis cut his own throat, which metaphorically was true enough."

She picked pepperoni out of the cold pizza, leaving craters in the cheese.

"Then twenty years later we've got this guy 'Captain Garth' being paid off by Charlotte's private secretary, Sir Herbert Taylor, because he was the bastard son of Princess Sophia. Which, all things considered, no big deal, right?" Her eyes twinkled. "Except Garth had proof his daddy was Sophie's *brother,* our Ernest again. Ernest had a thing for licking his grandchildren, particularly the girls. Big family joke, ha ha."

He grimaced.

"The whole Georgian era is full of this stuff, I can see why Chris loved it so much." She sobered. "I know she was researching a royal scandal, and there's plenty to choose from. She did say she thought Reece Wycombe refused to publish her work because it might offend the royal family." She looked at him with forlorn hope.

Keen shook his head. "Even if Chris had proof this duke was an incestuous child-molesting murderer, who am I supposed to arrest?" She was so crest-fallen, he added, "Don't give up, you've only been at this a day."

"This isn't my field," she protested. "Chris worked on this for two years, and I'm trying to redo her research in less than two *weeks* before my plane leaves. I don't even have the draft Dr. Wycombe read, and so far he hasn't been willing to tell me much."

His experience with interviews came in handy, her wording just vague enough to alert him. "So far?" he repeated. She looked at him sheepishly.

"I called him this morning. He'd told me at the funeral that he'd lent Chris a book and wanted it back. So I asked him to come over tomorrow around ten. I thought maybe we could make a deal; he tells me what was in Chris's manuscript and I let him look through her bookshelves without letting Max know about it."

"You should have told me," Keen said sharply.

"I just did."

He let it go. "What do you know of this Dr. Wycombe?"

She shrugged. "He's a professor at Cambridge, one of the editors of Georgian Historical Studies. Chris didn't much like him, but he edited her last book, *George the Third and the Gordon Rebellion*. It was pretty good, actually. If the riots had been more successful, England could have ended up a republic like America and France. See, what happened with the Catholic Relief bill . . ."

At his look of reproach, she faltered. "It's complicated, but you might find it interesting." He doubted it. "Anyway, Chris and Wycombe fell out over the book. Now with Chris dead, he's the only one who knew what she was writing, so there's nothing to stop him from plagiarizing her work and taking all the credit." She scowled. "Thieving bastard."

"Listen to what you just said, Jillie. He's *the only one* who knows what Chris was working on."

"You think *he* could have killed her?"

"I don't think *anyone* killed her. But how far do you think he'd go? Far enough to break into your room to search it once he knew Chris were dead?" Her mouth opened, then closed as she considered. "No Nancy Drew, remember? You're not meeting this man on your own, Jillie."

"If he knows you're a cop, he's not going to confess all with you hovering over my shoulder."

"I'll stay upstairs, out of sight. If there is any trouble, I can be right there. And no more argument, I'm staying with you as long as you're in that house."

"Okay," she said, oddly meek, the fight gone out of her.

"One more thing," he said as the idea occurred to him. "Have him either come in or leave by the back way through the kitchen."

"Why?"

"Because we're going to polish it spotless tonight."

" 'We' are, are 'we'?" she said with gentle mocking.

He smiled. "When he walks across that floor, he'll leave tracks we can compare with the one we found in your bed and breakfast."

"He could be wearing different shoes."

"I'm not looking for shoeprints."

She suddenly gasped and crouched down in pop-eyed horror. "Oh, my god . . . don't turn around!" she hissed. "Don't look, maybe she won't see us—"

"Who won't see us?"

"Iffy Rollins . . . Jesus, *don't look!*"

He did anyway. A plump woman in a hideously bright orange dress chattered enthusiastically at the waitress. Hardly anyone to be feared, in Keen's opinion.

"Oh no oh no oh no," Jillie moaned as the waitress pulled a menu from the stack and led Iffy Rollins toward them. At the last second, they turned down the opposite aisle and out of sight.

"Could you be a real *sweetie*," he could hear Iffy Rollins's razor-edged voice saying, "I'd really *much* prefer to sit away from the window, especially in this *awful* weather, not a bit like London's supposed to be, is it, I get heat flashes like about to pass out if it gets *too* hot, but thank heavens, it could be worse, it could be *pouring* down rain . . ."

"Get me outta here," Jillie begged.

So while he paid at the counter, Jillie crept away like a soldier under enemy fire. The cashier exchanged a bemused expression with him. Iffy Rollins seemed harmless enough, just a lonely, garrulous middle-aged woman.

"I don't mean to be rude, but do you wash your lettuce *really* thoroughly?" Iffy Rollins was still rattling on, her piercing voice carrying into every corner of the restaurant. "It's just I have these terrible *allergies,* and sometimes I get such a *dreadful* reaction, I mean, the least little bit of chemicals and oh, my goodness, I swell up and itch like crazy and my skin breaks out in the most horrible weeping *rash* . . ."

On second thought, Keen admitted, he began to feel sorry for the waitress standing with pen poised in case the woman ever did get round to ordering something. Outside, Jillie grabbed his hand and dragged him at a near trot toward the Tube station, not letting up her pace until they were safely past the turnstile and standing on the quay. Even then, Jillie kept glancing back in dread.

"Millions of people in London and I have to run into Iphegenia goddamn Rollins," she muttered. "I'd rather take on a dozen homicidal maniacs—"

"Who *is* she?"

Jillie's hair whipped her face in the stiff breeze of pressurized air pushed ahead of the train through the tunnel.

"Another history professor, believe it or not." She had to shout over the noise. "Met her in Leeds, friend of Lena's. She says Iffy's usually okay, whenever she hasn't forgotten to take her lithium."

Keen studied her doubtfully. "Is that a joke?"

"Wish I knew." They both started laughing as the train rolled to a stop, steel doors sliding open with an arthritic thunk.

"Mind the gap," the recorded man's voice warned with taciturn indifference. The crowd within poured out, and once spent, the tide surged in. "Mind the gap . . ."

Keen tried to ignore her body pressed up nicely against his, warm and soft, close enough to breathe in her perfume. It was both a relief and a disappointment when they'd reached their station, riding the clacking escalator up out of the stink of burning brake linings, old sweat, and pine disinfectant. The sky had faded to a cobalt blue, street lamps not yet on while neon storefronts glowed. The aroma of coffee and fresh pastry permeated the air as they strolled past the cafés up Regent's Park Road. A pleasant illusion, he thought, just out for an evening stroll with a lovely lass.

The illusion shattered as they turned the corner. Men in white dungarees shuttled cardboard boxes and furniture into a removals van parked in front of Chris's house. A heavily pregnant woman emerged onto the front steps, scowling. Celia Swinton. She glared as they approached before she disappeared back inside.

"At least it isn't burglars," Jillie said bitterly. "Just grave robbers."

They maneuvered past removal men carrying a huge chaise longue through the open doorway. Once inside, they found the rooms had been stripped, the floor littered with cardboard boxes, bubble wrap, and old newspapers. Pale squares on the wallpaper gave blank evidence where paintings had hung, the walls bare. Celia Swinton stood with her legs braced aggressively and smoking a cigarette.

"It all belongs to Max now," she snapped before either of them could speak. "And, if you'll recall, Mother did ask that I come over to take things in hand."

"I'm sorry," Jillie said sweetly. "I assumed you'd wait until the body was cold."

Keen rubbed his chin to hide his smile as the woman's nostrils flared. She glared down her long nose as she inhaled on her cigarette. Who was she trying to imitate, he wondered, Sharon Stone? Bette Davis?

"How frightfully witty," Celia sneered, "for an American. But Verona and I both felt Max was far too impulsive leaving a total stranger in charge. We decided it best to remove anything too valuable to leave until he returns; looters, I'm sure you understand." A heavy-set man grunted into the room with a frayed overstuffed chair. "Not that one," Celia growled. "I *told* you, the leather one in the sitting room."

The man shrugged, dropping it where he stood and shuffled off. "It belonged to Churchill, in Number Ten," she couldn't resist explaining. Not getting the awed reaction she'd expected, Celia Swinton raked Keen with a contemptuous once-over. "My husband would not be pleased the police are in his house without permission."

"I'm not with the Metropolitan Police, Mrs. Swinton," he said mildly. "I'm only here as a friend of Dr. Waltham's since, as you've pointed out, certain sorts of people might try to loot the premises."

His irony wasn't lost on her. She glanced pointedly at the shadow left in the dust coating the desk, streaked where the now vanished computer had once been. "Speaking of looters, perhaps you might advise me on how to recover the computer system the police confiscated?" Her disdainful tone was a shade too contrived for his policeman's antennae not to quiver.

"Why the rush? Is there something on it you need right away?"

She started guiltily. "Of course not. But as I'm sure you're well aware, it's worth several hundred pounds. I'd hate for it to be . . . accidentally misplaced."

"Well, I can only suggest you call up the station and ask." He smiled cordially in return, and after a moment, she turned her attention elsewhere.

"*Careful* with that," she snapped at the mover wrestling with a huge chandelier. "That's genuine crystal, you know."

"Yes'm, not to worry," the dark-skinned man assured her in a melodious accent. "We're always very careful."

She tsked her exasperation as he moved past them, crystal tinkling merrily. "My mother-in-law insisted on hiring them since they were the cheapest she could find," she snapped at Jillie and Keen, although he knew she was speaking to herself. "But when you hire *this* lot, you have to constantly keep your eye on them."

Her eye wasn't on the Asian as he glanced back with smoldering hostility. Roving around the nearly emptied room, Celia picked over Chris's antique knickknacks to examine them with an experienced eye.

"You may, of course, stay on until Max returns," she said to a porcelain vase, sneering at the stamp on its base. She dumped seaside pebbles out of a silver candy dish. "No doubt *you* could use the money you'd save on a hotel." She smiled, all tooth and no warmth as she stuffed the dish into her already bulging jacket pocket.

"No, thanks," Jillie said calmly. "Now that you've . . . *removed* any reason he wanted me to stay, I'll be out by tomorrow afternoon."

"No hurry, dear," Celia said with her frosty smile broadening. "Take your time." She crammed a couple of photos of Chris into an open cardboard box, more for their expensive frames than for any sentimental value, Keen suspected. "But we would like to have the rubbish cleared out before renovation work starts on Monday. There's *so* much to do before the baby arrives."

Celia looked up as another mover struggled down the staircase with a huge wooden sculpture. "No, no, *no*," she snapped. "I don't want any voodoo masks, no skeletons with sombreros, no cheap Persian rugs with Lenin on them, no dead animal heads, no weird insects pinned in boxes, and no Nigerian stick figures with penises. Absolutely none of that cheap ethnic crap. Have I *finally* made myself understood?"

"Yes'm." He struggled back up the stairs again, the swollen-eyed wooden statue thumping on each step.

"Good Lord." Fists on her hips, Chris Swinton's sister-in-law surveyed the room with contempt. "What a load of useless trash," she declared. "It's a shame having to pay death duties on *this*." She began tossing out rumpled dresses and squashed hats with silk flowers from a Victorian chest. Gingerly holding up a fur wrap as if afraid it was rabid, glass-eyed fox head and a moth-eaten tail, she eyed Jillie. "Help yourself to any of her clothing, dear. It's all going to Oxfam anyway."

"No, thank you," Jillie repeated through clenched teeth.

Dropping the pelt into the chest, Celia slapped the dust from her palms and shot Keen a glance with eyes too perfectly blue to be anything but expensive contact lenses. She ran her finger along the bookshelves lining the walls around Chris's desk. "I've had a book dealer come by, one of those people who buy secondhand books in bulk. Filbert Booksellers. He'll come round with a lorry tomorrow about half one. I shan't be here, doctor's appointment, I'm afraid. But if you're staying on, would you mind terribly letting him in? I don't expect he'll take long, and you can drop the keys through the mail slot when you go. I'll pop round to pick them up fivish." She smiled at Jillie with brazen hostility. "You *will* be gone by then, I assume?"

Jillie's face drained to a mottled white. Alarmed, Keen moved closer to her, ready to restrain her if she tried to strike Celia Swinton. Apparently, Celia realized it as well, eyes widening as she took a quick step back.

"No problem." Jillie's voice was calm if hoarse.

As if she understood it was time to hasten her retreat, Celia nodded and quickly strode out of the room. Keen watched as Jillie retrieved a shabby one-eyed teddy bear from the pile of refuse. She gently brushed the debris and scraps of thread off its worn fur before she sat down on the rejected chair and hugged the teddy, resting her chin between its ears, her eyes glistening although her face was perfectly still. "Will you be all right?" Keen asked.

She nodded without looking at him. He strolled into the atrium where Celia Swinton continued to harass the movers. "Are you nearly finished, Mrs. Swinton?"

"That's none of your business," she snarled. "You can't intimidate me, you've absolutely no authority here. This is *my* house now, and you were not invited."

"I understand," he said benignly, nodding as if in total agreement with her. "But I'm right surprised at you, Mrs. Swinton." He nodded at her swollen middle. "Knowing how excited you and your husband are about the new baby, I would think you'd have more sense than to be smoking during pregnancy."

She glared at him hatefully. "No one asked for your opinion. *You!*" Grabbing the porch railing for support, she shouted at the mover. He leaned against the van to light his own cigarette, hands cupped around the match, light flickering on his tired lined face. He looked up in surprise as she yelled. "I haven't hired you by the hour to stand around doing bloody nothing!"

The mover shook the flame out and flicked the dead match into the front garden with a flat, obstinate look.

As if embarrassed at being caught out, Celia hugged herself tightly. "I must apologize," she said with hollow courtesy, then dropped the cigarette and ground it out under her shoe. "This has been a stressful week for the family. Mother isn't up to seeing anyone and, with Max away, it's been left up to me to deal with this mess."

"It must be hard on you, Mrs. Swinton, especially a lady in your condition."

His conciliation softened her. "Dreadfully," she agreed, a whine of self-pity under her anger. "To top everything off, that horrible solicitor of hers, Schaefer, rang me this morning."

Keen said nothing, listening politely.

"I think he got some sort of sadistic pleasure out of ringing up so soon after the funeral to tell us about Chris's will, can you believe the utter insensitivity of the man? She left every asset she had locked up in a trust to my daughter, and nothing to the new baby, absolutely *nothing*." Celia pouted as if searching for sympathy or at least agreement. "And fifty thousand pounds to her darling goddaughter, Karen Waltham." She shifted her sulfurous glare toward the house. "We intend to contest it, of course. Are you staying much longer, Mr. . . . ?"

"Dunliffe. With your permission," he said carefully, knowing her consent was essential for him to continue legally searching the house while not wanting her to realize it. He offered her one of his cards.

He watched her nibble at her bottom lip, wondering at her uncertainty. After a moment's hesitation, she thrust it into a jacket pocket strained at the seams. "I suppose it's for the best, if only to keep an eye on *that* woman. And you can also tell her from me, she's never going to see one damned penny!"

Within fifteen minutes, the movers had removed the last of the plundered loot and drove off, Celia Swinton following in her bright yellow BMW. He watched until both vehicles were out of sight before going back inside.

Jillie's eyes were red, but her cheeks dry as her hands idly stroked the timeworn teddy. She looked shattered. He gazed at the shambles around him. Celia Swinton had left the house a dismal wreck. "You don't have to stay here tonight, Jillie," he said finally. "I'll help you with the kitchen, and then we'll find you a hotel."

"No." She hugged the toy bear and took a deep breath. "When I make a bed, I lie in it." He wasn't quite sure what she meant by that.

"Did you know that Chris mentioned your daughter in her will?"

She looked up sharply. "No. I didn't even know Chris had a will."

He answered her unspoken question. "Fifty thousand pounds."

"Jesus." The spontaneity of her reaction convinced him she had known nothing about it. Then, suspiciously, "How do *you* know?"

"Celia Swinton intends to contest it."

Jillie didn't answer for a long moment. She asked cautiously, "Just Karen. . . . ?"

"As far as I know."

"That's a relief." She grimaced. "I mean I don't want anything. I don't want to profit from Chris's death. It would be too . . . ghoulish."

That it also helped extricate her from a motive for murder, however improbable, apparently hadn't occurred to her.

After a moment, she stood up and placed the stuffed bear on the chair, tenderly smoothing its bent ear. "I'll go wax the kitchen floor if you want to look through what's left for any more clues or whatever."

"Give the door handle a wipe, countertop, anywhere you think he might touch."

"Anything else?" she asked cynically.

"No, that should be enough."

He'd seen drug-crazed burglars turn over a house and leave the premises in tidier condition. He sifted the wreckage with less care than he had the previous night, neatness no longer mattering. But he found nothing he hadn't already gleaned.

By ten o'clock, he'd given up and gone down to the kitchen, where Jillie was on her hands and knees on the floor, the tiles gleaming, immaculate. She sat on her heels, rag in one hand.

"There. Ready for tomorrow." She stood up and faced him, her eyes uneasy. "I'll get some blankets and make up the couch for you."

"That'd be fine."

Relieved, she busied herself making up a bed as comfortably as the short settee would allow, smoothing wrinkles from the sheet, shaking pillows into lace cases, tucking the duvet around the cushions, fidgeting unnecessarily.

"There you go," she finally pronounced, stepping back to gaze at the settee as if it were an exhibit in a museum. "I bought coffee and milk this morning. And bread for toast. I don't have any granola, though."

"Coffee and toast is fine."

"There's a fresh bar of soap in the bathroom, and I've got a package of disposable razors in my luggage."

"Thank you . . ."

She looked at him, eyes anxious. "I don't have an extra toothbrush."

"I'll survive. Jillie, relax. Everything's *fine*." She nodded stiffly. "Look, it's not that late, fancy a walk and a quiet drink before bed?"

Just as she had that first night he took her to dinner, she considered his proposal long enough for him to be sure she was about to decline, then surprised him. "I'd like that."

And, like that night, she looked startled by her own reaction.

The evening air was still warm, although London's city lights washed the night sky clean of stars. They walked by the same car he had seen parked by the corner tower, this time unoccupied. Keen chose the first pub they came to, seating her before he went to get half a pint of Webster's for himself and a glass of Chablis for her.

Jillie thanked him, sipping the wine with an expression he was beginning to recognize. He waited.

"I think I should tell you about something else . . ." She paused as if steeling herself for an unpleasant quarrel. "Someone called last night. Actually early this morning . . ."

"At the house? Who was it?" he said sharply. And felt bad as she flinched.

"I don't know. He didn't give his name. He didn't know she was dead, and he didn't sound like much of a friend." He realized she had meant someone had telephoned.

"Did he threaten you?"

"Not exactly."

"What does 'not exactly' mean?"

"It was just an obscene phone call," Jillie said, her nonchalance unconvincing. "It was really nothing. Probably some kid."

"Are you sure it couldn't have been Dr. Wycombe?"

The idea startled her. "No, it wasn't his voice."

"If he rings again tonight, are you up to speaking with him? I'll be right there, so there's no reason to be frightened . . ."

Whatever he had said, it hadn't reassured her. "I think I can handle it," she said tightly, with a look of white-faced anger. "You don't have to treat me like I'm a five-year-old."

He wondered what the hell he was doing in London, as everyone around him lately—Phil, Bernie, now Jillie—were doing their best to convince him they could handle everything on their own without him.

"Sorry." It was Jillie who apologized, before he had a chance himself. "I'm still spooked, I guess."

"Don't worry. After we get this sorted out in the morning, we'll find you somewhere else first thing tomorrow."

"Thank you."

They finished their drinks in silence.

VIII

THURSDAY

"Do you know you snore?" Her voice jolted Keen painfully awake.

His eyelids felt bloated as they opened against his will. The sheet had twisted into knots under him, most of the duvet slipped off onto the floor. Stifling a groan, he sat up and dragged the duvet up over his exposed legs. Already dressed in jeans and a LES MISÉRABLES T-shirt, she proffered a cup of hot coffee.

"I'm aware of it." His voice was hoarse. Burying his face in his hands, he rubbed at his fatigue. "Christ, what time is it?"

"Six-thirty. You did say to wake you."

"Thanks." He meant for the coffee. Although weak, it washed away the sour fur in his mouth and he was grateful enough to have it.

She perched on the arm of the settee. "You sleep okay?"

"Fine. Brilliant. Never better."

His entire body ached. Sinuses rebelled against the baked London smog, his headache a thin wedge of pain around his brow like the brim of a too-tight hat. Vertebrae popped as he rolled his neck. He was in dire need of a few aspirin and a proper workout. More than anything else, he wanted to be back in his own bed, Thomas a bothersome lump at his feet, and to have never *ever* heard of Dr. Christine bloody Swinton. "You're up early."

She looked around the pillaged room uneasily. "I can't sleep well here. I don't believe in ghosts, or spirits, nothing like that. But . . . that first night, I kept thinking she was just in the other room. Now, I can't *feel* Chris here anymore. Like she's really and truly gone." She looked at him, troubled. "Do you think that's crazy?"

He understood what she meant. "It's not crazy." He tried to smile reassuringly. "Only a few more hours, and we'll get you out of here."

She smiled back, relieved. "Want some toast?"

"No, best to leave the kitchen floor clean as you can." He yawned hugely.

"I hope that wasn't a criticism of my coffee."

"I'll get dressed and we'll go out for a proper breakfast." Scratching his unshaven chin, he said, "And I could do with one of those razors of yours."

"I think the Don Johnson look is cute, don't you?"

Cute? "No."

"No Ferrari, no Giorgio Armani T-shirts, no stubble. Some cop you are." She laughed and left him in peace to dress and shave.

Jillie's palms were sweating when Dr. Reece Wycombe rang the doorbell at exactly ten o'clock. Keen gave her shoulder a quick squeeze before he disappeared up the stairway.

When she opened the door, Wycombe muttered a quick greeting and elbowed past, his cast clunking on the parquet floor. She followed him into Chris's sitting room. The man scanned the bookshelves, his eyes avoiding hers. "Let's make this quick, Dr. Waltham, shall we?" he said shortly. "I want my book back."

"And I want to know what Chris was working on."

"I have no intention of haggling with you," he said irritably. She gazed back blandly, hiding her reaction; her ex-husband had taught her well. "That book is mine, I paid dearly for it, and don't care to see it flogged off to some amateur collector who won't appreciate its true value. And I'm sure you understand the gravity of your situation should you unwisely choose to hold on to stolen property."

"Call the police and press charges, if you want."

He tried to soften his expression, which only made him seem more deceitful. His tongue darted between tight lips, as fast as a chameleon swallowing a fly. "I'd prefer it didn't come to that. The provenance is a bit . . . well, awkward. Not that there's anything criminal involved," he hastened to add, "I simply wish to avoid any . . . embarrassment. For us both." He attempted an ingratiating smile.

She returned it sweetly. "Sorry. Can't help you."

His mouth hardened into a compressed line. "Then I'll have a look through these here, if you don't mind."

She barred his way as he stepped toward the shelves, aware of Keen listening, hoping he wouldn't misconstrue this as the time to "rescue" her. "Actually, I do mind. Max Swinton asked me to house-sit so nothing got stolen. If you touch one thing"—she leaned closer as if daring him to push her out of his way, oddly exhilarated by her uncharacteristic defiance—"including me, I'll call the police *for* you."

She'd expected Wycombe to quarrel with her. But to her amazement, he instantly crumbled. His overbearing arrogance vanished, and he looked like a guilty child, an expression that on his unattractive face was more grotesque than pathetic. He pulled a handkerchief from his pocket to mop his forehead. "My apologies, Dr. Waltham. This leg is killing me. Skiing accident. Would you mind if I sat down?"

She gestured at the scruffy chairs abandoned by the movers. "Be my guest."

He levered himself clumsily into a chair. "All I want is to recover my property. I don't have a copy of her manuscript. Without that, along with her references, there's no possibility of my completing her work and taking the credit, if that's what you're worried about."

Jillie remained standing, her arms crossed, intuitively understanding the psychological advantage she gained. "That's *exactly* what I am worried about."

"As much as I know you won't like to hear this, Chris was no stranger to stealing other people's work herself, you know."

"Now that *is* a lie . . ." Jillie flared.

He raised his hand appeasingly. "I don't mean plagiarism, I assure you."

"Then what do you mean?"

"One of my graduate students was an old school chum of Chris's. Marge Beecher. She worked with my colleague Dr. Jordan Arthur. Jordie was working on a theory that Queen Elizabeth the First paid off her medical doctors to certify her as a virgin when she was not. He'd traced two original letters; the first by one of Elizabeth's doctors, and the other from a lady-in-waiting, proving beyond a shadow of doubt that Elizabeth's affair with the Earl of Essex was quite consummated. Then Jordie's office at the university was burgled and all his original material was stolen."

"What on earth does this have to do with Chris?" Jillie demanded. "Her research was on George the Third, not Elizabeth the First."

Wycombe raised an eyebrow. "Rumor hath it, Chris and Jordie were lovers." He cleared his throat, commentary rather than necessity. "It didn't last, of course. Jordie was married, and he'd never leave his wife. Chris didn't give a fig about Elizabeth the First, but she knew how to hit Jordie where it hurt."

"Revenge? Chris wasn't like that . . ."

He smiled bitterly, his teeth crooked and yellowed, the purplish hue of his lips giving them a feral cast. "Of course she was."

Jillie wavered uncertainly as Wycombe smirked in triumph.

"Jordie was in line for a chair at Oxford, along with Dr. Roger Saunders, perhaps you've heard of him?" Jillie shook her head. "No matter. After Jordie published his theory, Saunders accused Jordie of forging documents to salt the records. And somehow he had gotten hold of Jordie's original source material to 'prove' it." Wycombe waggled fingers to indicate quotation marks.

"Not Chris," Jillie said doggedly.

"Marge told me that a week before Jordie's offices were broken into, Chris rang her out of the blue, asked her to lunch on the pretext of crying on her shoulder, moaning over her broken affair with Jordie, the sort of thing you ladies do."

Again, Jillie had no problem remaining expressionless.

"Marge believes Chris lifted the office keys from her handbag when she wasn't looking, and took a wax impression . . ."

"That is ridiculous," Jillie retorted. "Where did you come up with this, *Mission Impossible?*"

Wycombe managed to look hurt. "Complicated, certainly, but not ridiculous. Jordie's letters were examined by experts, and they were indeed forgeries.

The scandal ruined him. Saunders got the chair. His wife had a nervous break-down, the private hospital charges wiped him out financially. Jordie died a few months ago after a long illness. The kind that comes in bottles, poor man."

Wycombe's voice had lost its edge, his gaze distant. Jillie had a flash of insight. "Were you in love with Chris?"

His attention snapped back into focus. His already pale skin blanched further, leaving his cheeks a mottled pink. Then he laughed, strained. "A schoolboy crush, nothing more." He shrugged. "She was a beautiful, brilliant woman. That made it easy to overlook the fact that she was a thief and liar, with a mind like a snake pit."

Why was it, Jillie wondered, that brilliant and beautiful women could be both admired and despised in the same breath?

"Why would she steal this book you're looking for?"

"Coercion. Publish her book or mine perishes."

"So what's it look like?"

Thankful to let the subject of his infatuation with Chris drop, Wycombe relaxed. "About this size," he said, measuring with his hands, "and this wide. It has Etruscan calf bindings with a marbled center panel. The borders are stained terra-cotta, and decorated with black Greek palmettes, like those you find on Greek vases. It's a book of drawings of monuments and ancient art in Constantinople, Greece, and Egypt made by Richard Dalton during his travels there. Dalton had a special edition bound by a Yorkshire bookbinder from Halifax, William Edwards, in seventeen fifty-seven to present as a gift to the Prince of Wales, later George the Third."

Jillie started, then hoped her surprise wasn't noticeable. It was, but apparently Wycombe read something different into her reaction.

"So it's rather valuable, as you can imagine. Have you seen it?"

"Sorry, no." Although, she thought, it did sound oddly familiar.

"Would you mind if I took a quick look?" Wycombe asked politely, gesturing toward the untidy shelves of books. "It's quite unique, not easy to miss."

"No, go ahead." She didn't offer to help as he struggled upright and hobbled toward the books, scanning them quickly.

"The unusual thing about it is the fore-edges, they have a landscape scene painted on them. You can't see them, because it's hidden by gilt, you have to fan the pages before it comes visible." Wycombe pulled a book by its spine partway out from the rest, just far enough to examine the edges, then pushed it back into the stack.

"So why is the provenance a problem?"

Wycombe adopted what Jillie suspected was his "wise professor" pose: hands clasped behind his back, slouched with his feet apart. "Ah," he said, flustered. "Well . . ." He coughed, a nervous habit beginning to grate on her nerves. "This particular book belonged to the Spencer family library at Cannon Hall, near Barnsley. It's thought George may have presented it as a gift to one of the younger Spencer ladies he'd taken a fancy to while he was Prince of Wales."

Jillie imagined Keen rolling his eyes and suppressing a groan as he was subjected to yet more dull Georgian history.

"The Spencers later had a quarrel with Dorothy Fleming, Lady Worsley. She and a couple friends raided the Spencer library. Several books were carried off as booty and never returned. This being one."

Jillie squinted at him dubiously. "And?"

Wycombe cleared his throat again, and Jillie gritted her teeth. "Ah. You see, Lady Worsley was the daughter of Lady Jane Fleming. Edwin Lascelles's second wife." At her bewilderment, he sighed. "Lord Harewood?"

Her jaw dropped. "Harewood like in Harewood House?" Well, *that* might perk Keen's interest.

"Exactly." His purplish lips twisted in an apologetic smile.

"So what was Chris doing at Harewood House? And how did *you* get the book in the first place?"

"I bought it from an antique dealer in Abingdon, and I have the receipts to prove it," Wycombe said firmly. "He claims the book was part of an estate sale in nineteen forty-seven when the Lascelles were hard hit by death duties. But it was listed in the inventory of Harewood House when the trust was formed a few years ago, which would certainly contradict his claim." He shrugged.

"So you think it was stolen?"

"Unquestionably once. Possibly several times. Would you have a ladder? Ah, this will do . . ."

He brushed the litter off a footstool and stood on it with his good foot, cast dangling, as he stretched to inspect the top shelves. "However," he continued, "if one had gone missing, it would be ages before anyone discovered it." He probed the dusty spines, then rubbed his fingertips together with contempt. "Much like these." He looked toward the stairway hopefully. "There wouldn't be any others upstairs?"

"Sorry," she said, trying to sound indifferent. "Celia's got a bookseller coming today to cart everything away, so it's all down here." She indicated a small pile of books on George the Third she had selected for herself. "Those are all that's left."

He dismissed them with a glance before he cautiously lowered himself back down. Looking around, he hunched with hands in his pockets.

"Well." Wycombe sighed again, dejected. "I should be going."

She panicked as she realized she hadn't thought of a way to get him to leave through the back door. "Um . . . would you like a cup of tea?"

He studied her quizzically. "Very kind, but no, thank you. If you do find that book, you will let me know, won't you?"

"Certainly . . ." Suddenly, she remembered there were other books, in the kitchen, and just as suddenly realized she did not want him to look at them at all. She stared at him, then jumped as the front doorbell rang. "Oh, my god, that's probably Celia Swinton. She'll have a fit if she finds you here." Jillie leapt on the excuse like a starving dog on a discarded bone, thin as it was. He looked alarmed. "Quick, you can leave out the back, through the kitchen . . ."

She almost laughed from nerves as he scuttled through the kitchen. Steadying himself with one hand on the meticulously clean countertop, he overlooked the cookbooks directly over his head. "There's a gate to the right," she said, forcing herself not to glance at the cookbooks, "and I *promise,* I'll call you if I find anything."

"Thank you," he said as he grabbed the doorknob. "I appreciate that . . ." And he was gone. She exhaled in relief and sprinted for the front door as the bell rang again.

Lynne Selkirk smiled from the front porch. "Hello, hope this isn't too early," she said. "I've an address for you, Mrs. Flutes's bed and breakfast. I rang up this morning and there's a room available, if you're still interested. It's not far, she doesn't charge the earth, and it's women only. But I warn you she's a bit of an eccentric."

"That's wonderful, come on in," Jillie said, spotting Wycombe slinking past the gate. She nearly yanked the woman inside. As Lynne stepped past her, the man's walking cast made a loud connection with a trash can. He grabbed his leg in pain and Jillie quickly shut the door. The need to invent any on-the-spot explanations for the sudden clang was eliminated as Lynne scowled.

"I wish the council would do *something* about those damned cats."

Skulking was not much to his liking, Keen thought as he sat at the top of the stairs waiting for Lynne Selkirk to leave. But he had to smile when a flustered Jillie finally appeared. She looked lovely as she swept her hair out of her eyes, the color high in her cheeks. "How'd I do?" she demanded. "Police-interrogationwise?"

"Might have helped if he'd given you the name of that Abingdon dealer he bought the book from."

His criticism did little to dim her enthusiasm. "Well, maybe I know something to make up for that."

"What?"

"I know where the book is!"

"You're joking! Where?"

She giggled, all nerves. "In the *kitchen.*"

"Then it'll have to keep." He came down the stairs and picked up the telephone. "Bloody hell." He scowled at the dead handset. "Celia Swinton's already had the telephone disconnected."

He put in a call to Kentish Town's Scene of Crimes Office from a corner telephone kiosk, cursing himself for not replacing his own dead mobile phone still at home. He barely got through to the SOCO before BT devoured the last tenpence and cut him off. He'd have to buy a second mobile if he intended to keep on with this job.

The SOCO showed up half an hour later. "Gareth Burns." The wiry man with wiry hair set his scene-of-crimes kit down at the edge of the kitchen floor, cocking his head to study the barely visible prints. "Interesting." He glanced at Keen with a broad smile. "You want me to dust for fingerprints as well?"

If it had been Wycombe in Jillie's B and B, the lack of a match wouldn't mean anything. But he could get lucky with those in the Garth Moor Arms, or on Chris Swinton's computer. "Worktop, there . . . and there. And the door handle. Only other shoeprints are hers."

Gareth set out his jars and brushes, cans of aerosols, and rolls of plastic tape. He spun a brush between both hands to flare the soft bristles.

"You did exactly right, miss, walking well away from him, keep the prints separated," Gareth said. "Amazing how many times you find even coppers running in without thinking. It isn't like your dramas on telly." He pronounced it "drammers," the Birmingham not fully leached out of his accent. "We had this man'd been shot in a condemned parking garage, empty for ages? Found at least thirty shoemarks tracked through the blood, all belonging to police officers, bloody useless. One of 'em turned out to be a *very* senior officer, strolling around mucking up the evidence."

"You're kidding," Jillie said. Keen glanced at her warily, but she seemed more interested than distressed.

Gareth beamed at her. Behind Jillie, Keen pointedly raised an eyebrow at him. Gareth turned his attention to his work, but kept up his steady stream of conversation.

"Of course, you need the doctor to say he's dead, somebody to collect evidence, maybe a couple officers to keep order. But everybody else is just walking around out of curiosity and saying, 'Yup, he's dead, Jim.' Bloody useless." That appeared to be his favorite verdict.

Gareth dipped the brush into a jar, picking up dark powder on the tips. He squatted to brush the first print Wycombe's walking cast had left, the distinct pattern materializing under the bristles.

"Aren't you a police officer?" Jillie asked.

"Oh, not me. We just collect the forensic evidence, rest is done at the main lab over in Lambeth. Now, watch this, I can lift these shoemarks just the way I would fingerprints. Lucky for you this floor was so clean." Jillie exchanged a glance with Keen, amused. "That's very important. Fingerprints are all around us everywhere. Every time you touch something you leave a little bit and take away a little bit."

"Really." Jillie examined her own fingertips.

"But touch something dusty, you'll take away the dust but not leave anything. Well . . ." He paused to amend himself. "There *is* an electrostatic process, but I've never used it myself. Too expensive for anything less than murder."

Keen shot her a warning look while Gareth, oblivious, chattered on. "Then you got your shoemarks," he said, bent double to examine the print. "Anyone can have the same brand shoe, but you're looking for minute detail, like say he's walked on a stone and it's taken a chip out. But these are really unique, never quite seen anything like this."

Although nothing the man was saying was news to Keen, Jillie watched like an inquisitive child doing her best to stay out of the way. He smiled, wondering at how easily he'd forgotten his own fascination with forensics as a novice constable.

Then Keen recognized her look, the same as she had given Ronnie Norville, her attention focused on Gareth like a spotlight trained on an actor. Her ability to get people to talk to her was more than a genuine interest, he realized, but a clever way for her to stay invisible. He wondered if she was even aware she was doing it.

Gareth blew excess powder away and reached for his camera.

"Will a photograph be good enough?" Jillie asked.

Gareth favored her with his broad, happy smile. "Oh, don't worry, miss, I'm going to take the print up as well." He adjusted the tripod and squinted through the lens, focusing carefully. After he had taken two shots, he chose a roll of transparent sticky tape several inches wide. It *skreaked* as he pulled out a length and pressed it down onto the highlighted print, smoothing it with his finger to press out air pockets.

He peeled the tape off in one smooth, practiced movement, taking the print with it, then eyed it critically before flashing them both a grin. "God, I love this job."

He pressed the tape impression onto a sheet of thin transparent celluloid, sealing it permanently, and trimmed the tape. "And there it is," he said, holding up the print. "This'll stay usable for years."

He began dusting the worktop. Invisible fingerprints materialized like magic, black powdery kisses peppering the counter and door handle. It reminded Keen, as it always did, of his boyhood secret messages written in milk, appearing with a cigarette lighter held under the paper.

"Heard you're the bloke worked that slurry case," Gareth said as he worked. "Really intrigued me."

"Glad to hear it," Keen said impassively.

"Had a case last year might interest you. Young girl raped and strangled over in Cricklewood." Jillie started, and Keen glanced at her warily, Gareth oblivious.

"Thought he was one smart bugger, used a condom and took it with him, so there wasn't any semen to find. Then he took a handful of her own shi . . . ah, fecal material and smeared it all over her face, made a right disgustin' mess of her."

Gareth glanced up apologetically, not for his gruesome story but for his slip of the tongue in front of a lady. "He wiped his hands on his jeans, then got it on the seat of his car when he drove off. By the time we caught up with him, he'd washed his jeans and had the car professionally steam-cleaned, thought he was in the clear."

Skreak! One of Wycombe's fingerprints was now permanently preserved.

"What he didn't know is that everybody's feces has its own set of enzymes, as unique as fingerprints. Just like your load of slurry, every tank has a different composition. So I had the lab test the jeans and the car for trace enzymes, and there they were, just enough to compare to the girl's for an exact match, and he was done for rape and murder."

"You really caught him?" Jillie said, awed. Keen was oddly pleased by her reaction, and glad she wasn't squeamish. "He's in prison?"

Gareth looked massively proud of himself. "Bang to rights, he's going nowhere for a long, long time." Then to Keen, "You want any of these tiles lifting?"

Jillie looked at Keen with alarm. "Can you do that?"

"Hey, no problem!" Gareth said as he scribbled out the evidence tag. "Do it all the time. If they're too stuck to come up, we'll just saw them out of the floor."

That's not what she'd meant, Keen knew as Gareth handed the card to him to sign off on, and wished the man would stop talking quite so much.

"A crime was committed at your B and B in Leeds," Keen explained tersely. "Prints from that scene may match prints here, so as long as I'm lawfully on the premises and I've reasonable grounds to believe this is evidence in relation to an offense, I can take whatever I need in order to prevent it from being destroyed or lost. That would include the floor tiles, yes." He didn't add the degree of trouble should be proportional to the seriousness of the crime, as he knew a criminal damage case would never have warranted this much effort.

Jillie and Gareth both twisted to stare him askance, each for differing reasons. "Do they have to send you to a special school to learn to talk like that?" she asked.

Keen smiled. "Section nineteen of the Police and Criminal Evidence Act of nineteen eighty-four, chapter and verse."

Satisfied, she gazed down at the floor again. "Celia Swinton isn't going to like this." She seemed rather happy with that thought.

Lifting two of the vinyl floor tiles was easier than Keen had expected, to his relief, each of Wycombe's tracks sealed to them.

Gareth Burns repacked his equipment, putting the transparent sheets of lifted prints into a folder. "If your nick sends a fax of your track for comparison, I can probably make a preliminary judgment on these."

"As soon as you know, give me a ring."

Keen saw him out the door and returned to find Jillie pulling down cookbooks from a shelf, discarding several in her search.

"This is it, if it's what I think it is," Jillie announced with a large, heavy cookbook in her arms. "I was so close to finding it, just never opened it."

She set it on the table. The book wrapper declared it to be Alexandre Dumas's *Le Grand Dictionnaire de Cuisine*. The faded gilt on the page ends revealed the indistinct outline of something underneath. Jillie flexed the book in such a way that the pages fanned apart, trees and mountains popping into focus. She looked up in delighted triumph, and removed the book wrapper.

The leather bindings were scratched and darkened, but despite the book's age, it still retained a veneer of elegance. On the inside flyleaves, two stamped coats of arms had been garnished with colored ink and gilt; one familiar enough, that of a Prince of Wales, the other with a pair of chained bears standing on either side of a shield, a large gold cross on its face, a crown and horse's head above it. "In Solo Deo Salus" had been inscribed along a banner underneath.

" 'Only in God, salvation,' " Jillie translated, and flipped through the portfolio of beautifully rendered landscapes of exotic locales long vanished. "What's the big deal about this book. . . . ?" she murmured, studying the prints.

But Keen had been distracted by a bit of orange paper wedged in the crack between the bookshelf and the wall, half hidden behind the books. He worked it up, his nails too short and blunt, scowled when it tore, leaving him holding a scrap. Using both hands, he patiently eased it loose. Then he had it, ripping as he pulled it free, a thin folder from a local Kodak one-hour photo shop.

"What've you found?"

"Holiday snaps, apparently." He spread the photographs out on the table: a dark-skinned boy in scruffy shorts holding a fish, the top of his head cropped off. Blurred panoramas of sailboats in a harbor. An elderly, mangy donkey in a straw hat being fed a carrot by a woman, an unflattering angle of her backside as she bent over.

"Chris went to the Virgin Islands last year," Jillie said, picking up one of the photos. "She travels a lot." She winced. "Traveled."

"Know any of these people?"

"No."

He fingered one of Chris smiling serenely, the moment eternally frozen. She was sitting at a beachside bar, wearing only a skimpy bikini as she sipped from a straw sticking out of a pineapple. Beside her, a tanned man in an even tinier swimsuit, and who plainly spent much of his time lifting weights, sat with his arm possessively around her waist. He leaned into the shot to dazzle the camera with his perfect teeth.

"I think I know who that is," Jillie said. "His name's Don Tolver." She smiled at the photograph. "Chris always had great taste in men." Keen eyed the man's broad shoulders, the well-muscled legs, square chin, the prominent bulge in his tight swimsuit, and brushed aside his absurd twinge of envy.

"You knew him?"

"Never met him. Karen said he and Chris broke up just before her last visit."

"Chris talk about him much?"

"Not really. Chris always had boyfriends, but none of them ever lasted that long. She was too much of a free spirit." She studied the picture of Chris at the beach bar. "But she did love my daughter. Chris flew her over every summer vacation since she was a teenager, up until Karen went to college. I thought it was better than spending the summers at home watching her parents' marriage fall apart." She smiled sadly. "This summer was supposed to my turn, catch up on all the things we'd missed. But now I'll never get the chance . . ."

She stopped, breath shuddering. Keen put his hand over hers, which felt right. His fingers slipped under her palm, and after a moment, she squeezed them gently before pulling away. When he thought she'd recovered, he said, "Would you know who this is of?" and placed the last photograph onto the table.

Chris and a slightly heavier woman, who might have been the same woman with the donkey, stood on a beach with their arms around each other. Both wore outrageously garish sarongs and huge straw hats, the sort of thing tourists buy on holiday and never wear again. The dark woman had one hand on the ridiculous hat, laughing as the wind whipped her long hair across her face, partly obscuring it.

"No," Jillie said uncertainly. But the woman did look vaguely familiar, Keen thought, sure Jillie felt the same way. "Wait a minute . . ." Her finger pointed to Chris. "That's the necklace, the one I told you she was wearing up in Leeds."

He squinted, unable to make out more than a glint of gold suspended on a chain. Jillie checked her watch as a diesel engine rumbled outside. "And there's the bookseller."

As he replaced the photographs into their envelope, she rewrapped the book in its counterfeit dust jacket and carried it into the study to add to a small pile of books she had gleaned for herself.

The driver clambered out of a white removal van, its FILBERT & SON QUALITY BOOKDEALERS painted in rather less than professional lettering. Barely five and a half feet tall, with his beret slanted over one eye, curly ginger hair matching his full beard, baggy army green trousers held up with bright red suspenders, he seemed like a character out of some antiquated BBC comedy. A younger version with only slightly less exuberant ginger hair and beard climbed out of the passenger side.

"You the Swintons?" the older man said with a rich Glaswegian accent. The younger man began hoisting flat cardboard boxes from the back of the removal van.

"No, but we're expecting you."

Jillie hovered over her small pile of books as the men crated the rest and carted them away, neither sparing a glance at titles. Cradling the Dumas cookbook as possessively against her chest as she had the teddy bear, she said, "Excuse me . . . ?"

"Aye, miss?" The older man paused with a box in his burly arms, hefting the weight with ease.

"Could I buy some of these books from you now? The lady they belonged to was a friend of mine, and . . ." Her voice trailed off.

She could have simply taken them, Keen knew, and the book dealer would never have minded a bit. But Filbert senior eyed her curiously. "Spose so. Ye'll be wanting that cookbook, would ye nae?"

Her grip on it tightened. "These, too." She pushed the little stack of books toward him. "How much?"

Filbert set down his load and idly scratched his neck. "Well, dunno," he said, an amused gleam in his bright blue eyes.

"Textbooks on eighteenth-century history a popular item, are they?" Keen said dryly.

The man capitulated. "Tell ye whit I'm goan tae dae, I ken let ye take th'lot of them fer . . . fifty quid?"

Jillie gasped.

"Ten," Keen said.

"Thirty."

"Fifteen."

"Them books is old, antiques like. Could be valuable."

"Fourteen."

The bookseller laughed. "Done. You need a box?"

"Thank you . . ." Jillie said.

"Be a pound extra."

"We'll carry them," Keen said, reaching for his wallet.

Jillie stopped him. "I'll pay for these." She kept hold of the Dumas as she retrieved the money from her handbag, handing Filbert three fivers. The book dealer fished in his pocket for a pound change.

Half an hour later, Filbert and son slammed the doors to their removal van and drove off.

"Well, I guess that's it." Jillie looked tired and sad. Impulsively, he put his arm around her, regretting it as she stiffened. Then she relaxed and smiled wanly. "That mean I done good?"

"You done good." He hugged her again, a casual squeeze before letting his arm drop away. The tension was again palpable between them, and Keen wasn't sure why. "Let's get you moved on."

"I'm ready."

He carried her two small suitcases to the front door, where Jillie waited with her carrier bag of books, adding to it two wilted plants in ceramic pots she had decided to rescue, as well as the scruffy teddy bear and an album of sex ads. "For my daughter's collection," Jillie explained as she stuffed the album into the carrier bag and settled the bear on top. With its missing eye, it seemed to be winking at Keen. "But I'm keeping Darius for myself."

"How do you know its name is Darius?"

"Chris said her father gave it to her when she was little. She told me Darius was the only member of her family who ever really loved her."

He didn't know what to say to that. "Anything else?"

"No, that's everything."

She closed the door and locked it, then dropped the keys through the post slot. They jingled as they hit the floor. Keen found it disconcerting, this sense of closure, as if ending a partnership they had both found pleasurable.

The address Lynne Selkirk had given Jillie was in Camden Town, a genteelly aging white building with a roof garden overlooking the open market on Inverness. They weaved through the wagons as men and women called out bargains for peas and marrows and pineapples, fiver a pair. The neon colors of a billboard advertising a chocolate bar nearly drowned out the delicate hand-painted sign in the lower window:

MRS. FLUTE'S, FOR–LADIES–ONLY

Mrs. Flute took several minutes between answering her intercom and opening the door, fumbling with several security locks. Keen guessed she was well into her eighties, a tiny bird of a woman under gauzy layers of blouses and skirts, her stick-thin wrists laden with jangling bracelets. Her hair, pulled up into a neat, steel-gray bun, glittered with antique jet pins.

"Are you the young lady Lynne rang me about this morning?" She had an odd lilt to her London accent Keen couldn't place.

"Yes, Jillie Waltham. She said you have a room available?"

She eyed Keen distrustfully. "I'm sorry, dear; it's ladies only."

He hefted the suitcases. "I'm only the Sherpa."

"Well . . . I suppose that's all right, come in."

A long stairway led up to Mrs. Flute's flat over a ground-floor shop. Music played from the shop below, a subsonic throb of bass felt more than heard through the floor. The stairway continued up to a second floor, branching off to bedrooms on either side of the landing.

"You have your choice," Mrs. Flute said, "You may have the bedroom on the street where the traffic will keep you awake until two in the morning, or the garden where the market will wake you at four-thirty."

"It doesn't matter."

"Take the back one, then, dear." Mrs. Flute opened the door to a large, sunny room. Sheer curtains wafted from a window overlooking a rooftop garden. Filmy mosquito netting flowed down from the ceiling over a futon bed. Pier Export's best rattan and bamboo furnishings completed the set. Numerous paintings hung around the room. "These are lovely," Jillie said with genuine admiration.

Mrs. Flute smiled indulgently. "I don't paint as much as I used to, arthritis slows me down."

Keen set the suitcases by the bed, then looked at the paintings himself. A few had been simply framed, the rest were basic stretched canvases. His own taste ran to safe rural landscapes with sheep and priory ruins, or maybe the odd basket of grapes with an apple or two, but even to his untrained eye these looked upmarket and expensive. The figures had a dreamy not quite photographic realism to them, and he liked her unconventional style and rich colors. *Bohemian,* he thought, then supposed that probably wasn't the proper artistic term for it.

"When you've settled in, we'll have a nice cup of tea in the study." This for Jillie. "Pleasure to meet you." This for Keen, clearly a hint he should be off, before Mrs. Flute went downstairs.

"I'd better go," he said. "You'll be all right?"

She smiled politely, again that strange distance between them. "Yes, thank you. For everything."

It sounded so final.

"Right, then," he said with a forced cheerfulness. "I'll get on and give you a ring tonight. Dinner? Nothing fancy, just a curry or Chinese takeaway. Then you can tell me about whatever you find at the library today."

She stared at him, as if remembering there were still things to do. "All right."

Jillie didn't bother to look up as a dark-haired woman set a book down next to Jillie's stack. "Thanks," she murmured, too busy jotting down notations.

It lay untouched for another twenty minutes before Jillie glanced at the book, then frowned, puzzled. *Furniture Making in Early Victorian Ireland.* Obviously, it had been sent to the wrong table. She scanned the room for the librarian who had delivered the book, then spotted a yellow request form inserted in the pages. But when she pulled it out, expecting to see a researcher's name and seat number, it read, "If you want to know why C.S. died, be at the Cupid & Flora Tea Shop, Phoenix St. off Charing X Rd in ½ an hour. Be careful—you're being watched."

For a moment, Jillie stared at it blankly, as if trying to figure out the joke. When she looked around again, she gazed at a blond woman in a blue fish-print blouse who looked away too quickly to be casual. The hair on Jillie's arms prickled.

She got up, taking her purse but leaving her books on the table, and made a point of asking the man at the circulation desk for directions to the ladies' room, a little louder than necessary so as to be overheard. Jillie didn't pay any attention to his instructions, heading straight for the exit once she'd left the research rooms.

"Taxi!"

At first, when the driver dropped her off, she couldn't spot the tea shop, crowds milling past her on the sidewalk, newspapers hawked over the clamor of traffic and jackhammers, dust from a construction site filtering the air a hazy yellow. Then she spotted a teapot sign suspended over a doorway from a wrought-iron scroll.

She took a table away from the window, sheltered in the cool shadows, the street noise fading to a distant burr. The only other customers were a pair of elderly women, nearly twins in their sensible dress and sensible shoes. After a few minutes, she was already considering walking out when a dark-haired woman sat down across from her. "You're late."

Jillie found herself gaping at a pendant necklace, recognizing it with a chill shock. Chris had been wearing one exactly like it, the one in the photograph. Then her memory suddenly asserted itself. "You were at Chris's funeral."

"Yes." She smiled up at the waitress, who brought tea and a basket of scones without being asked. The fruity scent of Darjeeling steamed the air. "Thanks, Greta."

"Who are you?" Jillie said, alarm turning to anger. "What's this about?"

"My name's Dawn, Dawn Tolver." Her accent was Irish.

Jillie felt her jaw drop in astonishment. "*You're* Don Tolver? But I thought you were a man!"

The woman smiled thinly, without warmth. "It's D-A-W-N." She laughed gently as Jillie stared at her speechless. "And here I was jealous, thinking *you* were Chris's new lover."

"Me?" Jillie's voice squeaked. "Lover?"

Dawn held the pendant necklace out toward Jillie. "Didn't this give you an inkling when you saw her wearing one like it?"

"I didn't think anything, why should I . . . ?"

"Lambda. The Greek letter *l*. For *lesbian*." She pronounced the word with exaggerated precision.

Jillie blinked away tears, although she wasn't sure why. "But the photographs"—as she said it she understood—"of you and her. Oh . . ." She glanced again at the two elderly women, their gnarled fingers entwined lovingly amid their teacups. "I thought Don Tolver was the blond guy."

"What blond guy?"

"The tall blond guy in the red bikini."

After a moment, Dawn laughed. "Oh, right. *Him*." She sobered quickly. "Do you have them? The photographs?"

"No. A police officer from Leeds found them . . ."

"Bloody hell," Dawn hissed. The anger on her face frightened Jillie. "And you told him about me?"

"No, I didn't know it wasn't you, I mean, I told him the blond guy was you. I didn't recognize you with long hair." She felt confused.

"Good. Now listen; you've been under constant police surveillance ever since Chris died."

"You're wrong. The police think Chris drowned accidentally."

Dawn Tolver was shaking her head in disbelief. "*Think*. I couldn't talk to you at the funeral, not with CID there. Remember the white van? No doubt, they've got a video of everyone there. I only hope I spotted them before they spotted me."

"But," Jillie protested weakly, "those were just the funeral guys."

Dawn snorted her derision. "Sure they were. And the two CID cops sitting in a car all night round the corner are birdwatchers, and the people in the vacant house across from Chris's are just homeless yobbos found themselves a nice squat. That woman reading Proust in the British Library? She's there to improve her mind. Funny how she never turns any pages, or didn't you notice that, either?" She sipped her tea. "Convenient, that nice policeman bumping into you at the funeral? Not a bad-looking bloke. Has he gotten round to giving you one yet?"

Jillie stood up, angry. "You are so totally out of line—"

Dawn held up her hands in capitulation. "I apologize. Sit down, please."

Reluctantly, Jillie did. "Maybe they were watching for you," she said recklessly. "For all I know, you're an IRA terrorist—"

The woman's mouth narrowed. "Now *you're* bloody out of line."

Jillie flushed. "Sorry."

"Then we're even. So now he's got all he wants out of the house. Including you. But he hasn't ridden off into the sunset yet, has he?" The dark-haired women smirked knowingly as Jillie said nothing. But her smile quickly faded.

"I loved Chris, more than I've ever loved anyone. She was a woman it was hard not to love even when you knew it would end in disaster." Dawn's voice cracked and she inhaled before she could go on. "But she'd never accepted her sexuality. All those causes she fought for, went to *jail* for? She never once went to a Gay and Lesbian Pride parade, never marched with Act-Up against AIDS, wanted nothing to do with gay rights. If people thought she was promiscuous, fine. But never gay.

"Half the time we were together, she'd be out screwing men right, left, and center, trying to prove something to herself humping the sort of bastards she shouldn't have been mucking about with. When I couldn't take any more of it, I left. It didn't matter how much I loved her, I couldn't live with her craziness."

Jillie didn't want to be listening to this, feeling like everything she had ever believed about Chris had been a lie. The woman she mourned had never existed.

"If you loved her, and if you're not a . . . you know . . . why were you sneaking around at her funeral?"

Dawn Tolver sat back, glancing out the window as if making sure no one was peering in. "Chris got herself involved with some pretty nasty people, and now she's dead," she said bitterly. "I'd rather neither they nor the police came looking for me."

"You said you know who killed her."

Dawn snorted her disbelief. "I never said she was killed. But if you're smart, sweetie, you'll leave it alone."

"I'm not going to do that."

The darker woman gnawed her lip pensively. "All right, it's your neck. I'll give you some names, in return for your promise. You must swear you'll never tell the police *anything* about me. Not one word."

"But I can't just—" As the woman rose, Jillie blurted, "Okay! I promise!"

After a moment, Dawn Tolver settled back. "Talk to Richard Atherton at the Windsor Archives."

"Why? Who is he?"

"Tell him you're interested in Hannah Lightfoot."

"Lightfoot . . ." Jillie struggled with the slippery memory, an absurd juxtaposition of a folk song running through her head, "The Wreck of the Edmund Fitzgerald" . . . Then it came to her. "Hannah Lightfoot, the fair Quakeress. The woman George the Third was supposedly married to before he married Charlotte?"

"That's the one."

"And she's what Chris was working on?"

"Mmm-hmm. If he gets too snarky, just mention you're a friend of Vicky's."

"Who's Vicky?"

Dawn picked heat-swollen raisins out of the crumbled remains of her scone. "Ring 'Dungeon.' D-U-N-G-E-O-N. Ask for the Dragon Queen. But don't bother her unless Richard is being uncooperative. Victoria can be rather . . . temperamental."

Jillie was puzzled. "So where does Dr. Reece Wycombe fit into all this?"

"Wycombe? He doesn't."

"But . . . he broke into our bed and breakfast in Leeds!"

"Reece Wycombe may be a thief as well as an unimaginative, backstabbing prick, but I'd be surprised he did his own break-in job. He'd have to be desperate."

"Desperate enough to kill her?"

"Him? Not likely." Dawn snorted her disdain. "Look, Chris was well in over her head. And I'm not talking about Charter Eighty-eight, or spiteful academics or even the sort who scrawl Ay-Oh on the walls. The kind of animals I'm talking about are far more dangerous because they wear better disguises. Chris's mistake was to think she could outcamouflage *them*." Dawn sighed. "If I were your friend, I'd tell you to just let it go. It won't bring Chris back and you'll only be causing trouble for yourself. It's not worth it, not for you, not for anybody."

"But you're *not* my friend."

"True. I'm not. Neither are the police." Dawn glanced at her watch. "And that's all I'm going to say. Except . . ." She stood and slung her purse over her shoulder. "A word of advice: don't trust that lovely policeman of yours too far."

The Kentish Town Station's gymnasium could have been anywhere, anyplace, Keen thought as he lay on a slanted bench, hands clasped under his head. His heart beat hollowly, his breath hot acid. Sweat trickled down his sides as he considered whether or not he could get through another thirty curls. He loathed exercise, bullying his reluctant body with the same obstinacy with which he ate his muesli, and tried to take his mind off it by thinking of other things.

Phil had again vanished, off on his own. Keen didn't feel so much snubbed as ignored, peripheral to those busy with real police work. Lucky sod, wasn't he? All he had to do was hang about with a pretty lady all day.

But with Jillie Waltham buried up to her highbrow eyebrows in library books, he had precious little to do. He left a note on Phil's desk along with the photographs he'd found in the Swinton house to be copied, then made several futile phone calls trying to track down Marge Beecher. Wycombe's assistant lived in Cambridge during the academic term, and stayed at her parents' home in Richmond while they were on summer holiday. He left a message on her machine after listening to a woman's refined voice apologize for his inconvenience.

Then he sketched a rough outline of Chris's pendant before faxing it to Leeds with a note to check local pawnbrokers.

After that, Keen hadn't much else to occupy his time. To please Jillie, he'd plodded through John Clarke's *The Life and Times of George the Third* and William Massey's *History of England During the Reign of George III* with grim determination, his eyes glazing over within minutes. Except for a tactless statement the mad king had made ("A very ugly county, Yorkshire, Mr. Stanhope!"), Keen found it excruciatingly boring. He'd decided he loathed working out only marginally less than he loathed eighteenth-century British dynastic history.

He started another set of repetitions, eyes shut as he concentrated on the sounds around him: snatches of conversation, young laughter echoing, the squeak of athletic shoes. The smell of sweat and chlorine steam undercut the eucalyptus tang. Any gym in any police station in the country had the same smudged mirrors, the same fluorescent lighting, exercise machines scattered like museum exhibits of a medieval torture chamber, worn carpeting inevitably the color of snot. Where you could spend as much time and agony as you pleased grinding through push-downs and leg curls and lifting weights and where it didn't matter what waited for you on the outside.

Twenty-nine, thirty. Christ.

His body screamed reproachfully. He had another two machines to get through, but as he lay quivering with muscle fatigue, eyes still closed, he let his imagination try to make the leap. For a moment, he could almost envision he was in Leeds, believe himself in his own nick's gym. He was rudely jerked out of this pleasant fantasy by Phil's too-loud voice next to him.

"You know how they practice safe sex up in Yorkshire?"

He didn't open his eyes, refusing to respond.

"Mark all the sheep that kick."

Keen sighed tiredly. "What do you want?" His eyes flew open as the orange envelope of photographs slapped onto his chest. In street clothes, Phil sat on the bench opposite inspecting Keen clad in shorts and tank top.

"Thanks for caring and sharing," Phil said, amused.

Keen made no effort to sit up. "That it?"

"Got a report back on her computer, if you're interested."

Phil waited, making him ask for it. "I'm interested," Keen said grimly.

"Her hard disk was overwritten. Not erased, since anyone with even basic computer skills could *un*erase memory resident files. The file names are all there, and interesting titles they are, too. I'd have particularly liked to know what was in one marked 'Blakmale.' Unfortunately, all that's on it is about eighty megabytes of the Greater London Metropolitan telephone directory, over and over." Phil's smile broadened. "You can buy the software for thirty quid on Tottenham Court Road."

"Why would she have done that?"

"Doesn't seem she did. Fingerprints on the keyboard weren't Swinton's. Don't know whose yet."

"Huh." He wiped the sweat from his forehead.

"Lucky for some," Phil said, eyeing him with his ever-present sly grin. "Coo, I'd love being paid to keep my pecs in shape for a ladyfriend. Much overtime in it?"

Keen sat up and grabbed his towel. "Pack it in, Reaves," he snapped, then mentally kicked himself for letting his irritation show. The hell with the rest of his workout, he decided, and headed for the locker room. Phil strolled after him.

"If you're finished up here, don't take too long in the shower." Keen paused by the locker room door and eyed him distrustfully. "Darryl Guiscoigne finally answered his telephone, if you have a spare moment."

When Darryl Guiscoigne answered the knock at the small brownstone home he had shared with his mother, Keen caught Reaves's expression a split second before he saw the man standing in the doorway and instantly understood why the first interview had been so perfunctory. No one spoke in that tense, awkward moment.

"We're sorry to trouble you again, Mr. Guiscoigne," Phil said as he opened his warrant card. His fingers stiffened around it as Guiscoigne leaned closer as if he were about to take it from him. "We'd like to ask you a few more questions about your mother's death. Won't take long."

The skull perched on the man's bony frame smiled thinly, the expression grotesque. "Certainly," he said, his voice hoarse but soft. "Please, come in." His smile turned to a grimace of pain as he opened the door wider. He was dressed only in a bathrobe, blackened splotches covered the lead-white skin of his exposed calves, laceless trainers loose on his swollen feet. They followed as he shuffled down the hallway to a small lounge overlooking a postage-stamp-sized garden. The double doors were open, birdsong and the scent of flowers drifting into the room, brazenly alive, the fresh air not enough to erase the smell of sickness permeating the house.

Darryl Guiscoigne held on tightly to the back of a rocking chair and motioned them toward a sofa. "Make yourself at home." He slowly levered his
wasted body into the pillows and crocheted afghan swaddled in the chair.
Keen and Phil sat down on the sofa, the worn cushions too soft, and waited as
the skeletal man fussed with his pillows, even this effort seeming nearly beyond his strength.

As a policeman, Keen had done his share of the hardest duty, notifying
mothers of the death of their children, husbands their wives. But it was different to stare mortality in the face, to see death written on a living human being
and be impotent with the fear of it yourself.

Once settled, Guiscoigne cradled a stoneware mug in hands as fragile as spider's legs. "Would you gentlemen care for tea?" he offered knowingly. "Kettle's still hot. I'd make it for you, but I don't have much energy these days." He
waved toward the kitchen, the effeminate gesture a hideous parody.

Keen heard Reaves audibly swallow. "No bother," Reaves said. "We won't
take up much of your time, Mr. Guiscoigne." His normally good-humored
voice was strained.

"Oh, deary me." Guiscoigne cocked his head, the sunken eyes glittering.
"Whatever happened to the friendly neighborhood bobby always up for a
cuppa and a chat? It's all so impersonal now, no one visits a moment longer
than absolutely necessary." He spoke with an effete lisp that made no attempt
to hide the rage smoldering beneath.

Phil hid his reaction by making a production of readying his notebook before he cleared his throat. "Mr. Guiscoigne, you've lived with your mother for
how long?"

"Ever since I got too sick to take care of myself," he answered, all trace of
his supercilious affectation vanished. "I lost my job the day my boss found out
I was HIV positive, even though I was still healthy enough to work. Couldn't
find another, *quelle surprise,* and the dole wasn't enough so I lost my flat as well.
I moved back in to me old bedroom upstairs." He indicated it with his eyes.
"But when I couldn't manage the stairs, I ended up stuck down here. The
NHS doesn't consider me sick enough to hospitalize, and I don't qualify for
home care. But *someone* had to bathe me and help me change my clothes, get
me in and out of bed, mop up the vomit and clean my arse when I shit meself.
Well, what else are mothers for?"

They sat in silence for several long moments, Keen acutely aware of Phil's
uneasiness and Guiscoigne's furious satisfaction.

"I sympathize with your . . . unfortunate situation, Mr. Guiscoigne," Phil
struggled, "but could you be more specific about the dates?"

"Which ones?" Guiscoigne snapped. "The date I got AIDS, the date I lost
my flat and moved in with me mum, or the date she had to carry me down the
stairs by herself on her arthritic back?"

It wasn't just because the witness had AIDS which had made the first interview so short, Keen understood. Guiscoigne was not interested in the inquiry

into his mother's death, far too wrapped up in his own. He met the man's bloodshot stare evenly as Phil studied his notebook.

"I know what you're thinking," Guiscoigne sneered. Keen raised an eyebrow. " 'Poor silly bugger. Stuck it up the wrong bunghole and look where it's got him. But then, he shoulda known better,' right?"

"That's interesting," Keen said mildly. "I weren't aware having AIDS also made you psychic."

Guiscoigne laughed harshly, covering Phil's sharp inhale. "I don't have to be psychic to read it on your face, I see it every day."

"Uh-huh." Keen slid a few inches down on the sofa and stretched out his legs. "If you *were* psychic, Mr. Guiscoigne, what you would have read was me wondering how you cope on your own now that your mum isn't here to take care of you."

Guiscoigne stared at him for a long, suspicious moment. "Not well," he admitted. "Mostly I depend upon the kindness of strangers, those who aren't terrified shitless breathing the same air as me." The hostility was more subdued, as if it took too much energy for him to sustain. "I moved in two years ago. It only got bad about eight months back, Mum found me collapsed on the stairs and dragged me here by herself." He smiled bitterly, accentuating his death's-head features. "I'm six one, she was five foot three, this tiny woman, and I was so wasted she could still pick me up and carry me from here to bed like a child."

"She had health problems herself, I believe," Keen said. Phil leaned back, more than willing to let him take over the interview.

"Diabetes. We used to joke about it, so much medication in this house we could set up our own chemist shop. But she'd had it since she was twenty, never slowed her down. She watched her weight, no salt, no alcohol. She never even bothered with one of those medical alert bracelets, thought they were ugly. You could sit right next to her in a restaurant and she'd take out her kit, give herself an insulin injection, and have it put away before you'd suspected a thing. It was all very matter-of-fact with her."

"She was found at Kensington Palace." Guiscoigne's expression didn't change, no twinge of pain or grief. "Would you know why she'd gone out there?"

"I haven't no idea, except maybe she needed some time away from *this*."

Keen heard the man's guilt that he was to blame for his mother's death fueling his anger. If his illness hadn't created such a burden on her, she wouldn't have gone to Kensington that day, not fallen into a diabetic coma as people passed by her, tutting their distaste at another homeless bag lady sleeping it off in a park. Until the security guard tried to roust her when it was far too late to have saved her. His AIDS had killed them both.

"The day she died, did she tell you she were leaving for a while?"

Guiscoigne nodded dully. "But not for pissing about in a park. She always said she had her own garden if she wanted to stop and smell the roses. She'd gone out shopping, pick up my medication . . ." He leaned his head back, exhausted, the chair rocking as his eyes closed wearily. "Then some mince from the butchers for lasagna. Mum knew it's me favorite, lasagna is, and with my appetite . . ." His voice trailed off.

"How long was she gone before you started to worry?"

When Guiscoigne didn't answer, Keen realized he had fallen asleep. He exchanged a glance with Phil.

"Bloody hell. *Now* what?" the younger man asked.

"Now we wait."

After a moment's indecision, Phil set his notebook aside and sorted incuriously through a pile of magazines. When Phil offered him a year-old *Vanity Fair*, Keen shook his head, content to sit and observe the room and its occupant.

This was woman's territory, utterly feminine: the brass lamps with Art Deco stained-glass shades, walnut end tables laden with sentimental bric-a-brac collected from years of seaside holidays, 1930s mantel clock and sun-faded chintz curtains, a crocheted doily protecting the back of the armchair or, perhaps too late, hiding an oily stain from too many scalps. Even had he been healthy, Guiscoigne looked startlingly out of place in his mother's house, regardless of his sexual orientation.

Phil eyed the dozing man reproachfully, then opened a *House Beautiful* to glower at an article on "Exciting French Cottage-Style Makeovers for Spring."

Asleep, Guiscoigne's expression was as unguarded as a child's, and as frightening as a corpse's. Without his waking anger to animate him, he was so ravaged it seemed a callous miracle his body could still be breathing, his cheeks sunken so deeply Keen could almost make out where the jaw inserted into the skull.

Guiscoigne's eyes fluttered open. He stared at the two men as if uncertain whether he was still dreaming or not, fearful and disoriented. Then he remembered.

"Sorry," he said, the cunning smile returning. He flicked a glance at the clock. "I tend to nod off at inconvenient moments. Hope I didn't keep you gentlemen waiting long."

"No, but if you don't mind—" Keen stood up. "I'd fancy that cup of tea now. Yours must be stone-cold, and you look as you could do with a warmup." Guiscoigne looked startled but made no comment as Keen took the mug from his hands. "Phil?"

"Uh . . . none for me, thanks."

The quick look Keen exchanged with Guiscoigne was one of shared gallows humor. It was only another version of the timeworn good cop, bad cop routine, but still effective enough.

The kitchen wasn't dirty, simply untidy. Boxes and tins littered the worktop as if Guiscoigne had simply lacked the energy to lift them back into the cupboard, dirty dishes stacked neatly but neglected in the sink. Keen filled the kettle and washed out a mug. No one had spoken a word in the lounge when the kettle whistled. He steeped the tea in a dainty china pot before pouring two mugs and carried them back out.

When he returned, Phil stood examining photographs crowding the false mantelpiece over a two-bar electric fire. Guiscoigne watched Phil's back with amusement and contempt. As Keen handed him his refilled mug, his fingers brushed against Guiscoigne's. The man's dry skin was ice-cold. He held the mug until Guiscoigne had gotten a steady grip, ignoring the irrational frisson down his spine.

"Did you or your mother know a man named Daniel Barrow?" Keen asked. "A young plumber, lived in Surrey with a girl named Josie Bunts. She works at a Boots in the Farnham town center."

"Sorry. Don't think either of us knew anyone in Surrey." Guiscoigne sipped his tea and smiled as Phil picked up one of the photographs for a closer look.

"You didn't have any plumbing problems your mother might have called a repairman for?"

Guiscoigne's sardonic look returned. "I have *plenty* of plumbing problems, but I believe you're referring to the house? No, not since I've been here, anyway."

"Did you know a John Wortley?"

"No. Look, I've been over this before. Mum didn't socialize much, and not many dropped in to visit." He recited it impatiently to make it clear he was repeating himself. "The only people she saw on a regular basis were John Tees, her doctor, and Mr. Brooks, the chemist."

"Did your mother ever attend any community groups, Neighborhood Watch, anything like that?"

"Uh-uh." Guiscoigne's interest was still focused on Phil.

"Are you or any of your family Masons?"

"No." This with a scowl of irritation.

"Were either of you actively involved with something called Charter Eighty-eight?"

He got Guiscoigne's attention again, but the man's expression was more curiosity than recognition. "We haven't been *active* in anything recently. Mum played bridge with a group up until about two, three months ago, and I did a couple of marches with Act-Up summer last year, back when I could still walk."

"Did you know a woman named Christine Swinton?"

"Nope." Nor did he care, his tone implied. His eyes shifted back to Phil inspecting the gilt-framed photographs.

"Mr. Guiscoigne, did your mother carry on any correspondence on a regular basis?"

"She wrote letters." Guiscoigne nodded to a rolltop desk, closed and covered with a fine glimmer of dust. "I didn't pay much attention, not too interested in old lady's gossip about the neighbors. That's where she kept it, if you want a look. The first two coppers out here've already gone through it all, don't know what you're expecting to find."

Keen set down his mug and crossed to the desk. It was unlocked. Drawers overflowed with old bills and scented stationery, empty envelopes used for scratch paper covered with hasty notations. Keen sorted them methodically, examining return addresses, checking bank statements, keeping his mind open and not looking for anything specific.

Behind him, Phil asked, "This your Norton?"

"Mm-hm," Guiscoigne acknowledged. "Nineteen fifty-five, five ninety-six cc, everything original. Bought that when I was sixteen, took two years to restore."

"Lovely motorbike."

"That she was. One next to it, yeah, that one, seventy-six Triumph Trident one-sixty. Engine's a Les Williams. That's me standing next to it, the fat git with the stupid grin."

Keen examined the feminine old-school handwriting on the back of an empty envelope Alice Guiscoigne had used to list times and dates, long passed, for a church jumble sale collection.

"Mmm." Phil picked up another photo. "Harley Arien Ness special, isn't it?"

"Yeah. Not mine, though, much as I panted after it. That's what I did, mechanic. Restoring classic motorbikes, before . . . this."

Keen was about to discard another envelope with a reminder to call her optometrist when he turned it over. He stared at the return address neatly embossed in blue in the left-hand corner, then double-checked he hadn't missed the contents by mistake. The envelope was empty. The postmark was in late November of last year.

"Excuse me, Mr. Guiscoigne?" he said. "Did your mother have a solicitor?"

Resentful of being distracted from his motorbikes, Guiscoigne said shortly, "She might have done, but I wouldn't have no idea who."

Keen looked back at the embossed address. "Did the name Felix Schaefer ever come up? Of Schaefer, Burgess, and Lowenthal?"

At Schaefer's name, Phil turned with the framed photograph still in his hands.

"No."

Keen held up the empty envelope. "You wouldn't remember what was in this envelope then, by any chance?"

Guiscoigne's eyes barely flickered toward it. "No. We didn't discuss anything legal and I never asked." He looked up at Keen, his smile malevolent. "She might have been worried about her will, but I don't think it matters much now. Do you?"

"You were her only heir, then?"

Guiscoigne's expression hardened as he snorted in disgust. "*Heir*. Right. I confess, Officer. Y'got me. I bumped the old lady off so I could abscond to Costa del Sol with her millions."

"I'm more concerned with someone who might have tried to take advantage of the situation. There's any number of reasons she might want to see a solicitor."

"If she did, she didn't discuss it with me. It was hard enough on her as it was." He blinked rapidly, as if fighting tears. "I miss her, but in a way I'm glad she did go before me. Parents shouldn't have to watch their children die. It's obscene." The last was a whisper. He glanced at the clock. "If you're almost finished here, I'm expecting company. Excuse me if I don't see you to the door, but one trip a day is my limit."

"May we keep this?" Keen held up the envelope.

Guiscoigne shrugged. "Take the lot. What do I care?"

Keen nodded and picked up both his mug and Guiscoigne's. "If you'd like, I could do the washing-up in there for you before we go."

Both he and Phil stared at him in surprise. "What's all this," Guiscoigne said distrustfully, "part of the new police and community relations?"

Keen smiled. "Might say that. We are public servants, aren't we?"

Guiscoigne snickered, but didn't seem as hostile. "Much as I'd enjoy seeing that, leave it. Bonnie'll be by soon, she looks after me. She's from GLASS, the Gay and Lesbian AIDS Support Society. Might not like to find herself competing for my affections with a good-looking copper, she's the jealous type."

Phil replaced the photograph on the mantelpiece before handing Guiscoigne his card. He flushed when the man gingerly took it as if Phil had some loathsome disease that might have contaminated the card. "If you do think of anything else," Phil said stiffly, ignoring Guiscoigne's spiteful grin, "give us a ring."

"Oh, thertainly, Offither."

They were halfway down the hall when Guiscoigne called out, "I'm not gay, you know." When they turned back, he glared bitterly at Phil. "That Norton you were admiring? I was on it when a drink driver come out of a roundabout straight into me. Bike was a total loss. I spent three weeks in hospital. Had to have seven pints of blood during the surgery. One of them was past its sell-by date. But you get AIDS and people *assume*. Do you have any idea what it's like, having to ring every girlfriend you ever had? They never believe you, and they're scared and pissed at you. All your mates start giving you funny looks, those who aren't as quick to drop you as the rest."

Guiscoigne shook his head, frowning. "That's the thing that got to me, the friends I thought I could count on. Never come by anymore. And all those people I'd spent a lifetime thinking were disgustin', make me sick just to imagine one of *them* ever laying their dirty hands on me? Them's the ones who're here every day to make sure I'm still alive, see that I eat properly, get the doctor out when I need one, run me errands and clean the house. Helped me to bury my mother."

Neither Phil nor Keen responded. Guiscoigne's despairing anger was still palpable but he seemed desperate for them to understand.

"You spend your whole life believing you know right from wrong, then find it all turned on its head. What a laugh, innit? Finding out what's really important in life just when you're about to lose it."

Keen exchanged a look with Phil, but there wasn't anything much to say. "I'm sorry, Mr. Guiscoigne."

For a long moment, the dying man stared bleakly, then his mocking smile crept back. "Right. We're *all* sorry, mate."

They let themselves out, closing the door softly. Phil exhaled in relief. "I should know better, my wife's a nurse. But I can't help it, that gave me the shudders."

Keen nodded. "Why don't we try to find out if Mr. Schaefer ever did any legal work for Daniel Barrow or John Wortley."

A lime-green Lada pulled up to the pavement and a young woman climbed out. Her short leather skirt hugged her hips and slender waist, her blouse unbuttoned far enough to reveal freckles on her ample cleavage. Dark, angry eyes flashed at them as she brushed back a mane of permed bleached hair.

"Who the hell are you?" she demanded, and glanced toward the house in alarm. "Is anything wrong?"

"You must be Bonnie," Keen said. "We were just visiting. Not to worry, he's fine."

"He's anything *but* fine," she snapped, before she marched toward the Guiscoigne house and let herself in with her own key. Both he and Phil waited until she had slammed the door behind her.

"*She's* a lesbian?" Phil murmured. "Sweet Lord, what a waste."

"Not to her girlfriend, I'd expect."

Phil glanced at him dubiously, but Keen kept a straight face.

Jillie nursed a pint of cider in a pub a few streets from the British Library as she studied her meager notes on Hannah Lightfoot.

" 'Although George had a long-term romance with a beautiful Quaker girl named Hannah Lightfoot, the daughter of a modest Wapping shoemaker, no reliable proof exists that he married her . . .' " She skimmed down the page quickly. " 'Sir Joshua Reynolds painted a portrait of Hannah around 1756, which now belongs to the Sackville family at Knole in Kent . . . George the Third supported the Quaker 'persuasion' throughout his life, once even claiming he would have become a Quaker had it not been for his coronation oath binding him to the Church of England . . .' "

Blah, blah, blah. Precious little to go on, Jillie thought. She drained her glass and made up her mind. She found a pay phone at the back of the pub and flipped through her notebook for the number she'd jotted down. The glass door gave her scant privacy as she arranged her collection of twenty-pence coins on the shelf.

"Richard Atherton, please," she said firmly.

After several reconnections through other extension lines, a man's voice said, "Richard Atherton, may I help you?"

"Hello," Jillie said, trying to sound both confident and professional. "My name is Dr. Gillian Waltham from Cascade Pacific University. I'm in London for a few weeks and hoping you can help me with some research."

"This is in regard to?" he asked in a vaguely puzzled tone.

"I'm researching eighteenth-century English books and I've been told the Windsor Archives has a collection of fine bookbindings. Would it be possible to make an appointment and visit the archives?" She had decided on this lie as the safest bet to induce Atherton to see her. "I'm particularly looking for information on a bookbinder named William Edwards, from Yorkshire."

There was a pause before he said with a polite aloofness, "I'm part of the administration staff, not a librarian, so I don't think I can be of much help to you in that matter. In any case, the Royal Library is not open to members of the public."

"But you do allow scholars access to the archives, don't you?" Her heart was rapidly sinking.

"Of course, but I'm afraid no one is allowed into the library without a security check, which would take longer than a few weeks." Jillie blinked in surprise. Since when were libraries and books considered dangerous secrets? Now she knew what Chris had meant. "However, it's unlikely the archives have anything that isn't public record elsewhere. May I ask how you got my name, Dr. . . . ?"

"Waltham. You knew a colleague of mine, Dr. Christine Swinton."

The line went so quiet she thought they'd been disconnected. Then he said frostily, "No, I don't believe so. I'm afraid I can't help you—"

"Then you might know someone else, a lady named Vicky?" Jillie blurted hastily.

When he spoke again, his voice had altered, hollow as if he had cupped the phone to speak very quietly into it. "I don't wish to speak to you, Dr. Waltham," Atherton said, his voice quivering, fear behind the cold hostility. "If you bother me again, I shall be forced to ring my solicitors." He hung up, leaving her shaking as well.

She drank another cider for courage before she could dial the phone again. This time, when she punched out D-U-N-G-E-O-N, she got a recording informing her that the number was in error. She tried a different area code, and a young woman's voice answered cheerfully, "Dungeons and dragons." She wondered if that was the name of a pub.

"Could I speak to Victoria, please?"

"Who?"

"Uh, the Dragon Queen?"

On the other end, the woman shouted, "Oi, Vic! They's some flippin' Yank bint wantin' a wuhd wit' you!"

The offices of Schaefer, Burgess, and Lowenthal were near the prestigious St. James's Park, but closer to Picadilly than Whitehall. Felix Schaefer was due in court, he made it clear, and his time was valuable.

He leaned back, hands clasped together with the tips of both forefingers brushing his chin as he observed the two policemen with an air of amusement.

"Just a few questions, Mr. Schaefer. It won't take long," Phil said amiably. Content to have let Keen handle Guiscoigne's interview, Phil was reestablishing his authority. "We understand you were retained by a Mrs. Alice Guiscoigne this November last. Could you tell us what it was in regard to?"

"No."

Phil leaned forward as if he hadn't heard clearly. "Excuse me?"

"I said no. I can't tell you anything about Alice Guiscoigne." The solicitor smiled, clearly enjoying himself.

"Why would that be?"

"Client confidentiality. I'm sure you two gentlemen understand."

"But she *was* your client."

Schaefer crossed one thin leg over the other, and picked at invisible lint on the trouser fabric. "I'm not at liberty to tell you that, either."

"You handled the will for Christine Swinton," Keen put in, "in which she provided fifty thousand pounds to Karen Waltham, isn't that correct?"

"It's none of your business."

"Then could you tell us about the work you handled for Mr. Daniel Barrow or Mr. John Wortley?" Phil said. If he had hoped to surprise the solicitor into revealing anything, he failed miserably.

Schaefer's grin widened. "Nope."

"Mr. Schaefer," Phil said patiently, "we know Mrs. Guiscoigne received a letter from your offices around the twenty-second of November last year. Would you mind telling us what was in that letter?"

"Yes, I'd mind."

"Why is that, Mr. Schaefer?"

"Because I don't have to."

Phil exchanged a glance with Keen, unfazed. "That is correct, Mr. Schaefer, you don't. But we could get a warrant to search your files, if you'd prefer."

"Oh, come now, Detective," Schaefer replied. "We both know for you to get a warrant, you'd have to convince a magistrate you have reasonable grounds to believe a serious arrestable offense has been committed. As far as I'm aware, no one in our offices is under any investigation for a serious arrestable offense, nor are any of our clients." His mocking grin exposed a gleam of gold. "Moreover, you'd have to specify exactly what material you were looking for on said warrant which would be of substantial value as relative evidence supporting any inquiries on the aforementioned, nonexistent offense. Material, I hasten to point out, which is protected by legal privilege between any person and his legal advisor and therefore confidential."

He examined a Rolex on his bony wrist. "Now, having given you free counsel for which I generally charge by the minute, I am a busy man. You'll excuse me?"

"Mr. Schaefer," Phil said reproachfully, "I'm sure a man of the law such as yourself would want to cooperate with the police in what is, after all, our common interest." Phil's sarcasm matched Schaefer's own. "Surely you can see the liabilities of creating such a negative rapport?"

"You are referring, I suppose, to a possible deluge of parking summonses and being stopped every day for faulty lights or Breathalysers until I agree to 'help the police with their inquiries'? Tactics that will inevitably result in my protesting such harassment to the Police Complaints Authority? I think not."

He stood, gathering several microcassettes from his desk with one hand and picking up a briefcase with the other. "If that's all, good day, gentlemen," he said, and walked out into the foyer.

"Reschedule my two o'clock tomorrow to ten next Tuesday," Schaefer ordered his receptionist brusquely as they followed him out.

"Yes, Mr. Schaefer."

"Tell Lowenthal I won't be back until after four on Monday."

"Yes, Mr. Schaefer."

"And get rid of that decaffeinated crap, Helaine. If we're out of decent coffee, pick some up at Marks and Spencer on your lunch."

"Yes, Mr. Schaefer."

He slung the microcassettes onto her desk. She scrambled to catch them, but a few escaped, dropping onto the plush carpet by her feet.

"Have these transcribed and on my desk by the time I'm back from court."

"Yes, Mr. Schaefer," she said, her voice muffled as she retrieved the cassettes under her desk. He walked out without another glance or word, the glass Art Deco door wheezing shut behind him. Her face flushed with humiliation, she stacked the cassettes into a neat little pile.

"You know why solicitors wear their collars so tight, don't you?" Phil said and flashed Keen a quick grin. "It's to keep their foreskins from rolling up over the top of their heads."

It was the first time any of Phil's jokes had made him chuckle. He also mentally filed away Helaine's strangled laughter for future reference.

They walked down the stairs, enjoying the cool air-conditioning while they could. "Cor, fifty thousand quid? You didn't mention that. Tell you what; you keep the mother, I'll take the daughter." He sighed theatrically. "I think I've accumulated enough paperwork to keep me busy the rest of the afternoon. You want me to drop you anywhere?"

"Think I might get in a bit of shopping. Mind dropping me at Marks and Spencer on your way?"

Phil glanced at him wryly. "And what, pray tell, would you be wanting at Marks and Spencer?"

"Coffee. And none of that decaffeinated crap, either."

"I love it when you talk dirty," Phil said.

Outside, the interior of Phil's car felt like an oven. His mobile phone sang the theme from *The X-Files* as they got in, the leather car seat searing through their trousers. He rolled down the window before he answered it. "Reaves. Uh-huh. Uh-huh." He glanced at Keen. "Uh-huh. No, don't think so. Just do your best, then. Ta."

He put the phone back in his pocket. "Seems your girlfriend's gone walkies."

At four-thirty, Keen loitered across the street from the offices of Schaefer, Burgess, and Lowenthal with a package tucked under one arm. Keen Dunliffe was a patient man, still waiting at five o'clock. At twenty past, Helaine emerged. She looked tired. Her hair was clipped back and she wore sturdy trainers not matching her smart office suit, her pumps no doubt tucked away in the large bag on her shoulder. She turned right, walking at a pace suggesting she had begun a long hike home.

He pushed off the wall and crossed the road, dodging cars. "Helaine?" he called out.

She whirled around, walking backward warily as she shielded her eyes. Then she recognized him and smiled. "Hello. Did you forget something?"

"Remembered, actually." He held up the package. She glanced at it curiously, but didn't take it. "Fresh ground coffee from Marks and Sparks, chockfull of caffeine."

Her smile widened, knowingly. "That's very kind of you, but I couldn't possibly accept it."

Shrugging regretfully, he continued to hold it out. "It'll just go to waste then. Too fancy for the likes of me. I prefer my coffee weak, burnt, and out of a machine."

She laughed, her eyes twinkling with a wickedness he liked. "What do you want?" But still she didn't take the coffee.

"You have time for a drink and a chat?"

"My boyfriend's expecting me . . ."

"There's a pub on the corner. Surely he won't mind you having a cold drink in this heat?"

Pretending reluctance, she let him steer her into the cool pub and buy her a half pint of bitter. She ignored the coffee package on the table as he set the glasses down. "This isn't a free beer, now, is it?"

"It is if you want it to be."

Candy-pink lips twisted with mocking humor. "Everything that goes on in our offices is supposed to remain privileged information, Mr. . . . ?"

"Dunliffe. But call me Keen."

"Hm." She sipped her beer. "I could lose my job if my bosses knew I'd even been speaking to the police."

"Then don't tell them. And anything you do talk to me about will be treated with absolute confidentiality."

Her look told him she didn't believe him. "Just hypothetically, what are you interested in talking about?"

"Hypothetically, then, I wouldn't be interested in anything Mr. Burgess or Mr. Lowenthal are working on."

"Just Mr. Schaefer." It was a statement, not a question. "And what would you want to know about him? Again, hypothetically?"

"I'd like to know what you think of him."

Caught off guard, she laughed. "I think he's a prize jackass. He's a good enough solicitor, but he's not a nice human being."

"So why do you work for him?"

"I work for Schaefer, Burgess, and Lowenthal. It's only Mr. Schaefer who's the ruddy bastard." She shrugged.

"You're the only secretary for all three, then?"

"Oh, yes. And receptionist, clerk, and general dogsbody. I've had a couple of years of prelegal, as well." He heard the wistful resentment.

"Mr. Schaefer doesn't much appreciate you, does he?"

"No, not much."

"So you wouldn't be that involved in his cases?"

"I know *everything* that goes on in that office, Mr. Dunliffe. He may treat me like dirt, but that doesn't mean he doesn't need me."

"Then you'd know what he'd worked on for Christine Swinton and Alice Guiscoigne, wouldn't you? Or Daniel Barrow and John Wortley?"

She sipped her bitter, eyeing him over the rim. "Now we're getting into the not-so-hypothetical areas." He waited. Finally she said, "Sorry, it's not worth my job."

He wasn't surprised, and knew not to press. This wasn't like developing the usual informant, small-time criminals who could be turned with a bit of dosh slipped under the table. He handed her one of his cards, the Kentish Town nick's number on the back. "If you change your mind, you'll give me a ring?"

"I'll think about it," she said, and that gave him some encouragement. "Sorry you didn't get much for your beer."

"Keep the coffee," he said. "It's free, too."

Keen rang Jillie several times, receiving only Mrs. Flute's relentlessly cheerful response that, no, she hadn't returned yet. Alone, he felt a restlessness he didn't know how to alleviate. He nursed a single cup of tea in the canteen and watched the flux of officers, envying their easy companionship.

"Where've you been?" he demanded when he finally managed to reach Jillie, one finger in his ear to shut out the canteen noise.

"What do you mean, 'where've I been'? At the library," her voice snapped back. "Where do you think?"

He berated himself for his slip before he realized he'd nearly missed her lie. "Sorry, I'm tired and that came out wrong. I've been trying to reach you for over an hour. We were supposed to go for a curry, remember . . . ?"

"I'm sorry, I forgot." Her voice was distant. "I've already eaten."

He backed off carefully. "Doesn't matter. Now that I've reached you, did you find out anything interesting?"

She didn't answer for a moment. "Maybe. I'm not sure yet."

Her evasiveness didn't irritate him as much as it was so ineptly obvious. He was momentarily distracted by Bernie Pearson waving a sheet of paper as she spotted him on the pay phone. He waved back as she started toward him.

"Then let's talk about it over dinner tomorrow." He kept his voice casual, offhand. "I might see my way clear to something a bit more fancy. Something between McDonald's and the Ritz . . ." As he listened carefully to her awkward silence, he wondered what had happened.

But this time he wasn't surprised when she said yes.

Bernie reached him as he hung up. "You've got a message to ring your nick." She handed him the note with Nigel Mullard's name scribbled on it.

He turned his wince into a smile. "Thanks, love."

She returned it. "Pleasure."

But Mullard had booked off promptly at five, to Keen's relief, and he was happy to feed the coinbox while someone tracked down the message. Finally, he heard DI Roger Osborne's familiar voice. "Keen?"

"Lo, guv. You got any idea what Nigel were wanting with me?"

"Mm-hm." He heard Osborne shuffling papers. "You got a match on that print of yours. Uniroyals. Whoever stepped on that glass here is the same person stomping around down there."

"Brilliant. I need another favor. Could someone check with whoever's in charge of inventory at Harewood House? I'm looking for an antique book of drawings"—he checked the notes he had taken down while on the stairwell—"by Richard Dalton. It may have been sold in an estate sale in nineteen forty-seven, see if their records go back that far. If it were sold, find out who bought it." He listened to faint scratching over the telephone lines as Roger took down the information. "And if not, when were the last time anyone remembers seeing it."

"Speaking of Harewood," Roger said, "your friend there came up with the victim's handbag. A bit on the soggy side, but it's hers."

"Anything in it?"

"No wallet and no necklace, if that's what you're looking for."

"What about cannabis?"

"Huh," Roger said, surprised. "Funny you should mention that. We found traces; seeds and bits, but nothing in quantity. Were you expecting it?"

"Hoped, more like. You've made my evening, boss."

"Glad of it."

Bernie sat on the other side of the canteen reading a book, but smiled hospitably as he walked toward her with a fresh cup of coffee. "Mind if I join you?"

"It's a free country."

"Wherever did you get that idea?" he said as he slid into the chair across from her and nodded at her book. "What're you reading?"

"I'm doing an Open University course in applied criminology. You know, home study." She shrugged self-consciously, which told Keen quite a bit about how much ribbing she'd already endured from her colleagues. "They give you the books and videotapes, and the local tutorial group organizes night lectures." Bernie checked her watch, and drank the last of her tea. "Sorry to love you and leave you, but I've got to be at one in half an hour."

"What's tonight's subject, then?"

"Wine." She grinned. "It's a week-long seminar by an inspector for the Wine Standards Board on EC wine regulations in the wholesale trade."

"Bring me back some homework?"

"Red or white?"

He watched her go, a bit wistfully, before he had shepherd's pie for tea. By nine, he found himself back in his room in the station housing, in bed with Massey's *History of England* propped open on his stomach. Bored and staring out the window at the hypnotically blinking light of Canary Wharf, he let his mind drift.

The more he thought about it, the more he had to admit all this bother about academic rivalries or controversial mysteries around George the Third was total rubbish. But Keen couldn't help suspecting it was a useful smokescreen for something far more ordinary and malignant. He fell asleep a few minutes later, the neglected book slipping from his fingers to the floor.

IX

FRIDAY

Keen thought he might learn to like London after all, maybe just a little. For the first time in a week, he woke feeling rested. He showered and shaved, humming as he dressed. He combed his hair and checked his tie was on straight before he took the lift down and stepped out into dazzling sunshine, the morning air still cool.

Across the lot, Phil Reaves leaned against the wall, his face in the shadows, as Keen walked toward him. "Think we might be on to something," Keen said.

"Thrilled," Phil said, his voice unenthusiastic. Keen shaded eyes not yet adjusted enough to make out the younger man's expression.

"What's up?"

"Game's off. The job's been canceled."

"What?"

Phil pushed off the wall. "Case closed. The end. Roll the credits."

"Why?"

Phil shrugged. "I just work here, mate."

Keen shouldered past, heading for Galton's office. He knocked on the open door to gain the man's attention. Galton smiled up from his paperwork, exposing tobacco-stained teeth.

"Good morning, Mr. Dunliffe. What can I do for you?"

Aware of Phil in the doorway behind him, Keen said brusquely, "You could explain why the inquiry's been called off."

Galton looked as if he were enjoying himself as he shook out a cigarette and lit it. "The Swinton case has been ruled as death by misadventure. No further police inquiries are intended at the present time. You will be pleased to hear your assignment is no longer necessary, as I know how eager you are to return to Leeds."

Keen struggled to keep his anger from showing. "Sir, we've obtained evidence establishing a link between Christine Swinton and Alice Guiscoigne; they had the same solicitor, Felix Schaefer. He may also have represented Daniel Barrow and John Wortley—"

"Coincidence," Galton said dryly. "Unfortunately, being a lawyer isn't yet against the law."

Keen took the fax from his jacket pocket. "Secondly, tracks collected from Chris Swinton's residence match those taken from broken glass found at a break-in where she were staying in Leeds. They were both made by the same piece of tire cut out to use as a sole for a walking cast. Both marks were left by Dr. Reece Wycombe."

"Excellent detective work, Sergeant," Galton said without bothering to look at Keen's exhibits. "But if you want to charge him with breaking and entering, that's up to Leeds. As far as I'm aware, nothing was taken, so your attempted burglary is now down to simple criminal damage. It's a waste of time and money, Mr. Dunliffe."

"At least we can compare the fingerprints found on the woman's computer with those I collected at her flat—" Phil's embarrassed cough stopped him more than the dangerous glint in Galton's eyes.

"Allow me to save you the trouble. They're not your lame professor's. They belong to Celia Swinton. And you can congratulate yourself for that. You apparently gave her the impression you knew more than you did, and she came in quite contrite yesterday afternoon to confess all. She deeply regretted her sister-in-law's death, as she had hoped Chris Swinton would return alive and well, turn on her computer, and suffer a fatal heart attack when she saw what had been done to it."

"I don't understand—"

"Revenge, Sergeant. Swinton suspected her sister-in-law's frequent visits to her gynecologist were social rather than medical, the amniocentesis more to determine paternity than sex. Thus, the file marked 'blakmale.' Nice and tidy, wouldn't you agree?"

Galton leaned across the desk. "Christine Swinton died in an accident. She got drunk, she got druggy, she got drowned. The family isn't complaining and the case is *closed*. Go home. Goodbye."

"What does Mr. Scudder in Home Office have to say?" Keen demanded stubbornly. "Or Mr. McCraig?"

Galton chuckled, not with amusement. "Mr. Scudder has been . . . reassigned. His zeal overwhelmed his common sense and he exaggerated the facts to blow the Swinton death out of all proportion, causing a certain amount of embarrassment within the Home Office. Chief Superintendent McCraig has been a police officer long enough to know when and how to cut his losses. Do you?"

Keen pulled himself back with an effort. "Yes, sir."

"Good. Have a safe journey back, Sergeant."

It wasn't until he was out of the building and striding across the car park that Keen realized he had no idea where he was going. He stopped, fists clenched and his breathing ragged. Hearing steps, he turned to face Phil Reaves.

The younger man cocked his head, his teeth too white in the sun as he grinned. "I'm not sure I care for that look in your eye, pal."

"I don't bloody care what you like or don't like," Keen snapped. "This doesn't smell right."

Phil's sardonic smile widened. "Even if I agreed with you—which I don't, by the way—just exactly what do you plan on doing about it?"

"I don't know."

"Look, Dunliffe. You did a good job. Too bad that doing a good job around here is a lot like pissing in a wet suit. It gives you that lovely warm feeling, but nobody is ever going to take much notice. It's finished. Go back to Leeds and catch your sheep rustlers or slurry thieves or whatever the hell it is you do up there."

Keen's teeth ground, sick to death of Phil's hayseed ridicule. But his anger waned quickly; Phil's heart wasn't in it, the man looked genuinely unhappy as he dug a card from his wallet and scribbled a number on the back. "My home number. Next time you're in London, give me a ring. I'll have you round for drinks, meet the boss." Keen took the card. After a moment's hesitation he extended his hand. Phil shook it.

"Stay out of trouble, mate, eh?"

"Sure." Keen managed to smile. "Cheers."

The address Jillie had been given led her to a house in a maze of streets east of Chancery Lane. Security bars covered the windows on all three stories, their solidity not masked by the scroll-like motif. There was no name on the door as she knocked.

The spyhole darkened. Several heavy locks unlatched before a thin woman wrapped in a silk Chinese robe opened the door to look past the chain. At almost noon, her hair was a snarled mess and sleep-smeared mascara raccooned her eyes. "Yeah?"

"I'm Jillie Waltham, to see Victoria?"

"You that pr'fessor lady what rang? Jes' a minute . . ."

Raccoon Girl closed the door to slide the chain off and let her in. Inside the foyer, lackluster prints of country cottages hung on floral wallpapered walls, a drooping bouquet of tulips shed their petals onto a scallop-edged table. The tang of cheap perfume undercut the mustiness endemic to old houses. She followed Raccoon Girl down the hall to a sunny kitchen filled with the aroma of fresh toast and coffee. Rainbow shards of light sprayed the room through the beveled glass. It was all so cheerfully ordinary.

What wasn't so ordinary was the large woman hunched over a Formica table. Jet-black hair cascaded down an even more elaborate crepe de Chine robe than Raccoon Girl's, a huge embroidered dragon on red silk. Her elbows on the table, thick hands encrusted with heavy rings cupped around a steaming coffee mug, a bottle of whiskey next to it. Three-inch nails had been filed to sharp points and painted bloodred.

"Vic, it's that pr'fessor lady."

The woman grunted, her once sensuous mouth now hung thick and slack. Slowly, her toadlike bloodshot eyes opened to focus on Jillie blearily. Dark blue, they reminded Jillie of the heat-fractured marbles Karen had made as a child, startlingly vivid. "Excuse th' inconvenience, but would y'mind holding your arms out?"

Surprised, Jillie held out her hands like a child being inspected for clean fingernails. Victoria laughed, a cigarette-harshened chuckle. Jillie recoiled as Raccoon Girl roughly groped her body, pawing at her clothing. Gritting her teeth, she forced herself to submit to the search. Raccoon Girl squeezed both breasts but when she reached under Jillie's skirt, Jillie jerked away, resisting the urge to slap the woman's face.

"That's enough," she said sharply. Raccoon Girl grinned roguishly as she reached for Jillie's purse. She clamped it firmly under her arm as Raccoon Girl tugged at the strap.

"Sorry, luv, but we 'ave to be sure y'r not some police plant wif a wire," Victoria said, her hangover slurring the words. Her accent was identical to Raccoon Girl's, quite different from the one she had used on the phone the previous day.

Still trembling with anger, Jillie relinquished her purse. Raccoon Girl lifted it, preparing to dump the contents out onto the table.

"But if you don't treat the pr'fessor with more respect, Sanchez, I'll give you a thrashing you will *not* enjoy."

Raccoon Girl scowled, but rummaged through the contents before handing Jillie's purse back with exaggerated courtesy.

"Now then," Victoria said as she poured a large amount of whiskey into her coffee. "Jes' what the friggin' 'ell do you want wif us?"

"May I sit down?" Jillie's knees trembled.

"Please y'se'f." She sipped her coffee, eyes still shut.

"You were a friend of Christine Swinton's?"

"No."

Jillie blinked. "But you knew her, didn't you?"

"I know a lot of people I'm not friends with." The artificial regal tone Victoria had used on the phone was creeping back into her voice. "Sanchez, get the pr'fessor lady here a cuppa, will you?"

With ill grace, Sanchez poured a cup and banged it down on the table in front of Jillie with a glare. "Want i' livened up a bit?"

"Thanks, no. I take my coffee neat."

At that, the Dragon Queen coughed a hoarse laugh. "I like that." She nodded. "What were you wanting to know about Chris?"

"How did you know her?"

Victoria exchanged a look with Sanchez, Raccoon Girl sniggering. "It were business, tha's all."

"What kind of business?"

Raccoon Girl guffawed loudly, earning her a sharp look of displeasure. She cut the laugh short. "What kind of 'business' d'you *think* I'm in, love?" Victoria asked mockingly. "We provide a valuable community service here, like social workers. One, however, which is not generally appreciated by the Old Bill."

" 'Ceptin' f'them's which drop in fer a free quickie now and agin," Raccoon Girl put in. This time Victoria didn't rebuke her.

"We cater to a specific clientele. Dungeons and Dragons is a specialty service, if y'know what I mean."

Unfortunately, Jillie was certain she did.

"Fancy a guided tour round *our* London dungeon?" Raccoon Girl offered lasciviously.

"Sanchez," Victoria said softly, and the girl froze warily. "I'd prefer having this chat wi' the lady alone."

The snarl which briefly transformed Raccoon Girl's face made her appallingly feral. She swept from the kitchen, and Jillie could hear her stomp up the entire two flights of stairs.

Either the whiskey or the coffee had resuscitated Victoria, and she lounged on the chair with a practiced sensuality that fit her well despite her dissipated appearance.

"You don' look the sor'. So what's it to you, aye?"

"I'm sure you know Chris is dead. I was told you knew something about her and a man named Richard Atherton." The woman's cracked marble eyes were aloof, not a flicker of interest.

"The filth involved in this?"

"The what?"

"The police."

"I don't know," she said candidly. "But I'm not interested in causing you trouble. All I want is to find out what really happened to Chris. That's it."

"Yeah? Just how good a friend of yours was she?"

"She was my daughter's godmother." Jillie wondered if such abstract distinctions mattered to her.

The woman's fleshy lips pursed thoughtfully. "I'd prefer not to attract undue attention from the local constabulary. We have a cordial but fragile balance."

The ticking of a clock punctuated the quiet as Victoria considered. The Dragon Queen finally smiled, the creases of her face nearly obliterating her eyes. "On the other hand," she said, "all men are bastards. Screw 'em." She heaved herself to her feet. "Let's take our coffee into the drawing room, shall we?"

Carrying both coffees, Jillie followed Victoria into an average-looking business office, desk and filing cabinets, computer, shelves lined neatly with books. "Sit down," Victoria ordered. Jillie obeyed, sitting on a small chair as the Dragon Queen settled her considerable bulk onto a plush chaise longue and arranged the folds of her silk robe around herself carefully.

"Anything I tell you is confidential. I don't want any coppers coming by to ask me questions."

"Of course. Absolutely."

Victoria snorted skeptically, but said, "Men don't have names here, but they *do* have credit cards, and I maintain excellent records. I know Mr. Atherton."

"So what did he have to do with Chris?"

Victoria regarded Jillie with a withering look of jaded disbelief. "You *do* understand my business here, don't you?"

"I think so . . ."

"Uh-huh. I'm a whore, if that helps." Jillie's face heated with an embarrassed flush. "All women are whores, to one extent or another. Some of us are merely better businesswomen." Too daunted to protest, Jillie didn't reply. "We specialize in satisfying unusual fantasies what are natural for many people but which the law in its infinite wisdom has determined to be immoral and therefore illegal. We're not into rough trade, no one gets hurt. Much. It's perfectly harmless meck-believe."

"How did Chris know about your . . . business?"

"We're not in the Yellow Pages, but we have ways of advertising for them that wants finding us."

Of course. The sex ads.

"But no one gets into Dungeons and Dragons without references. I checked Chris out with . . . mutual acquaintances," Victoria said obliquely. Jillie grasped the relationship between Victoria and Sanchez, and knew what sort of mutual acquaintances she meant. "Chris and Atherton were here, what . . . ?" Victoria studied the ceiling. "Six months ago? I couldn't see what the attraction was to milquetoast like him, but I liked *her*."

Jillie swallowed hard. "Did they come here a lot?"

"Just the once. I got the impression it was a birfday present." Not Chris's, Jillie knew. "We do get quite a few one-offs, tourist trade, mostly, Japanese businessmen. Sometimes it's couples looking to put a bit of excitement back into their marriage. Sometimes it's people wanting an education. Sometimes it's just lonely men who need a sympathetic ear, more enjoyable than a psychiatrist, and for about the same price. A good many so-called sexual perverts are only overgrown little boys longing for cuddles from their mummies." She grinned. "Or spankings."

Jillie wasn't interested in Victoria's sociological analysis of sexual dysfunctions, more uncomfortable with a growing suspicion.

"Is it possible that . . . Was Chris blackmailing him?"

Victoria cupped her cheek into her palm. Jillie shivered, watching as her sharpened nails lightly stroked her face. "I don't much like that word, sounds cheap and sleazy. I doubt your friend was either." She stretched as languidly as a cat after its nap. "And if she were, that wasn't any of my business, was it?"

The Dragon Queen laughed.

* * *

The guest hotel straddled the corner of the Elizabeth Street bridge, a dingy white building not too different from those along the streets of Belgravia. But rather than overlooking sedate gardens in Eccleston Square, Keen's room had a deafening vista onto Victoria Station, multiple railroad tracks, rows of chimneyed flats, and a clock tower above bleak office blocks. And rather than wholesome backpacking Swedish students, the Cotswold Arms catered primarily to gaunt men with ravaged faces and faded tattoos on their arms and hands.

"Toilet and shower in the hall," the bored clerk said. He handed Keen two keys welded to a heavy metal ball. "Big key for the room, little key for the shower. Television's on the blink."

"Don't think I'll miss it."

"Tea makings in the room, breakfast at seven, four pounds extra."

At forty-five pounds a night, the room was dead cheap for London, which was about all Keen could say for it. It reeked of stale cigarette smoke, with water-stained wallpaper curling to expose a stipple of black fungus. The narrow bed nearly filled the entire room, and Keen had to duck under the shelf supporting the defunct television to reach the wardrobe. He inspected the twisted hangers with tattered dry-cleaning paper still intact, then placed his suitcase inside, not bothering to unpack.

A tiny sink dripped quietly to itself in the corner, the used sliver of soap slimy. The meager assortment of instant coffee, instant nondairy creamer, instant tea, and no sugar made the notion of a hot drink theoretical at best.

Glow-in-the-dark *Jurassic Park* dinosaur stickers concealed holes punched through the flimsy door. Keen examined the doorframe with interest; a long segment had been replaced, the ends not quite flush under the paint slapped over the wood. Large circles of the worn carpet had been patched. But the fabric was far newer, the colors still bright, and whoever had done the repair work hadn't bothered lining up the pattern. Something violent and messy had once happened in this room.

Hopefully, he wouldn't spend more time here than necessary, but he had to put his head down somewhere, Kentish Town Station housing no longer available to an officer supposedly on his way home. He headed out into the arid London streets.

His first order of business was to buy himself another mobile phone, and he checked it was working properly by ringing Mrs. Flora Wortley in Streatham. The elderly woman didn't know whether or not her husband had seen a solicitor. In any case, John Wortley left a will drawn up years ago. Mr. Philpots had been his name, Milton Philpots, Flora recalled. Nice man but had a dicky heart, like her own Jack. Ate too much and drank too much, but boys will be boys, whatever age they are. Dead and gone these past ten years. Mr. Philpots, she meant, not Jack . . .

When Keen asked about any letters or papers, she told him the police had only yesterday asked that very same question. Two young officers, ever so polite they were. She'd never heard of that Schaefer fellow, but of course she knew as well as the next that lawyers were as crooked as the day was long, weren't they all? So she'd been happy to let those nice gentlemen take all the papers they wanted, weren't no use to her, and if it could help someone else, she felt it her civic duty.

It was a repeat with Josie Bunts, Daniel Barrow's live-in girlfriend. The two nice policemen had to use a more aggressive tack with Josie, who was not quite as affable as Mrs. Wortley, or as gullible. After failing to sway her with a warning she could be charged with estate housing fraud, a more credible threat of nicking her for possession of cannabis coerced her to turn over what few papers Barrow left behind.

Unlike Mr. Wortley, there had been no will, since there had been no money. Josie's only legacy for five years of being Daniel Barrow's primary source of income was a flat full of charity shop furniture, a mangy dog she hated, and overdue bills she could not pay. She was in no mood to assist Keen in his inquiries, since she was busy moving out what few possessions she had before the creditors could catch up with her. She finished with a few imaginative comments expressing her opinion of the British police, and hung up on him.

"It's for you, dear," Mrs. Flute called up the stairs.

Jillie hurried downstairs, a towel wrapped over her wet hair. "Hello?"

"Hi, it's Keen." When she didn't answer, he said, "Everything all right?"

"Yes, fine, just tired." She winced, lies not coming easily.

"I've made reservations for seven. It's not far, if you don't mind walking."

"Walking's no problem."

"I'll call at six-thirty, shall I?"

"What for?"

"To take you to dinner?"

"Why don't you just come by here?"

She didn't understand his amusement. "Right. See you then."

"Okay." She couldn't see how she could call it off. She couldn't see how she could call *any* of it off, not now. "See you."

When she hung up, she found Mrs. Flute watching her knowingly. "Sit down, dear, I'll put the kettle on."

"Don't go to any bother, really . . ."

But Mrs. Flute had already banged a huge copper kettle onto a vintage 1930s gas stove, polished chrome and black iron, dainty flowers fired into the white ceramic.

"Nonsense," she said firmly. "That's why I let to young ladies, now that my Joseph is gone. New faces, new stories, keeps me young." She smiled slyly. "Sells a few paintings now and again, too." She settled into a chair by the massive wooden table. "Now, what exactly is the problem with this young man of yours?"

Jillie sat and tucked her terry-cloth robe behind her knees. She didn't know how to begin. "Well . . . he's a policeman."

"My, how *dreadful*." Mrs. Flute's irony made Jillie laugh in spite of herself.

"No, what I mean is . . ." Jillie wasn't sure what she meant. "I met him in Leeds, when I identified my friend's body after she drowned."

"Death and sex," Mrs. Flute said brightly. "A primal combination. Perfectly normal. That's simply the cycle of life; death making way for new life, the natural urge to vanquish mortality with procreation. Even when you're well past it like my Joseph and I were, the urge is always there. Although," she added speculatively but not sadly, "there's quite a bit more death than sex when you get to my age."

Jillie was baffled if amused. "I think it's a little more complicated than that."

"Oh, but course it is. We're human beings; we *like* things to be complicated. It makes us feel superior to the animals if we think our lives are complicated."

The kettle sang. "I'm ninety-two years old, dear," Mrs. Flute continued as she made a pot of tea. "I've lived through more changes than you could imagine, and one thing I've learned is that everything is basically simple. People would be so much happier if they only accepted how simple life is. But we're too busy telling lies to ourselves, trying to make things complicated so we can feel it all *means* something."

"It doesn't mean anything? Life?"

"Being alive and happy, that means something. The rest"—Mrs. Flute set the tea onto the table—"is useless complication no one needs."

Even at seven in the evening, the heat sizzled, not a cloud in the sky as Keen steered Jillie into an elegant bistro on St. George Terrace. She had on the same sheer dress she wore to Lynne Selkirk's party, while he suffered in his dark suit and tie. The tuxedoed waiter escorted them to a courtyard alcove at the far end of the building, the ceiling covered with hothouse glass, potted plants suspended by brass chains in the sweltering humidity. Even the ferns looked pitifully wilted.

Keen pulled out the heavy plush chair for Jillie. She slid into it carefully, her entire body tense. The waiter checked the menus before handing them out, Keen only realized after he had opened his, to be sure Jillie had the lady's; the one *without* the exorbitant prices. Then his heart sank even further; it was entirely in French, with no English translations. If he'd been with Laura, they'd have mangled it with glee, competing to see who could pronounce it the funniest. But he was reluctant to attempt speaking it in front of Jillie. Damn. He sweated until the waiter returned, flipping open his order pad like a summons book, pencil poised.

"What would you suggest?" Keen asked him hopefully.

"*L'entrée du jour chaude* is a *mouclade au Pineau des Charentes,*" the waiter reeled off rapidly, his accent sounding perfect to Keen's ear. "And *l'entrée froide* is a *terrine de foie gras irlandais avec cèpes, faite à la maison,* it's quite incredible. *Le plat du jour* is *selle d'agneau aux gousses d'ail en chemise.* Keen nodded as if he understood every word.

Thank you so much, he thought. You're a big help.

"I'll have the *mouclade* and *filets de cabillaud,*" Jillie said, and closed her menu, unaware she'd just rescued him from his quandary.

"I'll have the same."

As the waiter scribbled, Keen realized he hadn't quite made it to safety yet. He stared at the unopened wine list as the waiter smirked.

"Do we need a few minutes to decide on the wine?"

"Thank you," Keen said shortly, clearly a dismissal. Opening the wine list, he scanned a list of nearly every bloody vintage the French had ever bottled in the past two hundred years.

"This is a nice place. Have you been here before?"

"No. It was recommended by a friend." "Friend" being an extremely loose description of Phil Reaves. Keen reminded himself Reaves hadn't known the department wouldn't be paying his bills when he'd suggested taking Jillie here.

She draped the linen serviette across her lap. "Are you trying to impress me?"

"Is it working?"

"Very."

"Then I'm trying to impress you." He held the wine list out across the table in defeat. "Truth is, I don't know owt about wine. Be a love, and pick one for me?"

"What do you like, sweet, demi-sec, or dry?"

"I don't know. Dry, I suppose."

She examined the list. "Two glasses of Tokay pinot gris with the *mouclade* and a bottle of the Coteaux du Layon for the fish," she said, handing the list back.

When the waiter returned, he managed to pronounce it well enough to earn himself a raised eyebrow and a respectful nod.

He hadn't known what *mouclade* was, would never have ordered mussels otherwise. But to his surprise, they tasted better than they looked. The fish was delicious, and the wine wasn't bad, either. Of course, at those prices, it had damned well better be.

"Do you like French food?" Jillie asked.

"Love it." Everything except for the weird squidgy things the frogs scraped off the bottom of their boats. And escargots and head cheese. And frogs.

Their strained conversation trickled to a halt, which Keen credited to the formal surroundings. What a complicated woman, so hard to decipher, like trying to piece together a picture from the shards of a broken kaleidoscope. Then Jillie said, far too casually, "So who were the guys watching Chris's house the other night?"

He sat back, buying time by sipping his wine. "Police," he answered. "Which I think you already know."

"I thought no one was interested in Chris's death."

"No one is. It was a favor to me." He tried a light smile. "Max Swinton had a point; someone might have burgled the place. I wanted to be sure you were safe."

She didn't return his smile. "Is the British Library also in danger of being burgled?"

"Pardon?"

"There's a woman been following me around at the British Library. Is she a cop, too?"

Keen cursed Reaves's arrogant cheek, his team too cocky. "Probably."

Jillie nodded, not in agreement, but in confirmation of what she'd suspected. "That's a hell of a favor. Did you have to come all the way from Leeds to arrange it? Like you just happened to be at Chris's funeral?" Her tone was flat, without warmth but without anger.

His appetite had gone. "I don't know what to tell you, Jillie."

"How about the truth?"

"All right." He met her gaze directly. "I swear to you, on my honor, there is no police inquiry going on into Christine Swinton's death." The fact that he wasn't lying made it easier. Her certainty weakened, and he pressed the advantage. "I also swear the only police officer interested in her death is *me*."

"Then you do think she was murdered?" she demanded.

His honesty wavered. That invisible line was still too difficult to cross. "I'm not convinced, no. But I intend to do what I promised I would; find the truth."

"So what were all those other cops doing . . . ?"

"Christine Swinton's father was a well-known MP. Her mother is a very wealthy woman. If that house *were* burgled, or if anything happened to you while you were in it, the Swinton family has the kind of clout that could make things unpleasant for the local police authority. It's no big surprise they've been keeping a close watch out." She nibbled her bottom lip uncertainly. "What were you imagining they were there for?"

"First you tell me the police aren't interested," she said. "Then they're all over the place, watching me. What was I *supposed* to think?"

He suspected there was more to her sudden distrust than she was letting on. Pressing her would only confirm her suspicions, and drive her further away. No amount of sophisticated police interrogation technique would ever replace simple, human trust.

"There's no one watching you now," he said. "And if you tell me you'd rather not go any further, I'll leave off and it's done."

"Really?"

"I give you my word." He meant it.

She hesitated, wavering. *Talk to me, Jillie* . . . Then to Keen's irritation, the waiter returned.

"And how is everything?" he demanded blithely.

"Just brilliant." Keen cursed the man's timing silently as he whisked away their plates.

It wasn't until after they'd finished the chocolate torte that Jillie asked, "Why didn't you tell me the police were watching the house?"

"Because I felt you'd either be alarmed or jump to the wrong conclusion. Which you did. The police aren't supposed to give members of the public any more information than necessary. It's a hard habit to break. I'm sorry, I was wrong. I should have told you."

She averted her gaze, her expression unreadable. "I understand." When she looked back, he had the feeling she had made a decision, although still wary. "I phoned someone today, this guy I met on the train from Leeds. Martin Harding-Renwick. He was at the congress to demonstrate some computer software for prosopography databases."

"What kind of . . . ?" It sounded like a painfully intimate medical examination.

"Prosopography. It means studying the history of people related by different factors, like families, or by economics or politics. Things like that." Somehow, she had managed to explain it in a way that didn't make him embarrassed by his ignorance. Not that many people would have known what prosopro . . . possopagor . . . whatever the hell it was.

"Martin designed the software for medical labs. They use it to study genetic diseases by tracking different families with Parkinson's and Alzheimer's. But he also sells it for genealogical research."

"Sounds fascinating, but what's he got to do with what you're looking for?"

"I have a hunch that Chris was working on George the Third's first wife, Hannah Lightfoot." Again, she avoided his eyes, and he wondered just where she'd gotten this "hunch."

"Who?"

"A Quaker woman who's supposed to have married George when he was still Prince of Wales."

"What about her?"

"All I know so far is that she was the daughter of either a shoemaker or a draper and she secretly married George in April of 1759, and had children by him well before he married Charlotte."

"So what?"

"So, if George did marry her when he was Prince of Wales, it was before the Royal Marriage Act in 1772 forbidding the royal family from marrying commoners. The law can't be applied retroactively, which means his marriage to Hannah would have been legal. If he did marry her, he wasn't divorced when he married Charlotte, which makes him a bigamist. Any children he'd had by Hannah were legitimate, and any kids by Charlotte would be bastards, so the rightful heirs to the throne would have been his children by Hannah Lightfoot. And their descendants. Which mean every monarch of Britain since has been a usurper."

He considered it. "And *that's* what you think Chris was working on? Finding the heirs of Hannah Lightfoot?"

"Yes, I do."

He couldn't help laughing. "You don't really believe someone claiming to be a descendant of King George by this Hannah person is going to overthrow the queen and take her place, do you?"

"No." She wasn't amused. "Possession being nine-tenths of the law. But Chris was a passionate republican. She loathed the royal family, and I think she was looking for a way to use this as part of a campaign to get rid of the monarchy."

The entire concept was absurd. "And your friend Martin . . ."

"Harding-Renwick."

"Harding-Renwick, how can he help?"

"His business is genealogy. And selling titles. He knows how to research this stuff better than I do. Maybe he can help me find out more about Hannah Lightfoot and her children. I've got an appointment with him Monday."

Shrugging, he said, "It can't hurt, I suppose. Look, you work on this Hannah Lightfoot while I look into Chris's political activities. Maybe there's a connection somewhere." Although he doubted it. But at least Hannah Lightfoot would keep her occupied and out of trouble.

He enjoyed the diffident smile tweaking the corners of her mouth. "Maybe."

The friction between them lightened. He was sipping the most expensive thimble of coffee he'd ever bought in his life while trying to signal the waiter for the bill. When it arrived, packaged in a leather folder with two chocolate mints to sweeten the shock, Keen gulped at the total, and placed his Visa card inside the folder.

The sun had set, but the summer sky was still light. He hesitated as they reached the end of St. George Terrace. "Fancy a walk in the park?" he asked. When she smiled her assent, they crossed Regent's Park Road to Primrose Hill, a nearly treeless expanse of lawn cut with graveled paths.

"Chris brought me up here before we went to Leeds. You can see all of London from the top," Jillie said.

They were both out of breath by the time they'd climbed the summit. They shared the view with a boy on a bicycle, his wiry-whiskered dog beside him, tongue lolling. The boy waited until the dog had lifted its leg against the landmarker's stone base, then cycled off toward the twinkling lights of a high-rise, short-legged dog scampering desperately in his wake.

"There's St. Paul's . . ." Jillie pointed. A breeze brushed back her curls, and he studied her profile, nerves tingling in the pit of his stomach. "This is what I wanted," she said wistfully. "Just to see London. It's so different from the States."

"Think you could live here?" He tried to make it sound casual.

"What, in London?"

That wasn't quite where he had in mind. "Or England in general."

She understood him anyway, the silence prolonged. "I don't know. Karen is grown up now, but Oregon is beautiful and I have a decent job, boring as it is. What about you? Think you could ever leave Britain, go live in the States?" she countered.

Fair enough question, he realized, just not one he'd thought of himself. Women were expected to live wherever their men did, the reverse simply hadn't occurred to him, sexist git that he was.

He gave it serious consideration. Even outside the question of the twins, he had to admit he would be unhappy with the idea. "Never been to the States, no idea what it's like. I don't know as I could find work with the American police. Anyway," he added, "I wouldn't want to carry a gun."

"That would make it difficult. And dangerous."

"Armed police haven't made it any safer for you Americans. You have a hundred and fifty times more shootings every year in the States than in Britain, did you know that?"

"Believe me, I know." She leaned against the bronze marker, the London horizon at her back. The dome of St. Paul's had faded in the twilight to a hunchbacked beetle nestled in the forest of lights. "And cops carrying guns don't make me feel any safer. American cops don't carry guns to protect me; they wear them to protect themselves *from* me. Do you have any idea how easy it is for anyone to get a gun in the States?"

"I've read the statistics."

"I'm not a statistic. I own two hunting rifles and a handgun. One rifle I inherited from my father when he died." She pushed back her loose hair. "And the other I pulled out of a garbage can."

"You're joking."

"Nope. A neighbor's fourteen-year-old kid left it out in the rain. His mother said if he were going to treat his rifle like garbage, she'd throw it away like garbage. So I took it."

"Is that even legal?"

"Sure. Law-abiding, taxpaying citizens feel they have the constitutional right to two things, a car and a gun. Try to take either one away, and you'd have a riot."

He smiled grimly. "You've convinced me. I could never live in the States."

"I'm not sure that's what I was trying to convince you of," she said, her tone unreadable.

For a moment, he struggled against an intense urge to tip her chin gently toward him, wanting to kiss her. She glanced up warily, extinguishing his desire as thoroughly as had she rejected him outright.

"Well," he said, and smiled far more casually than he felt. "Let's get you back to Mrs. Flute's."

But that night, it wasn't just the stifling heat, or the lumpy mattress, or the piercing whistles of passing trains that kept him awake. The hands of the clock tower read slightly after three o'clock in the morning as he stood at the open window of his hotel, looking down at a dozen British Rail workmen in fluorescent jackets and safety hats busily jackhammering one of Victoria Station's many railroad tracks to bits.

He should have been home by now, he thought. Should have done the sensible thing, forgotten all about Christine Swinton and Jillie Waltham. He should check out of this miserable fleabag hotel and go back to Leeds where he belonged.

Masochistic sod, he thought, sighing as he wiped a trickle of sweat from his naked chest. Then he lay back down on the uncomfortable bed and tried to sleep.

X

SATURDAY

The zoo was crowded, people happy for the unusually hot weather even if the animals suffered for it. Laura arrived at their rendezvous point, as punctual as ever. Keen's heart caught as she waved, beautiful in a summer dress. They exchanged a kiss, chaste and safe, then sat on the bench and pretended to be mum and dad again.

"Thanks for letting me have the boys for the afternoon."

"They look like they've had a lovely time. Thank you for taking them, Keen." The twins raced around the seal pond, squealing in delight as they tried to keep up with the noisy animals. "You'll be going back tomorrow?"

When he didn't answer, she looked at him sharply, eyes narrowed. "What are you getting up to, Keen?"

"That assignment I'm here on . . ."

"Yes?"

"It's off." She knew him well enough to wait him out, and, he had to admit, he needed someone to talk to. "They've closed the case."

"Then you're shot of it. What's the problem?"

Always the practical one, Laura. "I'm not entirely convinced the woman weren't murdered."

"What woman?" Laura said suspiciously. She'd been a policeman's wife too long not to hear what he wasn't saying.

"Christine Swinton. James Witherstone Swinton's daughter."

"The one who got drowned up at Harewood House?"

"Mm-hm. First theory was she were a political activist got in over her head, Home Office wants a discreet investigation. I find a few things might actually support the notion of unlawful death and suddenly the case is yanked, slagged off on some idiot seeing terrorists and Liberal Democrats under every bed. Don't make any sense, none at all."

"I'm shocked," Laura scoffed. "Corruption in our high-minded government officials? Who'd have thought? Just what do *you* plan on doing about it, Mr. Plod?"

"I'm stopping in London for a while, make a few inquiries of my own."

Laura leaned over to stare at him, incredulous. "Have you gone completely out of your mind?"

"It's a possibility," he said acerbically.

"If your gaffers tell you it's finished, then it's *finished.* What's done is done, so pack it in and go on. Go home and leave well enough alone."

The old anger churned sluggishly, deep in his gut. "I don't need to be hearing that from you, Laura. You should know me better."

"I *do* know you better, and you're not telling me everything, are you?"

No, he wasn't. He realized, too late, confiding in Laura was a mistake. She could read into his silence whatever she wanted.

"What the hell are you trying to prove? Don't you have enough problems without creating more for yourself?"

He clamped his hands around one knee and studied the cracks of the pavement, watching yellow and black flies hovering over wildflowers. He should have known better, belatedly remembering their arguments had been much the same before their divorce; frustration making her shrill while he retreated into stony silence.

"Keen, you're doing all right now, why beg to have it all blow up in your face again? My God, you're still as daft as a dormouse!" The Yorkshire sneaking back into her accent was a clear indication how upset she was. "You *cannot* take on the bosses and win, you know that. You've put in too many years' service, why jeopardize your pension now?"

He said nothing, his head down not in submission, but like a recalcitrant bull looking for a target, his shoulders tense.

"Right then, go off and play at private eye on your own time. For all the good it'll do you." She lowered her voice to a sharper edge. "But when the wheel comes off, clever clogs, and it will, the only one who'll be left holding it is *you.*"

"Laura," he said softly, "I'm asking you polite, leave off. Please."

"No, I'm *not* going to leave off. What is it about this case you'd risk your job over? Don't do it. If not for yourself, then for the boys . . ."

At that his anger finally squeezed up like molten lead from where it burned inside him. He turned, one stiffened finger quivering under her nose. "Don't you dare use the lads like that, it's beneath you."

She glanced down at his raised finger in disdain. He dropped it, shamed. "Now I see the real reason," she said. "Your pride's been bruised, hasn't it, and you're bloody mad. You think because you've clamped a lid on it, that solves all your problems?" Laura persisted. "All it takes is an act of will?"

"I've done all right," Keen said quietly, but far from calm.

"Bollocks. That anger of yours has already dropped you in the shit once. What's it going to take for you to see that, before someone else gets hurt, maybe even you this time?"

"Laura—"

"*Listen* to me, Keen. You're my kids' father, and I care what happens to you. You're not some canteen cowboy, so don't pull this strong silent macho crap on me."

"I'm all right," he insisted. "There's nothing to talk about, so let's drop it."

She glared at him. "Right, then," she asked with mock innocence. "So what's Clive been up to these days?"

That had been a low blow. Keen watched the boys running around on the dry grass. "I don't know," he said flatly. "I haven't talked to Clive in a long time."

"Since it happened."

"Laura, he doesn't *want* to talk to me."

"You don't know that—"

"If he did, he knows where I work, where I live. I don't intend to embarrass either of us by imposing myself on him."

"Goddamn it, Keen. He spent three months in hospital and you never once went to see him, not so much as a bloody card! What is he *supposed* to think? Have you ever thought that if you throttled your ego back far enough, if you asked him to forgive you and he actually did, you might learn to forgive yourself?"

Keen sighed. "Laura, I have had so much crap psychobabble shoved down my throat already, please spare me any more of it."

"Or is it that you don't want him to forgive you?"

He stood up abruptly and walked away from her. She followed, grabbing his arm, and blocked his way. He stopped, gazing over her shoulder as the boys chased each other in erratic circles and shrieked with childish glee.

"I'm asking you, Keen, please let me help."

"There's nothing to 'help' with. I'm sorry, Laura. I know you mean well, but I shouldn't have brought up any of this with you. You've got your own life now. You're not a part of mine anymore."

His heart ached at the hurt on her face. But it was more than the truth, he resented her wanting to have it both ways. She'd given up her right to his intimate problems, abrogated her position as his chief confidante. "If I can't have you how I want, back again as my wife, then it's best we just stay friends and nothing more."

"What's that mean, 'friends,' aye? We'll go out for a pint now and again, talk about the weather? Isn't Liverpool doing well, how's your brother-in-law doing with the video shop these days? Is that it?"

He grabbed her by the waist, pulling her against him, and kissed her hard. Her hands pushed frantically at him before she simply froze, rigid. When he pulled away, but didn't let her go, she stared up wild-eyed, her hair disarrayed and lipstick smeared.

"The weather's too bloody hot," he said, his voice hoarse. She blinked against his breath. "I hope Leeds United kicks Liverpool up the arse, and Rick is pissing away good money after bad." He released her, aware of the boys staring. "Now *back off*, Laura," he warned, "before you hurt someone. Namely me."

She almost stumbled backing away. "That were really stupid, Keen," she said, her voice low, then called to the twins. "Come on, lads, time to go home."

As she marched them away, the twins twisted in her grip to wave goodbye, anxious and uncertain. It took an effort to smile and wave back with cheerful reassurance that all was okay.

But, strangely enough, he did feel the better for it, the pressure easing, breathing just a little freer.

The feeling lasted until he reached the car park. As he opened the Vauxhall's door, he sensed rather than saw a presence. A clean-shaven, square-chinned man crowded him in the open door. On the other side, the man's partner leaned against the car and rested his own, blunt chin on his forearm. Keen didn't return his thin-lipped smile. He looked back cautiously at the first man standing close enough to smell his mint-and-coffee breath. He suspected these were the same two policemen who had put the frighteners on Josie Bunts.

"Something I can do for you gentlemen?" Keen said more calmly than he felt. He also suspected this might end with him taking a beating. A prospect, surprisingly, arousing more excitement than fear, his youthful pub brawls having left him bloodied but satiated.

"You could start by going home, Mr. Dunliffe," the first man said amiably. "You seem to be having trouble getting the message. Your services are no longer needed. Stop bothering people."

Keen said nothing. Adrenaline sang along his nerves and he wondered how the man's nose would feel as it cracked against his fist. Then the other man remarked in a voice so soft it was nearly a whisper, "Cute lads you've got there. Have a nice time at the zoo today?"

Slowly, he turned, still wary of being assaulted. "Are you threatening my children?" His own voice was equally quiet, afraid it would shake with the rage he barely held in check.

The man's smile widened enough to show his teeth, eyes cold. "Of course not. Just want to put your mind at ease knowing we'll keep watch, make sure they're safe and sound while you're up in Leeds."

He locked eyes with him, his hands curled into fists.

"Go on home, Mr. Dunliffe," the first man said with almost gentle concern, then nodded to his partner. After a moment, the second man shoved the door of the Vauxhall lightly against Keen, and followed his companion at an indifferent saunter.

The thwarted promise of violence left him feeling sick. Fleeting fantasies of running them both down, bodies bleeding and smashed, surged through his head. It took him nearly ten minutes before he trusted himself to drive.

To Jillie's surprise, tracking down Richard Atherton's address had been easy. He wasn't in the London directory, but a simple check of the Windsor phone book verified her intuition. She took the Southeast train into Windsor and got off at the Riverside Station terminus.

At any other time, she might have crossed the Thames to see Eton, joined the throng of tourists taking photographs of their hideously dressed families marring the view of the castle. As it was, she barely glanced at the turreted bastions before she turned onto the main shopping street. She stopped to ask directions from a shop clerk selling postcards and T-shirts and water-filled paperweights that snowed on a plastic Windsor Castle when shaken.

Following the girl's arcane instructions, she searched for oranges carved in red brick on a rooftop, walked around a church, and passed a flower bed where a gardener yanked elderly daffodils out of the ground, flats of pansies waiting to replace them.

Richard Atherton lived in a small house off a narrow, tiled alley. As she walked up the front steps, Jillie began to panic. What if he slammed the door in her face? What if he . . . *hit* her? She rang the doorbell, chimes ringing out an unfamiliar melody, and waited, shaking with terror.

A woman answered the door. "Yes?"

"Is . . ." Jillie's voice cracked. "Is Richard Atherton home?"

"I'm Mrs. Atherton. Is he expecting you?"

Although Atherton's wife was about Jillie's age, their differences couldn't have been more striking. Mrs. Atherton's features had shriveled into something strangely fossilized, her thickened figure like steel armature under her austere dress. Her immaculate hair encased her head like a warrior's helmet carved out of granite. Even her makeup, although expertly done, seemed permanently tattooed onto her face.

"No, he's not," Jillie said. His wife raised one eyebrow without wrinkling her forehead, and Jillie wondered how she did it. "But I called him yesterday at the Windsor Archives. My name is Jillie Waltham, I'm a professor at Cascade Pacific University in Oregon. I have something I think he'd be interested in looking at."

His wife held out a hand. "I'll be sure he receives it."

Jillie gulped. "I'd prefer giving it to him myself. If he's not in, I can come back later."

Mrs. Atherton dropped her hand, more in contempt than defeat. "We prefer not to be disturbed on weekends, but I'll see if he can spare a few minutes. If you'd care to wait here, please?"

Mrs. Atherton closed the door behind her. It wasn't enough to keep her voice from leaking through, nor her husband's reply, although Jillie could make out nothing more than tones. Mrs. Atherton sounded glacially angry, while her husband seemed to be placating her. A wiry thin man with a wiry thin moustache opened the door, his wife glowering behind him. *Jack Sprat,* she thought.

Richard Atherton tried to smile and failed miserably. "Dr. Waltham," he said with false warmth. "How nice of you to call." Jillie blinked as he turned to his wife. "Darling, Dr. Waltham is a visiting professor from the States, on a research project . . ."

He was nearly babbling as the two women stared at him, one in confusion, the other with suspicion.

"You had something to give my husband, I believe?"

Richard Atherton blanched, his terror visible.

"Not exactly 'give,'" Jillie said quickly. "I wanted to know if he could tell me if a book is authentic or not . . ." She pulled the Dalton portfolio partway out of her shoulder bag, and glanced at him, wondering if her own expression matched his. He gaped at the book with open horror.

Again, Mrs. Atherton raised her amazing eyebrow.

"Yes, of course." Her husband belatedly picked up his cue. "I did say I'd give you an appraisal, completely slipped my mind, I'm afraid. Darling, why don't I walk Dr. Waltham through to the library, shouldn't be more than a half hour . . . ?"

"You do remember the Swains will be here at four?"

"I'll pick up some Taittinger at Odd Bins on my way home, shall I, darling?"

After a chilled silence, Mrs. Atherton said, "That'll do, darling." Jillie was certain she was not referring to the champagne. Richard Atherton bared his teeth in what Jillie realized a second later was supposed to be a smile. He clenched her arm fiercely as he steered her down the steps.

"*Ow . . .*" she protested as soon as they were far enough away from the house, and tried to shake off his hand. "You're hurting me."

"Frankly, I wouldn't mind murdering you right about now," Atherton hissed in fury. His hand clamped tighter, propelling her along at a fast walk. "How dare you come to my house like this . . ."

As they turned the corner, Jillie struggled to escape his grip. "Let me go, or I'll start screaming . . ." An elderly man walking a dachshund eyed them inquisitively.

Richard Atherton's hand fell away. "What are you doing here? And how did you get that book?"

Strangely, Jillie was no longer frightened, anger clearing her head. "I found it in Chris Swinton's house after she died. It belongs to you, doesn't it?"

"No," he said too rapidly. "It doesn't."

"The Royal Archives, then?"

"No . . . *Yes* . . ." He snatched at her shoulder bag. "*Give it to me . . .*" She jerked it away, and the two of them faced each other, glaring.

"Mr. Atherton, I talked to Victoria. She told me all about you and Chris."

He stared with naked fear in his eyes. "What do you want?" he demanded in a hoarse whisper.

She gestured toward a public park with a few benches and old tombstones propped up against a stone wall. "The truth. That's all."

They sat in hot sunlight on the only unoccupied bench, those in the shade of an ancient oak already staked out by elderly pigeon feeders ignoring openly groping couples. Girls chanted as they skipped rope, childish energy undaunted by the heat. *I see London, I see France . . .*

"God help me, this sort of scandal is supposed to happen to politicians, not to clerks," Atherton said in a low voice, anguished. "I suppose it was foolish to hope this would all die quietly when Chris did."

Her heart skipped a beat. She had to ask. "Did you kill her?"

"Of course not! It was an accident . . ." His certainty wavered. "Wasn't it?"

"It's what everyone thinks. I don't."

"I didn't murder anyone. Not that the thought hadn't crossed my mind, I'll give you that."

"Then she *was* blackmailing you."

He started, then gazed down at his clenched hands, knuckles whitened. "Yes. She was. But I'm finished with blackmail. I'm taking early retirement, and I've already confessed everything to my wife. We're . . . we're seeking professional counseling. So there's nothing further I can do for you."

Jillie's jaw dropped as she understood his implications. "I had no intention of blackmailing you!"

His bravado withered. "Then . . . what *do* you want?"

"All I want to know is what did you give Chris? I know it wasn't money. What did she want from you?"

He began blinking rapidly behind his glasses, took them off and paid careful attention to polishing them with his handkerchief. Sweat beaded his small bald spot, pink in the sun.

"Documents," he said in a monotone. "I gave her copies of documents from the Royal Archives."

"What kind of documents?"

He sighed, and replaced his glasses. "A marriage register dated the seventeenth of April, seventeen fifty-nine."

"Between George the Third and Hannah Lightfoot," she guessed. When he nodded, she said, "I don't understand. It's no secret Hannah Lightfoot married George, it's public record."

"Not all of it is public record. Some of it's sealed information. In particular, two baptismal records, one for Hannah's first child, a daughter named Sophia Amelia Caroline, born January sixth, seventeen fifty-eight, and the other for a son, George Edward William, born December ninth, seventeen fifty-nine, all bearing the Prince of Wales's signature."

"Anything else?"

"Letters. Court letters. The royal family's private letters. It's fairly certain that Hannah was murdered and that the crown went to a great deal of trouble to suppress information about her or her children."

"You mean King George had his own wife *killed*?"

"Doubtful. No, it could have been any number of people close to him, ministers, friends, even his mother, Augusta. Or Thomas Pelham, Duke of Newcastle. He had a huge spy network to keep him informed of everything concerning the royal family."

Richard Atherton had calmed, although his voice had gone flat, lifeless. "In any case, Hannah died, her children vanished. No one cared about the evidence until eighteen sixty-six. By then, Victoria was queen and Disraeli was soon to be prime minister. He had Sir Roundell Palmer, the attorney general, impound any documents relating to the case and locked in the Royal Archives."

Jillie listened quietly. Atherton's face had regained its color. "No one even remembered the documents existed until nineteen ten, when some sharp journalist got wind of it, but the archives denied him permission to examine them. The last thing the crown needed was the coals of an old scandal raked up."

He smiled, now completely calm. "But it won't go away. Two months before I met Chris, the home secretary signed a Public Interest Immunity Certificate to prevent any public release of these documents."

"To protect the royal family?"

"Well, that's one way of looking at it." He shook his head unhappily. "Bad enough I told her exactly *what* and *where,* down to the folio catalogue number, but I actually photocopied the documents. *Photocopied.*" Jillie understood his horror at risking damage to valuable manuscripts. "The personal papers and correspondence of sovereigns and the royal family are the private property of the crown. As a member of Her Majesty's private staff, I am under oath not to betray that trust."

"You mean it would be like treason?"

He blanched. "Technically, I suppose. Enough to earn me temporary residency in one of Her Majesty's prisons. Oh, God, I'm ruined." He bent his head and very quietly began to weep.

Such an ugly little man, with ugly inclinations, but all she felt was enormous pity for him. She took the book out of her shoulder bag. "But what does this book have to do with Hannah Lightfoot?"

He cleared his throat, wiped his face, and straightened. "May I?"

After a moment's hesitation, she handed him the book. He opened it from the back cover, flipping through the last pages quickly until he'd found what he was looking for. He pointed, and just above his finger, Jillie read the archaic script in faded ink. " 'To my Darling, allways Remember & Trust in God, Hannah Regina.' "

Goose bumps lifted on her arms.

"Hannah Lightfoot," Atherton said. "The same signature as the one on her will, which she also signed 'Hannah Regina.' "

" 'To my Darling,' " she read aloud. "Her darling *who?* George?"

He shrugged and returned the book to her. "That remains, I'm afraid, part of the mystery."

"If this book doesn't belong to you or the archives, whom *does* it belong to?"

"I have no idea. But it does make me wonder who else she was blackmailing for her to get her hands on it." His chin trembled and he looked away abruptly.

"How did you meet Chris?" she asked sympathetically.

It took him several deep breaths before he regained his self-control. "In a pub. By chance, or so I thought at the time. She was so beautiful, I couldn't believe my luck. She was . . . everything a middle-aged man dreams of. Sexy, passionate, wild. And an excellent actress, she had me convinced she actually was in love with me." He glanced at her, miserable. "Believe what you like, but I'd never had an affair before. And I'd never done anything like . . . *that* . . . in my life."

"You mean Victoria's? Why did you, then?"

He laughed, shakily. "Because it's what *she* wanted. It started with little things, nothing but a bit of spice, to make it more . . . exciting. I thought that's why she loved me, because I'd do the things she liked. I was willing to do whatever she wanted rather than lose her. It just got out of control." He cleared his throat, trying to reestablish his calm demeanor. "Even after she laughed at me, even when I knew it had all been a ghastly lie, I still loved her. I still do."

Jillie looked away at the children playing jump rope. She couldn't help but feel sorry for him, despite her better judgment. "Thank you," she said quietly. "That's all I wanted to know."

He stood and looked down at her. "Goodbye, Dr. Waltham. I hope you won't take this the wrong way, but I never want to lay eyes on you again. You understand?"

"Yes, I do." She smiled. "Goodbye, Mr. Atherton."

His mobile phone beeped and he answered it, expecting it to be Jillie. "Hello?"

"Sergeant Dunliffe?" A woman's cultured voice he didn't recognize.

"Yes?"

"You left a message for me to ring you. Marge Beecher. The Kentish Town Station gave me this number."

Ah, right. He wondered how to handle this, now there was no longer any case. "Thank you for returning my call, Miss Beecher. I wonder if I could come by and ask a few questions, whenever it would be convenient for you?"

The woman asked cautiously, "What would this be in regard to?"

"Merely routine. I understand you knew Dr. Christine Swinton?"

"Yes, I knew her. I heard she drowned."

"That's right. In any sudden death like this, the police have to make a few routine inquiries." He repeated the word "routine" to try to assuage her. "Make sure she weren't depressed or having any personal troubles, that sort of thing."

"Are you saying it might have been suicide?"

"Not for me to say, but we do have to check into these things, Miss Beecher. Would this afternoon do?"

"Actually . . ." He kept silent as she resisted. Then, "Fine. Four o'clock?"

He glanced at his watch, three-fifteen. "No problem."

He'd had to push the speed limit, but drove through the gates a few minutes before four, parking on the semicircular drive in front of a large brick manor deluged with ivy. Marge Beecher opened the door, restraining a large dog by the collar, one of those exotic inbred animals resembling a cross between a greyhound and a spaniel, all anorexic sinew and bone under sleek gray fur.

With her bloodless face, limp dishwater-blond hair cut bluntly at her chin, plain gray skirt and blouse, Marge Beecher was herself a good match for her parents' house, a not terribly attractive woman whose understated demeanor screamed of upper-class wealth. She wore no makeup, her blond eyelashes lending her a slightly vacuous expression, but her pale eyes were direct.

He opened his wallet at his warrant card, and she inspected it more out of courtesy. "Won't you come in, Mr. Dunliffe." She held the dog back to keep it from jumping on him, the animal's flanks quivering with excitement. "Go on, Podge," she said to the dog once Keen was inside. "Have a good run." She released the collar and the dog bounded hysterically across the expanse of lawn as if built of springs and elastic rather than flesh.

Inside, wooden floors creaked under enormous Persian carpets, luxurious but worn, as she led him through to a spacious sitting room. Bay windows overlooked a formal garden stretching to the horizon. She motioned him toward an overstuffed chair, dog hair clinging to the faded brocade. As he opened his notebook, he took in the room, antique furniture burnished to a silky patina by centuries of wax. Several dozen oil paintings on the walls that should be in a museum with proper lighting rather than moldering in a private house. For some reason this irritated him. She sat on a divan opposite and waited with a meticulously bored expression.

"Miss Beecher. I understand you're a graduate student working with Dr. Reece Wycombe, is that correct?"

"Yes." Her hands smoothed out the skirt over her knees and were now clasped demurely in her lap. Her nails had been polished with clear lacquer, a gold ring with a cluster of small rubies on her right hand.

"And before that, you were also a researcher for one of his colleagues?"

"Yes. Dr. Jordan Arthur." He paused, waiting for her to elaborate, but she was giving nothing away.

"You assisted in Dr. Arthur's work on Queen Elizabeth the First."

"Yes." Flat voice, flat eyes. "Are you here to ask me about Dr. Arthur's theories on Elizabethan England or Christine Swinton?"

"Both. How well did you know Christine Swinton?"

"We read at Cambridge together."

"Were you good friends?"

"We were acquaintances."

"I see." He didn't. "I understand Ms. Swinton and Dr. Arthur were having an affair round the time his office was burgled, his books and papers stolen?"

Her face drained to a translucent ash, but he admired her composure. Not a muscle flinched as she returned his gaze evenly. "I really couldn't say what his relationship with Christine Swinton was, Mr. Dunliffe."

"I believe Dr. Arthur was a married man, is that right?"

"He was, and he loved his wife very much."

Her expression didn't shift a fraction, and he had a flash of insight, and with it a handle on this remote, cold woman. "So he wouldn't have left her then, in your opinion?"

"Not for Christine Swinton." As he expected, the venom was there, barely controlled under the surface.

"But *you* were hoping he might have left his wife for you." He said it almost indifferently, but she reacted as if he'd slapped her. She flushed a mottled red.

She half rose from the divan, then sank back. Her eyes glistened. But her brittle anger didn't yield. "I won't even dignify that with an answer."

"It must have been upsetting for you, watching him fall in love with a woman who was not only beautiful but exceptionally clever as well . . . ?" He could tell he was hurting her, despite her efforts to hide it. He didn't relent. "But if he wouldn't leave his wife for Chris, what do you suppose she saw in him? Could he have offered her compensation of another sort to keep her sexually interested in him . . . ?"

She finally broke. *"Stop it,"* she hissed, all pretense of gracious manners gone. "He never promised to leave his wife for her, *never,*" she blurted, then realized her mistake.

"Then they *were* having an affair?"

Tears slid down her cheeks in a methodical stream that didn't match her austere expression, like tears from a child's plastic dolly. She ignored them. "Chris seduced Jor—Dr. Arthur at a time when he was terribly vulnerable; his wife was mentally ill, he was lonely and unhappy. They slept together once or twice, but I'd hardly call it an affair."

"Did that make you jealous, Miss Beecher? That it was Christine Swinton he turned to for comfort instead of you?"

She briefly shut her eyes as if in pain. "Not jealous. I wouldn't expect *you* to understand, but Dr. Arthur was a great man. A genius. But he was still a human being who needed someone who respected him and could appreciate his enormous talent and simply be a friend when he needed support."

"Someone like you."

"Someone exactly like me." She held her chin up, defiant, although the tears didn't stop. "His wife was a paranoid schizophrenic and Chris Swinton was a parasite. I wanted to protect him from them both."

"Chris Swinton rang you a few days before the break-in to Dr. Arthur's office. You had lunch together. What did you two talk about?"

"Now I know who's been spreading the vicious gossip around," she said with malicious triumph. "I would be skeptical about anything Reece Wycombe tells you, Mr. Dunliffe. He's a chronic liar." She laughed unconvincingly. "He's been telling the most elaborate story about how he broke his leg skiing in the Swiss Alps. But everyone knows he slipped in dog dirt."

"It weren't true, then, that Chris rang you or that you had lunch together shortly before the burglary?"

She had stopped weeping, brushing away her tears with a disdainful swipe. But her eyes avoided his, evasive. "No, that part is true."

"And what did you two talk about?"

"We just talked. I can't remember about what in particular."

"It wasn't to cry on your shoulder once her love affair with Dr. Arthur fell apart?"

She laughed again, the same high, fragile sound. "Chris never cried on anyone's shoulder in her life. She was totally incapable of loving anyone enough for them to ever be able to hurt her."

"So it were Chris who broke it off with him, not the other way round."

Realizing she'd made another error, she pressed her lips together stubbornly and didn't answer.

He made a pretense of scratching his neck in confusion. "Let me get this straight, Miss Beecher. A woman you claim was merely an acquaintance, someone you didn't even much like, rang you up unexpectedly, invited you to lunch. You knew she'd been sleeping with someone you cared for." She glanced at him warily. "Yet you agreed. You talked, but you can't remember about what. A few days later, Dr. Arthur's office is burgled, all his research stolen. Then this Dr. Saunders accuses him of forgery—"

"But it wasn't true—" she protested.

"It didn't have to be. The scandal was enough to kill him. Drank himself to death. And Saunders gets the chair at Oxford."

The tears were back, this time seeming more genuine. She stared at her hands twisting together in her lap.

"Chris somehow made a wax impression of the office keys in your handbag during that lunch," he persisted. "Have I got it right so far?"

"Yes . . ." She raised her head, her breath ragged with strain. "Chris was the one who broke in to his office. Then she and Saunders used his notes to trace the original letters he'd discovered and replaced them with the planted forgeries to destroy his career." It was said in a rush, far too quickly. His eyes narrowed.

"I have a few problems with this, Miss Beecher. Why would Chris Swinton want revenge on a lover she'd broken it off with herself? And I can also tell you it's not easy taking impressions good enough to make keys from if you're not an expert. I'd be very surprised if Dr. Swinton were."

She gulped air, panicking. "It hardly matters anymore," she insisted desperately. "They're both dead."

"That's right. So why don't you tell me the truth now?"

She sat motionless for a long moment before crumbling, like the illusory solidity of a sand castle washed away in the surf. Doubled over with her arms clasped around her waist, she sobbed as if in physical pain. He waited for the crying to subside. She stared at the carpet, exhausted.

"Miss Beecher," he prodded gently, "tell me what really happened."

"I did love him, but not the way you think. There was never anything sordid between us," she said simply, no emotion left in her voice. "But he was head over heels in love with Chris. The Golden Girl who could do no wrong."

"But when he wouldn't leave his wife for her, she broke it off?"

She smiled, a damp grimace more of pain than humor. "Chris didn't care if he was married or not. She had no morals at all, she'd sleep with anyone . . ." Tiny droplets of sweat dusted the fine hair on her upper lip, winking like jewels as she sneered. "No, she dropped him because she got bored. All her life, people gave her whatever she wanted because she was beautiful or clever or easy. She *expected* it. She took whatever she wanted, and when she lost interest, she threw it away. I hated her for hurting him almost as much as I hated him for hurting me."

He let the last statement hang in the air, letting it work its poisonous incrimination. She seemed to recoil from her own naked malice. Then he said softly, "There was never any lunch with Chris Swinton, was there?"

"No."

"You faked the break-in and took Dr. Arthur's papers."

"Yes." A whisper, a confession in church.

"You gave them to Saunders, and put the blame on Chris."

"No." It was barely audible.

"No?"

"No. I gave them to Reece Wycombe." She gulped back an escaping sob. "It was all *his* idea. He told me he would give the papers back to Dr. Arthur, as proof that Chris had tried to steal his work; we'd discredit her. I did it because she was destroying Jordie's life and I couldn't stand by and watch it happen any longer."

Once she had begun, it boiled out of her in an anguished rush. "But Reece tricked me. When I told him he had to give them back or I'd tell Jordie what we'd done, he laughed at me. He said I'd be the one blamed, not him. He would make it look like I did it to get back at Jordie and Chris, out of spite. I'd have ruined my career, and humiliated my parents. *He* gave the letters to Saunders. I don't know how, but he'd had forgeries made, obvious forgeries to make it look like Jordie had falsified the documents, but he *didn't*." She stared at him, pleading. "They *were* genuine!"

The truth was almost as Machiavellian and convoluted as the lies. "And Chris Swinton had nothing to do with any of it."

She covered her face with both hands. "No." The word was muffled.

"Why did Wycombe hate Dr. Arthur so much?"

She hiccupped, and he wasn't sure if it was a laugh or a sob. "He didn't. He hated Chris. She refused to collaborate with him anymore, walked away and took all her research with her. He never forgave her. Everyone knows he needed her far more than she ever needed him."

"So he destroyed Arthur's reputation, and used you to spread the rumor that Chris was to blame?"

"It wasn't hard. Jordie believed it. *Everyone* believed she'd done it." Her hands fell away as she glared in hate and defiance. "Who were they likely to believe? Me, or that slag?"

Keen didn't react. "And now you're working for Wycombe." Who would take her own research and put his name to it. Very neat.

Her shoulders slumped. "I have no choice," she said, subdued, eyes down.

He studied her for a long moment. Then he stood. "Thank you, Miss Beecher. I appreciate your help."

"I suppose you don't think much of me, do you?" she said bitterly.

"I think you're a young woman who allowed her passions to get the better of her common sense." She didn't respond, haggard and wretched. "But what you've done was more than unethical, it was criminal." She glanced up in alarm. The idea she could actually be arrested had obviously never occurred to her. He smiled grimly.

"I'll see myself out."

Jillie was preoccupied on the train back from Windsor, still unable to accept the idea of Chris as a thief and a liar who could have contrived a vicious blackmail scheme to ruin someone out of petty malice. A woman with a lesbian lover. The doubt Jillie had managed to suppress surfaced, like a boil gushing out noxious pus. She swallowed hard against her nausea. Had Karen known? Had Chris and Karen . . . ?

Young panhandlers and old drunks clogged the exits of the Underground at Camden Town. Black men in mirrorshades and huge knit caps had taken over the sidewalks with folding tables, hawking tapes and incense. Rastafarian rap music blasted out at volumes so loud the speakers crackled under the strain. Deafening music blared from every shop, and a man with a microphone and two huge speakers, not content with the electronic amplification of his voice, screamed out bargain prices, his face red as tendons in his neck popped in taut relief.

She shouldered her way through the crowd, passing shops selling identical leather jackets, leather bags and boots, leather whips and pot-metal handcuffs, then dodged traffic to cross the street. Diesel exhaust saturated the air already stinking of overripe bodies and patchouli incense. As she reached the corner, she was startled when someone brushed in front of her and a man's palm slapped against the building to cut her off. He grinned hugely at her, his teeth yellowed and rotten.

Sunlight glittered off the sweat in the pale brown stubble of his cropped scalp. His green T-shirt adhered like a second skin to gym-sculpted muscles while his jeans were so baggy they threatened to fall off his hips at any moment.

"Go' a fag, luff?" he demanded, his voice hoarse.

"What?"

"A fag. A cigarette, y'go' a ciggy for me, luff?"

She recovered her wits and said quickly, "Sorry, I don't smoke." But as she moved to walk around him, he blocked her way, still grinning. She stared at the tufts of armpit hair, his sour sweat odor ripe. A blue-green tattoo jutted from his sleeve, the letter *A* encircled in an *O*.

"Y'r American," he said with a glee that seemed more malevolent than cheerful. " 'Ere on 'oliday?"

Fright prickled her cheeks. "No. Excuse me—"

"What's yer 'urry, darlin'? I'm just haff'n a chat wif you, and you're not bein' very friendlylike . . ."

She pulled away, trapped against the wall. People hurried past guiltily, eyes averted, not wanting to get involved with anyone else's trouble. As he leaned over her with a predator's confidently lazy smile, she held herself rigidly still.

Then she forced herself to relax and smiled back, which startled him. But not as much as when she suddenly opened her mouth and began screaming at the top of her lungs, *"Fire! Fire!"*

It was enough to make him draw away in puzzled surprise, enough room for her to slip by and run, darting through a suddenly curious crowd scanning for the promised entertainment of a blaze.

She didn't look back as she sprinted two blocks then turned sharply into a fish and chips shop. A middle-aged East Indian couple behind the counter looked up in alarm, a half-dozen patrons stopped mid-chew. Breathless, she hurried to a table in the back and sat down, staring at the front door.

The woman glanced at her husband, an unspoken understanding between them. As he strode toward the door, his wife came around the counter.

"Everything all right, love?"

Unable to speak, Jillie nodded, trembling violently. "Pepsi?" she finally choked out.

Her husband clasped his hands behind his back, legs braced as he casually gazed out at the milling crowd on the sidewalk. The woman brought Jillie her soda, heavily laden with ice. "Drink this, you'll feel better very quickly," she said kindly.

She nursed the Pepsi for half an hour, but the young man didn't pass by. When she had calmed down, she thanked the couple—who graciously pretended not to understand what she was talking about—and left a tip twice the cost of the Pepsi.

Every nerve had been scraped raw as she walked to Mrs. Flute's. She scanned the street anxiously before she unlocked the series of security locks. Opening the door just far enough to let herself in, she slammed it shut behind her. Her knees wobbled as she stood in the atrium, waiting a moment before trying the stairs, but by the time she reached the top, she was certain she'd regained her self-control.

Mrs. Flute appeared in the doorway to the study, a gin and tonic in one hand. Her welcoming smile turned to a frown of concern. "My goodness, you look a fright! What's happened to you, dear?"

Overwhelmed, Jillie burst into tears.

⋆ ⋆ ⋆

Keen waited patiently for Mrs. Flute to unlock the door, security bolts clicking. When the small woman finally opened it, she looked up at him, unsmiling. "Hello, Sergeant Dunliffe," she said before he could speak. "Please do come in."

When she let him into the atrium, she clasped her hands in front of her as sternly as a schoolmistress. "Before we go up, you should know Miss Waltham is quite upset."

"With me?"

That got her to smile. "Oh, no. Not you. But she had an unpleasant experience this afternoon. A young man harassed her on the street, and she was badly shaken."

"She wasn't hurt . . . ?"

"She's fine. But she didn't want me to tell you." She raised her eyebrows meaningfully. "So I haven't."

"I understand."

Her look grew even primmer. "And should she feel more comfortable if you, well, kept her company, I shall make an exception and bend the rules. Just this once."

He smiled. "How much is your other room, then?"

"Thirty-five pounds a night, with breakfast," Mrs. Flute said promptly. As she watched him count the money from his wallet, she added, "You'll have to cook it yourself, and make up your own bed."

He murmured his thanks before following her up the stairs.

"If you'll wait in the sitting room?"

He sat in an overstuffed chair listening to squeaking floorboards and murmured voices. It took longer than expected for Jillie to appear, her puffy eyes red.

"Now, my dears," Mrs. Flute said brightly, checking her watch. "There's hot water in the kettle, help yourself to biscuits. I'm off, but I shan't be back until well after midnight, so don't wait up." Although the temperature was still abysmally hot, Mrs. Flute clipped a black cashmere sweater around her shoulders with a jet stone chain, and clumped energetically down the stairs.

Jillie attempted a casual smile. "It's still light. Would you like to sit out in the garden?"

"That would be lovely."

The rooftop behind the kitchen had been turned into an oasis of greenery. Sweet peas sprawled up trellises tacked to brick walls. Flower beds of weathered wood spilled over with alyssum and impatiens, tubs packed with lupins and aquilegias towering over pansies and dainty violas. He was wondering how the rooftop could support the weight when Jillie answered his unspoken question.

"It's part potting soil and part little Styrofoam pellets, designed specially for rooftop gardens."

A swinging bench hung by thin chains from a corroded steel frame. Jillie sat down confidently, Keen beside her with considerably more caution. The chains creaked ominously. Behind them, the Victorian men's hostel reflected the waning light, glowing like a castle in a child's fairy-tale book.

"It's a different world up here," Jillie said. "You can still be outdoors, but it's off the street. All the roofs sort of connect, like a little private village."

They sat in silence, swinging gently.

"Where's Mrs. Flute off to?" he asked finally.

"It's her coven's weekly meeting."

He studied her profile. "Is that a joke?"

"Nope. She's a devout member of Wicca. Her coven meets every Sabbath, which for them is a Saturday. There's supposed to be thirteen, but one lady died last year and another quit when she moved to her son's place in the Cotswolds."

"A witch's coven?" He couldn't help grinning. "Broomsticks and cauldrons, eye of newt and toe of frog, that sort of thing?"

"They don't like being called witches. Wicca isn't Satanism, it's animist, which doesn't mean animal worship, either. From what I gather, all they really do is brag about their grandchildren, spike their tea with gin, and cheat at mahjongg." She glanced at him stonily. "And I heard what she told you downstairs."

"Are you all right?" He tried to keep it casual.

"I'm fine. It happens in big cities. No different than New York or L.A."

"You don't mind if I stay here anyway, do you?"

Her face was pale. "That's up to you. Don't do it on my account. But it might make Mrs. Flute feel better."

He didn't challenge her. "Want to tell me about it?"

"There's nothing to tell." He waited until she shrugged, making the bench swing. "Some kid asked me for a cigarette. When I said I didn't smoke, he just hassled me the way kids do. I overreacted, that's all."

"What did he look like? Did he say anything?"

She frowned at him. "Can't you stop with being a cop for two minutes? I told you it was *nothing* . . ."

"Jillie—"

"Forget it, okay?" she said sharply. He didn't know what to say, while realizing his silence made her uncomfortable. "But I've been thinking," she added, chipping cracked varnish off the bench with her thumbnail. "Maybe you were right."

He was perplexed. "About what?"

"About it not being a murder. Maybe Chris really did accidentally drown. I think . . . maybe we should just let it drop." She looked at him and flinched at what she saw on his face.

He was certain the man who had intimidated Jillie had to be one of the pair he'd met that afternoon. Surely men who would stoop to threatening children wouldn't have any scruples about menacing a defenseless woman, either. "He frightened you that much, did he?"

"It's not that," she protested. "You don't believe she was murdered, and I know damned well you've only been humoring me, keeping me busy with Chris's research and out of your way."

"Jillie . . ." He hesitated, unsure of how much of the truth he could tell her. "I don't know if anything you find will be useful or not, and I can't do what you do, I don't know the first thing about it. But I can tell you this: Reece Wycombe was up to his neck in it."

She looked at him in curious surprise.

"I interviewed Marge Beecher today. Wycombe is a bloody liar and a black-mailer." He paused as she suddenly went white, visibly shaken. "Which doesn't mean he's a killer," he added quickly. "But Chris had nothing to do with Dr. Arthur's offices being burgled or forging any papers to discredit him. That was all Wycombe's doing, getting his revenge on Chris for her rejecting him, professionally. So I *do* want to know what she was working on and it's *not* to humor you."

She stiffened as he took her hand, her fingers cold. "Maybe it was nothing, that man. Or maybe not. But if you're too frightened, then let it go. You tell me what you want me to do."

She didn't pull away. "It's not that. Yes, he scared the hell out of me. But I don't want to be one of those spineless women terrified of bogymen under the bed."

"It's natural to be afraid, Jillie. You're hardly spineless."

She exhaled a silent laugh. "Thanks." She sounded far from convinced.

"Why would you even think that you were?"

After a long moment, she said, "My husband certainly thought I was. I never once stood up to him about anything, ever. But as long as things weren't too bad, I could pretend they were actually good. Funny, I was so angry when he left me for another woman, it took me ages to remember I never even liked being married to him. And it was so hard, learning how to cope on my own. I'm so tired of being scared."

"We're not all like that, honest. It's hard on men, too, you know. Divorce. Living alone," he said, wrestling with the words. "I've adjusted, learnt how to take care of myself. Doing all my own cooking and the washing-up and hoovering."

He looked out over the rooftops, studied the silver thread of a jet stitching through a russet-gold sky, and wondered what the hell he was going on about. This went against the grain; he was disciplined to keep his private life and his problems to himself.

He'd disdained all this moaning about accepting human weakness, believing those who chose police work should be expected to cope, willingly, competently, even proudly, with stressful situations. Even now, he couldn't rid himself of the guilt that he'd been tested beyond his endurance and been found wanting. But if he wanted her to open up to him, the price she was asking was fair enough.

He glanced nervously at her. She sat with one foot tucked under her, waiting. "The hardest part is missing my sons growing up. It's like one of those stop-motion films, every other week they shoot up another inch. I think if I were with someone again—not saying I'm looking," he added hastily, "but if I were, it couldn't be someone too much younger than me, someone who'd want to have more children."

"Why not?"

"Couldn't afford it." He tried to laugh. Her remote smile seemed more an acknowledgment of his effort than humor. God, he hated this, but wasn't yet willing to give up. "I wouldn't have the lads think I was trying to replace them. I couldn't anyway. And losing my boys hurt a lot. I don't want to go through it again."

"That's a pessimistic attitude."

This time his laugh was easier. "I prefer to think of it as 'realistic.' Not that it's much of a pressing concern. Even if I could remember how, it's been too long, all my best chat-up lines have gone rusty."

And, this time, her reaction seemed warmer. "There hasn't been anyone else since you got divorced?"

"No one I was serious about," he said. "You?"

She hesitated, then shook her head. "Me neither."

"Do you ever miss him? Your husband?"

"Honest to God, cross my heart and hope to die, stick a needle in my eye?" He nodded. "*Never.* I actually like living on my own now."

He wondered, with more than a little self-pity, if Laura felt the same way about him.

"Do you ever miss your wife?"

"Honest to God truth, cross my heart and all the rest of it?" He exhaled against the ache. "Every minute of every day."

"Oh." She looked pained. "I'm sorry."

"Don't be. My reasons are all selfish."

Unlike Jillie, he couldn't imagine living the rest of his life alone, abandoning all hope of being with anyone else again. He needed hope far more than he had ever needed love; the specter of his lonely existence stretching out like a dark road toward a blank horizon frightened him in its sudden intensity.

They sat silently for several moments before Keen sighed. "I'm sorry. I'm not much good at this"—he thought of Phil—"touchy-feely, caring-and-sharing crap you see on *Trisha* or *Kilroy*; 'Let's spew our souls out before we hold hands and sing hymns,' it's just not me."

"It's not a quid pro quo." She drew her legs up under her skirt, the bench swinging, and wrapped her arms around her knees. Like a drawbridge going up on a castle, he thought. Shutting him out. Bloody princesses.

He wished she'd been British, then there wouldn't have been a problem; it wouldn't have occurred to him to attempt bridging that yawning gap between them in the first place. He didn't want to have been attracted to her, and wondered *would* he have, had they met under normal circumstances? Then again, under normal circumstances, they'd likely never have met at all. Depressing thought.

He shrugged in defeat. "It's not just because I'm a police officer. Yorkshiremen're raised to be stoic, never explain, never complain." Although that myth had been hard for him to live up to over the years. But he was pleased to see her smile, even fleetingly. "It's hard work when you've got a temper bad as mine."

"You?" she blurted with open astonishment. "You're the calmest person I think I've ever met!"

He smiled ruefully. "I do my best to keep it under control. I'm not fond of angry folk, don't like to find myself being one of them."

She sat too still. "That was the problem between you and your wife?" He looked at her, puzzled. "Did you hit her, I mean?"

"God, no!" His face burned with instant shame although he knew he was innocent. "I've never hit a woman in my life, never would."

She nodded as if she accepted his word for it, but her expression appeared as resigned as an abused child, both irritating and saddening him. "Not even if you had to arrest a woman?"

"No . . ."

"What if she were hitting you? Not even then?"

"No . . ."

"What would you do?" she persisted, her expression still solemnly unmoved.

"I'd sit on her," he snapped. "I weigh fourteen stone. Look, I'll give you my ex-wife's number, you can ring her and ask."

"Don't be silly," she said, passionless, the lines under her eyes making her look exhausted.

"Jillie . . . did your husband hit you?"

Astonished, she laughed. "Oh, no. No, he didn't. I didn't mean to give you that impression."

"Sorry, that was out of line."

"No, it wasn't." She huddled deeper into the arms wrapped around her knees. "We never even argued; Robert wouldn't allow it. He considered it a character defect. Whenever things got too tense between us, he would just go off to his office and work. I think he believes if you don't talk about a problem, then it doesn't really exist." She bent her head and closed her eyes, drawing herself in tighter as if she could make herself small enough to disappear.

He wanted to break down the drawbridge, helpless. Then he remembered something, something that sent a visceral thrill of unease up the back of his neck. "You told me you own two rifles . . . and a pistol."

She said nothing for so long, he thought he'd blown it. Then she said, "A Heckler and Koch P7 ten plus one." Her calm voice recited the specs as casually as had she been talking about a particular brand of soap. The hair on his arms prickled. "I bought it a couple years ago. In Oregon, all you need is a valid driver's license and sign a form saying you've never been convicted of a felony. Which by the time they get around to checking out, you've already got the gun and gone."

"What did you need a handgun for?" he asked quietly, steeling himself for the answer. He had vague images of a jealous, deserted wife plotting revenge against her unfaithful husband.

"We'd had a few break-ins in the neighborhood. I bought it for protection," she said, and he knew she was lying.

"You think you could really shoot someone? Pull the trigger and end another person's life?"

She looked at him blandly before she stood up and walked to the rooftop border, her back turned toward him as he followed. "Oh, yes," she said lifelessly. "I could." He shuddered, but kept silent, waiting. "Five years ago I was raped."

That, he hadn't expected. He nearly sighed with relief before what she had said registered. Not knowing how to respond, he said nothing, not even sure if she was going to continue.

"I don't know who he was, he must have followed me to the house," she said, keeping her back to him. "Robert wasn't home, he'd gone to Atlanta for a business conference that week. It was only me and Karen. He climbed in the kitchen window about three in the morning, came upstairs, and woke me up with a knife to my throat."

The serenity in her voice as she recited the facts unnerved him.

"He told me if I didn't do exactly as he said, or if I called the police, he'd come back and do it to Karen."

"Jesus," he whispered.

"The strangest part is, afterward I thought I'd be more upset that someone had violated my body. But that was the least of it. What was worse is that I didn't do anything to defend myself, just . . . lay there and let him do it. I felt like such a coward."

"Jillie—"

"Don't," she said sharply, cutting him off. Still, she didn't turn to face him. "He made me . . . He said things that . . ." She stopped and again the silence stretched excruciatingly. "When he left, I went into Karen's bedroom to make sure she was all right. She was still asleep. Then I saw her Raggedy Ann doll. I made it when she was born, and she always took it to bed with her." She took a deep breath, and Keen could see her tremble. "He'd cut the doll's head off."

"Did you call the police?"

"Of course not." She lowered her chin, her hair falling forward to hide what little he could make out of her face. Her voice was eerily calm, dispassionate. "I spent the rest of the night sewing the head back on her Raggedy Ann so she wouldn't find out. I didn't tell anyone. Didn't *want* to tell anyone, not even Robert . . ." She laughed, a terrible strangled sound. "*Especially* not

Robert. I just wanted to forget it ever happened. But when the obscene phone calls started, I had to tell him. He was so angry. Robert, I mean."

"I can understand that, I'd have wanted to kill the bastard . . ." Keen said softly, and was startled when she did turn around, her features twisted in rage and grief.

"He was angry with *me*. I must have forgotten to lock the window, or I got picked instead of someone else because of something I did. I was too friendly, too careless. He said I hadn't been cautious enough.

"After the calls started, I didn't want to live in that horrible house anymore. I didn't want to live in that *town* anymore. We moved to a house that wasn't as nice as the one we had, one farther away from his work. The whole thing was just a real inconvenience for him."

Listening helplessly to her, he wanted to hold her and knew he couldn't, knew she couldn't bear him to.

"He made me call the police. They were very sympathetic, even though they couldn't do much about it. I had a medical exam, but it was far too late by then. Not enough physical evidence left." She smiled bleakly. "I was a very bad witness. I didn't describe him too well."

"You couldn't have seen him that well in the dark," he tried to reassure her.

She opened her mouth, closed it again, then brushed her hands across her face. "I saw him just fine. The cops could tell, I knew they were annoyed with me. But all I could think of was that he'd come back for Karen. And the calls stopped after we moved. But he's still out there. Somewhere. Hurting some-one else." She was staring off into the distance. "And it's my fault—"

"Jillie . . ." He fumbled for the words. "Why didn't you ring up one of those rape crisis lines, talk to someone . . . ?"

"You mean that touchy-feely baloney where we puke our souls out before we hold hands and sing songs?" He was ashamed. "No, I thought I could han-dle it, because I *had* to. You can do almost anything when there's no other choice. So I pretended it never happened and got on with my life. I never told anyone, ever. Not even Chris.

"Then . . . ah . . ." Her voice shook for a moment, then steadied. "My marriage wasn't great to begin with, but after that, Robert couldn't . . . he couldn't make love to me anymore." Her eyes blinked out twin tears. "He couldn't stand the thought of putting himself where someone else had been, someone so disgusting. It made him feel . . . dirty."

He stood without touching her, both of them staring down at the street below.

"I haven't wanted to be with anyone for so long," she said, unable to meet his eyes. "I thought that part of me had died, and I was *glad*." Now she was weeping in earnest, swollen eyes pale without makeup. "Then you were so nice to me . . . I really like you, but if I told you, if you knew . . ." She gasped, half laugh half sob, and blurted out, "I was afraid you would think I wasn't good enough for you."

"*Good enough for . . .*" Appalled, he swallowed back a laugh and gently took her by her shoulders. At his touch, she broke, huge sobs racking her body. "Oh, Jillie." At a total loss, he simply cradled her in his arms, rocking her like a child until her weeping finally subsided.

Two hours later, Keen rang Phil and waited in a pub. He nursed his second scotch until Phil showed up. The younger man slid in beside him with his usual mocking grin. "Thought you'd have gone back to the countryside by now, where men are men and sheep are afraid."

Keen nodded at the bartender, reaching for his wallet. "What'll you drink?"

"Pint of bitter's fine, since you're buying."

They said nothing while the barkeep poured a pint from the tap, tilting the glass to clear the foam. He set it in front of Phil and took the tenner Keen placed on the counter, returning with a third scotch and change. Phil drained four inches of his beer in one pull. "So, why are you still here, Dunliffe?"

"The job's not done."

Phil snorted. "I can't work out whether you're persistent or just stupid. It's *over*. Go back to Leeds. What have you got to gain by annoying people here, aye?"

Anger brewed deep in his chest, he knew it was bad, knew Phil was right. "Christine Swinton were murdered." Phil rolled his eyes. "I'm convinced of it. And to sit by while someone gets away with it goes against everything I've ever worked for."

"Oh, bollocks. People get away with crimes every day, and we *all* know about it. We *all* sit on our hands and hope they get stupid enough to balls it up bad enough so that even the CPS can't miss it."

"This is different . . ."

"Yeah?" Phil's mocking smile had dimmed, the edge of bitterness showing. "Just what the hell makes this one so special? I got a case of a seventy-year-old man's run over by this building society manager been out drinking. Backs up to see what he's hit and runs the poor bugger over a second time. Leaves him lying there bleeding to death. By the time traffic's traced the car, it's reported as stolen and torched back of an estate. All neat and tidy, slag it off on them giro hooligans. Then when I interview the manager, *I know*. His story doesn't add up, hands shaking, he can't keep anything sorted. But he's got a convenient alibi, and no witnesses to contradict him. Besides, he's an upstanding member of the community, old geezer's just a Jamaican panhandler. Who cares, right? Certainly not the Crown Prosecution Service."

"Phil—"

But he wouldn't be stopped. "Then there's this local drug dealer's done in his junkie wife, chopped her up and put all the bits in a bin liner. Only she don't show up until she's about three months ripe in the local tip. No fingerprints, no forensics, no nothing. He's already reported her missing, big show weeping and wailing when they scrape up what's left of her. Except I know he's done it, my guv'nor knows he's done it. Everybody on the damn *estate* knows he's done it. But no one is saying bloody nothing, not if they don't want to end up like her, they aren't. We can't touch him. Just not enough solid evidence to convict him . . ."

"This isn't—" Keen felt the dark anger swelling close to the surface.

"I've got at least twenty cases of people murdered where I know damned well who did it. And I know damned well there's not a thing I can do about it. You were the one who said if she'd been just another tart instead of some political agitator floating in his lordship's lake, nobody would give a monkey. So why do you care so much? Because she was a rich white woman?"

"No. Because I made a promise I'd get to the truth."

Phil laughed, a surly, contemptuous sound. "In case you missed the ten o'- clock news, chivalry is *dead,* my son," he said, smirking. "Of course, I don't suppose the fact you're shagging her has the slightest thing to do with it, now does it?"

Keen hit him.

His reaction had been spontaneous rather than intentional. Deliberate or not, the impact was solid. Phil's head snapped back. He stumbled, arms wind-milling as he collided into empty chairs and fell. His pint of beer toppled as well, shattering glass and foam. Phil sprawled on the floor, his outstretched arms and legs tangled in furniture, and stared up at Keen with eyes wide with astonishment. The pub had gone silent, as if all the sound had been switched off, other patrons expectantly alert. Keen noticed the bartender reaching un-der the counter where no doubt he had a three-foot oak peacemaker stored just in case.

Then Phil touched his fingertips delicately to his split lip and stared at the blood in disbelief. "Jesus Christ," he said quietly. The utter lack of anger in his voice was unbearable.

Keen turned on his heel and left the pub.

"Oi, you!" the bartender shouted. "What about the damages . . . !"

He ignored him, striding out into the night and gasping in air like a man drowning. He walked until his feet ached, wandering in no particular direc-tion. Well after midnight, he found himself in front of Mrs. Flute's. The streets were quiet, abandoned. He stopped as he spotted a figure hunched on the front steps. The man looked up. Phil.

They stared at one another for a long moment.

"How long've you been here?" Keen asked, monotoned.

Phil pulled a flat pint of whiskey from his jacket and squinted at it. " 'Bout half a bottle." He winced as he attempted to smile. "Can't complain as I wasn't warned about you."

Keen looked up at the darkened windows, hoping Jillie was asleep. He swal-lowed against a dry throat and glanced away, down the deserted street, colors pallid and washed out in the streetlight.

"I have never in my life *ever* struck another officer."

"I'll take that as a weird sort of compliment. Had no idea I was so effective winding you up like that."

"I'm not looking for excuses. There are none."

"Uh-huh. I'd surely love to know who you've been practicing on, then, if not your partners. You're good, had my eyes wide open and never saw it coming." He held up the whiskey bottle. "You still drinking with me or not?"

Keen took the bottle, untwisting the screw cap and put it to his lips. The harsh, cheap liquid burned, and he swallowed quickly before handing the bottle back. Then he sat down heavily on the steps and stared at the ground between his feet.

They drank quietly for several minutes, passing the bottle between them. "You could make a complaint," Keen said finally, still unable to apologize. He felt foolish even as he said it.

Phil stared at him before he burst out laughing. Sprawling back against the steps, long jean-clad legs stretched out on the pavement, he tucked one hand under his head and said, "Give me a bloody break. Sure, pal, that's *just* what I intend to do, trot down the hall to Galton and tattle on you." He grinned past a badly swollen lip. "You know what your problem is, Dunliffe? You take yourself too seriously. You take the *job* too seriously. I have to warn you, you won't survive down here trying to carry around that much excess baggage."

Phil swallowed another mouthful of whiskey. As he hissed with the pain, Keen winced against a flicker of guilt. "Look, mate, the job's tough enough as it is. Yobbos to the left of us, poovs to the right, and here we are, stuck in it again. So why do you want to go and make it even harder on yourself, aye?"

"I don't know," Keen admitted. "I don't know about you, but I joined the force to do the job for what it was. Doing good by doing right. Now . . ." He shrugged. "It's all changed. Probationers with ten weeks at a regional training center let loose on the public, not even trained properly before they're teaching their own sprogs. Those with any talent or experience quit for civvy jobs and more money. What's left sickens me."

He ran his palm over his scalp. "I'm running a hundred miles an hour just to stand still. I don't have any energy left for idealism, it's just been beaten out of me. Don't even matter if the government's corrupt; they're killing us just as quick with pig-blind ignorance and incompetence."

He stopped, feeling foolish with his bitter lecture, and covered his embarrassment by rubbing his fingers into the sockets of his eyes.

"You should have a soapbox," Phil said dryly.

"I put in for one. Not enough in the budget."

The younger man had the courtesy to laugh, taking the sting out of it. "You have an interesting way of insulting people, Dunliffe. What, only you dinosaurs ever joined up for love of queen and country? Us kiddies were only after the pension scheme and medical coverage?" He shook his head in disbelief. "You old-timers may be God's gift to the Police Federation, but I joined for much the same reasons you did. I'd bet that's true for ninety-five percent of the people I work with. I'm just doing the best job I humanly can. Key word here being 'humanly.' So if I don't bother chasing after hopeless cases, it's because I know it's time better spent banging down the ones I can. That's not cynicism, that's common sense."

Keen sighed, a long exhalation. "I want it back," he said simply. "That idealism. I want to be the man I used to be again, not some uniform carrier shuffling paper as fast as I can to keep from being buried in it."

Phil swirled the whiskey bottle lazily, watching the amber liquor spin. "You won't win." He passed the bottle to Keen.

"Don't right know if I care anymore." Keen took a judicious sip of his own. "But I don't expect you to understand."

Phil glanced at him, amused. "And why's that? Because you've done twenty years to my six? Things were so much better in your day? Methinks your memory is a bit rosy, there, pal. Remember Operation Countryman and Broadwater Farm? Those good old days, you mean?"

Keen's anger flared, a brief flash of kindling in the belly. "Don't be lecturing me, *pal*. How the hell would you know what being in a riot were like? You weren't even there. I was."

Phil's grin widened. "You think so? I was in Brixton, September twenty-ninth, nineteen-eighty-five. Except I was on the other side of that thin blue line." He laughed at Keen's astonishment. "Me and all me mates in solidarity with the blacks and the Asians, all us angry young men making a stand together. Them against us. I didn't know shit about politics, too complex to understand even if I'd had the patience to try. Simple minds want simple answers."

He took another sip of whiskey, swishing it like mouthwash before he swallowed.

"So there I am, spotty punk kid, big for my age and trying too hard to be bigger, a smart lad pretending to be thick. Off we go with the rest of the pack marching on the police station, waving our fists, shouting our slogans. We reach the police line, they tell us to leave. Okay, fine, we've made our point and turn around.

"Except they've cordoned off the other end of the street and next thing I know all hell breaks loose. I think, fuck this for a lark, be just as happy to go home and have tea with me old granny, thank you very much. Suddenly this bobby in riot gear starts whacking the shit out of me; it's fucking Robocop, he's so encased in armor can't be no real person behind all that. Blood's flying everywhere, and this little voice in my head is saying, 'I'm just a kid. Why is he doing this to me?' "

Keen listened with his hands clasped around one knee. Phil still sprawled on the steps, his face obscure in the gloom.

"Next day, I'm lying there still bleeding all over me granny's chintz sofa watching telly. And there's ol' Maggie pontificating about all us nasty hooligans and mothers crying over their young'uns been hurt by them fascist police, and there's a couple bobbies in hospital aren't in any better shape than me. It's all getting mixed up together, starts me thinking: them *is* us. Things aren't black and white, they aren't even shades of gray. It's a Technicolor world out there, Dunliffe, and if you start trying to sort out all the pixels one from the other, you'll end up going mad."

"So that's your answer, is it? Sit back and watch the show, flip it off when you get bored?"

"More or less," Phil agreed, unoffended. "Step back from it far enough to keep the picture in focus and send for the repairman when it goes on the blink. That's us, bloody repairmen."

"Marvelous motivation for joining the police."

"Part of it. Part of it was wanting to make things better and naïve enough to think I had all the right answers. And part of it was that if someone had to be thumped, I'd rather be the one doing the thumping." He grimaced, working his tongue against a tooth. "Hasn't always worked out that way."

He held up the bottle, an inch sloshing in the bottom. Keen shook his head. Phil screwed the cap back on and shoved it into his jacket.

"Still, it's strange, wondering, you know? Sometimes when I walk through the station, I can't help thinking, 'could of been *you,* mate, or you or you.'" He grinned at Keen, his smile lopsided from the cut on his lip. "Or maybe even *you.*"

"I weren't in Brixton and I didn't thump anyone." He didn't mention he'd been one of those bobbies who'd been thumped themselves. Phil looked mildly disappointed. They listened to the electric lines sizzle overhead in the misty night air.

"So, kemo sabe. What's our game plan?"

"You still in with me?" Keen tried to keep the incredulity out of his tone.

"Not if you plan on punching me in the mouth again."

Keen examined his knuckles where the skin had broken against the edges of Phil's teeth. "No. Your head's too hard on my fist." He studied the cracked sign above the grocery, neon light sputtering. "I don't get it, what's changed your mind?"

"Truth?" Phil chuckled. "For the hell of it. I like puzzles, it interests me. It's more fun than your usual run of handbag snatchers and dimwit druggies breaking into estate flats." His tone changed, more somber. "But it's not personal for me. Bad thing to do, take a case and turn it into something personal."

"Little late now."

"Uh-huh. So where do we go from here?"

"Phil, I think maybe this Wycombe character could have done it. Maybe just an argument got out of hand instead of some stupid anarchist conspiracy."

"I'm still not convinced there's any murder," Phil said, "but say he did. So why not bang him up for it? Why protect him? Just to save some petty bureaucrat's arse? Makes no sense."

"No, it doesn't," Keen agreed. "But whatever it's about, someone in the job is covering it up. Someone fairly high up, at that. And you and I both know it."

A car sped by with a soft shush of tires, the night so quiet Keen could hear the engine dopplering.

"If I enjoyed being despised and spit on, I'd move over to Complaints and Discipline. Why not let them sort it out?" Phil said finally.

Keen heard no conviction in the younger man's voice. "*Someone* on our side has been passing information on to Special Branch. Whatever connected Schaefer to Wortley or Barrow has been neatly cleared out. Then a couple of unfriendly young coppers made it a point to inform me they know where my little boys live."

Phil grunted in concerned surprise. "What will you do about that?"

"I don't know yet. Other than doing what they want, and back off."

"And you're too stupid to do that, aren't you?"

Keen didn't answer that question. "We're just a couple of ten-a-tuppence sergeants, you and me. We need someone further up the chain willing to give *us* information while being content to let it be our arses on the line."

"Not Galton," Phil said without malice. "He's too by-the-book. That sort is either too straight to be of any damn use at all, or about as bent as they get."

"Then I think the next thing to do is have a private chat with Chief Superintendent McCraig." Phil made a noise Keen wasn't sure was agreement or doubt. "He knows more about what's really going on in the Met and Home Office than we're likely to get elsewhere."

"What makes you so sure he's not in it himself? Even if he isn't, he must know enough already and still be willing to look the other way."

"I think he's clean. I'm not planning on making a lot of noise with this. A quiet word off the record, then we'll see where we stand. But we have to start by trusting someone."

Still lounging on the steps, Phil raked his hair with one hand and kept it there, his arm blocking the streetlight. Keen couldn't see his face.

"And if you're wrong, mate, we're fucked," the voice in the dark said cheerfully. "What we're discussing goes beyond a bit of naughtiness curb crawling or fiddling a notebook for extra overtime. Not that I'd mind shopping 'em if we find out some of our own governors are corrupt. Problem again is, how do you go about separating those bloody pixels? Say you're right—it can't be only one person. Wouldn't surprise me if the rot'll go well back inside Special Branch, maybe even Home Office. But them's the big boys, Dunliffe. We find out this or that one's bent, who do we tell? *He's* going to know who his friends are while we don't. No one will touch him and we're dropped right in it. What's left? Try running it up properly through the ranks? How sure are you that you can trust your own bosses?"

A reasonable question. Keen had been in the job long enough there were few bosses he'd started with, never mind trusted. The only one left was Harper, who had backed him when he hadn't had to. But even then he couldn't dislodge that small element of doubt. After twenty-odd years, the realities of his job had ossified his cynicism. He remembered with visceral clarity sitting in that interview room, his head bowed over hands clasped so tightly they ached, eyes locked onto the Formica tabletop as if searching for hidden messages in the fake wood grain. Keen had known the C&D officer for years, respected and even liked him. He'd maintained a stoical silence for hours as the man tried his hardest to help. If that experience had been so distressful, it wasn't likely those people he was after would be any more forthcoming with information about their own misdeeds.

"No offense, Phil, but I trust mine a hell of a lot more than I trust yours."

Phil snorted. "The Met's not any more bent than anywhere else. Maybe we're a bit crimped around the edges, but we're still legal tender. But yours or mine, bent or not, how far do you think we'll get before we bump up into that brick wall again?"

It would be difficult to even find someone who would *want* to know. Too many bureaucratic cover-ups were less a matter of criminal conspiracy than even the most honest of police officers reluctant to risk jeopardizing their retirement pension.

"What then? Go to the press or the telly?"

"I don't believe it's that bad," Keen insisted.

"You willing to bet your warrant card on it?" Phil asked softly.

Keen studied his hands. "Yes," he said finally. "Because if it *is* that bad, it's nothing I want to be a part of anyway. You can still back out, Phil, no hard feelings."

Phil grinned, sat up, and clapped a hand on Keen's shoulder. "Oh, what the hell. I never did think I'd make chief constable, anyway."

Absurdly grateful, Keen glanced at Phil's swollen lip. "Sorry."

Phil dabbed at it cautiously. "Yeah, well. All's fair in love and war. The only painful part now's going to be explaining it to the wife, especially rolling in at this hour with scotch on my breath." He chuckled. "She's not too sympathetic, my Gabby. I'm in for a good two-week grovel before *I* get any."

Phil stood, a little unsteady on his feet. "Speaking of which, are you, um . . . involved with the lady?" He was safely out of arm's reach. "Not meaning to pry," he quickly added as Keen looked up sharply. "Only asking out of professional interest here."

"No, I'm not shagging her." Although he desperately wanted to, he didn't dare admit.

Phil winced. "Sorry about that." Keen shrugged. "Well, see you tomorrow?"

"Yeah. Thanks, Phil. I appreciate it."

Keen watched until Phil had vanished around the corner before he unlocked the door of Mrs. Flute's flat as quietly as he could, not easy to do with so many keys.

Unfortunately, Jillie was awake, having never gone to bed. She sat at the top of the stairs, waiting for him. "Who were you talking to out there?"

"A friend." He preferred not to explain too far. "Didn't mean to disturb you."

"You didn't disturb me." She shuffled over to make room beside her. "Mrs. Flute's gone to bed. She was worried when you weren't here when she came home. Then this guy shows up and sits out front drinking for the longest time. She was about to call the cops when you came back and started talking to him."

He smiled. That might have been interesting. "We'd had an argument." Then he added reluctantly, not sure why, "I hit him."

"Was he hurt?" She didn't seem shocked or upset.

He cleared his throat. "Not seriously."

"What did you hit him for?"

"Nothing we couldn't work out."

"You don't want to talk about it."

"No," he conceded tersely. "I don't want to talk about it." He'd had enough of talking for one night.

"None of my business," she said far too reasonably.

"Damn it, woman . . ." Resigned, he sighed. "Look, I've always had a temper, schoolyard scraps, a couple pub brawls, that sort of thing. But after my wife left me, I'd lost everything I cared about. It made me angry. So I used anger like a drug, to give me the energy to keep going. I told myself that anger was good, helped me to cope. If I could just keep running, I'd be all right."

He sat with his arms balanced on his knees, addressing his hands. "And it *did* work. For a while. Until I got tired and dropped myself right in the shit. I screwed up, cut too many corners . . ."

He had fallen into speaking in a near monotone, not feeling much of anything behind the words. His memories had all faded to a distant black and white, like badly flickering images of an old movie: Clive, white-faced as he pleaded for Keen to calm down, for chrissake, just slow the fuck down. The crash that hadn't hurt either one of them. The silence of the rain as the radiator spewed white steam into the black night sky, while Clive stood on the pavement shaking his head in disgust. Keen remembered the fury boiling into an uncontrollable fire in his head as the joyriders in the stolen car squealed around the corner to laugh at them. Open mouths laughing, black mocking holes in white faces. He wanted to break those faces, kill that laughter. He'd leapt out into the street straight in front of the speeding car, thrown his hand radio into the windscreen as hard as he could in a blind rage.

He remembered the brilliant white spiderwebs of cracked glass, the car fishtailing on the wet road as the blinded driver skidded over the pavement. He remembered the look of surprise on Clive's face as the car smashed into him, no fear, not even pain, just surprise as he sailed over the bonnet, and fell a broken man.

But Keen couldn't remember any color at all . . . except one . . .

Funny how the streetlights turned the color of blood to violet, as dark as burgundy wine splattered across the rain-polished pavement . . .

He stopped and took a breath. "I almost got someone killed. A colleague. A friend." Suddenly so much pressed down on him he couldn't begin to describe what had happened, couldn't find words to explain the sleepless nights and recurring nightmares, his manic bursts of energy followed by depressed exhaustion, the irrational anxiety, and above all, the intense shame with being forced to accept psychological treatment or face medical retirement. He wasn't crazy, feared the stigma such therapy implied.

He shrugged, a gesture of frustration rather than callousness. "I nearly got the sack. I was lucky. It frightened the life out of me, made me stop and think. I can't afford to be angry anymore. I'd lost my wife and my kids, and that hurt. More than I'd have ever believed anything could. But if I'd lost the job as well . . ." He swallowed hard. "I think I would have lost myself."

"Work doesn't make us who we are, it's only what we do," she said softly.

He tried to laugh, but the effort was too strained. "That's what the counselors tell us, innit?" When she didn't respond, he looked away. He'd thought he'd navigated the long, painful road back as well as anyone could have, learned to accept less—from his ambitions, his life, himself. Now, the feeling he'd somehow been cheated roiled within him.

"I've been a police officer most of my adult life. I hate it sometimes and love it sometimes, and sometimes it gets me so discouraged I don't know what the hell good I'm doing. But I don't care what anyone bloody says, it's still what I *am*." He looked up in helpless anger. "I don't how to be anything other than a policeman."

He stopped, appalled. He had never said any of this to anyone before, not to any of his mates, not to his superiors, not to that condescending force welfare officer he'd had to see week after miserable week for stress counseling. Not even to Laura.

He froze as she did an astonishing thing. She turned to balance on her bare feet on the steps below him, took his hands in hers, and laid her cheek against them. Wordless, she looked up into his face. His mouth went dry, and suddenly he didn't want that, not this way.

"I can't, Jillie," he whispered.

Her eyes glittered as they scanned his face. He couldn't read the expression in her own, like a mask of translucent flesh illuminated by blurred emotions underneath; confusion, hurt, anger, fear, he couldn't pin any of them down. She started to pull away, and his hands tightened on hers, stopping her. "It's not that I don't want to. But we have to keep this professional. At least for now."

She smiled wanly. "I understand. I can wait."

He wasn't sure how long he could.

X I

SUNDAY

Keen sat on the park bench gazing out across the Thames as McCraig walked by, neither man acknowledging the other. A young couple threw a Frisbee for a black mongrel dog, red handkerchief tied around its neck. McCraig paused as the animal nearly knocked him over. The girl, a pretty brunette wearing a sheer summer dress and Doc Martens boots, apologized sweetly. Once McCraig had passed, Keen stood up, and ambled after him. He walked into the gent's public and took a urinal two down from where McCraig paid close attention to his own business. A toilet flushed, and a thin, pockmarked man in skintight jeans exited a stall. He gave them both a lingering once-over, smiling silkily. When it wasn't returned, he shrugged and left.

They were alone. Keen zipped and washed his hands in the small sink, the porcelain cracked, the soap dispenser empty. No hot water tap, the cold water barely a dribble. Crumpled paper towels soaked in a large puddle under leaking pipes. Graffiti had been sprayed onto broken tiled walls; BLAIR IS A SPIV; STUFF STRAW, DUNK BLUNKETT. The public toilet reeked.

"I don't care for meeting like this," McCraig groused beside him. "It's too much like crap television." The towel dispenser was empty, and McCraig shook his hands, air-drying them.

Keen laughed to himself, thinking crap television would have had them in Burberry trench coats on a deserted dock, Canary Wharf a chic backdrop, where anyone with a decent telephoto could snap the breeze artfully ruffling their razor-cut hairstyles. "Sorry, sir. Best I could think of under the circumstances."

"Then make it short," McCraig snapped.

"Christine Swinton were murdered."

McCraig's eyes narrowed. "It's been ruled otherwise, Mr. Dunliffe, and the police aren't making any further inquiries."

Keen slowly smiled. "You haven't said it *wasn't* murder." When McCraig didn't answer, he said, "In Leeds, you were the one trying to convince me this case weren't right. The water in her lungs, abrasions on her tongue, scopolamine in her blood. Then I start finding other suspicious particulars and suddenly the case is dropped, Scudder exiled to Siberia." He studied McCraig. "Look me in the eye and tell me it really was an accidental death; that for whatever reasons, Scudder tampered with the forensic evidence. I'll go back to Leeds and that's the end of it."

McCraig assessed him as carefully as a man debating picking up a scorpion. "You wearing a wire?"

Talk about crap television, Keen thought, and held his arms out from his sides. "Search me, then."

McCraig did, brisk and thorough. When he stepped back, he was only marginally more relaxed. "So what do you have for supposing the Swinton woman was murdered?"

"For a start, I've matched prints from the Swinton house to those taken from broken glass at her bedsit in Leeds. They belong to a Dr. Reece Wycombe—"

He stopped at McCraig's faint smirk. "Then you haven't heard."

"Heard what?"

"Wycombe committed suicide late last night."

For a stunned moment Keen absorbed it. "Convenient."

"Unfortunately, it looks convincing. Wrote a note, washed down a bottle of Gordon's for courage, and shot himself in the mouth. His housekeeper found him this morning in his study."

"What did the note say?"

"Not verbatim but on the line of being awfully sorry for what he'd done to poor Dr. Swinton."

"Typed or written?"

"Typed. Old-fashioned Remington, no computer. But his housekeeper says it's definitely his machine and his signature."

"Gun his?"

"Yes. Family souvenir." McCraig snorted. "Tiny two-shot three-fifty-seven Derringer, looks like a bloody toy. Housekeeper'd seen the damned thing in his desk any number of times, assumed it was one of those fancy cigarette lighters." He frowned. "Only peculiarity was he'd shot himself twice. Coroner said it's not too unusual, the second shot's a reflex pull on the trigger, man was already dead."

"Powder burns?"

"Textbook perfect."

"Shit."

McCraig watched him, eyes amused. "So if Wycombe *was* your murderer," he said, "not much more to be done about it, is there?"

"Then there's a connection between the dead woman's solicitor and one of the other victims, Alice Guiscoigne. I had reason to think the other two victims might also be connected, but a couple of busy policemen cleaned out any evidence which might have confirmed it."

"Yes, I know."

"*Is* there a connection?"

McCraig coughed gently. "Mr. Schaefer has given his full cooperation and satisfied the appropriate parties concerned that while his offices had indeed been in contact with all four of these people, nothing in his involvement was unethical or illegal, nor involved in any of the deaths, including Swinton's."

"Rather a long coincidence. Mind telling me what that connection was?"

"Yes, I would. You're no longer on any inquiry, so you have no need to know. Those authorities concerned have already ruled on it, and the case has been *closed,* Mr. Dunliffe." His tone was as gentle as a father rebuking a small child. Strangely, Keen took no offense, the sweep of anger clearing his head like a shot of good whiskey. It was remarkably easy to keep his voice calm.

"So I was reminded by two brave lads who found it necessary to tell me they've been watching my children."

McCraig grunted, displeased. The chief superintendent's reaction alleviated some of the tension in Keen's gut.

"Say you're right; Swinton was murdered. Wycombe did it, and he's killed himself." McCraig shrugged a shade too casually. "The rest is just another sordid incident blown out of all proportion by an overzealous bureaucrat. End of story. There's no more to be gained in further investigation except possibly embarrassing a few underhanded politicians. While you and I might personally find that gratifying, the increasing number of other investigations is already straining the limits of a *de*creasing police budget. It's just not on, Sergeant."

Keen didn't reply. McCraig's lecture had been delivered too smoothly, too sincerely to convince.

Inspecting his nails, McCraig said, "Your superintendent thinks rather highly of you. It seems you've been waiting an unwarranted length of time for your promotion to inspector."

"First threats, now a bribe?" Keen shook his head.

McCraig chuckled with unamused incredulity. "My God, an idealistic policeman." His expression hardened. "The system isn't kind on idealistic policemen, Mr. Dunliffe. If you want to keep chasing this case, that's for you to take up with your own CID. As far as the Met or Home Office is concerned, we're finished here."

He turned as if to go, but stopped when Keen said calmly, "I'd be doing it on my own time." McCraig looked back, intrigued.

"By yourself?"

"If necessary."

"*Not* recommended. How much do you make a year, Sergeant?"

"Thirty-two thousand pounds." Before taxes and child maintenance, which McCraig already knew.

"Hardly an adequate budget for conducting a murder investigation, is it?" When Keen didn't answer, he rubbed his chin. "I've met your type before, Mr. Dunliffe. Bulldog stubborn. Bulldog *stupid*. You sink your teeth into something and you don't have enough sense to know when to let go of it."

His eyes level, Keen didn't reply. McCraig fished a pipe and a pouch of tobacco from his coat pocket, paying fastidious attention to tamping the tobacco into the bowl and lighting it. He dropped the match on the sodden floor to sizzle into a blackened splinter. Aromatic smoke mixed with the odor of rancid urine. He inspected Keen shrewdly, eyes narrowed against the smoke.

"A word of advice," he said finally. "While I wouldn't mind seeing certain members of this government hanged by their hairy testicles, don't confuse incompetence with conspiracy. There might *be* nothing to find. If Home Office is sweeping a few dead cockroaches under the rug, it's more likely an attempt to conceal a political blunder, not criminal activity. They're bureaucrats, not policemen."

Keen's heart beat faster. "I understand, sir."

"However . . ." He looked away, clearing his throat. "There are a few anomalies about this case which I don't like any better than you do. Keep it legal, and don't involve yourself more than necessary. Or that American woman; let's keep foreign nationals out of it. No heroics." McCraig smiled tightly. "I can't protect you if you screw up, but I may be able to arrange a few things, send along this and that which may be of use. Strictly as a private favor. Just do your job, cover the ground."

"That's all I'm asking."

"And no more of these ridiculous clandestine meetings. Don't bother me again unless you've got something solid."

He jammed the pipe into his mouth before opening the door, almost tripping over the OUT OF ORDER sign. He glared as Phil quickly whisked it out of the way.

"Sorry, guv'nor," he said, grinning. McCraig scowled but said nothing, striding away. Phil looked at Keen questioningly.

"Wycombe's dead. Shot himself."

"My, oh, my," Phil said phlegmatically. "That do throw a spanner in the works, dunnit? Now what?"

"Now we look for proof that Wycombe killed her. And for who else was involved in it and why."

"God, you're a pigheaded bastard." He glanced at McCraig's retreating back, puffs of smoke trailing behind him like a small locomotive. "Still think he's clean?"

Keen shrugged. "Do we have a choice?"

Phil hadn't worked too many weekends since he'd been a uniformed constable. The detective's room was largely empty, but as Keen was currently less than welcome in the Kentish Town Station, they took over the vacant Pub Licensing Office to avoid the curious. This being London in the summertime, uniformed officers continued dragging in a surplus of GBHs committed between overheated neighbors, along with the usual handbag snatches, shoplifting, gang warfare, arson, burglary, and general mayhem. Shrieked obscenities echoed down the corridors as Phil and Keen sifted through a large box of files.

Phil claimed the only comfortable seat, tilting back with his ankles crossed on the desk. Keen made do with the sofa, a squat, sagging affair barely wide enough for very companionable Kate Moss twins.

Every other space not occupied by bums or feet was covered with paper: incident reports, arrest reports, SOCO listings of Submission of Articles for Examination reports, Support Unit files, Summary of Evidence files, Confidential Information forms, Exhibits List files, Initial Remand Application forms, faxes of photocopies of other faxes sent back and forth from various Force Records Offices, and reams of barely legible scrawled witness statements.

Anything and everything that could be dredged up which even remotely connected to Christine Swinton or Reece Wycombe.

They spent the afternoon in quiet reading, only the flutter of pages turning or another file discarded onto a growing heap. "I'm missing the last page on the Colette Preston statement," Keen murmured, the first words he'd spoken in two hours.

Phil glanced up from a file in his lap, rummaged through tattered blue folders, and surfaced with a sheet of paper with a corner missing where it had been ripped from the grip binder. "In James Preston's file." He propelled it toward Keen, the page sailing like a dead leaf to the floor. "Anything?" he asked with forlorn hope.

"Nope."

"This is a bloody waste of time," Phil grumbled, flipping another page on a witness statement. "This Giles Roxbury claims he's slept with so many Page Three girls, he can't keep straight which one he's had on what day. Look at this, *Dani Behr,* for chrissake. What is it with women and doctors, anyway?"

"Wrinkled green pajamas'll do it every time. Jealous?"

"Too right I am. If he's not a total lying wanker." Phil tossed the Roxbury file onto the discard pile and picked up another witness statement from a disgruntled neighbor who had had a dispute with Chris Swinton eight months previously over a rubbish skip. The details of this tenuous connection had been taken down by a PC with the worst spelling errors Phil thought he'd ever seen.

"Someone should check out his alibis." Phil was beginning to loathe Keen's laconic Northern accent. "Interview all those lovely lasses to make sure he were actually where he said he was."

"Fine. You do it," Phil said, rubbing his neck. "I'm in enough hot water with the missus as it is."

"She give you a rough time last night?"

"No." Phil grinned. "I wasn't conscious long enough for her to give me a rough time. She saved it up for this morning, goes great with a hangover. I had to promise her a romantic weekend trip to France before she'd stop doing my head in."

"How awful, France. Fate worse than death, that is."

Then again, sometimes he thought he might get to like this surly Yorkshire mug. "Yeah. No kiddies, no job, no hospital, just the two of us in bed the whole weekend drinking champagne and shagging ourselves blind. And I daren't let on how much I'm going to enjoy it; if she suspects I'm not properly repentant, she'll insist on dragging her mum along. Sightseeing and souvenir shopping." He shuddered.

Keen didn't respond, scanning his file before he closed it. "You know what's odd," he said, more to himself, "there's not much about her in any of this."

Phil raised an eyebrow.

"What I mean is, here she were, active for years with all these causes, Wildlife Foundation, Save Our Planet, Charter Eighty-eight, all the rest of it. Always going on marches, arrest record an arm long. And she's got a busy social life, family Christmas bashes with the Prestons, dinners with the Selkirks, all these high society dos for charities. Loads of boyfriends, drinks a bit too much but still the life of the party. Right?"

Phil rested his cheek in one hand, listening. "Okay, so what?"

"So everybody interviewed knows precious little about the woman. Boyfriends never last more than a week, no close friends, not even Jillie Waltham. Even that bunch of professors, they've all heard about her affair with this Dr. Jordan, her feud with Wycombe. But they're just repeating second-hand stories. Like she's somehow there but invisible."

Phil shrugged. "I give up. What's it mean, then?"

Keen stared around at the clutter. "I'm not sure."

Sighing, Phil let his feet slide off the desk. Dunliffe had to be pretty far gone on this American teacher lady, he thought, to be getting that weird look like a man chasing UFOs or the Yorkshire Moor Monster. And *he* was starting to be very sorry indeed he'd involved himself in this lunacy. On his days off, no less.

"When you figure it out, you'll let me know, won't you? I'm going home while I've still got one."

"Go on, I'll finish up here." Keen opened another file.

"Glutton for punishment." Phil unclipped a key from his Ferrari key ring, as close to an Italian sports car as his family Volvo would ever let him get. "Lock them in my desk when you're done, there's a good chap."

Jillie couldn't figure out the time zones; was it five in the morning or the afternoon in Portland? Or was it four? Or six? After three attempts to use her Sprint card, too many fumbled numbers, she gave up and called the operator. Even that wasn't easy, British telephone numbers for even the simplest things entirely different from what Jillie had always assumed to be "normal" rather than merely American.

Finally, she heard Karen's voice through the long-distance hiss.

"Hello, sweetheart."

"Mom!" Karen turned it into a three-syllable protest. "Do you have any idea what time it is here?"

She winced. "No, not really. Sorry, baby, did I wake you up?"

"Of course you woke me up," Karen groaned. "But I'm glad you called. How are you?"

"Fine. Better. You?"

"Okay." Jillie heard her daughter yawn. "Sorry, I'm not quite awake yet."

"Do you have a pencil and paper handy? I want to give you a phone number where you can reach me."

"You're not staying at Aunt Chris's house?" Karen's voice was shockingly steady; the resilience of youth, Jillie thought.

"No. Her sister-in-law wants to renovate before they move in."

"I take it you've met Her Royal Highness, the Grand Duchess Celia." Karen snickered. "What a total bitch. What did you think of her?"

"We didn't hit it off, either. Anyway, I'm staying at a bed and breakfast in Camden Town—"

"Way cool! That's a really great area, Mom."

"Well, it is pretty funky."

" 'Funky,' " Karen mimicked. "Is that, like, the same thing as 'groovy'? Is it a far-out happening fab marvy place, can you dig it?"

Jillie smiled in spite of herself. "Listen, kiddo. Someday, you too will be old and wrinkly, like, a so totally awesome concept, y'know?"

Karen laughed. "Okay, what's the number?"

Jillie gave it to her, then wasted more money on an international call on trivial things, the drip in the bathtub, cranky Mrs. Fianobello's mutt pooping on the front lawn again, what garage should fix the brakes on Karen's Toyota. Then Jillie asked with false casualness, "How's Carlos doing these days?"

"I haven't seen Carlos in *ages*. Not since I caught him sucking face with that snake-in-the-grass Anna Birkowleski."

"Oh, I'd forgotten," Jillie said, her chest hollow. "You haven't gone out with anyone since Carlos, have you?"

She listened to the puzzled silence, the subliminal chittering of ghost voices on the line. "No. I haven't been out with anyone since Carlos. What's this all about?"

"Karen . . ." Her face felt clammy. "Baby, I have to ask you something." But she couldn't, gulping for breath.

"Mom?"

"Are you gay?" she blurted.

Again, the silence stretched unbearably. "Would you stop loving me if I were?" Karen asked, her tone icy.

Jillie squeezed her eyes shut. "Of course not. I love you, no matter what."

"Well, I'm not. Okay? Feel better? Not that it would be any of your business if I were." Her relief was so intense she nearly missed Karen say, "I guess this means you've found out about Aunt Chris."

"You *knew?*"

"I've known since I was fifteen, Mom."

"And you never told me you knew she was gay?"

"She wasn't gay; she was bi. AC/DC. She liked it both ways. And if she wanted you to know, she'd have told you herself."

"Karen . . . How did you . . . ? Did she ever . . . ?" Jillie couldn't finish the thought, never mind the sentence.

"Jeez, Mom. Get real, of *course* not. Like, you're straight, right? But that doesn't mean you go to bed with every *guy* you meet, does it?"

No, it most certainly did not, she thought.

"Anyway," Karen continued, "she made me promise I wouldn't ever tell you."

"Why not?"

"Because she was afraid maybe you wouldn't let me stay with her for summer vacations anymore." Karen hesitated. "And I think she was right."

"Honey, that's not true," Jillie protested. "How can you say that?"

"Christ, Mom! Here you find out she's bisexual, and the first thing you worry about is whether or not she's seduced your precious daughter! I mean, you pretend to be all left-wing liberal, but *you* are so conservative, even worse than Dad. You won't get your ears pierced, you think only hookers wear short skirts or high heels, you won't even polish your nails!"

Jillie struggled not to cry, confused and hurt. "So I don't wear flashy clothes or paint my nails, what does that prove? When I was your age, I was busted for protesting against nuclear power, how is that being conservative?"

"Get off it, Mom. You've been milking those glory days for years, but you haven't done diddly squat since. I mean, yeah, Dad may be a Republican right-wing fascist, but at least he's a *consistent* right-wing fascist. You say one thing and do another. You married him, you must have liked him for a reason. I think you're secretly turned on by conservative guys because they're safe. Dependable. And preferably white, middle class, and totally blah."

"Karen! You make me sound like a bigot—"

"You *are* a bigot! So you didn't go out of your way like Dad to make Carlos feel like he just swam across the Rio Grande, but you weren't terribly upset when we broke up, either. Who was it said I only went out with him to get back at Dad, hm?"

"I thought the way he treated you was a bit heavy on the Latino machismo."

"He never acted that way when he wasn't around you guys. Carlos resented you treating him like he was only going out with me because I was white, and I resented you for being a hypocrite about it."

Jillie took a breath and willed herself not to rise to the bait. Long practice had perfected her skills. "I never meant for either of you to take it that way, Karen. But this isn't about Carlos, is it?"

Karen sighed. "No, it's not," she admitted reluctantly. "Carlos was a jerk, but that wasn't because he was Chicano. And I did enjoy sticking it to Dad.

And you. I just wished you could have been more honest about it, like Aunt Chris."

Jillie tried to keep her voice from shaking. "I used to wish I was more like her, too. I used to wish I *was* her, and now I find out I never really knew her at all."

"So are we through fighting now?"

"Oh, honey. We weren't fighting."

"Well, I was." She heard Karen chuckle softly. "You're no fun, you give up too easy. Sorry, Mom. I didn't mean all that stuff about, you know, being a bigot. I just said it because you pissed me off. Stop worrying. I'm completely heterosexual, and I'll probably end up marrying some boring white-bread boy with a name like Todd or Beau who'll kiss your feet and call Dad 'sir.' That'll make his day."

Jillie managed a laugh. "All I care about is that you're happy. And wait until you've finished college. There, that's the conservative in me."

"First I have to *find* someone. And I plan on living together first, the idea of marrying someone you don't know if you can live with is, like, major stupid."

"Something I should maybe have done myself. See? I'm not totally hopeless."

"Speaking of totally hopeless, Dad came by the house yesterday to be sure I was okay staying here by myself. And to give me some fatherly advice about that stuff in Aunt Chris's will and everything."

Jillie had regained enough composure to keep her voice neutral. "Really? How thoughtful of him."

Karen laughed. "C'mon! Give him a little credit for trying. But you should have been here, Mom. The man is, like, such a total wreck!"

"Over Chris?" Jillie was perplexed.

"No. Guess what . . . ?"

"What?"

"You're never gonna believe this—"

"What?"

"Beverly's pregnant!"

Jillie felt as if she'd been slapped, breathless with shock. "Oh, no." It was a statement of pain, not disbelief.

"Oh, *yes.*" Karen gloated from halfway around the world, oblivious. "You remember that bull Uncle Homer castrated, poor animal walking around two days later, completely spaced? Dad had that exact same look!" After a prolonged silence, Karen said, "Mom?"

"I'm a little spaced myself, honey. You're not bothered by the idea of a new baby brother or sister?"

Again, her *tsk* carried through the line clearly. "*Half* brother or sister. What's the big deal? I think it's ironic; eighteen years of Dad yapping on about being glad when I'm grown and gone, and here he is, stuck for another eighteen. Serves him right. I straight-out told him no way I'm his free babysitting service, fuck that."

Jillie winced. "Karen . . ."

"Yeah, yeah. Watch my mouth. But just because Dad got Beverly the Blow-up Bimbo knocked up doesn't mean I have to like her now. Or their sniveling little brat, even if we are related."

"Now who's not being fair, Karen? The child isn't born yet and already you hate him."

"Or *her*. Don't be so sexist!"

"Or her." Jillie giggled. "Your poor father."

Karen echoed her laughter. "Poor Dad."

"Poor Beverly."

"The hell with Beverly. Poor you. Poor *me*!"

"Poor everybody."

The laughter went out of Karen's voice. "Poor Aunt Chris."

"Yeah," Jillie said, her own humor extinguished. "Poor Chris."

"I really loved her a lot, Mom." The tears were back.

"I know, baby. I'll be home soon. Sweet dreams."

Keen stood in the doorway of Mrs. Flute's sitting room and watched Jillie, wondering whether he should disturb her. Dressed in jeans and a T-shirt, she lay in the overstuffed chair like a tired child, eyes closed, her head propped on one arm of the chair, her legs dangling over the other. Papers littered the floor, an open book on her stomach rising and falling with her breath. She looked lovely.

"I'm not asleep," she murmured, her eyes closed. "I'm just taking a break."

He smiled, and settled into the armchair's mate. When she opened her eyes, he nodded at the untidy pile of books and photocopies. "Been keeping busy?"

She rubbed her face tiredly. "Yes and no. Not much is open on Sundays, so I thought I'd go through this again, see if I missed something."

"Found anything in all that?"

"Are you really interested, or are you just trying to be nice?"

"I'm really interested." He injected as much sincerity as he could into his voice.

She smiled skeptically, then swung bare feet to the floor and sat up to rummage through the chaos of papers.

"Researching women isn't easy because most historical accounts are written by men. All you usually find is whether or not she kept a clean house, was she pious in church and obeyed her husband. Interchangeable tombstones, 'here lies fill-in-the-blank, loving wife and devoted mother.' Nothing about her hopes, her dreams, her life. I wonder sometimes what anyone two hundred years from now is going to know about me, or Karen. Or Chris."

That struck a chord, but he couldn't decipher why.

"It took me hours going through microfiches to track down a reference to a planned publication called 'The Letters of an Elder Brother to a Fair

Quaker.' *The Citizen* promised to publish an article in seventeen seventy-six called, and I quote, 'The History and Adventures of Miss Lightfoot, the Fair Quaker, wherein will be faithfully portrayed some striking pictures of female constancy and princely gratitude.'" The photocopy drifted back to the floor. "I don't know if it was ever published or not, another dead end.

"Then I found a court case, *Ryves* versus *Ryves,* which tried to prove Hannah was married to George. One side had documents they said were real and the other side said were forgeries, but the court decided they were fakes and impounded them. Where they are now, I don't know."

Keen wasn't interested in details, just hoping something would give him a clue as to why Wycombe would kill Swinton over it.

"The main authority seems to be Wraxall's *Historical and Posthumous Memoirs,* and a writer named Wheatley. All I can find is that she was a shoemaker's daughter from Wapping—"

Keen suppressed a smile at her pronunciation.

"—and the niece of a linendraper named Wheeler who had a shop on St. James's Market where she met George when he was still Prince of Wales. George married her in the Curzon Street Mayfair Chapel, sort of like this Las Vegas–style marriage factory. Secret marriages were all the rage then, it seems, everyone was getting one."

She sighed, discouraged. "Anyway, the chapel's not there anymore, torn down to build Sunderland House for the Duke of Marlborough. That's gone, too, by the way. Bombed in an air raid during the war. Doesn't matter, since all the marriage registers from the St. George's Church parish were transferred years ago to the Public Records Office on Chancery Lane."

She sounded as if she should have known better. But, he admitted, it was far more than he would ever have been able to trace.

"So I spent another hour talking some officious twerp into letting me look through them. I did find a marriage register for Hannah. But *not* to George." She flipped through her spiral notebook. "She married some guy named Isaac Axford. On the one hand, we've got Elizabeth Chudleigh, Duchess of Kingston, saying George and Axford are actually the same person. On the other, you've got Wraxall claiming George paid Axford to go through a phony marriage to get Hannah away from her family. 'Axford' then disappears while George secretly marries her later on."

Keen struggled to maintain an attentive expression.

"Then you've got Hester Thrale Piozzi who corrected the Wraxall *Memoirs.* She wrote a letter to Samuel Johnson claiming she knew a son of George the Third and Hannah Lightfoot was still alive. Supposedly Hannah had three children by George, including a daughter who married a man named Dalton."

"Dalton . . ." The name was familiar.

"As in Richard Dalton, the one who had that book Wycombe is so hot to get back." She didn't see him wince, and he decided he'd tell her about

Wycombe's death later. "So I looked up what I could find on him. Librarian to George the Third, Keeper of the Pictures and Antiquarian, Treasurer of the Incorporated Society of Artists, yada yada. He never got married. His older brother had affairs with Lady Luxborough and the Duchess of Somerset, whoever they were. But nothing to connect either of them to Hannah Lightfoot. So that's a dead end as well."

She yawned hugely. "All I can say is it's pretty certain George did marry Hannah and had children by her. But what happened to Hannah Lightfoot or her kids, I don't know. I don't know if Chris found out, either. So this has been a whole lot of work for nothing."

She grimaced apologetically. "Your turn. What have you found out?"

"Nothing good, I'm afraid." When she looked at him questioningly, he said reluctantly, "Reece Wycombe shot himself yesterday. Suicide."

She sat upright. "You're kidding! Christ, *why*?"

"He'd been drinking quite a lot that night, and left a note saying he were sorry for what he'd done to Chris."

She gazed around at the papers and books scattered around her feet, absorbing the news. "Well, that's it, isn't it? He killed Chris and now he's dead, it's over. At least we know now."

"There's still no proof he killed her."

"But he left a note . . ."

"Saying he was sorry for what he did to Chris, without saying exactly what it was he'd done. That could mean anything."

"But who else could it be? Who else had a motive?"

"Well, there's Celia. Chris was blackmailing her." At her surprise, he added, "The much anticipated son and heir to the Swinton fortunes may not be Max's."

"Really!" she breathed, and grinned. Then, reluctantly shaking her head, she said, "Yeah, but . . . I just can't see an eight-month-pregnant woman driving all the way to Leeds to bump her off. Can you imagine? 'Hi, Chris, I know you hate my guts but thought I'd just pop up and see if you want to go skinny-dipping in the middle of the night in some grimy fishpond, sounds like a hoot, whadya say?'"

Keen had to smile at Jillie's parody. "So there's a few holes with that theory."

"Big enough to drive a truck through."

"What about her brother? People commit murder for all sorts of reasons. Greed is right up there for a strong motive. Crassfield and Robyns hasn't been going too well last few years, according to the stockholders' reports. Maybe Max wanted the family business all to himself, inherit his sister's share of the company."

Jillie wrapped her arms around her knees, the toes of her bare feet curling over the edge of the cushion. When he glanced at the bright red nail polish on her toenails curiously, she blushed and crossed her legs as if trying to hide them.

"Two problems with that: one, Max was in Brussels that night, and two, she'd already been cut out of the family business when her father died. Max got everything. Most of Chris's income wasn't from Crassfield and Robyns anyway; she made a lot more from her own investments than she ever did from the company."

"She must have done pretty well at it, if she left fifty thousand pounds to your daughter and a whopping big trust fund for her neice."

"Bumping her off doesn't help Max out if she left everything in a trust to Jewel. He can't touch it, she'd have made damned sure of that. Chris was always the one with the business head, not Max. Her father only sent her to college to get the 'right' kind of education; boys become CEOs, girls marry them. The only reason she majored in history was to irritate her mother, something she considered to be totally useless. Which it is. Not much you *can* do with it except teach."

Her ambivalence baffled him. "Nothing wrong with that. You enjoy it."

Jillie snorted in disgust. "I *hate* teaching!"

"Then why did you become a teacher?"

"Because, unlike Chris, I wasn't born rich. I got the house and custody of Karen when Robert left me, but I'm still paying off the mortgage while he'd salted away most of the money where I couldn't touch it. He paid the absolute minimum he could for child support and stopped the day Karen turned eighteen. I had to get a job, *any* job, to make ends meet. Not much you can do with a Ph.D. in history. Four years ago, I got an offer to teach at Cascade. Okay, so it's not Harvard, but it was at least a full-time position." Her smile turned bitter. "It was hard, but you learn you can do anything, if there's no other choice.

"Look, I'm hungry," she said, brushing papers off her lap. "Mrs. Flute's not here, but she said it's okay if we cook dinner. I was planning on making myself a Karen Special."

"What's a 'Karen Special'?"

"Peanut butter sandwich with mayonnaise, fried bacon, and bananas." She grinned at his horror. "Or I can make grilled cheese and tomato on rye. Better?"

"Much. Mrs. Flute off sacrificing a goat tonight, is she?"

Jillie rolled her eyes. "It's Sunday. Goat sacrifices are on Tuesdays, everyone knows that." He followed her into the kitchen, watching her, as she had watched him cook breakfast, while keeping out of her way. "And you be careful she doesn't catch you making fun of her," she added as she piled cheese, mayonnaise, and tomatoes from the refrigerator onto the table.

"Or she'll put a curse on me?"

"Turn you into a big slimy green toad. With warts."

She closed the fridge door with a kick in the lower corner, already familiar with the idiosyncrasies of the flat. On the kitchen windowsill, even the two bedraggled potted herb plants she'd rescued from Chris's flat had rallied, sprouting pale green buds of new growth. He wondered what her own home looked like.

He leaned against the doorjamb. "Then I'll just have to find a princess to give me a quick snog, turn me back. Britain still has a few left, you know."

Her back was to him, hands busy slicing a loaf of rye bread, but he didn't miss how she stiffened, or how attentive she became to grilling their sandwiches, cheese melting over thin slices of onion and tomato. The sandwiches were good enough, washed down with two bottles of chilled Blackthorn cider.

But the illusion of intimacy had been marred, no matter how relaxed they pretended to be. She'd been hurt too badly, Keen thought. A shadow with a knife stood between them, and he had no idea how to fight a shadow.

Jillie took a shower before she went to bed, while Keen was in his own room, making more phone calls. But the hot water hadn't relaxed her as she'd hoped. She was miserable, lurid images of Chris floating in the lake, Wycombe's suicide churning in her mind. And visions of Keen lying naked in bed with only a door between them. It might as well have been a mountain. Death and sex, she thought wistfully as she toweled herself dry. She inspected her nude body in the steam-fogged mirror.

Her hips were too fat, her breasts too small. Her skin was rippled with childbirth stretchmarks and dimpled with cellulite no amount of dieting could remove. Her stomach was too soft, she should have worked out more, as Robert had nagged. Her skin was too pale, freckles dusting her shoulders. Her neck was too thin, her chin too short, her nose too long. Her hair was too frizzy. Robert used to call the color of her eyes shit brown because her head was full of it, although he'd insisted he was only teasing.

She was ugly, she decided bleakly, and pulled on her bathrobe to hide herself. Barefoot, she tiptoed past the other bedroom, and carefully shut her own door. A short time later, she heard running water in the bathroom, the squeak of floorboards, the click of his own door closing. Then silence.

He was only being kind, turning down her stupid, pathetic attempt at seduction with a courteous excuse to spare her feelings. Oh, she believed he liked her, but as a friend, nothing more.

No one wanted someone else's damaged goods. She had no delusions he could be turned on by her middle-aged, out-of-shape body. If *she* didn't like what she saw in the mirror, he would be disgusted. She cradled Chris's teddy bear, and curled into a tight ball on her side, quiet tears making her nose itch.

But crying herself to sleep didn't work. After an hour, she got up and stood at the window, black shapes cut out of the city's electric-purple sky. She had never wanted any man so badly in her life. The longing made her stomach flutter painfully.

By two-thirty, she'd worked up enough courage to open the door and stand in the darkened hallway. It took another ten minutes for her to cross the few feet to his door. She turned the knob carefully, hoping it was locked, and when it wasn't, hoping he would be asleep and she could retreat before he ever knew she'd been there.

He wasn't asleep. As the door swung noiselessly open, he turned his head to look at her without speaking, eyes half-hidden in the gloom. He lay propped up on the pillows of the low futon bed, one hand tucked under his head. The wan glow from streetlights cast odd shadows across his body. She closed the door and managed to take three steps toward him before she froze. He didn't move.

"I lied," she said, her voice shaking. He stared at her. "I can't wait."

She untied the belt of her robe with numbed fingers and let it slide off her shoulders. Trembling with her robe clutched in one hand, she watched his mouth drop open, his gaze travel down her naked body. She held herself still, terrified.

He could destroy her with a single word.

When he finally stared back up into her face, she had never seen any man look at her that way. His free hand lifted the sheet covering him, inviting her into his bed without a sound. Nearly weeping with relief, she dropped her robe on the floor and climbed in beside him like a child seeking comfort.

Any lingering doubt that he wasn't interested was dispelled by his already hard erection, curved upright and stirring to his heartbeat. She looked away in embarrassment, flustered. She'd never seen a man's penis other than her husband's . . . No, she reminded herself, that wasn't true . . .

He kissed her, first gently, then his mouth was as greedy as her own. Their lovemaking was inexpert, still strangers hesitant and clumsy in their ignorance, but somehow that made it all the more endearing. Robert had prided himself as a skilled lover while she'd learned to time faking her orgasm until it became a routine so automatic she found her mind totally disconnected, an out-of-body experience.

Now she had to push her husband out of her mind as Keen ran his hands tenderly along her stretchmarked skin, kissed her too thin neck, stroked her small breasts. His unfamiliar body made her hyperaware of her own, anxiously self-conscious. He was hard in places where Robert had been soft, smooth where Robert had been hairy. He smelled different. Fumbling as he slipped his legs between hers, their knees banged awkwardly, her hair catching under his elbow. They murmured "oops" and "sorry" until she suddenly giggled, horrified, and tried to stifle it before he became angry. To her relief, he smiled, then laughed softly himself.

"Shh, let's not be waking the landlady, now," he whispered in her ear, then she felt his teeth nibble at it, making her shiver. Her nervousness melted as heat made her skin deliciously sensitive. She hooked her too knobbly ankles around his back, enjoying how the muscles along his spine rippled as his hips rocked.

He may not have been as consummate a lover as her husband, but Keen was far more attentive, which aroused her far more than Robert ever had with any technique he'd found in his stupid sex manuals. Keen took his time about entering her, concentrating on other things until she was afraid he'd never do it. With the second burst of unexpected boldness of that night, she reached down and grasped him gently to direct him, something Robert would never have tolerated.

Keen shuddered and held himself still, balancing on his elbows above her. He waited with his forehead pressed into the hollow of her shoulder, his ragged breath fanning alternately hot and cold against her breasts. Amazed by his willingness to let her guide him, she hesitated, not intentionally prolonging the moment as she held him captive. Then, tentatively, she drew him into her, the velvety glove of skin over the solid shaft hot against her palm, pressure filling her as he slid easily inside.

It didn't take but three or four strokes before she gasped in astonishment, a tingling anticipation rippling through her. Then she came with an intensity she had never experienced before. Her back arched under him as she cried out softly. Her legs tightened around him, muscles in her thighs contracting, drawing him in deeper.

"Oh, sweet Jesus," he whispered hoarsely. His hands lifted her hips to urgently thrust himself against her until he muffled his own moan against her neck.

They lay entangled on sweat-dampened sheets, his body too heavy atop hers, before he realized and tried to move to one side without withdrawing. It didn't work, and his softening penis slithered out. The rush of cooling air between her legs felt oddly pleasant.

He lay beside her for several minutes, saying nothing, then ran a finger to brush aside her hair and kissed her chastely on the forehead. For a moment, she was fearful he'd say The Words, as if that lie was now something required.

She was grateful when he didn't. He simply closed his eyes and fell asleep with his arm over her waist.

During the night, in the intersection between dreams and waking, Keen had the eeriest sensation that he was back in his own bed at home, could actually feel the warmth of Laura's body next to his, the heavy lump of Thomas nestling between their feet. That somehow, by some miracle he didn't dare to question the logic of, the past two years had never happened. That even while aware he was dreaming, if he could just somehow take hold of this world and believe in it hard enough, he could bring it with him into the waking reality. He opened dream eyes and saw his own bedroom, every comfortingly familiar detail with vivid clarity. He could even hear the sheep calling in the fields, smell the breeze off the moors as the curtains stirred in the cool morning air. He had a flash of wild hope that it could actually be possible, if he wanted it badly enough he really could make it true.

He opened his eyes to the dark, disoriented by alien surroundings as his dream dissolved away. For a moment, the sense of loss was so sharp he couldn't breathe, a weight pressing down on his chest with ruthless force. Then he inhaled against the pain, a quiet gasp of grief, and another until the rush of adrenaline sickness had faded. He was awake, squarely so, and it was unlikely he'd soon get back to sleep. Lying on his back, he stared up at the ceiling through the gloom and listened to the slow breathing of a stranger beside him.

He hadn't wanted all that much, he thought, had never asked for more than anyone might have reasonably expected. What had he done wrong that it had to be so hard, then? It was unbearable, this suspension between what he'd lost and whatever came next. He'd lied to Jillie; he'd never stopped being angry, just better at hiding it, was all. This rage at the unfairness made him feel childish, but he didn't know *how* to stop being angry. He couldn't, he didn't want to.

It wasn't even so much that he still loved Laura. Not the person who had been his wife. He understood he had taken her for granted, but that was exactly what he missed the most, that dependability of being able to trust in daily routines. He desperately longed for the comfort of all the everyday habits he could follow as easily as the road home from work without the worry of how to get where he was going.

Selfish bastard, he thought. Selfish bastard lying in the dark next to a lovely woman and feeling sorry for yourself. Somehow, his self-reproach made him feel a little better. Selfish, lazy, stupid, obstinate, masochistic moaning bastard, that's what you are. He smiled ruefully, the pain gone.

The night heat had made cuddling uncomfortable, and, once asleep, they'd wormed their way apart, sweating limbs sprawled. He rolled onto his side and placed his palm against her back, the warmth of her smooth skin something real and solid, if of uncertain permanence. She started. *"Mmmph."*

"Sorry," he murmured, but kept his hand on her back.

"S'kay." A few minutes later, her breathing deepened, asleep.

Outside the window the sky lightened. He opened his eyes to early morning city traffic noises, the rumble of vegetable carts, and the rough voices of men singing as they set up for market, and realized he too had finally been able to sleep.

XII

MONDAY

They sat across from each other like an old married couple in their respective robes, identical bowls of cereal, matching cups of coffee. But the shy glances and awkward smiles wouldn't have been out of place on new lovers half their age, Keen thought wryly. Nor were they fooling anyone, as Mrs. Flute appeared, looking first at a blushing Jillie before winking at him.

"Good morning, dears. Sleep well?" was all she said before she poured herself a cup of coffee and disappeared into her studio from where the biting scent of turpentine and linseed oil soon emanated.

"I think she likes you," Jillie said, sotto voce.

"Ree-deep." He grinned as she shook an admonishing finger.

Her appointment with Martin Harding-Renwick was for nine o'clock. By half eight, they were in the thick of morning traffic crawling toward Battersea. Jillie had her hair pinned up in a schoolteacher's roll, which might have been more comfortable in the heat, but Keen much preferred those defiant curls loose around her shoulders.

Martin Harding-Renwick's offices were on the seventh floor of a modern eight-story building, an L-shaped structure enclosing a landscaped courtyard. A huge gnarled chestnut commanded the center of clipped lawn, cobblestones in the footpaths arranged into artful swirls. Flowerbeds overflowed with perfectly maintained blossoms.

Harding-Renwick buzzed the security door to let them in, and met them as they came up the lift, a glass birdcage sliding up the exterior of the building. Jillie had oohed at the sheer vertical drop while Keen kept his attention studiously focused on the polished steel door, back to the rapidly dropping ground.

"Jillie, lovely to see you again." Harding-Renwick kissed her cheek and held her by the shoulders long enough to make her blush. "And a pleasure to meet you . . . Mr. Dunliffe, is it?" he said in a pleasant voice making his cultured public school accent astonishingly sincere. His handshake was firm and warm, but not aggressive. Keen wanted to dislike him and failed.

Harding-Renwick wasn't what Keen had expected. Although taller than Keen, he hunched slightly as if embarrassed about his height. In his early fifties, his expensively tailored suit didn't camouflage his athlete's shoulders and slim torso, honed from a lifetime, Keen assumed, of tennis and skiing and polo. His thick halo of prematurely white hair heightened an unusually tanned face for a Londoner. He smiled, wrinkling the skin around his eyes. "Please, make yourselves at home."

But his flat was as far removed from what Keen might ever call "home" as an Eskimo igloo. Heavy brocade drapes drawn back from high windows revealed a panoramic view of Battersea Park, glass doors opened onto a long balcony overlooking the Thames. Red geraniums and pale yellow petunias cascaded from large pots on the balcony. The breeze carried their thick scent into the room and played tiny notes on the crystals of a chandelier sculpted like a cascading waterfall.

The Steinway grand piano perfectly matched the curve of a spiral staircase, skylights pouring sunlight down the steps. Harding-Renwick escorted them across a carpet plush enough to leave footprints to cream sectional sofas running the entire length of the windows. A low table made of a four-foot slab of glass as thick as Keen's arm counterbalanced on a massive bronze base, polished to an immaculate shine. Not a smudge or fingerprint marred the reflection of three silver saltcellars, very old, Keen was certain, and very valuable.

Cabinet shelves of leather-bound books covered the remaining walls floor to ceiling, a rolling ladder for access, brass keys in the locks. Beside an antique desk, a colonial terra-cotta pot held an arrangement of strangely twisted branches, the bark nearly black, pale pink blossoms just beginning to open. Classical music played in a discreet undertone, but Keen could observe no stereo system or speakers anywhere.

It was as perfectly designed and color coordinated as an *Architectural Digest* article, pristinely beautiful, and utterly sterile. Keen felt intimidated by the room, afraid to touch anything.

"Nice flat," he said, wincing at his own understatement.

"Thank you," Harding-Renwick acknowledged. "I can give you the grand tour, but there's not much to see. This room I use as the office. Bedroom and bath upstairs and a small kitchen through there." He gestured toward a door open far enough to hint at a kitchen larger than Keen's bedroom. "It's an adequate pied-à-terre for whenever I'm in London. I live a rather peripatetic life; my research takes me all over Europe. But I prefer spending the winters in more hospitable climes. I have a villa on the coast of Spain, not far from Gibraltar." He smiled as if they were sharing a kindred secret. "And of course the tax situation is more favorable there."

Keen nodded as if in total agreement with him. *Prat,* he thought, then wondered which of them he meant.

"My secretary doesn't come in until noon. I was just putting up a spot of tea, won't be a moment . . ."

Keen sat self-consciously on the sofa, back to the view, still mildly uneasy with vertigo. Jillie inspected the shelves, more impressed by a bunch of old books than Harding-Renwick's incredible flat.

"God," she murmured, "I'd *kill* for some of these." Realizing what she'd said, she gave Keen an apologetic grimace.

"Help yourself," Harding-Renwick said from the doorway, bearing a tea tray. "It's not locked. There's a lovely edition of Bede's *Historiae Ecclesiasticae* just there, on your right. And one shelf over, I have a four-volume set of the *Domesday Book* folios." He settled the tray onto the glass table and began to set out the cups and teapot. "One of the 'Record Commission' editions, John Nicholls designed the type and Joseph Jackson did the cut. First two volumes issued in seventeen eighty-three, the other two in eighteen eleven and eighteen sixteen." As she took a calf-bound book from the shelves, he finished arranging the tea and sat down at the angle from Keen, even his sprawl seeming poised.

She opened the book reverently, and said with awe, *"Psalterium Davidis Latino-Saxonicum vetus."*

"Oh, that. A first edition of an Anglo-Saxon psalter, sixteen forty, and the only remaining copy of that particular edition."

"You're an expert on books, then, a collector?" Keen asked.

Harding-Renwick was paying more attention to Jillie with an amused half-smile. "Not as such. Most of my collection is reference works I need for my business; Burke's and Debrett's, of course, the Rolls series, *Les Chroniques* of various French nobilities, that sort of thing. But as for being a collector, it's more a matter of personal taste, not investment. I enjoy books for what's in them, not the object itself."

"Would you know anything about Richard Dalton's work?" Jillie asked. "He was an eighteenth-century artist and a royal librarian."

"I'm afraid not. As I said, I'm no expert." At her disappointment, he added, "But you might be interested if you look just there"—he nodded with his head—"that rather plain, dreary old thing beside the large red one. You'll have to use the ladder . . ."

Jillie glanced at him, as eager as a child at Christmas. Keen paid attention to his tea, struggling with his irrational sense of rivalry. As he reached for what he thought was rock sugar—large, opaque crystals in the silver cellars—Harding-Renwick stopped him.

"Sorry, those aren't edible," he said, and handed Keen a small bowl of sugar from the tray. Feeling even more foolish, Keen studied the rough white stones in the silver cellars, suspecting he knew what they were and didn't want to ask. Harding-Renwick didn't enlighten him. Keen tried not to react as he heard Jillie's gasp of delight and pasted on a smile before he looked up.

"The Life and Works of Alexander de Sancto Albano," she said breathlessly, and added for Keen's benefit, "Alexander Nequam."

"A little-known Thomas Hearne. Seventeen thirty, but not a first edition, and in dreadful condition," Harding-Renwick said. "The calf binding isn't original and there's bit of damp-staining on the last few signatures. The hinges are cracked and the joints are split. Not an overly impressive gift, I'll admit, but I felt you might be more interested in the contents than the cover." He smiled at Jillie's wide-eyed surprise.

"Oh, no, I can't accept this, really. Thank you, but it's far too valuable . . ."

"Not at all. It's rare to find someone who appreciates books as I do, as something to be read and enjoyed. And I know no one else who has a better use for that particular work. Please."

After a moment's hesitation, Jillie held the book to her chest reverently. "Thank you very much."

"My pleasure." Harding-Renwick turned his brilliant smile on Keen. "Well, then," he said to them both as he guided Jillie toward the sofa. "To what do I owe this pleasure? Have you changed your mind? I have a lordship for sale in Norfolk, close to Wells-next-the-Sea, which retains a limited right to salvage shipwrecks. Although I daresay one would have to be quite creative to find something to do with a few tons of sodden Japanese televisions washing up on one's doorstep."

Jillie laughed. "No, thanks. I'm hoping you can give me some advice on how to do genealogical research on the Quakers."

"Quakers? In England rather than America, you mean?" His eyebrows, darker than his white hair, rose in doubt. "I don't know much about the Quakers. The genealogy I do is pretty much restricted to heraldic studies, tracing nobility to substantiate titles. I suggest you try the Friends' House on Euston Road."

"Actually, this *is* about the nobility. I'm looking for a woman named Hannah Lightfoot. She was a Quaker who supposedly married George the Third."

At the name, Harding-Renwick's expression cleared knowingly. "Yes, I know the story. I don't mean to discourage you, but I wouldn't expect much success with that, frankly. There was never any more to it than rumors and gossip." He looked pensive. "But this is the second time I've been asked about Hannah Lightfoot."

Keen looked up at him sharply. "Is it, now?"

Harding-Renwick mused, tapping his lips with a forefinger. "What was it, about . . . five or six months ago? A woman rang up, came to the office. Couldn't do much for her, either, I'm afraid."

Keen fished the photographs of Christine Swinton from his pocket. "This woman?"

Martin-Renwick studied a photo of Chris on her Virgin Islands holiday. "It could be, I can't say for sure. I only met her the once." He looked up, glancing from Keen to Jillie with interest. "If it's important, I could find her name for you."

"That would be greatly appreciated."

Harding-Renwick crossed to his desk and pulled open the top drawer, revealing a built-in computer system as the screen popped up. Keys clicked, the hard drive hummed, and a moment later, he said, "That was in early February, on the eighth. Christine Swinton. Hm . . . That name is familiar . . ." He looked up, startled. "The woman who drowned at Harewood during the conference!"

"She was a friend of mine," Jillie said in a subdued voice.

"Oh, Jillie. I'm so sorry. I didn't realize." He glanced at Keen shrewdly. "And I gather *you* must be a police officer?"

"From Leeds. Weetwood Police Station."

"I see. I had the impression it was an accident. Is there more to this than the press is telling us?"

"Just a few routine questions to clear up, is all."

"Anything I can do to help, naturally."

"Do you remember what Christine Swinton come looking for that day?"

Harding-Renwick frowned. "It was months ago. She came at two o'clock for an hour's consultation, and she paid by check. That's all the facts I can give you. I do recall it was in regard to a book she was writing. I told her the same thing as I've told Jillie, her best bet would have been the Library of Friends."

"I've tried that already," Jillie said. "The only record they have on Hannah Lightfoot is in the Minute Books of the Westminster Monthly Meetings. Hannah used to go regularly until seventeen fifty-four. One reference in seventeen fifty-five says she was married by a priest instead of a Quaker ceremony, and another said she'd left her husband. The committee visited her mother, but she either couldn't or wouldn't tell them where Hannah was. She did say it was true Hannah was married by a clergyman, but wasn't sure if she'd left her husband or not. No mention who he was.

"I've also checked through the Draper's Hall Company Records, but all I could find was a will by Robert Pearne probated in seventeen fifty-seven which left a trust fund to Hannah Axford née Lightfoot, niece of John Jeffrys who was a watchmaker in Holbern. Jeffrys was on the committee trying to locate her. When she didn't come back, the Quakers disowned her. I don't know if she ever got anything from the will or not. And that's it."

"Then you already know far more than I do," he said admiringly.

"How did it happen that Christine Swinton come to you for advice?" Keen asked.

"I'm in the Yellow Pages, as well as on the British Library's list of genealogical researchers." Harding-Renwick looked back at his computer screen. "But if memory serves me correctly . . . I think she was a referral. Mrs. Grace MacFalgan. She's an amateur historian." He grimaced. "Of sorts. She has come up with some remarkably astute insights in the past, although I should caution you, her putative sensitivities can be a bit, well, shall we say, 'umbrageous'?"

Keen stared at him. "Do you have an address and telephone number for her?"

"Certainly." Harding-Renwick tapped a few keys before scribbling on a pad of paper. He shut off his computer, then crossed the room to give the note to Keen.

"I don't know what else I can do to help you."

"You've been right helpful, Mr. Harding-Renwick."

"Martin," he corrected as Keen shook his hand. "If there's anything else, please don't hesitate. And I wish you every success with Mrs. MacFalgan," he added with a knowing smile that did not set Keen's mind at ease.

As Jillie set her empty cup down in the saucer, she asked, "How much do we owe you for the consultation?"

"Don't be silly. It's not every day I have the pleasure of 'helping the police with their inquiries,' so to speak. However . . ." He slipped his hand around Jillie's waist as they walked toward the door. "If you'd care to have dinner with me?"

Again, Keen forced himself not to react, but Harding-Renwick didn't fail to note Jillie's anxious glance toward Keen, reading it accurately.

"The three of us, of course," Harding-Renwick amended quickly. "And I'm sure Fiona would love to join us. My secretary."

"Can I call you?" Jillie offered tentatively. "I'm leaving on Friday, and I'm not exactly sure what I'll be doing until then."

"Certainly," Harding-Renwick said smoothly, letting her off the hook.

She turned to leave, then remembered. "And thank you again for the book, it's really sweet of you," she said shyly.

"Don't mention it." Keen found something else to look at as Harding-Renwick kissed Jillie on the cheek.

They didn't speak on the way down in the lift. The problem, Keen decided, wasn't only because Jillie was a foreigner. It was that she moved in a society he had limited experience with, as alien as another planet. Nor was it a disparity in intelligence; Keen knew the difference between being clever and being academically inclined. He knew policemen with only two O levels who did more writing than most university teachers. The average copper was quick enough, street smart rather than taught from textbooks how to handle arrogant legal experts and cunning solicitors during cross-examination in a magistrate's court.

But Keen was painfully aware that he had little with which to compete with the intellectuals who populated her world. Especially rich, handsome, sophisticated people like Martin Harding-Renwick.

"Just what the hell does 'umbrageous' mean, anyway?" he grumbled as they crossed the garden toward the car park. He hadn't meant his tone to sound so sour.

"Easily offended. Like in 'taking umbrage' at something."

"Oh."

He looked at her sharply as she giggled, uncertain if she were laughing at him. "Was that my imagination, or did he just hit on me?"

"Pardon?"

"He *was* making a pass, wasn't he?"

As they reached the Vauxhall, he opened the passenger door for her. "Looked that way. Watch your skirt." He slammed the door shut.

She was still grinning when he got in and turned the ignition key. "I think I could get to like this country after all."

He smiled ruefully, swallowing his jealousy for the childish nonsense it was. "Why shouldn't he, Jillie? You're a lovely woman."

"*Me?*"

Her surprise was so earnest it made him laugh. "Yes, *you*. Hasn't anyone ever told you how beautiful you are?"

Even with his eye on the traffic as he pulled out of the car park, he caught how her face froze, as pale as marble, before she turned away, gazing out the window.

"No," she said quietly. "They haven't."

And he knew he'd seen a fleeting glimpse of the shadow.

You're beautiful. For a sickening moment, Jillie could feel the cold edge of the knife again pressed against her throat. *If I had such a beautiful woman, I wouldn't go off and leave her on her own.*

Karen was wrong. She didn't dislike short skirts or skimpy blouses because she was too conservative. It was because she was too scared. Afraid of sending the wrong message to strange men passing her on the streets. Afraid of being blamed if creeps and perverts assumed she might be easy. She had to do everything possible to avoid drawing attention to herself. To be safe.

I'd never let you out of my sight, we'd stay in bed and I'd f—

She shuddered, and pushed the memory down. Hard.

Mrs. MacFalgan's address in Shadwell was a tiny duplex in the shadow of Tower Bridge, the crenellated tops and flags beyond just visible. A dog yapped as they rang the bell, and Grace MacFalgan had it in her arms when she answered the door. The Yorkshire terrier panted, tiny bows in the hair shrouding its eyes. Mrs. MacFalgan was a sweet grandmotherly woman in her seventies, with rosy cheeks and creamy white hair. She smiled, blue eyes bright.

"Mrs. Grace MacFalgan?" Keen asked.

"That's right."

She looked at his ID card with polite interest. "I'm Sergeant Dunliffe from Weetwood Police Station in Leeds, and this Dr. Gillian Waltham. Could we have a moment of your time to talk to you about a woman you may have assisted with some historical research?"

"Of course," Mrs. MacFalgan said, and invited them in. Bright chintz covered the windows and furniture, crocheted doilies everywhere, a collection of china Yorkies on a lowboy. The potpourri scent reminded Jillie of her own long-dead grandmother, childhood memories indelible.

"Would you care for a cup of tea?"

"Thank you, no, we've just had one," Keen replied. It seemed to Jillie like a ritual, acceptance or rejection of the offer perfectly acceptable. As they sat on her sofa, Mrs. MacFalgan settled into an armchair, the terrier wriggling in her lap.

"Curious, isn't it; the police taking an interest in historical research?"

"The circumstances are unusual," Keen said. "We've talked to a colleague of yours, Mr. Harding-Renwick? He tells us that around six months ago you helped a woman named Christine Swinton who was doing research for a book she were writing. Do you remember her?"

"Oh, yes," Mrs. MacFalgan said promptly. "The poor girl who drowned up in Yorkshire."

"That was the lady. Could you tell us what you did for her?"

"Certainly. She was looking for material connecting Hannah Lightfoot with George the Third."

"And you had information that could help her?" Jillie interrupted, unable to keep the eagerness out of her voice.

"Of course. I'm an expert on Hannah Lightfoot. Miss Swinton came to me for advice, and I was delighted to be of assistance." Mrs. MacFalgan stroked the dog's head. It blinked sleepily, the hair masking its eyes flicking from time to time. "Specifically, she wanted to know about the three children Hannah had by George. First, of course, was her daughter, Sophia Amelia Caroline, born in January of seventeen fifty-eight. Then in December of seventeen fifty-nine, Hannah gave birth to George's first son, whom Hannah had baptized as George Edward William. In September of seventeen sixty, she had her last child, Henry Augustus Frederick."

Mrs. MacFalgan paused indulgently as Jillie lunged into her purse for her notebook and a pen.

"George did love Hannah; and she was quite a beautiful woman, although she was several years older than he. But after three children the difference in age began to show, and by then, he'd fallen in love with Lady Sarah Lennox. Unfortunately, when George became king, Lord Bute informed George's mother of her son's marital state. The Princess Augusta was furious. She had her ministers put pressure on Hannah to agree to an annulment."

Again, Mrs. MacFalgan waited patiently as Jillie frantically took notes, her hand starting to cramp.

"Hannah was understandably reluctant. She claimed that as a Quaker, she could swear no oaths, not even to the king, thus limiting her involvement in the court were she to become queen. But neither could she swear to an annulment, nor to a morganatic status of her children. She wanted George to publicly legitimize her children, since she wasn't willing to be the mother of bastards. Negotiations came to an impasse, and Hannah fled England with her two baby sons. She had to leave behind her daughter, Sophia. A few months later, George married Queen Charlotte."

Jillie flipped a page over, still scribbling as she asked, "Without an annulment of his marriage to Hannah?"

"Not one she ever agreed to, no. When she was told that George had gone through some form of divorce and a private remarriage to Charlotte, she responded by making out her will in seventeen sixty-two, pointedly signing it 'Hannah Regina' and commending her three children into the care of their royal father. So without Hannah's consent, the legality of any divorce is rather dubious."

The Yorkshire terrier had gone to sleep in her lap, snoring loudly for such a little dog. Jillie noted Keen blinking, unable to mask his own drowsiness.

"The guilt did weigh on George's mind. His daughter Sophia 'Axton' or 'Axford,' as she was otherwise called, grew up in the foster care of Richard Dalton and his brother, John."

Jillie noticed as Keen perked up at the name Dalton, as did Mrs. MacFalgan, rewarding his interest with a warm smile.

"Sophia was educated and acquainted with members of the court, but treated as an unwanted bastard, barely tolerated as a servant. After Richard Dalton retired in seventeen seventy-five as royal librarian, he and the king arranged for her marriage to a distant cousin, Jonathan Dalton, whose financial difficulties made him quite happy to profit from a dowry settled on her by the king." Mrs. MacFalgan turned her smile on Jillie. "A secret marriage, of course, one secret to keep another. She was shipped safely off to the countryside in Eaglesfield, near Cockersmouth in Cumberland, where she had six children. Three died in infancy, the others grew up and married, totally ignorant of their royal lineage."

"This is wonderful," Jillie breathed, glancing up at Keen. He smiled back, as obviously pleased for her as he was waiting for the history lesson to finish before he could begin his more pragmatic questions.

"Hannah died in seventeen seventy-three, alone and impoverished. *Without* ever having been properly divorced from George. And there's a strong possibility she was poisoned."

"Poisoned? Why? By whom?"

"Good question. Elizabeth Chudleigh, who witnessed George's marriage to Hannah, was making life awkward for the king. She'd also been secretly married, but her estranged husband wanted a divorce. Elizabeth was by then engaged to the Duke of Kingston, and afraid the scandal might prevent her from becoming a duchess, she, like George, concealed the proof of her first marriage. She swore an oath she had never been married and never had children, both lies. The court ruled in her favor, and she married her duke. Four years later, her first husband demanded a new trial, accusing his wife of perjury, which naturally made George very uneasy. Then the Duke of Kingston died only days before Hannah Lightfoot, in suspiciously similar circumstances. Elizabeth believed she was the target of an assassination gone wrong.

"When she was found guilty of bigamy in seventeen seventy-six, it had a direct bearing on the validity of the king's own marital state. The poor man's mental health began to decline, worried his children by Hannah might reappear to challenge the rights of his children by Charlotte. At one point, he even threatened to abdicate, have 'all his marriages' annulled and go to live in America."

"Oh, wouldn't we have *loved* that," Jillie murmured as she scribbled.

"It also left the king open to blackmail. The Quakers constantly berated him in public, which he endured, hat in hand. He paid several hundred pounds for a herbarium collection of willows and sedges from a naturalist named John Lightfoot who just happened to be a distant cousin of Hannah's from Uxbridge. It's still in Kew, if you're interested."

Jillie couldn't believe her luck; all the research she had worked so hard on, the meager clues dead-ending, and now the details were simply pouring out into her lap like a shower of gold coins. "So where did Hannah go after she left England?"

"To Paris, hoping the French king would acknowledge her children by George. But then she died, and her sons were caught up in the Revolution. They both survived the Terror, both married and had children, and their descendants are alive today."

Jillie finished scribbling and looked up excitedly. "This is so incredible! What are your sources? Where did you *find* all this?"

"Oh, she told me herself."

"Who did? Chris?"

"No, Hannah. Hannah Lightfoot."

For a stunned moment, Jillie's mind went blank, unable to absorb what Mrs. MacFalgan had said. "Hannah Lightfoot told you?" she asked, keeping her voice neutral, hoping she'd heard it wrong.

"Yes. You see, I've always had an enormous passion for history, and could never understand why I felt so driven by the past until I finally accepted my gift. I'm exceptionally sensitive to metaphysical vibrations which make it possible for me to contact the dead, sometimes with individuals themselves, sometimes through the aid of cooperative spiritual messengers."

"Right." Even horrified, Jillie's voice sounded colorless to her own ears. She ignored the strangely quivering look on Keen's face, as if he were doing his utmost to keep from exploding into laughter.

"There are spirits who have a strong connection to the living because their own life force has been interrupted or violated on this side. Murdered children have especially intense spirits, or people who have suffered from a wrong that has never been resolved. With the help of my guardian angel, I'm able to link in those who have gone over to 'the other side,' to be receptive to psychic airwaves of those restless spirits who require my help in order to find completion. Hannah's spirit is troubled, she and her children have been the victims of a profound injustice."

"Uh-huh," Jillie responded in sinking dismay. Mrs. MacFalgan seemed so *normal.* There were no New Age crystals or tarot cards in evidence, nothing about this nice matronly lady in her flower-print dress and blue cardigan to show she was a lunatic. Keen had turned away, one hand rubbing his face to hide his expression.

"It's been a boon to my historical research, but it's an even greater pleasure to give comfort to relatives of those who have died too abruptly before being properly prepared for their translation to the other side."

Mrs. MacFalgan smiled, indulgent and benign. With her rosy cheeks, twinkling eyes, and frothy white hair, she looked the perfect Christmas card granny sitting with her gnarled hands caressing the dog in her lap.

Stark raving bonkers.

"I see by the change in your auras that you are not the most open-minded of people, are you?" Mrs. MacFalgan admonished mildly. Jillie felt a headache coming on. "And I take it Mr. Harding-Renwick didn't mention that I'm a clairvoyant?"

"It does seem he neglected to inform us of that fact," Keen said, while Jillie woodenly replaced her pen and notebook into her purse without another word.

"I've been a registered medium for over twenty years," Mrs. MacFalgan said. "And I've worked with the police on many cases, with documented success. They've come to *me* after exhausting all other conventional means for finding the suspect, or the body of the victim for that matter. There are even one or two psychic police officers about, we're not all 'weirdos' and 'freaks.'"

"I don't doubt that, Mrs. MacFalgan. Would you mind if I asked how Christine Swinton happened to come to you for advice?"

"The same way you did, Mr. Harding-Renwick referred her to me."

Keen frowned. "I had the impression you referred her to him."

Mrs. MacFalgan's certainty wavered. "Well, that could be," she admitted. "I am getting on and my memory isn't what it used to be. In either event, Mr. Harding-Renwick's approach to history is more orthodox than my own, and Dr. Swinton had objections to my methods similar to yours. Hearsay from the beyond wasn't sufficient to cite as documentation for her book."

"Nope," Jillie said fuming. "It sure isn't." She ignored both Keen's warning glance and Mrs. MacFalgan's chiding look, not giving a damn what her aura looked like.

"Anyway, she only came the once. I did try to contact Hannah's spirit directly, but it's not like simply picking up the telephone and ringing a number, you understand. Spirits can't be commanded. I'm receptive to communication, but there are days when spirits aren't in the mood to be cooperative."

"I can sympathize completely." This time Keen's glare was enough to get Jillie to bite her tongue.

"It's been some time, but I do remember she was trying to help one of Sophia Dalton's descendants search for information about his family."

"Did she come alone, or was anyone else with her?"

"She came alone. Mr. Dalton lives in Gloucester, I believe. I don't know much about him other than they'd been in correspondence. She showed me his letter, giving as full an account of his family history as he could. He was definitely a descendant of Sophia Dalton, the records back to that point were quite reliable. But connecting Sophia to George the Third was far more difficult. I'm afraid I wasn't able to help her much. I did suggest she bring Mr. Dalton to a session, it might have facilitated things. Blood calls to blood. She said she would consider it, but I could tell she was merely being polite." Mrs. MacFalgan gave Jillie a significant look.

"Do you remember Mr. Dalton's first name?"

"I'm afraid not. It's been too long."

Jillie had stopped paying much attention, disgusted with being made a fool of. She was only glad when Keen stood up and shook Mrs. MacFalgan's hand.

"Thank you for your time, madam."

"Not at all, Sergeant."

Mrs. MacFalgan left her dog asleep on the chair and accompanied them to the door. "The letters *AD* might be of interest, Sergeant. Possibly someone's initials?"

"Thank you very much," Keen said, with what Jillie thought far too much courtesy for a kook. "I'll keep it in mind."

As Jillie passed her, Mrs. MacFalgan said, "Your friend, Chris, is another with a strong spirit. I sense her presence all around you, and I know she's worried. She has been wronged"—she glanced at Keen meaningfully—"*greatly* wronged. But she's torn between seeking justice for herself and concern for your safety."

The hair on the back of Jillie's neck prickled.

"What did you expect?" Mrs. MacFalgan said dryly. "Eye-rolling trances and flying furniture?" She shut the door.

Jillie said nothing as they walked back to the Vauxhall. She slumped in the seat, arms crossed, and glared through the windshield.

"When the goin' gets tough, who you gonna call?" he said in a bad American accent. She glanced at him warily, his laughing eyes not matching his somber expression. "Ghostbusters!"

"Shut up and drive," she growled.

By the time they'd reached Camden Town, Keen was happy to see Jillie had recovered her good humor.

"I give up," she said plaintively, "I've done all I can. I'm a *medievalist,* for God's sake. I don't know what she was working on, I'm not going to find it, which doesn't matter because it was a stupid idea to begin with." She glowered at him. "But whatever else Chris was, she was a legitimate historian and she wouldn't have given the time of day to that woman's garbage!"

"Oh, I don't know. There could be *something* to Mrs. MacFalgan's story," he said with a straight face.

"Come *on*! You don't believe in that supernatural mumbo jumbo, do you?"

"No, not much." Although he'd had times when little things he couldn't pinpoint seemed off, when he'd played a hunch, felt a tingle of "bad vibes" with a policeman's sixth sense. "So what do you want to do now?" he asked.

"Go shopping," she said darkly. "Do touristy stuff, visit the Tower, gawk at Buckingham Palace. Buy a suitcase full of tacky souvenirs. Take photographs to prove to Karen I really was here after all."

That hadn't been quite what he'd meant. His own good humor clouded. "Just be careful, then, won't you?" By the look on her face, he expected her to argue. "I don't want to have to worry about you."

Her expression softened. "Okay. What are you going to do?"

"Thought I might go see my boys." He had just driven past the Camden Locks, coming up to the open market. "Let you off at the corner?"

"Here's fine." He pulled to the curb and waited with the engine running as she unsnapped her seat belt.

"I have a few more ideas before I give up on my own theories," he said. "Look, meet you at the Blue Tulip about four? We'll have a drink before dinner." The Blue Tulip was the café next door to Mrs. Flute's, largely frequented by trendy couples sipping chardonnay on the terrace while watching the homeless wander past.

"Fine. See you then."

She hesitated, then leaned across to kiss him, to his delight. When she pulled away, she was blushing furiously.

The warm glow of pleasure lingered as he drove to the other end of Regent's Park, searching for somewhere to park the Vauxhall. He found a space several streets from Laura's, barely enough room to jockey into.

He paused at a bookshop display, then stepped inside and bought a book. *Ten Words a Day,* the cover title blazed, the "EZ Learn Method" promising to increase his vocabulary aptitude quickly and painlessly.

Laura was out, no one answered his knock. She and the boys should have been home for elevenses. He checked his watch, and waited on the steps while studying the distinction between "tortuous" and "torturous." He was finding it torturous to concentrate.

To his relief, he heard the boys before he saw them, and put his book into his jacket pocket. The lads careened around the corner, caught sight of him and squealed as they rushed toward him. They'd mobbed him when Laura appeared, arms full of groceries. She smiled, their argument at least forgiven if not forgotten.

Forgiveness, he knew, which would likely be short-lived.

"Hello, Keen," she called out. "You're looking pleased with yourself."

He was startled, unaware his expression could reveal so much. He hid his reaction by bending over his sons. "Nah, then, what's this? A couple of big strong lads like you letting your mother carry all that by herself? G'her a hand, aye?"

The twins swarmed onto the bags, quarreling over who had to carry what load, and dragged the groceries up the steps as Laura unlocked the door. "Just set them on the table," she called after them. Then to Keen, "Did you want to come in?"

"I'm not stopping, love," he said gently. "I only come by for a few minutes to talk to you."

"What about?"

"This job I'm doing . . ."

Her look darkened. "So it's not finished, then."

"No, it's not. I need to ask you to keep a watch out on the lads."

Her face drained of color. *"What?"* It came out as a stunned hiss of anger.

"Just for a while," he said, avoiding her eyes. "It's probably nothing to worry about, I only want you to be a little extra cautious. Don't let them go off by themselves, and even if someone tells you he's a police officer, even if he shows you a warrant card, don't go anywhere with him. Lock yourself and the boys in the house and ring me right away, promise me you'll do that . . ."

"You bastard," she breathed in shock. "You've put your own children in harm's way because you won't back away from this bloody case, haven't you?"

He hadn't expected her to react otherwise, but the sheer fury twisting her bloodless face unnerved him.

"If one hair on those boys' heads is touched, if anyone so much as looks at them cross-eyed . . ." For a moment she was speechless, nothing but a dreadful animal growl squeezing past her throat. She shook herself, face twitching in rage. "So help me God, Keen, *I'll have you.*"

Jillie sat rigidly, her expression in the mirror terrified. A thin man with fluorescent orange hair smiled in sadistic contempt as he held the gun to her head. Screwing her eyes closed, she dug her fingernails into the cushions of the chair.

"It'll be over before you know it, love, you'll hardly feel a thing," the man said scornfully, and pulled the trigger.

She jumped as the gun went off. Her eyes flew open, and she stared as the man wiped her ear with a tuft of wet cotton. A glittering gold stud with an amethyst stone had been stapled through her earlobe.

"That didn't hurt much, now did it?" he scolded her.

At worst, it had been a sharp pinch, which the two complimentary glasses of truly awful champagne had taken the edge off. The man repeated the process on the other side. "Twice a day," he lectured as he handed her a small tube of cream, "with a little dab of hydrogen peroxide. Turn them to keep the skin from closing over. Don't try changing earrings for a few weeks until you've had a chance to heal. Okay, love?"

She nodded, unable to speak.

Her knees were wobbly, either from the champagne or the ordeal, but she found herself fascinated by her reflection in shop windows as she walked by, the tiny gleam of gemstone winking in her ears. No one else paid the slightest bit of attention.

By noon, the vegetable market was in full swing. She smiled and waved at Teddy, who had the fruit stand just in front of Mrs. Flute's. He waved back cheerfully. She juggled her shopping bags to get the door unlocked, and carried her loot up the stairs. She heard voices in the kitchen, and as she peeked in the doorway, Mrs. Flute caught sight of her.

"You've got a visitor," she said. "Tea's hot."

Lynne Selkirk turned around and smiled.

"Well, hello!" Jillie dumped her shopping on an empty chair and sat down. "A pleasant surprise."

Lynne kissed her cheek as Mrs. Flute poured Jillie a cup of tea. "The last time I saw Edith was, what? Two years ago?" Lynne ruefully held up a small painting of a woman, a 1930s gasoline pump, and a scaled lizard in soft blue and yellows. "I can't afford to come too often, because I can never resist buying something."

Mrs. Flute set the cup in front of Jillie and took the painting from Lynne. "I'll go wrap this up for you."

"This is nice of you to come by," Jillie said.

"It's on my way to collect Ashley from playschool." Lynne riffled through her purse. "You read French, don't you?"

"Yes."

Lynne pulled out a letter with several colorful stamps on it. "I kept on taking in Chris's post after she died, didn't know what else to do. I've been tossing the obvious rubbish and sending the bills and such on to her brother. The postman knows I've been collecting her mail, and this morning he knocked on my door with a registered letter from France. He didn't know what else to do with it, either."

Lynne winced. "I don't think Celia Swinton is the sort to bother with informing any of Chris's friends who don't know yet. It looks like a personal letter and I thought I'd just send a note back to whoever it was to, well, break the news gently."

She handed to letter to Jillie. "I barely passed my O levels in French, *and* it's handwritten. I can't make out a word of it. If it's somebody who should know, could you help me to write the letter?"

"Sure, no problem." Jillie unfolded the letter and scanned the first paragraph, then her heart thudded high in her throat. "It's from a priest," she said slowly. "He's responding to a letter Chris sent about a month ago about her research. She was supposed to make a trip to Paris to see him." She read through it quickly, trying to hide her growing excitement. "Look, why don't you let me write the letter? To tell him about Chris?"

"You wouldn't mind?" Lynne said gratefully. "I don't want to put you to any bother . . ."

"It's no bother." She slid the letter back in the envelope before placing it into her own purse. She sat and chatted with Lynne, drank her tea, and tried not to look at her watch when Mrs. Flute returned with the painting swathed in bubble wrap.

"I'm so glad you don't mind," Lynne said with obvious relief as she took her painting. As she stood, she picked up the one-eyed stuffed bear on the chair beside her where it had been hidden from Jillie's view. "Oh, and thank you ever so much for rescuing Darius. Ashley's been frantic for weeks, couldn't think where she'd left him. Chris must have found him and it was sweet of you to remember what with everything else on your mind. Ash will be so thrilled to have him back."

Shock washed over Jillie, but she forced herself to smile. "My pleasure."

"What do you call a midget psychic who's escaped from prison?" Phil asked after Keen had recounted their morning's adventures. "A small medium at large."

"Why don't you go hold a séance with the PNC and run some names through that crystal ball, hmm?" Keen said, the confrontation with Laura leaving him irritable. "Mind if I use your phone?"

"Don't let Galton catch you in here, or we'll both be doing our communicating from the other side," Phil said, taking the notes from Keen. "And I've received a few spirit messages from the Great Powers Beyond myself. It seems the coroner believes Wycombe's death to be suspicious."

Keen was surprised. "Does he now?"

"In his opinion, definitely murder. I was allowed a sneak preview of the blood screens. The amount of alcohol alone in Wycombe's system would have made him comatose, but he'd been drugged as well. A scopolamine cocktail identical to the mix they found in Chris Swinton's body. I've got someone tracking down that particular medical brand. No way he would have been conscious enough to shoot himself. Someone got him doped and legless, propped him up in that chair, put the gun in his hand, and helped him to stick it in his mouth and pull the trigger. Pretty nasty."

Keen digested that before Phil added, "Anyone could have written that note on his typewriter. It's electric, no way to tell who was typing. No fingerprints on the keys, wiped clean. And the signature on the suicide note was off."

"A forgery?"

"Traced off a letter he'd written about two months ago to Marge Beecher. The letter was in a drawer of his desk, shoved under some papers. But the clincher is something the killer missed. Wycombe had his own photocopier, one of those small Canon jobbies. He'd been making a copy of a manuscript, and forgot to remove the last page of the original. Crafty bugger as well; he used a strip of paper with his name and the page number at the top over the name of the real author, to make the photocopied page look like it was his own work."

"Christine Swinton's missing manuscript."

Phil's grin widened. "Bull's-eye. That act doesn't quite jibe with someone who supposedly was so sorry for what he'd done to her he then blew his brains out."

"So where's the rest of it?"

"Vanished into thin air. Probably destroyed."

"Rather careless of him, was it?" Keen mused. He meant the overlooked evidence of theft and plagiarism.

"Or *her*." When Keen glanced at him, Phil added quickly, "Just listen a minute, okay? Wycombe and Swinton are found with the same drugs in their systems, scopolamine, right? The other three weren't. Alice Guiscoigne died from an injection of too much insulin, could have been an accident. Wortley had too many tabs of nitro under his tongue, he could've panicked during a heart attack. Barrow's system had traces of cocaine his girlfriend claims he never touched. He might have been sneaking it behind her back. The only thing they have in common is a rather flimsy connection to royal real estate and a dodgy lawyer."

"But both Swinton and Wycombe died leaving a lot of questions behind. Even leaving out the drugs, the *modus operandi* isn't the same, not unless you consider Wycombe's landlord as being the Duke of Westminster along with half of London."

Keen said guardedly, "So what are you saying?"

"So whoever killed Wycombe did a sloppy job of it. Hardly seems like a professional killer, does it? But suppose it *isn't* a pro, suppose it's someone who hated Swinton enough to wish her dead, aye? Wycombe has already forged papers once to ruin a rival and blackmail his researcher. Who benefits most by his death? Marge Beecher's not going to be unduly distraught over his sudden demise, now is she?"

"Marge Beecher."

"Say she and Wycombe were in it together, killing Swinton. Poetic justice if Beecher then slips *him* the same drug he used on Swinton, shoots him, and cobbles it to look like suicide."

Frowning, Keen reached for the telephone and flipped open his notebook for Marge Beecher's number. No one was at home, but Keen didn't bother to leave a message on her machine.

"Makes sense, doesn't it?" Phil asked impatiently as Keen hung up. "Have we finally got ourselves a *real* suspect?"

Keen didn't answer for a long moment. "We're looking at this wrong," he said finally. "It's too easy. Wycombe has too much drink and drugs in his blood, two shots through the head when one would do, wiping fingerprints off the typewriter keys without pressing Wycombe's fingers on them after he were dead to make it look like he wrote the note. A vague suicide note along with a bad forgery. Two, actually, if you count the doctored page left in his photocopier. Wouldn't the paper line be visible on a photocopy? All the sort of mistakes a reckless amateur might make."

"Which is why my money's on Marge Beecher," Phil insisted. "Most murderers *are* amateurs, that's why they get caught."

"But it's not sloppy. Not sloppy at all. Wycombe's killer knows we're still looking for him. So do the people covering up for him. They dress up the scene so even the thickest of coppers can figure out it's a murder, and point the finger of blame in the direction they want."

"For fuck's sake!" Phil slapped his desk in frustration. "You're starting to sound as conspiracy crazy as Scudder! Why go looking for the hard answer when the easy one makes sense?"

"Because it's the wrong answer," Keen said doggedly. "And it don't change the fact that someone already tried to cover up the Swinton death. Think about it; we come up with a convenient suspect, a crime of passion to cover both Swinton and Wycombe, the other three ruled accidental, everything is tidied up nice and neat and everyone goes home happy. Case closed."

"You've got an annoying Machiavellian bent to you, Dunliffe, you know that? I'm telling you, it's *her*."

"It could well be. Let's look into it."

Phil sighed. "Right, then, if it *isn't* her, who is it?"

"I don't know. But somebody does. Someone on the inside protecting him."

"Great," Phil said cynically. "Now all we have to do is nick every bent copper in London, piece of cake."

"Something else to think about," Keen added. "If it's not Marge Beecher, if it isn't a crime of passion, then we're dealing with a serial killer who may have the idea this protection makes him fireproof."

"Bloody marvelous." Phil scowled. "Thanks for making my day, pal."

If he hadn't stopped on his way back from the loo for a good-natured flirt with Bernie Pearson, Phil would have missed seeing Felix Schaefer coming out of an interview room entirely. As it was, he spotted the lanky solicitor wittering into the ear of a lad with the ugliest hair Phil had ever seen on a white boy, matted ropes of bleached dreadlocks hanging limply by dark roots around a pinched face. Schaefer didn't notice Phil, too busy beleaguering his client who looked equally unhappy with whatever the solicitor was telling him. Trevor Bramwell was trying to lead the lad toward the detention cells, impatient with being hampered by Schaefer's insistence on advising his client.

Jack Brewer exited the interview room with interview tapes on top of a file. Phil nodded toward the odd couple. "What's he doing here?"

Jack followed his gaze. "Burglary. He and another lad broke into an old lady's flat and pinched her video recorder." He grinned. "She's more upset because her Rosemary Conley aerobics tape was in it at the time."

"No, *him*. Schaefer."

Jack looked at Phil, curious. "You know him?"

"Yeah. What's a two-bit thief doing with flash like that instead of having to make do with a duty solicitor?"

Jack shrugged. "Maybe he likes doing pro bono work?"

Phil snorted, and eyed the tape. "You mind if I give that a listen?"

"Help yourself, skip."

Tape REF/ZZ/98/441-00298-6

This interview is being tape-recorded, and it may be given in evidence if your case is brought to trial. My name is PC John Brewers. This is my colleague . . .

PC Trevor Bramwell.

Can you give us your full name, your date of birth, and your home address, please?

Raymond Burle Delwyn. March sixth, nineteen seventy-six. Nine Streatham Terrace, Tuftnell Park.

Thank you. We're in a private interview room at Kentish Town Police Station, and the time now is twelve minutes past noon. Before we go any further, Ray, I must remind you that you do not have to say anything unless you wish to do so, but anything you say may be given in evidence. Do you understand that?

[Silence.]

You nodded. Can you just speak up just for the purpose of the—

Yeah, yeah.

—microphone. You've taken your right to legal advice, and representing you today is . . . ?

Felix Schaefer of Schaefer, Burgess, and Lowenthal. I'm here to protect . . . ehm . . . Mr. Delwyn's basic and legal rights. I may interrupt the interview if Mr. Delwyn requests or requires legal advice, if you ask about matters which I have not been made aware of, or if you ask him about matters for which he is not under arrest.

Thank you. Now, Ray, when you were arrested by myself and my colleague, you were told you were being arrested on suspicion of burglary, is that right?

No. All you said was, "We'd be wanting a word with you, mate," and grabbed hold of me jacket 'cause, I don't know, maybe you thought I was gonna do a runner. Then that one there handcuffeted me . . .

But what did I say to you just before you were handcuffed?

Um . . . you said . . . "I'll just have one of them ciggies you got."

[Laughter.] I don't think so, because neither of us smokes. You were told you were under arrest on suspicion of burglary, because I was the one who cautioned you. We're now going to tell you that the premises we've suspected you've burgled is a flat on Maryhill Road. So would you tell me what you were doing yesterday evening?

No comment.

We have witnesses who saw two young men answering the description of yourself and another lad on Maryhill Road this morning in possession of a blue and white carrier bag which we believe contained stolen property. You were then seen half an hour later by other witnesses going into your flat on Streatham Terrace with a blue and white carrier bag. So you were initially arrested on suspicion of burglary because of the circumstances in which you were found in possession of these articles. Do you understand?

[Silence.]

Is that "yes," because we don't have a camera in here to see you going . . . okay? So is that a "yes" or a "no"?

Yes.

Okay. Your flatmate, Mark Lisson, has already spoken to us. Now, obviously you don't have to, but this is an opportunity for you to give your side of the story . . .

No comment.

No comment?

You heard me. No fucking comment.

[Pause.] Is it right to say that you have a drug addiction?

Fuck you! If Mark told you that, he's a lying prick bastard—

So if you're not committing crimes to pay for your drug habit, then how do you account for witnesses who saw you last night on Maryhill Road with Mark, and the two of you found later to be in possession of stolen articles?

I didn't commit no crime and I don't have no drug habit!

All right. Would I be accurate in describing your hair as bleached in a spiky dreadlock fashion?

Yeah, so what? You think it's funny?

I'm not trying to be funny, Ray, but would you accept that your hair is unusual? It stands out, right? And your flatmate's got hair shaved quite close, and a big Ay-Oh symbol tattooed on his right arm.

Look, there's loads of blokes got blond dreds walking around. Nothing to say that was me last night.

Two lads, one with hair like yours and the other wearing a green army T-shirt and an Ay-Oh tattoo on his arm, were seen together at three o'clock in the vicinity of a burgled house on Maryhill Road. Other witnesses identified you and Mark as the two people they saw carrying a blue and white carrier bag which turns out to contain a stolen video recorder. Then there's other video recorders in your flat which I think we'll find were also stolen. Now, the coincidence of that— You're shaking your head, but if you disagree with anything I'm saying, then challenge me!

No comment.

No comment. [Pause.] Have a look over there, please. Officers found this Sony video recorder inside that Tesco carrier bag in your flat. That silver aluminium powder on it is where our scene of crimes man has highlighted prints and used cellotape to lift off the marks.

Look, I don' know where that come from—

We know exactly where this video recorder has come from. It's come from that flat which was burgled early this morning on Maryhill Road. So why are your prints all over it, eh?

Yeah, well. I didn't nick it, I just found it in the rubbish. You can find loads of things in the rubbish or like at Oxfam—

Oxfam. You find video recorders like this at Oxfam?

I don't know what you find at Oxfam, all's I know is I found it, maybe someone's tossed it 'cause it don't work no more, see?

Okay, exactly where did you find this video recorder, then?

I don't remember. Mark and me were walking around, and we seen it . . . um . . . on top of this rubbish bin for when the dustmen come by.

So you were walking by, you and Mark . . . what time was this?

I don't remember.

People would leave their rubbish out to be collected before they went to bed, wouldn't they, so it would have to be late. Or early this morning? Which was it, Ray?

I don't know. Early this morning, maybe.

Well, see? That might account for the witnesses who saw you on Maryhill Road. You were walking around with Mark at three o'clock this morning, right?

Yeah.

So what was Mark wearing? A dark green T-shirt, wasn't it?

Don't remember.

You don't remember. [Sigh.] It's not a huge mystery, because he was wearing it when he got nicked.

I weren't with him when he got nicked, so how am I supposed to know what he's got on?

I didn't ask what he was wearing when he was nicked. I asked what he was wearing when he was with you at three this morning.

Don't remember.

Okay, let's back up a little. Where were you before you found the video recorder? [Pause.] If you're happy to tell us where you were at three this morning, why can't you tell us what you were doing before then?

Don't remember . . . Fucking hell . . . ?

[Loud obscenities, several people shouting and scuffling.]

For the benefit of the tape, Ray, would you just confirm we're not duffing you up or anything, it's somebody outside the interview room who's making all the noise. Isn't that right? . . . Ray?

Well, um . . . I guess so.

I'll corroborate that as well.

Thank you, Mr. Schaefer. So, Ray, where were you and Mark going at that time of night?

I told you, I can't remember where exactly. I wasn't paying no attention to nothing like that.

I see. So you were just walking along, don't know where, don't know for how long, not paying the slightest bit of attention to anything around you. Ray, how long have you lived in Tuftnell Park?

Couple weeks, a month maybe.

Where did you live before that?

Hackney.

And how long did you live in Hackney?

Don't know. Maybe four, five month.

Excuse me, but I don't see how this line of questioning has much bearing on your investigation.

I believe your client has lived in the area for a sufficient amount of time to know his way around, Mr. Schaefer. [Pause.] So tell me, Ray, how long have you lived in London?

Um . . . On my own, you mean? Just in London?

On your own, or with friends, or family, anyone. How long have you lived anywhere in the London Metropolitan area?

Don't know. Lived all over, never in one place for long, though.

Where do your parents live, Ray? Do you have any family in London?

Just my sister—

As my client is not a minor, the whereabouts of his family would not be germane to your inquiries.

[Pause.] We'll leave it there for the moment. Police officers found six video recorders in your flat. That's a lot of video recorders, Ray. So what're you doing with six video recorders?

They're not mine. Best to ask Mark.

It's your flat.

Not my flat, his girlfriend's flat, Francie's.

That a council flat?

Yeah.

Council know you're in there?

Yeah.

They do, do they? Are you a tenant?

No, it's just like somewhere to put my head down.

So who pays the rent?

It's from, you know, the social . . . Mark and Francie wants to get married, just not right away or nothing. You got to put down that you're living separate before it's all right. But if Mark says they're living together, they get less money, you know?

Uh-huh, I see . . .

I have to stay with friends 'cause I don't have no job. Can't get a job when you don't have no proper clothes, and you smell nasty, can't shower, can't shave, who's going to give me a job? I didn't get my giro money for two weeks 'cause I was living rough, then I get a chance to get cleaned up and all—just look at me hands here, I get pulled and then I've got this other court case—

We're not discussing . . . Look, forget your other court case, we're only talking about this morning . . . Ray, don't do that, sit down . . .

I got a sister in London, but she don't want to know me. They're not the sort want me popping round unexcepted and all, so it's not like I can go stay wif me family—

Sit down, Ray. I accept you have unfortunate domestic circumstances, but . . . listen to me, you have to just bear with us here, okay? Now *sit down*! [Pause.] You okay now, Ray? Let's change the subject and move on. What time did you and Mark leave the flat? Were you in the flat all day before you went out?

Yeah.

So what were you doing, you and Mark, before you went out?

Just the usual. Watching telly.

Can you remember what you were watching on telly?

Dunno. Francie mighta been watching the news.

That'd be what, ten o'clock, eleven? Then what?

I think Mark put a tape on the video.

Okay, what videotape were you watching?

Watched a couple, don't remember which ones.

So it was after you'd watched a couple of videotapes. Would it be fair to say it was probably sometime around three in morning, then?

Yeah . . . Well, maybe closer to two.

Two o'clock. Then what did you do? [Pause.] Witnesses saw you in the Holloway area around three in the morning.

Wun't me. Weren't there. Didn' go nowhere.

[Sigh.] Ray, you've already told us you and Mark were on Maryhill Road this morning at three A.M. . . .

Just because I don't have no job, maybe I just—you know—like having a smoke and watching the sun come up, you lot assume I got to be up to no good. That's just prejudice, is what it is, that's police harassment—

All right, all right. So did you watch the sun rise this morning?

Yeah, I guess so.

Sun comes up around when? Five-thirty? So what were you doing between the time you left Mark's flat at two this morning until you watched the sun come up?

[Pause.] No comment.

We're back to "no commenting" now, are we? Jesus, Ray, can't you think up anything better? You've already told us quite a lot, nobody's tricked you into it, nobody's forced you. It's a bit late now to be "no commenting."

What can I say?

The truth. I think the reason for the both of you going out at two in the morning was to do a burglary—

You're trying to fit us up because you don't got nobody else—

I also think it's highly unlikely you found that video recorder lying atop somebody's rubbish. I think you and Mark weren't out having a smoke and watching the sun come up, but breaking into a flat. *You* committed this burglary, Ray. You and Mark together—

You can accuse me of whatever you want, but that's all just your hypeth-hypocka-thestic—

Hypothesis.

Whatever! I *didn't* do no burglary!

Okay. When the police searched your flat, they also found a driving license which doesn't belong to anyone at that address. So what's *that* doing in your flat?

A driving license?

A driving license. [Pause.] It's a piece of paper about so big, says you're qualified to drive a car.

Oh, yeah. That's not mine.

I know it's not yours, Ray. That's why I'm asking what it's doing in your flat?

Mark's girlfriend's been using it.

Francie?

Yeah. But not to drive, or nuthin', just to get in the pubs, is all.

So she's in possession of stolen property. That's a crime, Ray. Seems I'll have to go arrest Francie now.

But she didn't have nothing to do with no video recorders!

I'm not talking about the video recorders, I'm talking about the driving license.

Who said it was stolen?

The woman it belongs to.

Look, Francie's got nothing to do with it—

It's *stolen*. Even if she's just found it somewheres and didn't turn it in . . . Look, you find a quid on the street, no way you're going to know who lost it, right? But this is an official document belonging to a Margaret Atkins in Knightsbridge. You need to take reasonable steps to find the owner, easy enough to do with her name and address written right on it, and Francie hasn't done that. That means she's been handling stolen goods, now, hasn't she?

But it's not stolen! It's my sister's.

[Pause.] Margaret Atkins is your sister?

Yeah. It wasn't no good to her anyway, not after she got married 'cause the name was different, so I give it to Francie. But she's not using it to drive, it's just for ID in the pubs! Nothin' wrong with that!

I think we need to go speak to your sister. What's her married name?

Excuse me, but unless my client is being charged with this particular offense, I don't see where your questions are relevant.

Mr. Schaefer, we're investigating all stolen property found—

Would you turn off the tape? I'd like to confer with my client in private.

No problem there. We're suspending the interview, the time now is twelve eighteen.

That's fine there, yeah. We are recommencing the interview, the time is now twelve twenty-five. You've had a consultation with your solicitor, Ray. Are you happy now to continue on with the interview?

Yeah.

And is that all right with you, Mr. Schaefer?

It is.

Okay, Ray. Are you now able to give us an explanation for your being in possession of stolen property found in your flat?

No comment.

Did you take part in a burglary on Maryhill Road?

No comment.

Where were you going?

No comment.

Where had you been?

No comment.

Is there anything else you'd like to say?

No comment.

[Pause.] All right, I think we'll have to leave it at that. Ray, here's a notice which ex-plains your rights to a copy of the tape in the machine at this moment. I've ticked that box for you and, basically, if you want a copy of the tape, tell me now or get in touch later and we'll supply one. Okay? Ray?

I didn't do no burglary and I don't care what fairy story you're making up, because . . . ah, that's . . . um—

Just sign this for us, please. Right there. Thank you. Mr. Schaefer, would you like to add anything for your client?

No.

The time is . . . twelve twenty-nine, and we'll conclude it there.

Half an hour later, Phil was in the charge room. "Come on, Phil," the custody sergeant was saying wearily, "I have to do things properly, or it's *me* going to be sitting on the radiator."

"Come in with me, Mel," Phil cajoled. "I'll take him a coffee and sand-wiches, have a friendly chat, and you can be there the whole time to keep me kosher."

The custody sergeant frowned, relenting. "You've never been kosher a day in your life." He picked up the keys. "You sign in and sign out, and if anybody takes offense at what you're up to, I'll be first in line to put my boot up your arse."

"Fair enough."

Phil bought the plastic wedge of sandwiches and a cup of instant coffee, and followed the custody sergeant down the corridor of scruffy cells. Noses and fingers poked out of tiny rusted slots in the metal doors, eyes peering out at the intruders into their strange world. The sergeant checked inside before he unlocked a cell and held the door open. "Kosher," he insisted firmly. "And I mean *orthodox*."

Raymond Burle Delwyn looked up suspiciously from where he sat on the narrow ledge, thin plastic mattress underneath his skinny bottom. He accepted the sandwiches and coffee from Phil with ill grace.

"Don't like chicken," he pronounced. He bit into a triangle of bread any-way, chewing openmouthed. "And I don't like powdered coffee, neever," he said from around a mouthful of chicken.

"I'll make a note of it," Phil said. The custody sergeant stood in front of the door, arms crossed.

Delwyn's eyes shifted from one to the other. "What d'you want?"

"Mind if I ask a couple of questions, son?"

Delwyn sneered, leaning back against the wall. "I knew it. All the nicey-nice questions when there's a solicitor and a tape recorder going, but the real questions come when you can knock me around cuz nobody's about. Fucking pig bastards, you're all the same."

"Don't believe everything you read in the papers. I'm not going to touch you." He thrust his hands in his pockets to emphasize the point, then added, "Besides, it's too late in the month."

"Aye?"

"The police've had to pay out too much compensation lately, so they've reduced the number of people we're allowed to beat up. This month's quota is filled, sorry. But get yourself nicked in a week or so, we'll see what we can do for you."

As Delwyn puzzled that over uncertainly, Phil heard the custody sergeant's warning cough. He nodded toward Mel. "He's here to keep *me* sweet, not you. Anyway, I don't want to ask anything about that sneak-in job you did this morning—"

"I didn't do nuffink . . ."

"Sorry, the *alleged* burglary you were arrested for."

Delwyn tilted his head on his bird-thin neck, still wary. "Then what do you want to ask me about?"

"All I want to know is who's paying your solicitor?"

The lad's eyes narrowed as he took another bite of his sandwich. "What do you want to know that for?"

Phil shrugged. "Here you are, living rough and collecting your giro, and yet you can afford an upmarket solicitor like Mr. Schaefer to defend you on a simple burglary charge? Looks a bit . . . *suspicious*. Think what a magistrate's going to make of it, you go into court pleading poverty with a brief like that standing next to you . . ."

Delwyn scowled, and washed down the detested chicken sandwich with the reviled instant coffee. "I'm not paying him."

"Then who is? *Somebody* must be paying him."

"He's told me all I'm supposed to give you lot is 'no comment'. So . . . No comment. So if you're not here to thump me, piss off." The lad smiled broadly, revealing crooked teeth, bits of white bread and chicken stuck in between the gaps.

"No comment?" Phil made a pretense of being perplexed. "Does that mean there *is* something illegal you don't want to discuss?"

"Nothing's illegal!"

"It's just for our records, Ray, like your name, date of birth, address. You don't say 'no comment' to those questions, do you? It's just an ordinary sort of question; who's paying your solicitor?"

"My sister, okay? But leaf her out."

"Your sister. That would be Margaret Atkins?"

And Delwyn supplied the answer to Phil's second question. "Sutton. She got married last April." He glanced away, his scowl bitter. "Sir Timothy Cavendish Sutton. Right fookin' prat, 'e is."

"I see. You and your sister aren't close, then. That's why you're staying with Mark Lisson instead of with your family."

An expression as impenetrable as armor plating fell over the boy's face. "Don't wanna live wif her, is all. What kind of grown man lives wif 'is sister, aye?"

"I can see your point. What with her being newly married—"

Delwyn rolled his eyes. "'E ain't her first, like. She just acts like she's the Virgin Mary. She ditched the first one five year ago, another rich prat too good for the rest of us, just like this one."

"I had assumed she'd been married before."

"You did?" Delwyn looked genuinely surprised, which genuinely confused Phil.

"Well, yeah. Her name being Atkins and yours being Delwyn . . ."

Again, that unreadable look settled across the boy's features. "That *is* her real name. First bastard's name was Knox. She took her maiden name back when she were shot of him. She's my half sister."

"Different fathers, then."

"Different mothers."

"Ah." This time, the boy's anger was palpable, and it told Phil Reaves a good many things. Like why a well-bred woman from Knightsbridge wouldn't be too pleased to have a bastard half brother show up on her doorstep with one boot still dragging in the gutter. It also told him it was time to back away from this subject. "Well, that's all I wanted to ask. Wasn't too painful, was it?"

Delwyn shot him a hostile look, then crammed the remainder of his sandwich into his mouth. Phil waited for the custody sergeant to let him out before he smiled innocently. "Kosher enough?"

The sergeant's expression was remarkably similar to Ray Delwyn's, but without the sandwich. "Do it the right way next time, okay?"

"If we always did it the right way, Mel, we'd never have time enough to get the job done. Think of what that would mean. Anarchy in the streets, looting and rioting and pillaging and all. Wouldn't want that on your conscience, would you?"

The sergeant walked away shaking his head, ignoring Phil's grin.

Near to the shift change, he went in search of either Brewers or Bramwell before they booked off. It took him a while, finally drawn to muted laughter in the civilian staff's coffee room. When he opened the door, the man nearest turned quickly, half blocking his way, half blocking his view along with four other uniformed officers, all male.

"It's okay, it's just Phil," the PC announced sheepishly.

He glanced over the constable's shoulder. Now he saw why they had crowded into the tiny room; the typists had their own video player to make transcriptions. It wasn't showing any courtroom scenes or child witness statements, however, but a video of quite a different nature which, Phil realized, was why they'd shut the door and posted a guard for any stray senior officers or women passing by.

"What's all this?"

Brewers grinned boyishly. "Evidence from that burglary on Maryhill Road, skip. We found a lot of tapes with no labels, thought what with all those video recorders in the flat maybe they'd been pirating films. You know, rent a Blockbuster videotape, break the decoding, make a dozen copies and sell them for a quick quid." He laughed. "But these aren't exactly your average Blockbusters . . ."

Phil could easily see that, the video in the machine at the moment bearing little resemblance to *Who Framed Roger Rabbit*. He stared, his mouth slack, at the three people writhing around on a rumpled bed engaged in a remarkably complicated sexual act involving chains and ropes and elaborate machinery, before Brewers nervously glanced behind him and said, "Come in and shut the door, won't you, Sarge?"

"Oh. Right." It didn't occur to Phil to demur.

"Ouch," another man murmured with his head twisted sideways. "I wouldn't have thought *that* was humanly possible . . ."

The amateur pornography had little regard for camera technique, flattering lighting, or even a basic story line. The sound quality was muffled and tinny, and immobility of the angle made it look, in fact, like a hidden camera behind a one-way mirror. A hunch confirmed when Trevor Bramwell changed tapes, the actresses different, but the stage setting yet another grotesque design straight out of a Marquis de Sade comic. And the leading man starring in this episode was a notably prominent senior police officer.

"Oh shit, oh dear," Jack Brewers whispered. The rest of the audience exchanged awkward glances.

Phil cleared his throat. "Trev, mind switching that off now?"

The PC hastily punched out the tape from the machine. The room was eerily quiet, the men watching him. Phil exhaled slowly. "I don't have to lecture anyone here on the virtues of discretion, do I?" A chorus of *No, guvs* rippled through the small room. "Don't you lot have things to see, people to do . . . ? Jack, Trev, you stay."

The room emptied out in seconds. Phil held out his hand and Bramwell gave him the videotape. "How many of these are there?"

"'Bout fifty, sixty. Not sure how many are dupes, though."

"Sorry, lads, but I'm about to yank this nice juicy case away from you."

Jack chuckled quietly. "Normally, that might tick me off. But on this occasion, CID's welcome to it."

"Good nick. I'll remember you when the time comes."

"Frankly, I'd rather you didn't." Trevor nodded at the videotape in Phil's hand. "Don't think I could keep the smirk off my face that one ever come round to pin any medals on *my* chest."

"Mark Lisson. Schaefer handling him, too?"

"No, duty solicitor."

"What'd he say in interview, then?"

"Solid 'no comment.' He's gone through the dance steps before, nasty piece of business, that one."

Phil tapped the videocassette thoughtfully.

"You pull this girl Francie yet?"

"Francine Jenkins, no. Lisson knocks her about on a regular basis, we've had two complaints gone nowhere because she was too afraid to testify. She's probably at her mother's quivering under the bed."

"Jack, give some thought to cultivating Ray Delwyn as a snout."

The look of incredulity on the PC's face was comical. "*Him?* You're joking! If brains were cotton, that one wouldn't have enough to stuff a Tampax up a flea's fanny!"

"Informants don't have to be that bright to grass their mates."

"They have to be bright enough not to grass *themselves*. C'mon, skip," he whined, "I can deal with snouts who're greedy, sneaky, psychotic, and hazardous to my health. But not *brain-dead*. He wouldn't last fifteen minutes on the streets."

"Yes, well . . ." Phil wasn't really listening. "Stop moaning and give it a go anyway. Somehow, I can't see him as the budding film mogul type, can you? Like as not, these are proceeds of a previous burglary, one which wasn't duly reported by the outraged citizen." He thought a moment. "Trevor, go see what you and the IO can find in the suspect files on local girls working the knocking shops, specialty houses in particular. Get me some faces for comparisons." Trevor's none-too-subtle glance at his watch jarred him out of his musings. "Soonest done, soonest you can book off."

"And what are you going to do?"

"Jack and I are going to sit here in the dark and watch a lot of very bad porn." He ignored Trevor's scowl as Jack grinned. "This thing got a fast-forward?"

At two o'clock, he rang Gabby at the hospital to say he'd be home late. He didn't make excuses, she'd heard them all too often to care. He'd try to make it up to her later on, when he had time. She knew his heart was in the right place. He hoped.

Then he settled back in the only comfortable chair, Jack making do with a plastic stool as the two watched one pornographic video after another. Most of them were merely tawdry, pathetic really, yet hardly shocking. But a few . . .

He answered a knock on the door, and accepted a large stack of suspect index cards from Trevor Bramwell. The PC stared past him, his eyes popping. "Gwah! No fair, Sarge, give us a turn!"

"Out."

Phil handed half the cards to Jack, put the rest in his lap. The pile of videocassettes on the left side of the television mounted, as those on the right shrank. Several were copies, which did seem to indicate Delwyn—or more likely Lisson—had been involved in a low-budget cottage industry. The girls (and some of the boys, for that matter) in the videos were heavily made up, which made comparisons to the sullen black-and-white suspect photos a challenge. On the other hand, Phil recognized a few of the punters all too easily, as photogenic on bad videotape as they were on the ten o'clock news, even if severely underdressed.

Once, Jack muttered, "Christ, skip! Do you know who *that* is?"

To which Phil had replied casually, "Nope. And neither do you. Worry about the punters later, Jack. For now, just find me the girls."

An hour later, he studied one of the suspect cards, then the face of a woman on the freeze frame. Trudy Grumms, alias Genevieve Westlake, alias Gloria de la Reina, alias Paloma Sanchez, had a CRO list for several convictions. He handed the card to Jack. "Know her?"

Jack studied the photo. "Not one of our regulars."

The rest went quicker, Phil playing each cassette only long enough to compare the woman on the tape with that on the card. Trudy Grumms, by whatever stage name she preferred, was more often than not the leading star. And one tape in particular startled him; this cassette didn't join the discard pile.

It was a relief to finally turn the telly off; he was not so much disgusted as bored silly by the sordid acts of bondage, buggery, masturbation, fellatio, and a few things he didn't even know the correct terminology for. Phil wondered vaguely how they'd managed to train the rottweiler. Slumped in the chair, he rubbed sore eyes. Next to him, Jack yawned and kneaded the small of his back.

"What now, skip?"

"Now, you're going to make double sure these are all correctly logged and locked away tight and proper so none of them just happens to go missing 'by mistake,' you understand?"

"Mm-hm," Jack said, unimpressed, and nodded at the tape Phil had singled out. "You just keeping the one for a souvenir, then, are you?"

Phil grinned. "Thought I might go ask for an autograph. Go on, put in for your overtime and go home." Which was more than he was going to do, he realized, checking his watch. He grimaced, knowing it would take something a bit more imaginative than his standard chocs and roses to make it up to Gabby.

Phil studied the house east of King's Cross with a policeman's jaundiced eye. It had been painted and the trim in good repair, the garden weeded, nothing to stand out from its neighbors. But if the antiburglary window bars disguised as wrought-iron scrollwork weren't much different from any of the other houses, Phil didn't miss the more unusual wires attached to the glass, or the motion sensors in the doorframe.

He rapped the brass knocker, the sound telling him the door might have a typical walnut veneer, but the interior was solid steel plating. He didn't hear anyone on the other side as the spyhole darkened, which also told him the house had been fitted with soundproofing. Smiling with toothy cheerfulness, he held his warrant card up close by his head.

The spyhole snapped shut. Heavy locks thunked back and a thin woman in an oversized T-shirt over black leggings peered out past the security chain, her pinched face sulky.

"Paloma Sanchez?" When the woman made no reply, he added, "Or should I ask for Trudy Grumms?" which made her scowl.

"Whadd'you want?"

"I'm DS Phil Reaves, from Kentish Town police. Open the door, Miss Grumms, and let me in." *Or I'll huff and I'll puff and I'll blow your door down.*

"You go' a warrant?"

"Why? Is there a reason I need one?"

She took her time as if her brain fired on less than the normal number of cylinders. "Depends."

"I'd like a chat with you about a burglary. Some videotapes that might have been stolen?"

"Wha' are y' going on about?" she whined in bewilderment. "We didn't steal no videotapes."

"I didn't say you did. But I think your boss might be interested in a few from her collection that've gone missing. Are you going to let me in now, love?"

"I'll have to talk to Vic first," Trudy said, and slammed the door none too gently in his face.

He shrugged, and took in what meager scenery the street provided for nearly ten minutes before the door unlocked and opened noiselessly on well-oiled hinges to reveal a formidable woman as Trudy hovered behind her. In her severely tailored schoolmistress skirt and jacket, she looked more like Margaret Thatcher than a whorehouse madam.

"You must be Victoria," he said, knowing that wasn't her real name any more than Trudy's was Paloma. Again, he displayed his warrant card. She barely glanced at it. "Might I have a private chat?"

"It's that bloody American bitch," Trudy grumbled. The larger woman's eyes flickered in anger, but she said nothing. "I told you she weren't going to keep no promises, went straight to the filf, she did. You shouldn't ha' trusted her, Vic, I told you so, din' I?"

Oh shit, oh dear, is right, Phil thought. He had a hunch he knew exactly which bloody American bitch Trudy was referring to.

Keen's mobile beeped just as they met at the door of the Blue Tulip café. Jillie seemed impatient, grimacing as he fished the mobile phone out of his pocket.

He kissed her cheek, and said, "Dunliffe." He listened for a moment. "Hang on, the reception isn't good." Clamping a hand over the phone, he said to Jillie, "Why don't you snag us a table? I'll just be a tick."

The reception had been fine, but he walked out onto the pavement before he said into the phone quietly, "Go ahead, Phil."

"As I was saying"—Phil's voice was bloodless over the connection—"Jillie was definitely here on Friday. How she knew, I can't figure. This Queen Victoria, or whatever the hell she calls herself, wasn't saying. I'm lucky she was in the mood to be cooperative at all, because I guarantee you, she does *not* have to be. She makes videotapes of certain of her clients as insurance, and a few are in a position to make damned sure she doesn't get herself nicked by the likes of me and thee, pal."

Keen listened without speaking. Jillie waited at the table as the waiter delivered their drinks, lager for him, red wine for her. She waved, lovely with the sunlight shimmering in her hair. He managed to feign a smile. His chest hurt.

". . . security systems all over," Phil continued. "Those two dimwits couldn't have gotten in with just a screwdriver or breaking a window without setting off alarms, so it's got to be an inside job. Only connection I can come up with is that neighbor, Lynne Selkirk."

"Why her?"

"Well, funny thing: Felix Schaefer's representing one of the scrotes who happens to be the brother of one Margaret, eye ee 'Molly' Sutton, a name on the list of people you met at that Charter Eighty-eight meeting. According to Victoria, Molly Sutton's husband is a regular customer. Just a bit too coincidental, wouldn't you say?"

"Possibly. You going to interview Molly Sutton?"

"If I don't get to it tonight, first thing in the morning."

"This tape, you're sure it's of Chris Swinton?"

"Positive. In one of those, what do you call it? *Ménage à trois.*"

"And the other two?"

"The woman is Trudy Grumms, calls herself Paloma Sanchez. The man's name is Richard Atherton. Lives in Windsor. I'm heading out to have a chat with him now, but I'll give you odds on, your lady friend has already paid him a visit as well." His electronic laugh came through the line painfully shrill. "If that woman ever decides to quit teaching history, we should offer her a job in CID. *Damn,* I'd love to know how the bloody hell she did it!"

"So would I, Phil. Cheers." He was less amused as he slipped the mobile back into his pocket. He gazed down for a moment, bridling his anger before he walked into the café and toward the terrace table.

She smiled as he sat, but it faded as he stared at her without returning it. "What?"

"Who did you go to see on Friday?"

She paled. "What do you mean?"

"Don't mess about with me, Jillie." He hated the ashen fright on her face, hated himself for causing it, but releasing his anger came almost as a relief. "Who did you go to see on Friday?"

"I can't tell you," she said unsteadily. "I'm sorry, but I promised—"

"You made me a promise, remember? You promised you'd let me do my job and not go off playing at Nancy Drew. But you've lied, and gone behind my back and possibly ballsed up any useful information I might have been able to get."

She hung her head like a penitent child, looking as wretched as he felt. He ignored the curious glances from other tables around them.

"You talked to a woman named Victoria, didn't you?" When she nodded, he leaned on the table. She drew back in alarm. "And Richard Atherton? Did you go to Windsor to see him as well?"

"Yes."

"How did you find them, what did you talk about?" he demanded relentlessly.

"I'm sorry, I really am, but I gave my word I wouldn't say anything to the police—"

"Right," he said with vicious scorn. "Your word. You'll keep your word to a whore and a sexual pervert, but not to a policeman. Not to *me*." Her mouth pressed together in a thin line. "Why, damn it? Why couldn't you have trusted me?"

"I'm sorry—"

"I don't want to hear 'sorry.' I want to hear the truth." He tried to surprise her. "Who told you about Victoria's? Was it Lynne Selkirk?"

"Lynne?" she said with genuine surprise. "Why Lynne?"

"Come on, Jillie. I know about the videotape. The police have it. It's been *seen*, she's been recognized."

She stared at him in confusion. "Who has? What videotape?"

"*Stop it*," he snarled, and watched her flinch. "Stop pretending to be so bloody ignorant. I expect that sort of crap from lowlife thieves and drug addicts, but not you. The police picked up a couple of lads for burglary last night. One of them just happens to be Molly Sutton's brother. You remember Molly Sutton, Lynne Selkirk's friend? Her brother had a bunch of stolen videotapes. Tapes Victoria made to blackmail people, including one of Richard Atherton and Chris Swinton. So who was Victoria trying to blackmail, Chris or Atherton?"

Her pale cheeks flared red as her own anger surfaced. "You told me no one was watching me anymore. You and the cops keeping an eye on Chris's house, the men in the van at Chris's funeral. Were they following me on Friday, too?" His unwilling silence gave her all the evidence she needed to convict him. "You expect me to be honest with you, but *you* haven't been honest with *me*. How long has this been going on? As long ago as Leeds? When you asked me to dinner that first night, was that already part of the plan?"

"No," he said sharply. "I wasn't—"

"And that guy who harassed me, he another cop friend of yours?"

He made a mistake, caught in the trap of his own anger. "No, and don't try turning this around on me, because it won't work. This isn't a game, Jillie. At the very least, you're breaking the law by withholding information on a burglary. So don't think I can't drag you down to the station and have you charged with obstructing police business. Then you'd be doing all your talking from the inside of a cell!"

She was breathing shallowly, eyes glistening, but she was shaking now with outrage rather than fear. "You're no different from the rest, are you?" she said, her voice low. "You think being a cop gives you the right to bully people just because you can get away with it?"

The strength of her fury was a match for his own. Startled, his anger retreated. "No," he said softly, "that's not—" She didn't listen, too upset to hear him.

"Go ahead, then, arrest me. The *law* is on your side. Who cares about promises to a prostitute or a pervert? Who cares about some stupid American college teacher? The ends justify the means." She blinked, and covered her mouth in dismay. "You even slept with me," she blurted in a whisper, as tears streamed down her face. "Now I understand why. You son of a bitch."

"For God's sake," he objected, appalled. "It weren't like that! *Jillie*—"

She stood and, far too angry, wrestled with her handbag snagged on the chair. The strap broke as she gave it a final wrench. For a moment, she couldn't speak, then choked out barely coherently, *"Go to hell."* She whirled around and collided with her chair, knocking it over. She kicked at it savagely before storming out, pushing past the waiter who backed hurriedly out of her way.

Keen stared down blindly. *"Shit!"* The word exploded from him, as his fist slammed down on the table. The impact toppled her glass, a red stain soaking into the tablecloth. Suddenly, he was acutely aware of the silence, and looked around at people watching him with wary interest.

His head cleared, he lifted a finger and called out calmly to the waiter, "Could I have the bill, please?"

He spent the next half hour walking around the block, both to curb his own temper and to give Jillie time to cool off.

That had been another mistake.

When he returned to Mrs. Flutes's he found the flat deserted and Mrs. Flute alone on the roof garden, a conical Oriental hat defending her from the sun as she watered her flowers. She looked up curiously as he stood in the doorway.

"Where's Jillie?"

"Oh," she said, surprised. "Then you're not going to France with her?"

"France!"

Mrs. Flute twisted the stopcock to turn off the water. "Lynne Selkirk called by today to give her a letter from someone in Paris about documents relating to Chris's research. Jillie was very excited, said she was going to tell you all about it at the café. She didn't, did she?"

Keen exhaled his frustration. "No," he said tiredly. "She didn't. Do you know where she's gone?"

"On the express train for a ferry from Dover to Calais."

"Excuse me, if you don't mind," he said, and woodenly punched numbers into his mobile.

Phil answered on the first ring.

"Where are you?"

"On the M4 to Windsor, why?"

"You wouldn't have your passport with you?"

There was a bewildered pause. "I wasn't aware I needed a passport to go to Windsor."

"You don't. You need it to go to France. Jillie's on her way to Dover for a ferry to Calais."

"Damn," Phil said in amazement, "when your girlfriend goes walkies, she doesn't mess about."

Keen ignored him. "I'm hoping you can get there afore she does."

"Why don't you go after her, then?"

"Because my bloody passport is in Leeds, that's why!" Keen shouted. Phil didn't reply, only muted traffic noise on the line. He calmed himself and offered Mrs. Flute a contrite smile. "I've blown it, Phil."

"How bad?"

"Bad enough. We had a row . . ." He hesitated before admitting, "I might have given her the impression she could be arrested if she refused to tell me how she knew about Victoria's and Atherton."

"Well, that was pretty friggin' stupid, wunnit?" Phil said, the contempt in his voice making Keen wince.

"Now she's got a letter Lynne Selkirk give her sent to Chris from Paris, something about that damned book Swinton were writing. She's not thinking straight, too blind mad at me—"

"So what? She's a big girl, Dunliffe, let her go—"

"Phil, I think one of the two bastards who threatened my kids may be the same man who put the frighteners on her Saturday."

For an anxious moment, Keen listened to the hiss of the open line. Then Phil sighed. "You want me to try and stop her?"

Keen tried to keep the relief out of his voice. "If you can. Don't let her get on that ferry, or if she does, bring her back, don't let her get off."

"I'll have to stop off home for my passport. What about Atherton?"

"I'll go out there and interview him now."

"Okay. Ring you later."

He hung up. "I'm sorry for the trouble," he said to Mrs. Flute. "I don't know if Jillie'll be back tonight or not. But if you'd prefer I left . . . ?"

Mrs. Flute smiled broadly. "My goodness, no, Sergeant. I haven't been so excited since they dragged the canal for Dirty Den. This is far better fun than *Eastenders,* I wouldn't miss it for the world!"

★   ★   ★

A sprawling lounge took up the entire front bow of the ship. Jillie bought a paperback from the duty free, a comfortingly mindless bodice-ripper, then ordered a Pepsi from the bar and sat alone by the window. The sea sparkled in the waning sunlight through the clouds, wind ruffling white breakers of foam. It was farther than she'd imagined to France, no land yet visible on the horizon. She was idly watching gulls swooping around the prow when her view was blocked by a man with a beer bottle in one hand and an empty glass in the other.

"This seat taken?" he said with an English accent and a smile.

The lounge wasn't crowded, there were plenty of other tables unoccupied, she noted. She opened the paperback she'd been ignoring for the past fifteen minutes. "Actually, I'm rather busy . . ."

He sat down across from her anyway. "Don't be like that, love," he said as he poured himself a glass of beer. "I'm bored and I don't speak French, looking to pass the time, that's all." He wiped the condensation off his palm on his jeans before holding out his hand. "Name's Phil."

Reluctantly, she shook it, not wanting to offend him. Then she wondered why she could never muster the nerve to tell a man to leave her alone. "Jillie," she said unwillingly.

"First time to France?"

"No." She didn't elaborate, trying to send him the message he wasn't wanted, but he smiled and nodded cheerfully.

"I'm only going as far as Calais, how about you?"

"Paris." She glared at her melting ice cubes.

"Paris! Never been there myself. You going on holiday, then?"

"No," she said, gritting her teeth. "Look, I'm not really in the mood for company." She smiled, trying to take the confrontation out of it.

"Oh, right." He reached to take his wallet out of his back pocket. "Could I just show you something?"

Stifling her resentment, she waited for what she expected to be photographs of his wife and kids to prove he wasn't trying to seduce her. Instead, she gaped at police identification.

"I'm a Metropolitan police officer, Ms. Waltham. And I'm asking you to come back to London with me."

She swallowed hard, heart pounding. "You're the man on the steps the other night," she said, recognizing him.

"That's right. I'm a friend of Keen Dunliffe's. We're trying to help you and it's not smart going off on your own. Please come back, and let's do it the right way."

"Am I under arrest?" Her voice sounded tight and small.

"No, of course not."

"Then I'm an American citizen." She shoved her book into her purse. "And you have no right to stop me from going any place I want."

"That's true, but—" He frowned ruefully as she stood. "Oh, come on, love, let's just talk this over."

"Piss off," she said as coolly as she could, her uncharacteristic swearing giving her a rush of exhilaration.

He gulped down half his beer before leaving the rest. "There's no harm done in talking to me," he said, keeping in step with her as she walked out of the lounge. "Be reasonable here. We're on a ship in the middle of the English Channel, where do you think you can go?"

She realized he was right; glancing around uncertainly, she saw she couldn't escape. Then she glared at him with unfeigned dislike. "To the ladies' room," she retorted, and strode toward the toilets.

"Well, you got me there," he said behind her. "But you'll have to come out sometime . . ." The swinging door cut off the rest.

Half a dozen slender young women around the mirrors and sinks chattered in rapid-fire French, adjusting blouses, repairing makeup. Jillie waited for a free stall and peed, then washed her hands slowly.

What *could* she do, she thought. She couldn't hide in the women's toilet forever. And he'd still be out there when they got to Calais. Could she make a scene? Would he try to stop her if she screamed and ran? Would the French authorities take his side because he was a cop?

Don't be an idiot, she thought, scowling at her reflection. Then to her horror, tears rolled out of her eyes. A young woman in a short red leather skirt stopped teasing her hair into fluff and glanced over in concern.

"*Tout va bien, madame?*" she asked gently. Her friend leaned over to look past her at Jillie with sympathetic eyes.

"No," Jillie replied in English, wiping her eyes in embarrassment. "Everything's not okay." She switched to French. "There is a man outside who is bothering me."

"He is your boyfriend?"

"No," Jillie said, and hesitated before lying. She definitely didn't want to say he was a policeman. "Not any longer. He is trying to prevent me from going to Paris because he is very jealous that I am in love with a French man." Then she added, honestly, "I am also very afraid of him."

"*Qu'est-ce qui se passe, Nathalie?*" A third girl joined the troupe gathering around her.

"*C'est un mec qui la dérange,*" Nathalie explained. Then she grinned with a merry wickedness. "You are wishing to go to Paris tonight, yes?" she asked Jillie in English.

"Oh, yes. Very much."

"Maybe we can help you."

Jillie was astonished. "You don't even know me!"

The girl laughed. "But we know men! I have a friend on the ship who is a, *comment dit-on 'routier' en anglais?* A driver of a big truck. He can take you to Paris tonight in his truck."

"The man outside, he'll follow me . . ."

"I have an eye-dee. Monique, Marie-Claude . . ." She spoke in rapid French too heavily sprinkled with slang for Jillie to follow. Her friends nodded, giggling, and, to Jillie's amazement, began stripping off their clothes. "Madame, you remove your dressing also."

"Why?"

"We make you into a disguise." She tugged at Jillie's skirt. "We change clothings, *oui*? Then we to make your hair different and put the *maquillage* on your face. It will be like a show, a fashion show. That is what we do . . ." She waved her hand at her slender, pretty friends. "*Les mannequins*. It will be *très chouette!*"

The girl's short skirt barely fit, far too snug across the rear end. Monique brutally attacked her hair with a brush as a fourth girl, Céline, artfully twisted and fastened a blouse over Jillie with safety pins dredged from the bottom of someone's purse. A round-robin of trying on each other's shoes left Jillie tottering on three-inch heels. The girls' chattering was interrupted by a knock on the toilet door.

"Jillie," he called out. "Can you hear me? Come out, now. Please? All I want is to talk to you."

The girls glanced wide-eyed at each other, stifling their giggles.

"Go away!" Jillie shouted. "Leave me alone!"

"This is *silly*, the boat'll be docking soon," he retorted. "Then what? I'm not leaving until you come out of there . . ."

Another rushed consultation between the French girls resulted in Céline unbuttoning another button of her blouse and checking her lipstick in the mirror. She grinned and left the toilet.

"We are nearly finish," Nathalie said. "Céline will be distracting with him, and then we . . ." She made a sound and gesture indicating a quick getaway. She shoved Jillie's purse inside her own huge rucksack, then caught her worried expression. "Don't worry," she said. "That skirt is a Jean-Paul Gaultier original, and I very much want it back."

"*Et voilà,*" Monique announced proudly, turning Jillie toward the mirror.

Jillie stared pop-eyed. Her hair had been pulled up tight against her scalp, tied with a bright pink scarf with the remaining curls arranged in a perky bouffant twenty years too young for her. Bloodred lipstick had entirely reshaped her mouth, blush making her cheekbones stand out in sharp relief. A liberal application of eyeshadow, liner, and mascara had transformed her eyes, seemingly twice as large as they'd ever been. She wore Nathalie's skirt, Marie-Claude's shoes, and Monique's blouse, unbuttoned far enough to expose an uncomfortable amount of pale, freckled flesh.

"Good, *non*? Think he will recognize you?" Nathalie grinned at her in the mirror, hands companionably on Jillie's shoulders.

"I don't think my own daughter would recognize me," Jillie murmured, fascinated with her changed appearance.

For a final moment, the girls looked at one another in conspiratorial glee. "Everybody ready . . . ? *Bon, allons-y!*"

"Come on, love, give a poor man a break, won't you?" Phil checked his watch again. He leaned against the wall next to the small duty-free kiosk. "What the bloody hell can anyone *do* in there for twenty minutes?"

He started in expectation, then frowned as a blond girl left the toilet. She crossed to the duty-free shop, chatting briefly in French with the man behind the counter, and bought Galoise Jaune cigarettes. He was only vaguely aware of her, his attention still on the ladies' room. Then she said something to him.

"Ah . . . jay no parlay fransay," he said helplessly.

She reacted with sheer delight. "You are Eengleesh?"

"Yes, I am."

"Oh!" She moved in front of him, indicating her cigarette. Startled, he could see down her blouse quite clearly. "I ask eef you 'ave zee briquette . . . zee fire?"

"No, I don't smoke, sorry."

She put her cigarettes in her handbag. "Zen I weel not smoke. Where are you coming from een Eengland?"

He tried to find something else to look at rather than the bare flesh being wriggled in front of him. "London."

She responded as if he'd just made love to her. *"Londres,"* she breathed in ecstasy. "I 'ave always wanted to make za visit to zee Buckeeng'am Palais. I like your Eengleesh accent very much, I seenk it eez very sexy, *non?*"

Phil wiped his forehead, glad Gabby wasn't on this trip with him. God damn you, Dunliffe. "That's . . . that's nice. I think your accent is very charming, too."

"Maybe you like to drink a caffee weez me?"

"No, thanks, sorry . . ."

She suddenly pouted. "You don' like me?"

"I'm waiting for someone," he said hurriedly.

Instead of taking the hint, she slithered closer, the wall pressed against his back leaving him no room for retreat. He glanced up as the door of the women's WC opened, but it was a group of four girls, smartly dressed, arms around each other as they babbled in high-speed French and walked away.

"You are married?" the blond girl persisted.

"Too right there, love."

"And you are waiteeng for your wife, *n'est-ce pas?*"

"Ah, no, she's not my wife."

"Ohhh," the girl said knowingly, her smile widening. "I *see!*"

"No, that's not . . . She isn't . . ." Christ, he realized belatedly. She was on the game, working the damned ferry! And it had taken him this long to figure it out, like a daft fool. "Look," he said, exasperated. "I think you're a very nice girl, but really, I'm not interested. Goodbye now. Right you go, orry vwar, ta . . ."

He waggled fingers at her then slumped with relief as she shrugged and walked away. A minute later, two women went in and a few minutes later when the same two came out, he checked his watch uneasily. A woman with a small girl entered, and he stopped her when she came out. "Excuse me, do you speak English?"

She gave him a sulfurous look. *"Non."*

"I'm waiting for a lady?" He did his best to pantomime, "Could you"—he pointed at her—"see"—he pointed at his eyes—"if she"—he pointed at the restroom door—"is still in there for me?"

The mother scowled even further. *"Non,"* she snapped, and dragged her little girl away.

He smiled at the child, still staring at him over her pinafored shoulder with wide-eyed fascination. "Righto. Thanks ever so much."

He glanced around, then ducked inside. A quick inspection proved the WC deserted. Jillie Waltham had vanished. *"Shit!"*

A stout elderly woman coming in ran into him coming out, and drew herself up with formidable indignation.

"Ah . . . cleaning crew. You can go in now," he invented hastily.

She let loose a torrent of shrill French, all of it astoundingly outraged, and ended with the only word Phil understood. *"Pervert!"*

When his mobile beeped, Keen jumped, keyed up waiting for Phil. But it was PC Malcomb Bealle.

". . . going on about there not being enough money to take care of all them books properly," the young constable was saying in a rushed voice. "Funny an earl having the same budget problems as us, innit? Anyway, they do get took down and cleaned every year, but there's nobody reads them. Except for a lot about opera. But she did come up with the inventory reference. A book of drawings by Richard Dalton, bound by William Edwards, is that right, Sarge?"

"That's the one."

"Well, Mrs. Frunzell, that's the librarian lady, she says it weren't part of no sale, so we went to see if it were on the shelf, check it'd been stolen, right? Except it's still there. But this is the interesting bit: it don't exactly match her inventory description. It's supposed to have two of these heraldry shields inside, only it don't. It's got just the one, so she says she'd look at the records. But that was going to take another half hour, and I couldn't drink another cup of tea or I'd burst something."

Keen sighed and glanced at his watch, wondering where Phil or Jillie were at that moment.

"So I think, right, why don't I go see Mr. Kearne, that's the gardener who found the handbag. I come round the lake and see Mr. Westley up a ways, give him a shout. He turns round, takes one look at my uniform, and goes about fourteen shades of white. I think, hang on, what's *his* problem? So I get all serious and say, 'Isn't there something you should be telling me, Mr. Westley?', like I already know what it is, and he's gobbin' off that it weren't him, we can't stick him with nothing, he only found it and flung it in the water after he spotted the woman.'"

"Hold it, back it up there, Malcomb," Keen said, confused.

"The handbag," Bealle explained. "That morning, he found the woman's clothing, but he don't see no one around. So he goes through the handbag, and comes up with a Baggie full of cannabis. He decides to nick it along with the money and a gold necklace, thinking whoever owns the handbag isn't likely to complain, not with the marijuana being there, are they? Then he leaves the handbag. But when he finds the body, he panics, sure we'll find his fingerprints on the handbag and think he's the one topped her. So he runs back and flings it into the lake. But when he sees me there after Mr. Kearne turned it in, he assumes we must've got his prints off it and I'm come back to arrest him for murder!"

Keen slowly smiled. "Have you got the necklace?"

"That were a bit tricky. Turns out he give it to his mother for her birthday. Right scene that were, I come by to confiscate it, him trying to explain it to his mum. For a minute, I thought I might have to nick *her* for murder!"

"And the book?"

"They're two different books. The one you got does belong to Harewood, but they don't know where this un's come from. Sorry, skip."

He mentally adjusted his earlier appraisal of Bealle; it seemed the lad would turn out to be a decent copper after all. "Good job, Malcomb."

"Thanks, but I just got lucky, and tried to handle it the way you would've."

And that touched Keen more deeply than he could have ever admitted.

By the time Céline arrived on the deck below, Nathalie, Marie-Claude, and Monique had stripped and exchanged clothing back with Jillie. The driver, Jacques, leaned out of his tractor-trailer rig to watch the girls undress, ignoring Nathalie's sharp admonishment that if he were any gentleman at all he would avert his eyes. The other girls seemed oblivious, fashion models too used to stripping near naked, Jillie assumed. The deserted cargo bay echoed their voices.

Nathalie tossed her head haughtily, and slithered back into the red leather skirt. "Do not worry about Jacques. He does not speak English, but he is a nice man and will try nothing naughty." She flashed dark eyes at the man, switching to vehement French to warn him to behave or risk losing various parts of his anatomy. He grinned, his unshaven face making him appear even more sinister. She wondered what on earth she had gotten herself into, but it was far too late now.

And, to her surprise, she was more excited than scared. She was having a real adventure which, if she survived it, would give her a story to astound Karen.

Céline's high heels clanged on the metal deck. "*Les rosbifs!* I near to throw myself on 'eemself and ee do nozeeng, *c'est incroyable!* Ee sinks I am a 'ooker!" The idea filled her with trembling wrath. "*Moi? Une putain! Merde!* Edith Cresson is right, all focking Eenglishmans must be payday!"

"Payday?" Jillie asked, tucking in her blouse.

"'Omosexual," Jacques called down helpfully, pleased to be of assistance.

Shortly after six, Keen rang Richard Atherton's doorbell, the chimes tinkling out the first few bars of "Rule, Britannia." An imposing woman answered the door, wearing a floppy cloth hat and a pair of secateurs in her hand.

He showed her his warrant card. "Mrs. Atherton?"

She studied it shrewdly. "Yes?"

"I'm Sergeant Keen Dunliffe from Weetwood Police Station in Leeds. Could I speak with your husband? I won't take up too much of his time."

Although not a muscle in her face moved, she seemed to be smiling, coldly. "Aren't you a bit far afield from West Yorkshire, Sergeant?"

"I'm investigating a crime committed in Leeds which your husband may be able to shed some light on."

"I very much doubt that." Mrs. Atherton made no motion to allow him entry. "It's rather late. My husband is ill and shouldn't be bothered. Doctor's orders."

"I quite understand, but he may be crucial in assisting the police in our inquiries." Her smile this time was perceptible, clear she understood the threat behind the traditional bland phrase. It was enough, however, to get her to allow him in.

He followed her into a grimly austere lounge, furnishings meticulously tidy. But any color seemed accidental; black-and-white photographs of unsmiling relatives in silver frames along a gray marble mantelpiece, lithographs hung on the muted gray walls. He sat on a beige sofa, and glanced around at faded lilies in an ivory Chinese vase, sunlight bleached through white linen drapes. Even the potted ficus in one corner seemed sallow and lifeless.

"I'll see if he's awake . . ." she said primly, before a man with a moustache that looked like it had been drawn on with an eyebrow pencil appeared on the stairs.

"Who is it, darling?" he asked, eyeing Keen.

"It's a police officer from Leeds, darling," she said with jaded distaste. "He'd like to ask you a few—"

She got no further before her husband's face drained as completely of color as the room, eyes rolling up as he pitched headlong down the stairs.

Startled, Keen jumped to his feet. Mrs. Atherton gazed down at her husband sprawled on the carpet. "Oh, my." She seemed more irritated than concerned. "I did warn you he was feeling poorly."

Keen knelt beside the man, rolling him onto his back. Atherton inhaled and his eyes fluttered open. He stared at Keen before he scrunched his eyes firmly shut, as if hoping Keen would be gone when he opened them again.

"They must train you how to deal with this sort of situation," his wife said, still unruffled. "Would a small amount of port be called for, do you think?"

"Excellent idea," Keen said tightly.

"I'll pour him some, then," she said, and left the room unhurriedly.

While any police inquiry tended to give even the most innocent witnesses sweaty palms, Atherton's reaction seemed rather over the top. "Mr. Atherton," Keen said gently. The man flinched while still trying to feign unconsciousness. "Let's get you to the settee, all right?"

"I shouldn't be moved. I'm a sick man," Atherton whined, eyes still shut.

Mrs. Atherton returned with the wine. She gazed down at her husband calmly. "A nice glass of port should soon sort you out, darling," she said; then to Keen, "It's just a touch of gastroenteritis."

Deflated, Atherton allowed himself to be helped to the settee. Mrs. Atherton handed her husband a tiny glass of port. "If you'll excuse me, I'll be out in the garden, darling. I simply *must* get those hydrangeas in before they wilt." She seemed utterly indifferent to her husband's fainting spell, or a policeman questioning him about a crime, an attitude Keen found rather peculiar.

He waited until she had gone. "Mr. Atherton, if you feel up to it now, I'd like to ask a few questions."

"About what?" His voice was dull.

"Did you know a woman named Christine Swinton?"

Atherton shrank back, clutching his glass of port like a talisman to ward off evil spirits. "Is this an official inquiry?"

"You are not under arrest, and you don't have to answer any of my questions if you don't want to," Keen said, avoiding the issue. "But if you don't, it will make me wonder what it is you have to hide."

Atherton thought it over, then said, "Yes, I knew Christine Swinton."

"How did you meet her?"

"In a pub," Atherton said. "With friends."

"How long ago?"

"I don't remember. A year or so ago, I think."

"And how often did you see her after that?"

"About once a fortnight."

"Were you having an affair with her?"

Atherton looked at him steadily. "No. Absolutely not."

"That's not what you told Jillie Waltham, now, is it?"

Atherton glared into the shallow depths of his port. "All right, I did have an affair with Chris, but it's been over for a long time."

"How long?"

"I haven't seen her in months."

"You know she's dead."

"Of course I know she's dead," Atherton snapped in irritation. "But I had nothing to with that, so why are you bothering me?"

Keen studied Atherton, aware his silence was making the man increasingly uncomfortable. "Do you know a woman named Trudy Grumms?"

Atherton blinked. "No, I don't believe so—"

"She's a prostitute, Mr. Atherton," Keen added mildly, and watched the man cringe. "You may know her as Paloma Sanchez."

"I don't wish to answer any more questions," Atherton said stonily.

"You might want to know that a videotape of you with Christine Swinton and Trudy Grumms is in the possession of the police. It was made at a brothel you visited in London, run by a lady named Victoria. You remember her?"

"Perhaps I should have my solicitor present, Sergeant."

"Perhaps you should. I'll wait if you'd like to ring him."

After a moment, Atherton said in an oddly detached voice, "It does look so . . . ridiculous on film, doesn't it?" Keen didn't respond, not having seen it. "Chris didn't care much for sex with men, did you know that? That's why Paloma had to be with us, to get her excited enough. It was so . . . *humiliating*." Keen caught the embarrassed flick of the man's smile, barely visible before it was gone. "But I paid for that tape. She swore it was the only one."

"That's the problem with videotapes," Keen said. "It's so easy to make copies."

Atherton ran his fingers across his thinning scalp. "I assume Dr. Waltham must have told you what Chris was blackmailing me for?"

The man's distress seemed a shade overdone. Keen settled back, eyelids half closed, although he wasn't sleepy in the least. "I don't mind hearing your side of it."

Atherton took a quick breath, like a runner preparing for a sprint. "Christine Swinton was obsessed with a woman named Hannah Lightfoot, who supposedly was married to King George the Third who—"

"I've had the history lesson, thank you. Let's keep it closer to the here and now. What was Chris Swinton wanting from you?"

His interruption threw Atherton off. "Ah. Right. Chris was after privileged information. Sealed documents. The kind of thing that would cost my job, possibly even time in one of Her Majesty's prisons." He looked back down into the glass he still clutched. "But I was in love with her, and desperate for that videotape."

"Hold on," Keen said, puzzled. "I thought Victoria sold you that tape."

Atherton looked alarmed, then recovered, shaking his head. "No, it was Chris. She promised to swap the tape for a book from the Royal Archives."

"What book?"

"A folio of drawings by Richard Dalton. Dr. Waltham has it now."

Keen raised an eyebrow. "That book isn't from the Royal Archives." Atherton swallowed, his Adam's apple bobbing. "Why are you lying to me, Mr. Atherton?"

"But I'm not," Atherton protested. "I stole that book out of the archives—"

"Stop," Keen said quietly, and although there was no menace in his voice, Atherton froze, mouth open. "*You* were blackmailing Christine Swinton, not the other way round." He was guessing, gratified when Atherton inhaled sharply. "She didn't like sex with men, isn't that what you said? You had the video with her and another woman, three of you together. But you weren't doing much other than watching, were you?"

Again, he was guessing, having only Phil's description to judge by. "You had the tape and wanted to exchange it for something she had." Atherton didn't answer, his eyes shifting desperately as if searching for places to run. Keen's heart jolted; another piece clicked into place. He tasted anger like acid in the back of his throat. "That's what you were doing in Leeds two weeks ago, isn't it?"

"I was in London that night, nowhere near Leeds."

"Witnesses saw you both at the Olde Oak Tree. You had the special: duck in raspberry sauce, salmon caviar, and apple tart."

Keen knew by Atherton's reaction he'd guessed right. "They're mistaken," he said defensively. "Even if I were there, having dinner with someone isn't a crime—"

"You raped her," Keen said bluntly, deriving an ugly satisfaction as Atherton's face mottled, the blood drained.

"You don't understand!" Atherton managed to squeak. "If you saw the tape, then you know it was just a charade, it was never real—"

Keen seized Atherton by the collar and jerked him to his feet. The glass of port fell, wine splashing their shoes, soaking into the carpet like a bloodstain.

"You raped her that night, and then you killed her." The rage sang in his ears, arms trembling as he resisted the urge to beat the living shit out of the man.

Atherton stared, eyes widened in fear. "I didn't!"

"We don't need the witnesses to hang you with," Keen lied grimly. "All we have to do is check the semen left on her body against yours."

"Test it then, it wasn't me!" Atherton's hands fluttered at the fist bunching his shirt tightly around his throat. "Damn you, let me go!"

Keen released him, and watched the man straighten his collar and tie with a shaky bravado.

"I should make a complaint," Atherton protested. "You could be in a good deal of trouble for that."

Keen smiled unpleasantly as he called the bluff. "Allow me to convey you to the nearest police station and help you fill in the proper forms myself." The man blinked, defeated. "And I'll be just as happy to bang you up for murder while we're there. At the moment, you're the only credible suspect I have, unless you want to give me a more reasonable explanation."

"Yes, please do, darling," Mrs. Atherton said from the doorway. Both men turned, one surprised, the other terrified. She stripped off her gardening gloves and placed them in the basket hanging from her arm. Wilted weeds, naked roots pale, hung over the edge. "I'm sure it would be vastly entertaining." She turned toward Keen. "His excuses usually are." Keen suspected she had never been in the garden, but listening all the time from behind the door.

It took several more glasses of port before Atherton could manage. He had tried to blackmail Chris. He had driven up to Leeds and had dinner with her. Chris had thought it was to be the usual arrangement; he would give her more precious information from the archives as payment for quick sex in a hotel room.

"Why Harewood? Why not a hotel closer to the university conference?"

"I have no idea. Chris made the hotel reservation, not me."

"That book came from Harewood House," Keen told him, and gauged the man's reaction.

"But it couldn't have . . ." Atherton said, bewildered. "It was mine."

"Then why did you tell me it came from the Royal Archives?"

"As evidence Chris was the one blackmailing me."

That was only partly the truth, Keen was certain, but let it go for the moment. "What happened, then, between the two of you?"

Atherton glanced at his sphinxlike wife, then gulped audibly and stared at his entwined hands, knuckles whitening. Over dinner, Atherton had told Chris about the videotape and what his new price was. And it wasn't sex.

"All I wanted was for her to return some documents I'd given her. I told her they weren't of any use because they were all forgeries."

"Forgeries?"

"There never *were* any 'real' documents. I had fakes made. I went to Leeds to tell her I wanted to break it off with her, that it had all been a scam. At first she didn't believe me. Once I convinced her, she was devastated, started drinking heavily. I drove her back to the hotel in her car, she was in no condition to drive. I got her into the room, and I did take her clothes off and put her on the bed. But I swear I didn't take advantage of her condition. Drunks aren't terribly appealing," he added while gazing at his wife. Her ominous smile widened, her eyes glittering like ice. "There was no point in trying to talk with her any further that evening, but she was alive when I left."

"And the videotape?"

"I burned it as soon as I'd heard she was dead." He looked at Keen anxiously. "It was *suicide*. All this talk of rape and murder is only to shake me up, isn't it?"

Keen didn't answer his question. "How was that videotape made, Mr. Atherton? You took Chris to Victoria's—"

"I didn't," he protested. "She took me." He ducked away from his wife as if expecting a blow. But the woman hadn't so much as blinked, as immobile as a lizard basking in the sun, reptilian eyes impassive. "She said she'd been there before with a friend, someone she trusted."

"Who?"

"I don't know," Atherton said quickly, and Keen knew he was lying. "But a man rang up a week later and told me about the videotape, and how much it would cost to buy it. I was horrified."

"How much?"

"Two thousand pounds. Cash."

"Did you pay it?

"Of course I paid it."

Keen glanced at Mrs. Atherton, who still seemed indifferent to her husband's behavior, as well as his paying to cover it up.

"To whom?"

"I don't know. I was instructed to go to a public phone box where I would be told where to put the money. I dropped the envelope with the money into a rubbish bin in Charing Cross station, then went back to the same phone box. The videotape was taped underneath the shelf. I never saw anyone."

The pieces didn't fit as neatly as they should, but he wasn't sure where the lies were. "Did you do the forgeries, Mr. Atherton?"

"No." He smiled bleakly. "I'm not that talented. I knew a man, we were boys at Harrow together. He'd made forgeries to sell to other students, handwriting mostly. Notes from mothers to excuse boys from exams, forged doctor's scripts, letters from the headmaster to parents. Eventually he was caught and expelled.

"Chris did chat me up in a pub, knowing who I was, where I worked, hoping I could help her gain access to the archives' confidential records." He exhaled a tired sigh. "Of course I couldn't give her anything of the sort, but she was losing interest in me. I had to do something."

Again, Atherton risked a quick glance at his wife with the odd self-satisfied glimmer of a smile. She returned it, an intimate spark flashing between them. What a very strange couple they were.

"Then I ran into my old schoolmate in the same pub. We talked over old times and somehow I got round to telling him my problems. I don't even remember whose idea it was, mine or his, but he agreed to fake documents on Hannah Lightfoot for me. I could easily supply him with the blank paper; I removed vellum flypages from old books, one here and there will never be missed. A week later, he gave me baptismal certificates for each of Hannah's children, as well as a letter, one from 'Lord Bute' to 'Princess Augusta,' informing her of George's marriage to Hannah.

"At first I could only risk giving her photocopies. But she insisted on seeing the original documents, wanting to have them tested. I finally gave her one, sure the game would be up, planned on claiming even the archives had been duped." He shook his head in disbelief. "But when she had it appraised, not even an expert could tell the difference. She was ecstatic; she honestly thought she had the real thing!"

Atherton had regained his composure while his wife remained inanimate. Keen felt an undercurrent he couldn't interpret, not sure he wanted to interpret.

"It started out just a harmless lark. I would have told her, eventually. But she was taking it all so seriously. Then she refused to give it back, claiming the monarchy shouldn't keep such a valuable secret, the public had a right to know, all that silly drivel. I gave her another fake, hoping her expert would catch the forgery this time. But when still he didn't, it had gone too far. I told her I'd exchange the documents for something far more valuable; in this case, the truth."

"And the videotape?"

Atherton lost some of his zeal. "Was a terrible mistake. I only intended it as leverage if she were unwilling to return the forgeries."

"Was she?"

"It didn't matter. I found the fakes in her handbag and took them with me when I left."

"Do you still have them?"

"I burned them with the videotape. I wanted nothing to connect her to me."

"Who was the expert she took the forgeries to?"

"I don't know, I didn't ask."

"This old school chum of yours, what's his name?"

Atherton looked uncomfortable. "That's the funny part. His name is also Dalton. Arthur Dalton."

A.D., Keen thought.

"He knew I owned that book Dr. Waltham has now, and that's what he wanted in payment for his forgeries." Atherton regarded him curiously. "I don't know where you've got the idea it's from Harewood House, Sergeant."

"Where did you get it, then?"

"I bought it years ago, spring of nineteen seventy-three, I think. We were touring in Wales, weren't we, darling?" He turned to his wife, placing his hand lightly on her knee with palpable nervousness. "That little bookshop in, what is it?"

"Hay-on-Wye, darling," his wife supplied obligingly. Her hand settled over his as she smiled.

"That's it. Hay-on-Wye."

"Where can I find Arthur Dalton?"

"Haven't the foggiest. I was in rather a panic after Chris had the first forgery authenticated, and I tried to ring him back. But he'd moved and his telephone had been disconnected. That was about six months ago. I haven't seen him since."

The two of them smiled knowingly, their expressions as alike as bookends. His anger spent, Keen swallowed against the revulsion left in its place.

★ ★ ★

Keen's phone beeped on his way back, and his heart sank as soon as he heard Phil's voice.

"She was already on the ferry by the time I got to Dover. Now I'm in bloody Calais. I've lost her."

"How?"

"I don't *know* how," Phil said heatedly. "She gave me the slip, I didn't see her get off the boat. I've no idea where she is now. You got any other bright ideas?"

Keen sighed. "No. Come back, there's nothing more to do."

"Yeah, well, I won't get home until well after midnight now. You owe me one hell of a favor, pal." The anger in Phil's voice traveled the distance well.

"Anytime."

"How about now? I want you to go get your hands on the fanciest bunch of roses you can find."

"Okay . . ."

"Then you buy the biggest fucking box of Cadbury's dark chocolates they make."

Keen had his notebook open to jot down notes. "Cadbury's . . ."

"Then go to a sporting goods shop and buy a cricket bat."

He stopped writing. "A cricket bat?"

"A cricket bat. Then you go give it all to my wife and explain to her what the hell I'm doing in France without her. Tell her she's to use the cricket bat to beat the crap out of you so that hopefully she'll be too tired to use it on me when I get home!"

Keen started to laugh, then winced as Phil slammed the handset down.

XIII

TUESDAY

Keen waited on the crowded pavement as Phil ordered lunch at a kebab stand. Phil handed him a paper plate of skewered kebabs and onions, and they stood out of the way of pedestrians as they ate.

As soon as he had arrived to work—Phil informed him around a mouthful of dripping meat—he'd asked Bernie Pearson to run Arthur Dalton's name through the PNC to check for any vehicle registration. Then he'd rung the Beecher house. The housekeeper had answered. Miss Beecher had taken a plane late Sunday evening to stay with her parents at their villa in Italy, and didn't say when she might be back. The housekeeper knew nothing about Miss Beecher's movements on Saturday as that was her day off.

"Not quite the behavior of an innocent person, is it? I'm telling you, she's it."

Keen didn't want to argue. "Did you check with the airline?"

"Of course I checked with the airline." Phil sucked on his fingers. "Alitalia confirmed Marge Beecher was a passenger on the eleven-fifteen flight to Milan Sunday evening. No reservation, just walked up to the counter and asked for the next flight out, paid on a Visa card."

"Did you ring the villa?"

"I tried this morning. Got someone on the other end babbling away a mile a minute." He grinned maliciously. "Besides, I don't speak any Eye-talian, do you?" Then, as Keen started toward a rubbish bin with the remains of his kebabs, Phil said, "You're not going to eat that last one?"

It took some doing, but Keen managed to ring through to Milan, sprinkling his English with the only two nonfood Italian words he knew: *grazie* and *prego*. A shrill Italian operator rattled incomprehensively until, through the crackling of the international lines, he heard Marge Beecher ask cautiously, "Who is this, please?"

The operator babbled before he had a chance to reply, then heard Marge Beecher say something back to her in Italian.

"Go ahead, please," the Italian operator said, the first words of English she'd bothered to use.

"It's Sergeant Keen Dunliffe, do you remember me, Miss Beecher?"

The delay in her response was due to more than just airwaves bouncing off satellites. "Yes, of course."

"Miss Beecher, I have some bad news. Reece Wycombe is dead."

The pause seemed longer than necessary, and her response, when it came, oddly indifferent. "Yes?"

Phil leaned his head closer to the mobile to listen in. "Could you tell me where you were Saturday evening?" Keen asked.

"At home, alone. I don't have an alibi, but I didn't shoot him."

Keen exchanged a startled look with Phil.

"I hadn't said he'd been shot. How did you know that?"

"Are you recording this conversation?" she asked, her anger discernible. "I sincerely hope you are. Someone claiming to be a police officer called me Sunday morning to tell me Reece had been shot and that enough evidence had been planted to make it likely I would be arrested for his murder."

"This police officer, did he give you a name?"

Her dismissive laugh crackled through the line. "Of course not. He just said he knew I was innocent and wanted to give me fair warning."

"You realize leaving the country only makes you look guilty."

"I may be naïve, Mr. Dunliffe, but I'm not stupid. If you plan on framing me for murder, I intend to make it as difficult as possible. You'll have to extradite me before I'll come back."

"Would you have any idea why Reece Wycombe was killed, who would want him dead?"

"Just about everyone who ever knew him, so I'm sure it won't be hard for you to find someone else to frame. Sorry to be an inconvenience."

She put the phone down before he could ask her anything further. Keen flipped up the end of the mobile and looked at Phil. "She did know he'd been shot, Phil," he admitted. "It's your call."

Phil finished Keen's kebab, tossed the wooden skewer into the rubbish bin, and licked the sauce from his fingers. "Okay, so it's not her. Let's go have a chat with Molly Sutton. Should be good for a laugh."

Under any other circumstances, Jillie would have enjoyed being back in Paris, the city strangely familiar, alive and bright. At half past noon, she sat down on a wooden pew in St. Gervais of Jerusalem. As bells rang, monks and nuns filed into the Lady Chapel, nuns in blue and white habits, monks in long brown robes, both sexes wearing sandals. She was surprised by how young most were, the women with scrubbed round faces, the men devoid of wrinkles and gray hair. She tried to imagine Karen giving up parties, makeup, rock music, and boys for the monastic life. And failed, with some relief.

One of the nuns began to sing in a clear, vibrant voice. She was answered in beautiful four-part harmony, a chorus in French. Jillie gazed at the statue of the Virgin Mary with baby Jesus in her arms, painted filigrees and gold borders, the sweet music and the melodic French sermon wrapping around her like a comforting quilt.

It lasted only half an hour, and she stood as the monks and nuns began leaving the chapel. They talked freely with each other, the sexes mingling with ease. Nervously, she approached one of the young men no older than twenty-five, cheeks still as round as a baby's.

"Excusez-moi," she said awkwardly. *"Mais je cherche frère Géraud?"*

His hands folded in his sleeves, he nodded toward a group of three elderly monks. *"C'est lui, là-bas."*

"Merci."

He smiled with an earnest piety that, while she did believe it genuine, seemed abnormal on anyone so young.

She waited patiently, until a monk with a neat white beard turned to her curiously. With his solemn, lined face and blue eyes, he looked straight out of Hollywood central casting.

"Frère Géraud?"

But it was another who responded, a bald, gaunt man with a cheerful face who couldn't have been less monklike. *"Oui?"*

"Bonjour, je suis désolée si je vous dérange. Je m'appelle Jillie Waltham et je suis une amie de Christine Swinton . . . qui vous avez écrit. Si vous avez quelques minutes de parler . . . ?"

At Chris's name, his smile dimmed, but he said, *"Bien sûr,"* before he nodded his goodbye to the other monks. "If you prefer," he said with a light accent, "we may speak English."

"I'm sorry, my French isn't that good—"

"Mais, non. Your French is fine. But I feel you may be more comfortable in English." He took her by the arm, as if they'd been friends for years. "And if you don't mind, I'd rather we didn't speak here." He opened a door. "Would you be interested in seeing our private chapel?"

Nonplussed, Jillie nodded. Stained-glass windows opened onto a tiny courtyard the Catholic monks shared with Jewish residential apartments. A beaten-copper altar with two square candelabra had been made by the same artist who created the altar for Notre-Dame, Brother Géraud informed her like a tour guide. Except for a long sculpture of the virgin and child to one side, the room was barren, nowhere to sit down.

"We may speak in private here." Brother Géraud tucked his hands into his sleeves and waited.

Jillie extracted the letter from her purse and held it out to him. "You sent this to a friend of mine, Christine Swinton."

"I did," Brother Géraud acknowledged frostily. "But if you've read it, you know I made it clear my responsibilities here come first. I have some papers in my possession that I agreed she might examine, papers relating to her research. But only on condition of anonymity. She was supposed to come alone, on the date we had agreed, and not to send other people. If this is how she chooses to respect my privacy, then I would prefer if she left me in peace."

"She's dead," Jillie said simply.

That at least surprised Brother Géraud out of his detached calm. *"Mon Seigneur . . ."* He bent his head as if saying a quick prayer, then looked at her sharply. "What happened?"

"She drowned two weeks ago."

"Ma pauvre. Please forgive my rudeness, Madame Waltham."

"It's okay. But all I know from your letter is that you have proof she needed to confirm her theories. Would you mind if I looked at it for myself?"

"Are you planning to continue her work?"

Jillie laughed softly. "I don't think so. For one, I'm a medieval scholar; it's not my field. I'm just trying to find out what she was working on, and if it was something someone wanted kept concealed badly enough to kill her."

"I see. Then it was not an accident." Brother Géraud gazed at the altar pensively. "Perhaps it is better forgotten."

"And if she was killed, you'd let her murderer get away with it?"

"If there is a murderer, he won't go unpunished," Brother Géraud assured her. "God judges us all."

"I'm sorry, Brother Géraud, but I'd rather it be in this world instead of the next."

He smiled wryly. "Your friend wanted to publish documents which have been in my family for several generations. As a monk who has taken a vow of poverty, I should not have kept them, and I suppose I am guilty of the sin of vanity as well. But I am the last of my family and there is no one to pass them on to. I had thought to burn them, but to destroy history is a sin the Church has been guilty of too often. They may have some value to a collector, perhaps I will bequeath them to the Church. But at the moment, I choose to keep silent because while the documents may themselves be valuable, what they contain might do more harm than good."

"What are they?"

"I took my vows thirty years ago," he said obliquely. "But I have not always been a monk, and although I have dedicated my life to God, my reasons were not all spiritual. My only desire is to do God's work, and now that I have cancer, I have no wish to waste what little life remains with political intrigues."

Jillie was startled, suddenly able to read what had been obvious: his gaunt face, the wispy hair left after chemotherapy. "Oh, I'm so sorry. I didn't realize . . ."

Brother Géraud shrugged. "I am lucky, there is little pain. The doctors say I could live another year, or die in two months. As much as they pretend to be God, only He really knows."

It was Jillie's turn to smile ruefully. "Brother Géraud, I'm not interested in causing scandals. I'm only looking for the truth."

"As should we all." He studied her astutely. "Whatever I tell you, I would prefer it to go no further. At least while I live. Do I have your word you will keep my confidence?"

"You and everybody else," she said tightly. "An English policeman is investigating Chris's death. I might have to tell him something, but I promise to keep you out of it as much as I can. Fair enough?"

Brother Géraud's smile widened. "That convinces me more than had you given me your sworn vow to absolute silence. Come . . ." He led her out of the small chapel and into one of the offices, a small portrait of the Virgin Mary above the desk.

"Will you wait here a moment, *s'il vous plaît?*"

When he returned, he carried a wooden box in his arms. He glanced at the Virgin Mary, as if addressing his words to her.

"I am the younger of two sons. I was with my father in Montrejeau, near Lourdes, when the Germans invaded Paris. My mother and Jean-Pierre were trapped. My father left me in the care of an old childless couple, good Catholics who raised me as their own son. When my father was shot by the Germans during the occupation, they adopted me. I was only six, and after the war, my mother couldn't find me. I grew up believing all my family were dead, a lie which my adoptive parents, understandably, encouraged. But Jean-Pierre never stopped searching for me. We were reunited only last year, thanks to Our Lord." He again bowed his head briefly, almost unconsciously.

"Six months ago, Jean-Pierre died. As my brother had no children, his estate was left to me. In his effects, I found letters and documents which had been in my mother's family. All my mother's ancestors since the Revolution are well documented in the National Archives, every one of solid country *fermiers* stock . . . with one very notable exception."

He handed her an old paper, yellowed and written in the calligraphical style of the nineteenth century. It was a "Déclaration de Nationalité" dated 1821, from the Directeur des Affaires Civiles in the Ministère de la Justice to one Henri Guillaume, born the twenty-fourth of March, 1798 (4 *germinal an* 6), in recognition of his contribution to the French war against the English. His parents were listed as Comtesse Marie de Renier and Georges Eduard Guillaume, "le fils du Roi."

"The king's son?" Jillie mused aloud. "But not Louis of France?"

Brother Géraud shook his head. "George Edward William, who called himself George Rex, son of George and Hannah and heir presumptive to the English throne."

Jillie's heart bump-bumped hollowly as she handled the ancient document carefully.

"Three years later, he left Paris for South Africa."

"Why South Africa?"

"It was safer there than in France, at least for a pretender. France was swarming with pretenders. Many claimed to be the son of Louis Sixteenth and Marie Antoinette smuggled out of prison by his guardians. Who knows? Somewhere, there could be the descendant of Louis and true heir to the French crown."

"If there still was one."

He chuckled. "We have a strong monarchist party in France with its own pretender. But as for Henri Fils du Roi, the danger came more from an Italian woman named Maria Stella who claimed to be the daughter of Louis Philippe, Duke of Orléans, switched at birth with a lowborn son of a Florentine police constable. She had credible evidence and eyewitnesses, including a local priest and two servants. Even the Bishop of Faenza's investigation convinced him she was the real heir to the French crown. Many influential people supported Marie's cause.

"So Louis Philippe had little motive to support Henri's claim to the English monarchy, not with Marie declaring similar circumstances cheating her of the throne. The king suppressed copies of a book Marie published, and nearly had her executed for treason. Henri decided it wiser to retreat to a large, comfortable estate in the Cape Colonies."

He smoothed open another yellowed, brittle document. "The son of Henri Guillaume," he said, turning it around for her to read an Act of Baptism from the Bishop of Saissons for a Jean-Denis LeRoi, listing his parents as Henri Guillaume Deleroi and Madeleine de Tournai.

"The son of Jean-Denis." This was a Certificat de Bonne Conduite from the Corps d'Armée, la Commission Spéciale du 130th Régiment d'Infanterie, given to a Lieutenant Jean-Maurice Auguste Leroi for his exemplary service under the French flag.

"His only child, a daughter, Odette." She examined the Certificat d'Études Primaries and a Certificat d'Instruction Religieuse, degré élémentaire, the ink browned with age, but clear enough.

"My brother." A Carte d'Identité issued in 1935 for Jean-Pierre d'Alarville.

"Myself." An "extrait des Minutes des Actes de Naissance" from the Préfecture de Paris, Mairie du 20ème Arrondissement.

When she looked up, stunned, he placed his hand on the rest of the documents in the open box. "There is much more, wills and accounting ledgers, property sales, invitations to family weddings, letters complaining of late payments of military pensions, awards given by local priests for childhood accomplishments, certificates for violin recitals, et cetera, and so on and so forth."

This wasn't spirit messages from the hereafter, this was solid, reliable documentation. The Real Thing. Her skin rose in goose bumps.

"You might have been king of England," she said, not completely teasing.

He blew his breath between pursed lips with Gallic indifference. "Never. To me, there is only one king, the King of Kings."

"How did Chris find out about you?"

Brother Géraud shrugged his shoulders in another purely French gesture. "I assume through my brother. After the war, Jean-Pierre went to university in England, to Oxford." He grinned with a very unpriestlike boyishness. "I, on the other hand, lived in New York for many years. I have always loved Negro American jazz and it was difficult to choose between the Church or being the only French saxophonist in Harlem." He laughed at her astonishment. "I made the right decision; I am a much better priest than saxophone player. Now I study philosophy. Mopping floors at night gives me plenty of time for prayer and meditation. And I am happier than any king.

"In any case, while Jean-Pierre was at Oxford, he met another student who by chance was a distant English cousin of ours, Anthony Dalton. They became interested in our mutual genealogy."

"Dalton!" Jillie exclaimed. Was it possible that dingbat psychic had known something after all? "Would he have been a descendant of Hannah Lightfoot's daughter, by any chance?"

"Her great-great-grandson, so he claimed. I never met him, and he's dead now. My brother mentioned a son, Arthur, I think was his name." As he spoke, he refolded the documents and replaced them in the box, all but a folded paper and a brittle newspaper clipping. "But as I explained to your friend, *my* papers are private. I agreed she could examine them, but I was not interested in her dispute. However, one of these letters was from Monsieur Dalton, who was very displeased with Jean-Pierre." Brother Géraud handed her the newspaper clipping.

Tiny squares of disintegrating paper stuck to her fingers as she unfolded it. A Wednesday edition of *Le Figaro,* 28 May, 1924, listed various art sales, an exposition of eighteenth-century watercolors, drawings, and gouaches, and other objets d'art held in the Galérie Georges Petit on the rue de Sèze. A receipt had been paper-clipped to it, rusted metal staining the paper.

"My mother was a collector. Not in the league of the Rothschilds or Guggenheims, but she had a good eye for old books and reasonable paintings. Most of her collection vanished during the German occupation, but a few things were salvaged. When Jean-Pierre went to England, Anthony Dalton loaned him a valuable letter in exchange for a book from my mother's library—"

"A book of drawings made by Richard Dalton while on his trip to Greece and Egypt," Jillie guessed.

Brother Géraud's eyebrows shot up in surprise. "As a matter of fact, yes. How did you know?"

"I have it."

Brother Géraud laced his hands and regarded her with renewed interest. "It seems this book was also the cause of their quarrel. All I know about Anthony Dalton is that he lived in Gloucester. Or did at the time he wrote to my brother." He handed her an envelope, the postmark dated 1972, with a terse one-page note inside. Anthony Dalton insisted Jean-Pierre immediately return the letter he'd had now for several years, or Dalton would retaliate by selling the book.

"Do you mind if I take the address?" she asked, jotting it down when he nodded.

"Although I doubt it will do you much good. I wrote to Monsieur Dalton after my brother died, but the letter was returned, marked 'deceased.'" I don't know what answer my brother gave, if any, but this was still in his possession when he died."

He handed her the document he had not replaced in his wooden box. It was much older than the clipping, written in quaint idiomatic French with a flowery hand.

"It's a letter from Madame de Duffand written to Horace Walpole. If you have a problem with the old French, I can help translate."

"Thanks, but I understand eighteenth-century French better than I do the modern," she said, thinking of Nathalie and Céline and Jacques. She read:

> Paris, ce dimanche 28 mars 1768, 11 eures du matin,
>
> . . . dined yesterday evening with *la grand'maman,* we were twelve. Among the company present was a Mme Anna Axfurd, who all remarked to be a handsome woman, if unnaturally quiet and shy. Such a subdued cover for so amazing a book, indeed made even stranger, as it was left to chère Milady Pembroke to recount her story to me this morning. The mysterious English lady is a friend of the widow Mme de Bretaigny with whom she is travelling to the country, accompanied by her two young sons, the eldest a boy of eleven and his brother ten months younger. They were as solemn and silent as their mother, as if burdened at such a tender age with a great tragedy echoing your own *La Mère Mystérieuse,* or perhaps bearing under a great injustice, which, as I shall recount to you, may indeed be so.
>
> Milady tells me the lady is a Quakeress who had been secretly married to your king George and these two boys both his royal sons! A daughter remains in England as hostage to her mother's good behaviour. Several gentlemen present remarked, although not within Mme Axfurd's hearing, that her eldest, a boy also named George, so resembled the portraits of your king as to be his twin, having the same intelligent eyes and most noble brow. Mme Axfurd is said to be penniless and hopes to petition le Roi to receive her, but with the Queen so ill (although one says she has been feeling slightly better as of late), her prospects are bleak.
>
> Yet for Mme Pembroke to be a vehicle of such a tale is almost as astonishing as the adventure of Voltaire and his niece Mme Denis which I recounted in my previous letter to you. Mme Pembroke's compassion for *la pauvre* Anna Axfurd's plight is but further proof of Milady's exemplary character, her sweetness and her modesty, as much of Mme Axfurd's claim depends upon the witness of another far less agreeable English lady, Mlle Chudleigh, who was once Milady's own husband's mistress! Currently Mlle Chudleigh favours the Duke of Kingston, and is notorious for drinking so much wine as to stagger about when she dances. All the more ironic that M Pembroke's former mistress is now

the plague of a certain Hervey, who claims to be Mlle Chudleigh's secret husband! *Ah! les Anglais, les Anglais ont bien des singularités!*

But I should tell you I did see the five comedies chez Mme de Villeroys after all . . .

Jillie read the rest of the letter, which while full of gossip and name-dropping, had nothing further to add about "Anna Axfurd" or the fate of her children. But she knew she was holding the proof Chris had searched so long for, Hannah Lightfoot and her children by George the Third were not only real, but had survived to produce their own heirs. Heirs to a stolen crown.

"I think you might be right about your papers," she said quietly. "They could cause trouble if they were made public."

Brother Géraud's eyes crinkled as he smiled. "I don't think I have long to worry." He nodded at the de Duffand letter. "In any case, that does not belong to me, and to keep it would be wrong. I've tried several times to find Monsieur Dalton's son, but without success. Now that I'm ill, I agreed to cooperate with your friend in exchange for her promise to search for him on my behalf. Madame Waltham, if I have been of any help to you, perhaps when you return to England, you could find Anthony Dalton's son and return his property for me?"

He chuckled as she stared at him, speechless.

Molly Sutton smoothed her skirt over crossed legs as Phil inserted the video-cassette into her VCR, black and chrome equipment hidden behind a carved walnut cabinet. The hair on Keen's arms prickled; the Suttons' majestic Knightsbridge home was uncomfortably chilled.

"This was one of several stolen videotapes which were recovered by the police, Mrs. Sutton," Phil said calmly. "If you recognize anyone in the video, could you please identify them for us?"

The leader showed only a bubbling sheen like fine champagne, then cut to a man and a woman, already naked and fully engaged in a sexual act. The sound had a strange back echo, but was distinct enough to understand the dialogue, such as it was.

Molly Sutton smiled, slow and amused, but said nothing. She looked away, not to avoid what was on the screen, but to pick up a gold cigarette case from the table beside the chair. She paid more attention to lighting a cigarette with a matching gold lighter before she leaned back to watch the entire videotape.

She might have been Celia Swinton's sister, the two equally frosty. But where Celia Swinton's mannerisms had a studied theatricality, Molly Sutton's seemed a natural part of her temperament, as if she were well aware of the effect she had but honestly couldn't have cared less.

Having seen none of the tapes, Keen had no way of knowing how banal this performance was by comparison. Nor did he recognize the old school ties being utilized in a fashion they hadn't been designed for.

Once the tape was finished, nothing but dancing electronic snow, Molly Sutton turned one arched eyebrow on them. "At least my husband had sense enough to use a condom," she said dryly; "that girl does *not* look healthy. Would you gentlemen care for coffee?"

They stood up when she did, and exchanged glances as she walked out of the room. *"Brrr,"* Phil said quietly. He was not referring to the temperature of the house.

The kitchen was far warmer than the lounge. She waved them toward a conservatory off the garden while she busied herself at an espresso machine.

"Please makes yourselves comfortable."

Keen sat but found it difficult to make himself comfortable. Low, gray clouds moved sluggishly across the sky, doing little to cool the air, but much to make it stagnant. Choked with a jungle of potted plants, the conservatory was unpleasantly humid and smelled of overheated earth and decaying flowers.

"Mrs. Sutton . . ." Phil began as she carried a tray with three demitasse cups of strong coffee into the conservatory.

"It's Lady Sutton, actually," she corrected him.

Keen suppressed a smile as Phil's confidence wavered. "Pardon, *Lady* Sutton. Were you aware of your husband's involvement with Dungeons and Dragons?"

"I assume that's the whorehouse in question?" She distributed the coffee, then sat down, placing her gold cigarette case beside her saucer. "No, Sergeant, I was not aware of it. I assume you were hoping this tawdry little film would so shock and outrage me that I would wish revenge on my husband and blurt out any malevolent knowledge I might have to harm him. I am *so* sorry to disappoint you. Sugar?"

"Yes, thank you," Phil said, recovering his self-assurance. He spooned several heaps of sugar out of the bone china bowl into his coffee. "Would you happen to know where your husband is at the moment?"

"At his club, enjoying rare roast beef and Yorkshire pudding served with a generous portion of smug self-righteousness, I would expect."

"I take it you and your husband aren't close, if you don't mind my asking?"

"Oh, but you're wrong; I adore my husband." She smiled brightly. "He's a charming man if not terribly clever, but well bred with such lovely manners. He's also very attractive, the blond hair and blue eyes go superbly with every dress I own. We look fabulous together, he's the perfect fashion accessory."

She sipped her coffee, ignoring the bemused look that passed between Phil and Keen.

"So it doesn't bother you someone might be blackmailing your husband?"

She considered. "Not really. *If* he is being blackmailed, which I doubt. I manage all our finances, and I'm certain I would have noticed if large amounts of cash had suddenly gone missing. Timothy has a small monthly allowance, but he has no control over the investments or stock portfolio, which are in my name alone."

"This video was part of a burglary," Phil said. "One of the lads we picked up for it is a young man named Ray Delwyn." She merely gazed at him expectantly. "He claims to be your brother."

"Half brother." It was the first time anything Phil had said breached her armor of amused contempt.

"At the time of his arrest, we also found your driver's license, which you reported stolen two months ago."

"Along with the rest of my handbag. I assume he's already sold off the credit cards?"

"There were no credits cards found."

"I didn't expect so."

"Do you know his friend, Mark Lisson?"

"Mark?" Her eyes looked past him vaguely. "Large chap with short hair, weasely face, tattoo on one arm and smells bad? Rotten teeth and rotten temper? Yes, I've met him once or twice whenever Ray dropped by to extort a bit of spare change to make him go away. But to give the boy a little credit, I wouldn't describe Mark as being a 'friend.'"

"Would it bother you to know that Mark and Ray were selling copies of these tapes as pornographic entertainment?"

Her mask slipped before she recovered. "Now that *would* concern me, Mr. . . . Reaves, was it? After all, I might have to sue them for my share of the royalties."

"Lady Sutton, your brother is sleeping rough and living off his giro money."

"And . . . ?" She seemed entirely unconcerned.

"Your own flesh and blood?"

"You'd like to know, if I'm so bloody loaded, why haven't I been more charitable to, like it or not, my brother?" She smiled acidly. "Because I loathe the little bastard, 'bastard' merely fact, rather than insult. As a caring socialist, I prefer spending my money on those who not only deserve it but will make better use of it."

"Then why are you paying Felix Schaefer to represent him?"

Keen detected a momentary surprise, sure this was news to her, before she deftly covered it. "I may not approve of my half brother's avant-garde lifestyle, but I can't allow him to cause too much damage to the family name."

"Which you don't share," Phil pointed out. "If you're concerned about the family name, why didn't you hire a solicitor for Ray when he was done for selling cannabis two years ago? Or for the criminal damage case he's still in court for?"

"Possibly because I didn't know Mr. Schaefer then."

"How did you meet him, Felix Schaefer?" Keen asked quietly.

It was the first time he'd spoken, and her eyes flickered to him with curious interest. "The same place I met you, Mr. Dunliffe. At one of Lynne Selkirk's meetings, about six months ago. One does meet *so* many interesting people there."

"You and your husband were together?"

"No. Timothy had a prior engagement, as usual. He's a solid Tory supporter, I vote LibDem. He doesn't agree with any attempts to change narrow-minded, unjust laws made by gray men in gray suits enforced by white men in blue suits."

"Your political differences don't cause a problem?"

"Never. Whatever else you may think of him, Timothy is a genuinely virtuous man. He doesn't like to think badly about anyone, possibly because he doesn't like to think. It makes him that rarest of all creatures, an honest Tory."

"Did you know Mr. Schaefer were Christine Swinton's solicitor?"

"Mr. Schaefer is quite a few people's solicitor."

"*Specifically,* Lady Sutton, did you know what Mr. Schaefer was doing for Chris Swinton?"

She set her cup down and leaned back, crossing long legs casually. "Perhaps he was sleeping with her," she said carelessly. "A good many people were."

"I see," Keen replied blandly. "Was your husband having an affair with her?"

Molly Sutton laughed, barely more than a smile over a soundless chuckle. "No, he wasn't," she said. "I was."

Phil gazed at the woman with a distracted look Keen found amusing. "*You* were?" Phil asked, as if unsure he'd heard correctly.

Molly Sutton's attention shifted back to him. "Yes, *I* was. You see, we really do have that uncommon commodity, the perfect marriage. He has the title, I have the money. I don't interfere with Timothy's pleasures, he doesn't interfere with mine, and we enjoy each other's company famously. For people like ourselves, public appearances are dreadfully important. But in private, friendship is more vital to a good marriage than is sex or even love."

"How long did your affair with Chris Swinton go on?" Keen continued, although he was unsettled to find he secretly agreed with her.

"A few weeks. It began when Felix brought her to a charity dinner raising money for medicine to send to orphaned children in Somalia. Or maybe it was Sierra Leone, somewhere in Africa, I really can't remember now. Several MPs were there, mainly Labour, naturally, but Timothy can't resist sniffing the knickers of the rich and powerful. A number of actors, mostly television, but Bob Geldof put in a three-minute appearance. Max and Celia Swinton were there, but Verona was feeling poorly. She feels poorly any night there's a possibility she might have to part with money. Let's see . . . Oh, yes. Celia's darling doctor, Giles Roxbury, came with his latest totty draped over one arm, just to annoy Celia, I think. And the Prestons, although Felix didn't speak with them, he suffers from professional jealousy."

"Did Chris attend many of the same parties as yourself?"

"Of course. It's de rigueur for people like us. But society parties only seem like great fun, until you've been to enough of them they all to start to look alike. Chris and I both preferred to get drunk as quickly as possible, which is the only way these things are remotely tolerable. She'd snagged a magnum of champagne and was hiding out with the caterers when I ran into her. We shared the bottle, although she'd already drunk half of it. Then she kissed me." She smiled at Phil's flat expression. "With her tongue," she added, enunciating slowly. "I kissed her back. She slipped her hand under my dress. Should I go on, Sergeant, or will that be sufficient?"

"Ah, no, that's fine." Phil recovered, shaking himself. "I don't think the details will be necessary, thank you."

Underneath Phil's mocking worldly façade, Keen realized, was a decent man unused to the same moral depravity and sexual promiscuity he expected from street scurve among respected members of society he was employed to protect from such uncouth riffraff in the first place.

"Who ended it, you or her?" Keen asked dryly.

Molly Sutton held out her gold case. "Cigarette?" When they both shook their heads, she placed one in her mouth and raised a finely plucked eyebrow as Keen picked up her lighter. Leaning forward, she cupped one impeccably manicured hand around his as he lit her cigarette. She blew out a cloud of smoke and said, "She did."

"Amicably?

"Completely."

"May I ask why?"

"You may ask." She inhaled from her cigarette before she added, "Christine was a strange woman, and very private, Mr. Dunliffe. But she was also passionate, *with* if not *about* people. She and I also had something else in common; the only people we really love are those we don't want to sleep with. Chris had a wonderful childlike quality in that she craved novelty. The problem with novelty is that sooner or later, it isn't new anymore. I suppose she got bored with me."

"What was Mr. Schaefer's reaction to all this, or did he know?"

"Oh, he knew. He liked to watch, found it highly erotic." She smiled.

In the uncomfortable silence, Phil regarded her with puzzled fascination and Keen studied his coffee. It disturbed him that, in spite of his better judgment, he found himself liking Lady Sutton.

"May I ask, other than gratifying any prurient interests you may harbor, why exactly are you asking all these questions?"

"Your husband wasn't the only person videotaped at Victoria's," Phil said. "So was Chris Swinton, with a man named Richard Atherton. Do you know him?"

"I know the name. Timothy has mentioned him."

"In what circumstances?"

"He's a client of Felix Schaefer's. Felix introduced him to Timothy, I believe. Got him in as a member of Timothy's club."

Keen mentally kicked himself for not thinking to inquire who Atherton's solicitor might be when the man had threatened to ring one.

"The three of them shoot together. Nothing like stamping wellies around countryside which doesn't belong to you and blasting small birds full of buckshot to cement that male bonding urge."

"Is it possible either Chris Swinton or Richard Atherton were being blackmailed?"

"By whom?"

"By anyone."

"Anything's possible, Mr. Reaves. If I knew, believe me, I would tell you."

"Do you know anyone named Arthur Dalton?" Keen put in.

"I know *of* Arthur Dalton, although I've never met him. He's a senior partner in the drugs company sponsoring that charity dinner, A and D Pharmaceuticals. I'm a shareholder, which is why I was there."

"Would you have an address for him?"

"Not a personal address, no. The company has a branch office in London." She smiled dryly. "I'm sure you'll able to find it in the telephone directory."

"We'd like to talk to your husband as well, Lady Sutton."

"Try his club. It's where Timothy spends his afternoons poisoning his body before he goes to his health spa to sweat it all out. If you hurry, he should still be there."

They did, and he was.

It was the sort of West End gentleman's club Phil despised, not that he'd ever been inside many, with murky wood paneling, oil paintings of floundering yachts, and an altar-sized portrait of the Queen. Moroccan red leather chairs were occupied by portly men perfuming the stale air with cigars and sipping brandy while pretending they were living in a more beloved era, back in the Golden Age when women and blackies and the aspiring middle classes knew their proper place and cutthroat Thatcherite capitalism was God.

Felix Schaefer steadfastly refused to notice them until his companion, a man with astonishingly clear blue eyes, looked up with friendly curiosity.

"Sir Timothy Sutton?" Phil asked politely, although he recognized him immediately from the videotape.

He waved the distinction away airily. "Please, don't bother with the 'sir,' a bit too patronizing for these liberal times."

Phil wondered if that was for Schaefer's benefit, not missing the solicitor's brief smirk.

"Detective Sergeant Reaves, Kentish Town police." Phil nodded toward Keen. "My colleague, Sergeant Dunliffe."

Sir Timothy glanced at their warrant cards, and smiled, his teeth movie-star even and white. His wife's description of his decorative charm had been spot on. "My, my. The day might not be so tedious after all. Please, do sit down. What can I offer you, gentlemen? Cognac, scotch?"

They declined his offer, but joined the cosy circle, leather creaking. Keen sat back with his eyes half-closed and let Phil carry the interview with Sir Timothy. Schaefer's angular body seemed at odds with his surroundings, a square wooden peg jamming itself awkwardly into a soft, round hole.

"Mr. Sutton," Phil said, deliberately ignoring the man's title. "As Mr. Schaefer may have already told you, your brother-in-law was arrested yesterday morning. He's representing your wife's brother against charges of burglary."

"Half brother, actually," Sir Timothy corrected without rancor, then glanced at Schaefer. "No, Felix hadn't mentioned it."

"I'm on a family retainer, Tim, it's automatic. It isn't unusual for Ray to get himself into these scrapes, and I hardly thought it worth bothering you with."

"Except according to our records, Mr. Delwyn didn't ring you, didn't even know you *were* his solicitor until you showed up. So how did you know he'd been nicked?"

"As I thought I'd made clear to you before, Sergeant," Schaefer sneered, "I don't have to answer questions about any of my clients."

"You know these officers?" Sir Timothy asked, perplexed.

"Regarding a totally different matter, Tim," Schaefer said darkly. "Nothing to do with you."

"I thought you might say that. So I checked our records, and found it was actually Mark Lisson who rang you." Phil turned his gregarious smile on Sir Timothy. "You know Mark Lisson, Ray's flatmate? Sort of a largish bloke, short hair, tattoo on one arm? Not terribly hygienic?"

Sir Timothy's smile diminished as he glanced between Phil and Schaefer. "I've met him. But why should he ring you, Felix?"

"Exactly what I was wanting to know." Phil turned toward the solicitor. "Especially since you're *not* representing Lisson, just Ray. Peculiar, innit?"

"Tim," Schaefer said quietly, "as your solicitor, I advise you not to volunteer information to these gentlemen, nor answer any questions. And I would suggest to *you,* Sergeant, that if you wish to proceed any further with this inquiry, you make an appointment to see me properly at my place of business. At the moment, you are unduly disturbing members of a private club."

"Mr. Sutton," Keen said in a voice that by now Phil knew was deceptively indifferent, "are you familiar with an establishment known as Dungeons and Dragons? Or a woman calling herself Paloma Sanchez?"

Sir Timothy's jaw dropped. "How did you—?"

"Don't answer that," Schaefer said sharply.

"But how do they know about—"

"Tim, keep your damned mouth *shut.*"

It was easy to see who had bullied whom all those years ago in public school, forging a lifelong relationship of intimate malice. Sir Timothy struggled to recover his benign air of superiority. "Terribly sorry, but I'm afraid my lawyer is paid handsomely to be tyrannical about protecting my rights, the law being the harsh mistress that she is."

"Speaking of harsh mistresses, Mr. Schaefer," Phil asked brightly, "how long were you rogering Christine Swinton before she jumped into bed with Sir Timothy's wife while you wanked off watching the two of them licking the cream?"

The solicitor's astonishment quickly shifted to bristling indignation. Sutton brayed into embarrassed laughter, choking it to a snort as Schaefer glared poisonously. But Lady Sutton had been right; her husband was not the jealous sort.

Schaefer spoke through clenched teeth. "Your deliberate effort to be offensive is counterproductive, Mr. Reaves. I insist you leave this club immediately." He signaled to a porter.

Phil shrugged. "Being polite hasn't gotten me anywhere, either, Mr. Schaefer." He addressed Sir Timothy. "We know about you and Paloma Sanchez because a videotape was made of the two of you in bed together. Were you aware of its existence, Mr. Sutton?"

Schaefer sighed, exasperated. "Don't answer that question, Tim."

But to judge by Timothy Sutton's expression, the answer was clearly "no."

"It was evidence collected from the burglary, along with other videotapes of people I found quite familiar." He turned to the solicitor. "So while I was watching these tapes, it occurred to me to ask, how many are clients of yours, Mr. Schaefer? And how many of them are members of this club? And how many were aware they were being videotaped *in flagrante delicto*?" Phil grinned boyishly and faked a shiver. "I get all aroused by that exotic legal jargon, don't you?"

The porter arrived, standing expectantly. "These gentlemen were just leaving, Halliwell," Schaefer said starkly. "Would you be so kind as to escort them out?"

"Certainly, sir."

Sir Timothy's smile had vanished, his blue eyes narrowed. "Actually," he said slowly, "these gentlemen are my guests, Halliwell. Sorry for the misunderstanding."

The porter nodded, unconcerned either way, and walked away. Schaefer stood up abruptly. "If you continue on ignoring my professional advice, Tim, I'll simply have to wash my hands of the entire affair."

Phil exchanged a look with Keen as Schaefer snatched up his briefcase and stalked off. After a moment, Keen got up, stretched, and sauntered after him.

Sir Timothy did his best to repair his affectation of cool detachment. "Are you sure you won't have a drink, Sergeant . . . Rhys, was it? Any relation to Sir Wendell Rhys?"

"Reaves," Phil corrected, unoffended. "And no, thank you." They looked up as Keen returned.

"Made a call on his mobile," Keen confirmed as he sat down again. "Saw me, hung up, and left the club in a hurry."

"Didn't get whoever he was talking to, did you?"

Keen shook his head.

"Any idea who Mr. Schaefer might be contacting, Sir Timothy?" This time Phil used his honorific.

"No, sorry." He leaned forward, as eager as a housewife for salacious gossip. "But I'd like to hear more about this videotape you mentioned. Any chance I could get a copy? Is it in color . . . ?"

On the drive back, Phil seemed uncharacteristically quiet. Then he said, "Sometimes, I do think about what it might be like being a policeman somewhere way out in the country, with one of those picturesque stone-and-thatch nicks like in *Heartbeat*. Where the people are all ordinary, normal, respectable church-going folk."

Keen glanced at his profile. Phil didn't look at him as he signaled, pulled out, and passed another car.

"Except for the odd sheep shagger here and there, of course," Phil added.

Keen turned his head away to hide his grin.

Phil had just dropped him off at his Vauxhall when Helaine, Schaefer's assistant, rang and asked Keen to meet her at the same pub. The promise of rain had finally materialized; his windscreen wipers squealed against fine drizzle. She'd sounded tense, and looked it sitting alone by the window with an empty pint glass.

The pub was nearly deserted. A pair of wizened pensioners huddled over their lagers, the barmaid wiped the counter lethargically, and a lone man in a plaid cap studied a racing form.

"Hello," he said, and nodded toward her glass. "Fancy another?"

She looked up, expressionless. "No, thank you." She stood before he had a chance to sit down. "I just wanted to give you this."

She pulled a half-empty bag of Marks & Spencer coffee from her handbag. Then she hit him in the face with it.

He jerked back as she swung the bag but it still connected solidly with his nose. The bag ripped open, coffee grounds spraying in an arc over the tables and floor.

"Aye, aye, aye!" the barmaid shouted in protest, leaning on the bar counter with hefty arms as if to vault over it. "What the bleedin' 'ell d'you think you're doing!" The three men had looked up with interest.

Keen dodged as Helaine swung the quickly draining bag again, her face twisted with tearful rage. "You lying son of a bitch!" The now empty bag hit him impotently. "You cost me my job, you bastard!"

He grabbed her wrist, spinning her around to restrain her in a tight hug that lifted her off her feet. "Hang on, there! For Christ's sake, Helaine, calm down . . ."

"*Aye, aye, aye!*" The barmaid was still bellowing, her face red. Now all three customers were grinning, enjoying the unexpected floor show. With her heels kicking wildly at his shins, he carried her out the back door of the pub to deserted picnic tables behind a chain-link fence. The wood gleamed with wet as he pushed her down on a bench. She had stopped fighting, panting heavily, but he didn't release her.

"Let go of me," she demanded, her voice hoarse.

"Are you going to behave, then?"

"I'd like to beat the crap out of you, is what I'd like," Helaine growled, tears streaming down her face.

Cautiously, he sat down next to her, ignoring the dampness seeping through his trousers. "Do you mind telling me what this is all about?"

The fight had gone out of her, if not her anger. "You know damned well what this is about. You told Felix Schaefer I'd blabbed all about Alice Guiscoigne so now he should cough up about the others. Then he sacked me! Six years I've been with that firm, six bloody years, and I'll not even get a recommendation!"

The last trailed off, hiccupped into a quiet sob.

He put a hand on her shoulder, which she shrugged off angrily. "Helaine, I didn't ring Felix Schaefer, if that's what he told you."

"Then it was that other one. *Somebody* told him I'd been talking to you."

"If someone did, I swear it weren't my partner, and it weren't me."

"So what?" She wiped at her face roughly. "If you hadn't shown up with your stupid bag of coffee, this would never have happened. It's still all your fault."

"I'm sorry," he said quietly. "I was only trying to do my job."

She turned a bitter, red-eyed snarl on him. "Yes, well, *fuck* your job. At least you still have one."

He waited until she'd settled down before he asked, "What *did* Schaefer do for Alice Guiscoigne, then?" When she stared at him, he added, "You don't have any further loyalty to Schaefer, Helaine. Why not tell me what you know if it can help?"

She laughed, a short bark of incredulity. "God! That just beggars belief! Did you do this on purpose, set me up to lose my job so you could cross-examine me without a conflict of interest?"

She hoisted her handbag onto her shoulder and stood up, brushing fiercely at the dampness on her skirt. He remained sitting, looking up unhappily.

"Helaine . . . please?"

"I don't have to tell you sod all," she retorted, not looking at him, her chin trembling with anger. But she hadn't walked away.

"No, you don't."

"Talking with you has gotten me nothing but grief."

"That's true, it has."

She glanced around the ugly garden, at the sparse weeds growing between cracked concrete, brown plastic rubbish bins, the chain-link fence, avoiding his eyes. "It's wet out here," she complained.

"We can go inside, if you prefer."

"No." She sat down again stiffly. But she still said nothing.

"Can I buy you a drink of anything?"

"No," she said curtly. Then, more softly, "Thank you." She sighed. "I only know some of what he was working on for Mrs. Guiscoigne. That was one part of his work he kept separate from the rest of his caseload."

"What was he doing for Mrs. Guiscoigne?"

"Preparing a lawsuit for her with a few other people involving some sort of wrongful death and fraud."

That surprised him. He'd expected a change in her will leaving everything to a bogus charity or a confidence trickster. "Against who?"

She smiled thinly, as if she didn't quite believe it herself. "The queen."

"What?"

"Well, not against the queen *herself,* of course. Technically speaking, she's above the law."

There was no "technically" about it, as Keen well knew. Once as a young naïve constable, he'd served traffic duty for a royal escort leading the queen's convoy. He'd started moving as soon as the headlights of the Leeds City Police appeared behind him, slipping in front as the Leeds car peeled off. To his horror, the royal car began to tailgate dangerously, flashing headlamps. With a normal limit of thirty miles an hour, he'd watched his car's needle creep past eighty-five miles per hour. His radio crackled as the junctions were notified of their approach. They blurred past, his hands clenched painfully to the steering wheel during that brief nightmare drive.

A North Yorkshire patrol car was already moving to take over the vanguard as he approached. But it took another mile before Keen could finally pull over to collect his shattered wits. He breathed a prayer of thanks that no poor sod had chosen that time of night to stroll across the carriageway. Red taillights bobbed once or twice over the darkened hills, all he ever saw of Her Royal Majesty.

"You can't sue the queen, not directly. But the suit was being filed according to the Crown Proceedings Act of 1947, against the Comptroller of the Royal Household, I think it was. And against the Prince of Wales, since he's not immune to prosecution until he's king."

"Wrongful death and fraud, you said? Whose death?"

"That's the weird part . . ."

Puzzle pieces clicked into place. "Let me guess," he said, "does the name Hannah Lightfoot have anything to do with it?"

She stared in surprise. "How did *you* know?"

"Would you believe me if I told you I heard it from a clairvoyant?"

"At this point," Helaine said sourly, "I'd believe just about anything. Schaefer was representing Alice Guiscoigne and John Wortley, who claimed they had proof King George the Third and this woman Hannah Lightfoot were legally married and that they were his direct descendants and real heirs to the crown. According to the Treason Act of 1351, it's a capital offense to attempt to hinder the succession to the crown to anyone entitled to it under the Act of Settlement. He was preparing a suit accusing the royal family of actively and knowingly suppressing documents which could prove conspiracy to usurp the crown."

"Only Alice Guiscoigne and John Wortley. Wasn't a third person, was there?"

"No, those were the only ones I know of," she said, making him wonder about Daniel Barrow. "Anyway, Schaefer used to date that historian woman, Christine Swinton. She was helping him gather evidence for the lawsuit. But the case never went anywhere because Alice Guiscoigne and John Wortley died. Then Christine Swinton drowned, which I suppose is where you came in."

"But what was he hoping to accomplish?"

Helaine snorted her contempt. "I have no idea. Other than to make Felix Schaefer famous by raking up a silly scandal and get his name plastered all over the tabloids, I can't see how this would do any good for anyone."

"Does the name Arthur Dalton mean anything to you? Or A and D Pharmaceuticals?"

Helaine mulled it over before shaking her head.

"What about Richard Atherton or Timothy Sutton?"

"I know Mr. Sutton. They went to public school together, Old Boys. Schaefer makes fun of him behind his back. He really is a baronet, I think; he's very sweet."

"Do you know his wife, Molly Sutton?"

"I've never met her personally."

"She has a half brother named Ray Delwyn, do you know him?"

"No."

"Schaefer is defending him in a burglary case."

She reacted with incredulity. "*Burglary?* He never handles that sort of thing."

"Can you think of any reason he would? A favor to his old school chum, Mr. Sutton?"

"Schaefer doesn't do favors. He's a backstabbing, unprincipled, sneaky little shit, and if he's defending somebody on a burglary charge, it's more likely to save his own skin than someone else's."

"Quite likely." He smiled at her. "Thank you very much, Helaine, you've been right helpful."

"I wish I could say it was a pleasure." He stood when she did. "But it wasn't."

*   *   *

Keen stopped dead when he spotted the Vauxhall. Every window had been smashed in, tiny cubes of safety glass glittering like diamonds on the road. In that moment of shock, he had all his attention focused on the car, leaving himself vulnerable to attack.

So it was relatively easy for the two men to jump him. He recognized the mint-and-coffee breath before he ever saw the man. Caught by his thumb, Keen had his arm twisted up behind his back, making him gasp more in astonishment than with the sudden pain. A policeman's technique, he recognized as he began to struggle. The second man appeared in front of him, fists pumping several hard jabs into his stomach. Then he brought his knee up sharply into Keen's groin.

Keen stopped fighting after that.

But they'd apparently finished; Mint-and-Coffee Breath lowered him to the pavement with gentle courtesy. The other man smiled with disdain as his partner squatted next to Keen, holding him upright to keep him from falling over.

Keen drew his legs up, the worst of the pain subsiding into a searing ache. Tears blurred his sight, and it was difficult to get a proper breath into his lungs.

"What do we have to do to convince you, Mr. Dunliffe?" Mint-and-Coffee Breath asked sympathetically. "Disobeying, omitting or neglecting to carry out any lawful order, to wit, 'be a good lad and trot along home now,' is in direct contravention of police regulations."

"So is willful neglect of your health," the second man put in, his voice whispery soft.

"Please. Don't make it necessary for us to take disciplinary action again."

Keen hadn't breath enough to answer, even had he wanted to. He hunched with his hands protectively tucked between his legs as the two men walked off. It took several minutes before he could manage to get to his feet. He swallowed against the rising bubble of nausea, and fumbled for his cellular phone.

It was broken.

He stared at it stupidly before putting it back in his pocket and looking around. A woman, dark hair in curlers, held a curtain aside far enough to watch him. He tried to smile. "I'm a police officer. Could I use your phone?" he croaked out.

She didn't answer, her face a blank as she drew the curtain. A glance around the street caught other faces vanishing behind their drapes.

"Fine," he rasped to himself. "Sod the lot of you."

He staggered down the street in search of a phone box.

Twenty minutes later, Phil pulled over at a bus stop where Keen slouched, and helped him into the car. Keen's breath hissed as he sat down gingerly, sharp pain shooting up his spine and down both legs.

"Tow truck will come for your car," Phil said with untypical gentleness. "I'll get the rest sorted out tomorrow. Meantime, you're coming home with me."

Keen didn't protest.

Phil Reaves lived in a small, brick duplex in Barnsbury, between Paradise Park and the prison. A plastic yellow tricycle guarded the front path, along with a scattering of half-naked dollies and stuffed toys Phil scooped up with habitual ease.

"Excuse the mess," he said as he unlocked the door. "Gabby! We've got company."

The slender woman who appeared in the kitchen doorway, drying her hands on a dishtowel, could not have been more different from Keen's expectations. Still in her nurse's uniform, she had removed her cap to allow a thick braid of black hair to hang down to her waist. Her skin, the color of polished olive wood, contrasted against the white of her uniform. She was a stunningly beautiful Asian woman.

"Hello," she said pleasantly, but unsmiling.

"My wife, Gabriella," Phil introduced her with pride. "Keen Dunliffe."

"Pleasure," Keen managed to mumble, and tottered over to the sofa, sinking down onto it gratefully.

She shook her head in disapproval. "I'll check him over. Finish putting the tea on, will you?"

"Yvonne in her room?" Phil disappeared down a hallway, arms still laden with children's toys.

Gabriella Reaves retrieved a pressure cuff and a stethoscope from the top of a bookcase filled with children's books. "Yes," she called out. "Watching *Snow White* for the millionth time. If I hear 'hi-ho, hi-ho' once more, I'm going to run screaming mad into the streets. Get her to turn it off, will you? Where does it hurt?"

She sat next to him to peer into his face, checking his pupils for dilation, he assumed. "I'm fine," he tried to protest, a bit breathless.

"Mm-hm," she said, unamused. "Unbutton your shirt."

He obeyed meekly, wincing as she prodded his abdomen. "This doesn't seem too bad, no deep bruising, just tender? Phil says you also took a good kick to the nethers." She wrapped the pressure cuff around one arm and pumped it up.

"I'm not about to unzip my trousers."

She snorted while listening to his pulse through the stethoscope. "I doubt you have anything I haven't seen before." The cuff deflated with a hiss. "I'll make up an ice bag, and you sit with it for a while. But if your scrotum starts to swell or turns blue, you could have a hematoma. Then you should see a doctor immediately, especially if you wee any blood."

She went back into the kitchen as Phil carried his daughter into the lounge. "And this is Yvonne. Say hello to my friend Keen, honey." He set her on her feet.

The three-year-old was a miniature version of her mother, brown eyes framed with thick lashes, black hair in two mussed ponytails. Keen could see the promise she would grow up to be a beautiful woman. She jammed her thumb in her mouth while staring at him, eyes huge and unblinking.

Gabriella returned with a towel and an ice pack. She draped the towel over Keen's thighs and handed him the bag of ice. "You can do this part for yourself," she said, then turned to Phil scoldingly. "The *tea,* Phil."

With both parents busy, his only audience was Yvonne, sucking her thumb vigorously. Screened by the towel, Keen unzipped his trousers and settled the cold pack where it would do the most good without embarrassing himself in front of the child. But not without several teeth-grinding gasps of shock. Once he'd managed to relax slightly, he attempted a smile at the little girl. It wasn't returned.

"Nothing fancy," Phil announced as he carried a tray out into the lounge. "Chicken korma. Thank God for Patak's." He put the tray down on the coffee table, and set out two plates. "Yvonne, do you want some chicken?" he tried to coax her.

She shook her head.

"How about some of Mummy's rice, darling? It's yummy," he wheedled. He made a production of tasting the rice. "Mmmmm!"

She shook her head.

Phil sighed, defeated. "Jelly sandwich?"

She nodded.

When Phil went back into the kitchen, Yvonne took her thumb from her mouth with an audible pop. "Where do you keep all your feathers?" she demanded gravely.

"Feathers? Why should I have feathers, love?"

"Daddy said you're a pillow."

Phil returned with half a sandwich, but stopped, wincing. Keen grinned. "I think your daddy meant 'pillock,' honey."

"What's a pillock?"

"Your father," Gabby said sourly, as she whisked the girl up with one hand, and snatched the sandwich from Phil with the other. "I'm sure you two must have better things to discuss?"

With Phil's wife and daughter out of the room, Keen quickly recounted the incident with the same two men who had threatened his boys. Phil didn't recognize descriptions of either one.

"You're certain they're police?" Phil scraped the last of the chicken curry from his plate. Keen left most of his, his appetite quashed.

"That, or ex-police."

"Y'don't suppose that was the call Schaefer made?"

They sat in silence for a moment. "Phil, if it were your family, your daughter, they'd threatened, would you leave this case alone?"

"Absolutely," Phil said without hesitating. "I'd forget I ever heard the name Christine Swinton. Then I'd spend every off hour I had tracking down the bastards who threatened my family and break their fucking kneecaps."

Keen nodded.

"So what do you want to do?" Phil asked.

"I have a small problem with my car at the moment," Keen said dryly. "Think you might give me a lift back to Camden Town?" Then he furtively removed the melting ice pack from under the towel and readjusted his clothing before standing up. "And if you don't mind, I should just check to see if I 'wee' any blood before I go."

He didn't. But he was going to be walking bowlegged for a while.

XIV

WEDNESDAY

Jillie had taken the train to Calais from Paris and found a transit hotel near the harbor. She slept better than she had in years, and the next morning, ate her *petit déjeuner* in the hotel's sunny garden. A woman with an apple-cheeked smile and a mouthful of gold served her hot croissants and cold jam, juice and coffee, and a copy of *Libération*. Jillie read the newspaper but understood little of the convoluted French politics.

At ten, she walked onto the ferry, feeling oddly at peace with herself. Standing out on the deck, she watched the coast of France dwindle into a thin blue line behind her before she faced northwest, the wind whipping back her hair, and waited for the white cliffs of Dover to appear through the mists.

"Sorry, skip," Bernie said. "PNC came up with four Arthur Daltons, but none of them's the one you want." Phil scanned the printout; two Arthur Daltons in the Met area, both under twenty-five, a seventy-year-old vicar in Devon, and the other currently doing porridge on the Isle of Wight. He crumpled the sheet into a wad.

She'd also checked with the late-shift information officer, a WPC she jogged with on weekends. Arthur Dalton, fifty-two-year-old son of the late Anthony Dalton, had inherited his father's position on the board of directors of A&D Pharmaceuticals, had no current known address, no registered driver's license, no outstanding warrants, no past history of any criminal activities.

"But I did come up with something else interesting. Did you know your favorite porn starlet has a younger sister named Corinne?"

It didn't surprise Phil she knew about the videotapes. Bernie handed him a suspect card with the photograph of a child's pouting face made harsh by her severe eye makeup. "She's a chronic shoplifter, nicked a dozen times since she was eleven. She turned sixteen in April."

Phil studied the card quizzically. "So?"

"So look at the address." Phil looked at the address. "You still don't see it? She lives with her mum on the same estate as Francine Jenkins's mum. Corinne and Francie are best mates."

A slow smile broadened across Phil's face. Mark Lisson was the insider to

Victoria's knocking shop, not Ray Delwyn. "Well, I'll be buggered. But for now, Bernie, let's just keep this information between the two of us, all right?"

She grinned and walked away with jaunty triumph.

Then he ran into Jack Brewer, the constable on his way to storage lockup with a pair of bloodstained trainers sealed in a plastic bag. "Good thing you got that video put back with the rest in lockup last night, skip," he announced as he passed Phil. "Had me sweating doing the count before we sent them off this morning."

Phil jerked to a stop. "What are you talking about?"

Jack paused, as if unsure whether Phil was having him on. "You know. The dirty videotapes from that burglary?" he prompted, obviously hoping Phil would know what he was talking about.

Phil's stomach lurched, suspecting he *did* know. "Sent off to where?"

"Lambeth. We got orders to send them in for computer enhancement on the punters' faces. For possible suspect identifications?" By the tone of his voice, they both knew what had happened. "Oh shit, oh dear," Jack said sadly.

"Jack, the only anatomy needing enhancement on any of those tapes wasn't anybody's bloody face, now was it?"

Of course, when he rang Lambeth Crime Laboratories, the videotapes had never arrived nor did anyone there know anything about computer enhancements. He tracked down the order sent in to Kentish Town Police Station, and with one look at the Home Office stamp of approval beside an illegible signature, he knew the videotapes had vanished down the White Rabbit's hole forever.

Replacing the windows and the windscreen on the Vauxhall would take at least a day. And a few more before Keen stopped inhaling sharply every time he sat down. Phil at least had the courtesy not to snicker too loudly every time he did.

"Your girlfriend find her way home yet?"

"No. She hasn't rung, either." Keen suppressed a wince as he got into Phil's Volvo. "Mrs. Flute is manning the telephone, she'll ring through on your number should anything happen."

The man from Cell-U-Lease Phones was none too pleased with one of their brand-new mobiles returned in fragments. He dourly informed Keen the soonest it could be mended would be twenty-four hours, and he didn't care that it had been damaged during the course of police business. So, for the day, Keen would be both phoneless and carless, much to his irritation.

Phil pulled away and blended into the sluggish traffic along Camden High Street. "Gabby likes you." Keen raised an eyebrow. "It's hard to tell sometimes, but I know she does." Phil glanced at him, amused. "Were you surprised?"

"What about?"

"Give over, you know what."

"Gobsmacked. She's too intelligent and beautiful to be married to the likes of you."

"That she is, you have me there. She's Indian, not Pakistani. I mean she's British, born in London, but her folks were originally from New Delhi, and not that that makes a damned bit of difference to me. Or to the blokes in the station."

"Ever a problem?"

Phil shrugged. "Not really. You know what gets said in the canteen and what gets done on the street are two different matters. Well, most often, anyway. They all know I don't care to listen to it, though. And no one from the nick has ever, *ever* been anything but sweet to Gabby." He was silent for a moment. "My own family is another matter," he added flatly. "I go see me old granny, I have to sneak in the back, my father doesn't want me in the house." His tone was noncommittal, but Keen could hear the pain underneath.

"And your granny?"

"She had a stroke years ago. Can't remember who I am now. Thinks I'm her husband been dead forty years." He chuckled wryly. "Bless."

A City of London doubledecker belched a cloud of diesel fumes before pulling over at a bus stop, blocking traffic behind it. Phil inched the Volvo's nose out far enough to force the car beside him to stop, driver honking in protest. Phil smiled benignly at the angry driver.

"Give it a rest, mate," he said pityingly to the red-faced man mouthing silent curses. "Life's too short as it is." The driver jabbed two fingers after them as they cut into his lane and passed the bus.

"On the other hand, my wife's folks have been lovely," Phil continued, flashing a quick grin at Keen. "They were skeptical at first, can't blame them, really. Now they treat me like I'm the next best thing to Vishnu. Her mum's a fabulous cook, thinks I'm too skinny. Her dad spoils Yvonne rotten, loads of toys and candy. When the whole family gets together, all the brothers and sisters and aunties and uncles and cousins, you'd go out of your mind with the noise, everybody talking at the top of their lungs in two languages, neither of which I can understand. But it's great. Big families." He looked over at Keen. "You should come for dinner sometime."

Phil maintained eye contact until Keen said, "Thanks. Maybe I will." Then the younger man went back to navigating the heavy traffic, leaving Keen to wonder what the hell that was all about.

"By the way, those videotapes have gone. Home Office had them sent over to Lambeth, but they never arrived."

Keen absorbed it. "Interesting."

"Isn't it just?" The Volvo crawled to stop, and Phil used the pause to stretch. "Galton bumped into me this morning, making a lot of mouth music about not seeing me round the nick much, whatever have I been up to?" Now Keen understood Phil's invitation. "Seems to me, pal, we're running out of time. If we don't come up with something soon, all the evidence is going to be swept clean anyway."

"We need to find Arthur Dalton." He tried to gauge Phil's reaction.

"Mm-hm," Phil said, unimpressed, glancing at his rear mirror.

Keen sighed. "Jillie's plane leaves Saturday morning."

"All right," Phil agreed. "Until then."

A&D Pharmaceuticals wasn't far from the Barbican, on the top floor of the faceless chrome-and-glass tower so beloved of seventies pseudo-Bauhaus architects. A lone receptionist sat enthroned in a semicircle of bleached oak, telephone at her right hand, oversized appointment book at her left. Her professional smile remained as impenetrable as concrete as they displayed their warrant cards.

"Mrs. Maytree might be of assistance," she said serenely. "If you gentlemen would like to take a seat, I'll see if she's available." She tapped the phone with an articulated fluidity better fitting a movie robot. After a considerable wait, the receptionist gave directions to her office with the same mechanical graciousness.

Mrs. Maytree had none of the receptionist's poise. An overweight woman in her early fifties with carrot-red hair, she seemed harried and nervous. "You're the police?" she greeted them, while glancing both directions down the corridor for eavesdroppers. "Please, come in."

Her office was even smaller than Galton's, and with about twice as much paper. She shifted files off the chairs, then slithered through the small gap between wall and desk, sat down, and shoved another stack of papers out of her line of sight. "What can I do for you?"

"Mrs. Maytree, we're trying to locate Mr. Arthur Dalton," Phil said. "He's a senior director in A and D Pharmaceuticals, I believe?"

"He's not here." She wasn't intending to be rude, Keen realized; simply not enough hours in the workday to waste time on pleasantries.

"Would you know where we could find him?"

"South Africa."

"I've been told he was in London ten months ago and that he'd been living in Gloucester," Keen said.

She looked from one to the other, as if waiting for the punch line of a not very funny joke. "That's highly unlikely. The company headquarters is in Bleisner, South Africa. I don't believe Mr. Dalton has been in this country at any time in the past eleven years, or if he has, this office hasn't been aware of it." Her hands folded into a tight knot in front of her. "Why? Is there a problem?"

Phil shook his head reassuringly. "We'd just like to ask him a few questions about a personal matter."

She flinched, and Phil exchanged a puzzled glance with Keen. "If it's a personal matter, we can't help you. You might want to speak with his solicitor. Or his wife." She winced again, amending, "Ex-wife. She lives in Gloucester. But I seriously doubt he was visiting with her."

Keen played a hunch. "Would his solicitor be Felix Schaefer, of Schaefer, Burgess, and Lowenthal?"

"No. James Preston, of Preston and Associates on Wellington Road." She searched through a Filofax, and pulled a card. "He still handles all the Daltons' personal business although he's retired." She jotted down the address, tore off the note, and handed it to Phil.

"Would you have his ex-wife's address or telephone number, Mrs. Maytree?" Keen asked, and again observed her pained wince.

But she didn't protest, searching the cards to write down another address. She smiled wanly as Keen thanked her. "Mrs. Maytree, have you ever met Mr. Dalton?"

"I met them both, father and son, when I started work with A and D. Dalton senior died five years ago, and his son took over his seat on the board of directors in Bleisner."

"A and D Pharmaceuticals," Keen asked. "Is the *D* for Dalton?"

"Digby. Thaddeus Arlington and Jeremiah Digby founded the company in eighteen ninety-three. They'd made a fortune in diamond mines, who didn't in South Africa? Cashed in their stock just before the Crash and bought out a drug company. Did very well, until thalidomide nearly killed the firm. Dalton senior took over the company, a good hands-on manager. His son . . ." She frowned ambiguously. "The past few years haven't been easy."

She wouldn't say more than that, and ushered them to the lift. The receptionist buzzed them out with the same plastic smile.

"We'll save time if we split it," Keen said as they reached Phil's Volvo.

"That mean I get the wife?"

"You've got the car."

They swapped addresses Mrs. Maytree had given them. As Phil drove off, Keen headed for the Tube station.

The former Mrs. Dalton lived in the postcard-picturesque village in Brickleswold, just over the Oxfordshire border. Phil parked behind a Mazda with Gloucester registration plates, *W 453 AAD*. Bloody letters seemed to be everywhere.

The pretty cottage at the end of the lane was hidden behind a large hedge. The postbox nailed to the gate bore the name "F. Wickford" rather than "Dalton."

He inhaled the cool air, grateful to get out of the car, and strolled up the neatly raked gravel path. He rang the doorbell and waited, a shadow passing behind the squares of lead glass. The door opened and a boy grinned up at him, blue eyes like speckled robin's eggs under his sandy-brown fringe of hair.

"Hello. Are you the policeman what rang up before?"

Phil noted the child's epicanthic eyes, the round face with a high, flattened forehead. The unmistakable telltale signs of Down syndrome.

"Yes, I am. Is your mum about?"

"She's here." The boy stared intently behind Phil, his head bobbing. "Where's your police car?" he demanded skeptically. "And where's your uniform?"

A woman appeared behind the boy. "Detective Sergeant Reaves?" She was less interested in his warrant card than was her son. "Ricky, give the gentleman back his wallet now, please. Won't you come in?" Her voice was pleasantly cultured.

Ricky closed the door once Phil had followed his mother into the cottage. Timbered beams and whitewashed walls made the interior seem larger than it was, the room warm and cheerful.

"Do sit down, Sergeant. Tea?"

"That would be lovely, thank you."

Ricky continued his inspection as his mother made the tea. "You don't look like a policeman," Ricky complained. "Why won't they give you a uniform? Don't they have enough to go round for everybody?"

"Not all policemen wear uniforms, Ricky. I'm the sort that doesn't."

"Oh." The profound disappointment on the boy's face was comical.

"Ricky, love," his mother said, carrying out a tray with the tea. "Why don't you go color while I have a chat with Mr. Reaves?"

Obediently, Ricky trotted into the kitchen, the table covered with children's crayons and paper. Ricky climbed onto a chair and began to draw, engrossed in his task. His mother set out the tea before she sat on the edge of the sofa.

"Mrs. Dalton . . . ?"

"Wickford," she corrected him. "I took my maiden name back after my divorce. But please call me Faith."

"Thank you. Faith, we'd like to talk to Arthur Dalton, if it's possible. Would you know where he is?"

"Bleisner, South Africa," she said promptly.

Phil sipped his tea and set it back into the saucer on the table. "He wouldn't have made a trip to England around last October?"

"He hasn't been to England in eleven years. He has no reason to."

Phil glanced at the boy in the kitchen. Ricky hunched over his drawing, crayon held in one stubby hand. The tip of his tongue protruded from his mouth, wriggling in concentration. "Not even to see his son?"

Faith chuckled dryly. "*Especially* not to see his son. Nor would I allow it. Arthur hated his own son from the moment he was born. He made much of his being descended from royalty, and couldn't bear that a child of his might be defective. It was all the fault of bad blood." She smiled thinly, tired lines under her eyes. "Mine, naturally. Two months after Ricky was born, I caught Arthur trying to smother the baby in his crib with a pillow."

She had dropped her voice, low enough that the boy in the kitchen couldn't hear. "He even tried to talk me into it, saying we could claim Ricky died of cot death. That it would be kinder to the child. I couldn't believe Arthur wanted to murder his own son." She looked away, oddly detached. "When I threatened to ring the police, he broke my nose and three ribs, cracked my head against the floor, then choked me until I passed out. Then he left. I never saw him again, nor do I ever want to."

Phil had to clear his throat. "And that was eleven years ago?"

"Yes."

"Would he have friends or family in England he might stay with?"

"Family, no. His mother's family refuse to have anything to do with him and his father is dead. My father-in-law was very good to me and his grand-son; he knew what Arthur had done. He'd had to extricate Arthur from trouble before, and this was the last straw. Anthony had made it clear that if Arthur wished to inherit anything, he would have to stay in South Africa. As for friends, Arthur kept in contact with a few people he knew from university."

"Was Richard Atherton one of them?"

She shook her head. "I wouldn't know."

"Sir Timothy Sutton?"

"Sorry."

"Felix Schaefer? He's a solicitor."

"No, Arthur's solicitor is James Preston. James takes care of Arthur's business in Britain, including my income from the company, child support, med-ical bills, and physical therapy. Ricky had surgery to repair heart defects, and his joints are loose, which can make physical exertion quite painful for him. It can be expensive."

"You said Arthur had been in trouble before. What sort of trouble?"

"Theft, mostly. Arthur has considerable talent, but used it to counterfeit stock issues. He forged his father's signature and left my father-in-law to pay off an enormous debt that nearly bankrupted the company. After that, Arthur left for Bleisner with the understanding that he was never to come back to England."

"But Arthur was never charged with anything?"

"No. It was a family matter, nothing to concern the police."

Phil didn't challenge this as she glanced again at the child sorting through his crayons. Ricky's broad face creased in a huge smile before he again scribbled on his drawing. "They're wonderful children," she said absently. "So full of love and affection." She turned her bleak smile on Phil. "I sometimes think the world would be a nicer place if there were more children like Ricky, not less."

"Would you have a photograph of your ex-husband?"

"Not a recent one. The only one I didn't burn was our wedding portrait. I suppose I keep it to remind me not to do anything quite so foolish again."

"Could I see it, please?"

While he waited, Phil wondered how he would have coped had Yvonne been born with a handicap. Ricky looked up and grinned blissfully. Phil smiled back with a dull ache in his chest.

Faith returned with a photograph, wiping dust from the gold frame, and handed it to Phil without a word.

Faith Wickford had once been a happy woman, her younger face untroubled as she smiled for the camera, eyes sparkling. The newlyweds posed in front of a village church, the bride's train in a froth around her feet. She clutched a bouquet of white roses and baby's breath. Her husband had been older, looking massively pleased with himself. He was much taller than she, his thick hair with graying wings cut in a longer style popular a decade before. Sunlight bouncing off black-framed glasses partly obscured his eyes. A full moustache curled over his smile. Nothing about these two joyful people hinted at the violence to come.

"Could I take this with me?" Phil asked.

Her eyes widened. "I'd rather you didn't. But I can make a copy for you at a shop in the village and send it out in tomorrow's post."

"That would be fine," he agreed, and handed back the photo. She held it as if trying to remember what it was she had once so loved about him. Then she laid it facedown in her lap.

"Thank you very much," Phil said, standing up and holding out his hand.

She shook it. "Sorry I couldn't have been of more help to you."

"Wait!" Ricky cried from the kitchen, realizing Phil was about to leave. He scrambled off the chair and ran into the front room, clutching his drawing. "Don't go yet, I made this for you!"

Solemnly, Phil accepted the crude illustration of a man in a police uniform with more brass buttons on it than it really needed, and wearing a tall pointed hat three times too big for his head.

"That's you. And that's your police car." A boxy vehicle with a severely compressed bonnet to make it fit onto the paper sported a blue light the size of the policeman's helmet.

"And what's this?" Phil asked, pointing to something hovering overhead like some bizarre insect about to devour the figure.

"That's your helicopter, but I didn't have time to finish it."

"A helicopter, well! Fancy that."

"I made this for you to show your boss. I bet if he sees this, then he'd let you have a uniform and a police car so that you could be a real policeman."

Phil's face quivered under the strain not to laugh. He looked from the boy's earnest face to his mother also suppressing a grin. Once he trusted himself to speak, he said, "I'll be sure to show it to him."

He held out his hand, expecting to shake the lad's hand, and was unprepared as the boy launched himself at him, hugging him tightly around his waist. Taken by surprise, Phil lifted the boy off his feet to fiercely return his hug. Ricky's arms squeezed around his neck, the child giggling with delight. Then he pulled away far enough to kiss Phil on the end of the nose, laughing unabashedly.

Over Ricky's shoulder, Phil caught Faith Wickford's unguarded look, and for a brief moment, he could see that happy woman with the love sparkling in her eyes.

Preston kept his law offices on the ground floor of the Preston family house, a large, rambling Victorian brick affair dominating a corner of Wellington Road. The offices shut, a sign directed him around the back to the Prestons' private entrance.

An imposingly stout woman answered the bell, examining him with suspicious contempt. Keen's smile wasn't returned. "Mrs. Preston?" She didn't look anything like the woman in Phil's photographs from the funeral.

"Missus Preston is not in." Her thick accent sounded Slavic to Keen's untutored ear. "She is gone to shopping."

"It's Mr. Preston I've come to see, actually." Keen showed her his warrant card. She seemed unimpressed. "Would he be in?"

"I see if he is awailable." She held the door open but her glare stopped him within a few steps inside. "Stay here." She pointed to the floor menacingly as if commanding a border collie before she clumped up the stairs.

After cooling his heels in the service entrance, surrounded by mops and brooms and shelves of cleaning products, he heard people arguing.

"Oh, for pity's sake, Gerda," a man's exasperated voice complained, "this isn't Bucharest and he's not from the Securitate." An elderly man in pajamas and bathrobe appeared on the stairway, Gerda glowering behind him. "I'm terribly sorry," he said, then froze, alarming Keen as he stared pop-eyed and fumbled desperately in one pocket. He managed to drag out a rumpled tissue in time to sneeze explosively into it.

"Sorry, I've the most awful summer cold," Mr. Preston said, wiping his reddened nose before stuffing the tissue in his pocket. "Do come up, won't you?"

Keen followed him to a dimly lit sitting room, curtains drawn as a football match played on the television. Preston picked up the remote to mute the sound, but left the game on. A marmalade cat had seized the opportunity to curl up in Preston's armchair, glaring as Preston pushed him off and settled into the chair with a box of Kleenex to hand, balls of used tissue scattered on the rug by his feet.

"What can I do for you, Mr. Dunliffe?" Preston asked as soon as Keen had identified himself.

"You were a friend of James Witherstone Swinton's, would that be correct?" Keen scratched the cat's ears as it sniffed his ankles.

"Oh, yes." Preston's eyes strayed regretfully to the game. "I've known the family ever since James married Verona, in fact." He blew his nose loudly into a tissue, crumpled it before dropping it to the floor with the rest, and pulled a fresh tissue from the box. The cat halfheartedly batted at the discarded wad of damp tissue, then sauntered out the door.

"And would you say you knew Christine and Max Swinton well?"

"Known them both since birth. Dreadful shame about Chris, her mother is heartbroken. Holding up well, though, strong woman."

Keen wondered if Preston was going through some meaningless formulae or if he didn't know the family as well as he thought. Preston squirmed in repressed excitement as a player in a striped green shirt tackled and the ball rebounded off. A player in blue intercepted a poor back pass, collecting the ball in midfield to sprint across the field. The crowd cheered, waving banners and scarves silently.

"You still represent Max Swinton's legal business, isn't that right?"

"That's right. I've been with the family for years, and when I retired five years ago, Max asked if I would continue to handle his affairs rather than changing to someone new." Preston's concentration again drifted toward the television.

Keen's eyes also strayed as the defending midfielder picked up the ball just inside the half and made a solo break deep into the penalty area. The shot was cannoned back with a spectacular overhead kick to another striker who slipped the ball past the goalkeeper and into the net from the narrowest of angles. The crowd surged to their hysterical feet, and Keen wished Preston would switch the game off.

"But Chris preferred to go with Felix Schaefer. Can you tell me why?"

He regained Preston's attention, the elderly man frowning. "I suppose his views were slanted in a direction she felt more comfortable with."

"Did you know she was having an affair with Mr. Schaefer?"

Preston scowled. "That would have been none of my concern, one way or the other. I will say I did find Mr. Schaefer's general practices to be rather disreputable, reflecting badly on our professional standards as a whole. If he were carrying on with Chris, it wouldn't surprise me."

"He may have been involved in more than an affair."

"What exactly is it you're investigating? I've already spoken with a constable they sent round after Chris's death. If Schaefer is involved in that, I'd certainly be interested in knowing."

"The coroner has ruled it death by misadventure, Mr. Preston. There's no further police inquiry into that matter."

"Then what's this got to do with Schaefer?"

"Apparently, Mr. Schaefer planned to sue the crown."

"On what charge?"

Keen said reluctantly, feeling foolish, "It's supposedly a capital offense under the Treason Act to hinder the succession to the crown of a rightful heir. He claimed there were legitimate descendants of George the Third by his first wife, Hannah Lightfoot, and that the palace was knowingly suppressing documents that could prove it. Documents he engaged Christine Swinton in helping him to find."

"Utter poppycock," Preston pronounced, and wiped at his nose with the tissue, muffling his voice. "No sensible lawyer in the country would touch such a load of rubbish, not even Felix Schaefer."

Keen shrugged. "It's what I've been told. And Chris Swinton did have a thing about the monarchy."

The midfielder slid the ball to a teammate who struck a screaming free kick just wide of the left-hand post. After a moment, Preston picked up the remote and flicked off the television, the screen going dark as Keen repressed an absurd pang of regret.

"She was an academic," Preston said. "She'd written two books on George the Third, so her interests were hardly a secret."

"She sometimes went beyond academic passion, didn't she, being an activist in antimonarchy campaigns, supporting republican causes?"

"Chris was involved in absurd causes all her life, Sergeant, as you no doubt are aware if you've checked her arrest record for the past twenty years. If she wasn't out saving poor little baby seals, it was to feed all the starving nig-nogs in Ethiopia. But it was a *game* to her, a hobby. She changed causes as often as she changed hairstyles, and with about as much reason."

Keen scratched his ear, close to the patch of white hair. "Did she meet Arthur Dalton through you?"

Although the question had been asked easily, Preston rocked back, dumbstruck. "I beg your pardon?"

"Arthur Dalton. Anthony Dalton's son, of A and D Pharmaceuticals. He's supposed to have been in South Africa for the past eleven years, but we know he was in Britain ten months ago, and in contact with Chris Swinton. Now, considering you've represented both the Swintons and the Daltons for years, it seems logical you were the connection."

"Arthur Dalton was in Britain, ten months ago? Are you *sure*?"

"I've reason to believe so, yes. Would you know where I could find him?"

"I'm afraid not." Preston blew his nose again, dropping another discarded tissue to the floor, then stood up to cross the room. He picked up a cut-crystal decanter. "Brandy?"

"No, thank you."

Preston poured himself a large helping before sitting back down, gulping at the liquor. "This is bad news, very bad news indeed."

"Why would that be, Mr. Preston?"

"Under the terms of his father's will, Arthur retains his seat on the board of directors only so long as he remains outside the United Kingdom. He could travel anywhere else in the world he liked, but he was never to return here or he would lose all rights and monies."

Keen weighed this. "Would it be a reasonable assumption, then, if Arthur Dalton did come back to Britain he wouldn't have done so openly? Come in secretly or under a false passport?"

Preston cradled the brandy in his hands, troubled. "It's possible. But Arthur seemed content in South Africa, I can't imagine why he would risk everything by coming back here."

"Why was he exiled, Mr. Preston?"

Preston sighed. "If Arthur hadn't had family connections and money, he'd have been in prison long ago. Even as a child, he was a bully and a thief, although Anthony did his best to instill the boy with some sense of honor. There are just some things you can't do with bad blood. Then there was that awful incident at Harrow."

Preston fidgeted, sniffling, obviously loath to discuss the past. "A boating accident. A lad drowned after their rowboat capsized, knocked unconscious when Arthur attempted to reach out to him with an oar. Arthur was only twelve, and the other boy was his eleven-year-old cousin. No one dared openly accuse Arthur of having purposely killed his own kin."

The skin on Keen's neck chilled. "Do *you* believe he murdered his cousin?"

Unwillingly, Preston nodded. "One doesn't like to believe that possible in a child of that age, certainly not someone of his background at any rate. He was an odd boy, large for his age and quite strong, but not terribly interested in sports. Bookish lad, quiet, very polite. He could be ever so charming, but he had this unnatural coldness even then. And the glaring fact was his cousin's skull had been bashed in several times. It was hardly an accident. The first legitimate excuse the school could find, they chucked him out.

"He did settle down after that. But after he married, there was some unpleasantness with his wife and baby son. It was only a matter of time before Arthur would do something his father couldn't put right. Sending him to South Africa was as much to protect the rest of the family as it was to protect Arthur. I drew up the settlement we both hoped would keep Arthur out of harm's way. He was Anthony's only child, after all."

"Arthur Dalton sent Christine Swinton a letter from Gloucester. He apparently thought himself to be a descendant of George the Third and Hannah Lightfoot. So how did he know Chris Swinton?"

"Not through me," Preston said unhappily. "Or if it was, I wasn't aware of it."

"Mr. Preston, do you know Richard Atherton? He was at Harrow with Arthur Dalton when they were boys."

Preston deliberated before he shook his head.

"Timothy Sutton?"

"Of course I know Sir Timothy. Likable old boy, but that wife of his . . ." His mouth made a moue of distaste.

"Have you ever met her brother, Ray Delwyn?"

"Wasn't even aware she had one."

Keen was running out of prospects. "Had you ever met any of the people Chris Swinton was involved with academically? Reece Wycombe?"

"That's the chap who topped himself the other night? Read about it in the papers. I'd met him once or twice, can't say much about him one way or the other."

"He had a research assistant, Marge Beecher."

"Sorry."

Keen exhaled in frustration. "Excuse me if this sounds a bit off, but are you familiar with a place called Dungeons and Dragons?"

"Isn't that one of those arcade parlors where kids play on boards with dice, what do they call that? Where they pretend to be wizards and trolls and whatnot?"

"No," Keen said dryly. "It's a whorehouse."

Preston's eyebrows shot up, but he was more intrigued than offended, and laughed. "Good Lord, no." He studied Keen quizzically. "What on earth would a whorehouse have to do with Chris?"

"It's where she were videotaped having sex with a man and a prostitute by the name of Paloma Sanchez."

"*Chris?* You're not serious?" When Keen's expression told him he was, he snuffled into a damp tissue. "Oh, dear. You haven't said anything to her mother or Max, have you? Who else knows? Good Lord, the scandal would devastate Verona," he continued without waiting for an answer. Keen was certain Verona Swinton would suffer far more from what the neighbors thought than from her own daughter's death.

"Would you say that was out of character for her, Mr. Preston?" At the retired solicitor's worried look, he pressed, "Were you aware Christine Swinton was also involved in homosexual love affairs?"

"My God," Preston said quietly. He downed his brandy. "I did warn him."

"Warn who?"

"Her father. He did love Chris, you know. He was proud of her, the investments she'd made, the books she'd published. I think he was aware of her . . . intimate life, but she was still a well-bred woman, no matter what sort of public spectacle she made of herself with her harebrained liberal causes. She understood that certain things had to be kept private. The same as she did her drinking problem."

"Was she an alcoholic?"

"She drank too much, and in five or six years, she might very well have become one. But she kept it under control. People of her class do, you know. As it is, I'm not surprised by the way she died, either too drunk to know what she was doing, or simply committing suicide."

He looked up from his empty glass. "It deeply hurt her that when James died, he left her nothing, gave in to Verona's demands and bequeathed it all to her brother. Oh, it wasn't about the money, she had plenty of that. But she felt he'd betrayed her, we both had. I drew up her father's will. That's why she went with Schaefer, we were a couple of gutless old hypocrites, in her eyes."

"Do you think Schaefer took advantage of her in that state? Maybe persuaded her to do things she might not ordinarily have done?"

"Entirely." Preston blew his nose again. "And if you find he's involved Chris in any illegality, I'd be grateful to be kept informed. It would give me the greatest pleasure to see him struck off."

Keen didn't estimate there was much else of use he could elicit from James Preston. "Would you mind if I used your telephone?"

Preston ushered him into a separate sitting room unquestionably his wife's domain. Keen closed the door and picked up a pink telephone, the intense smell of perfume making his eyes water.

"Where are you?" he asked once he'd reached Phil.

"On the M40, just passing Beaconsfield." Keen could hear the rush of traffic and faint bleating horn of a lorry. "Arthur Dalton is one very naughty boy."

"I'm aware of it—" Keen said, quelling the urge to sneeze.

"I've got good news and bad news," Phil cut him off. "The good news is that Busy Bernie's come up with another tidbit. She talked to the technician tracking down where the scopolamine compound came from. Guess what company makes it?"

A shiver slid down Keen's spine. "A and D Pharmaceuticals."

"Who's a clever boy, aye? Veterinary subsidiary. They use it to conk out dogs before they cut their goolies off."

"So what's the bad news?"

"Atherton's had a heart attack, he's still alive. Brought on, his wife claims, by you manhandling him. She's filed a complaint with the PCA." Keen closed his eyes and leaned his forehead against the doorjamb.

"And as if you didn't have enough to worry about," Phil continued, "your Mrs. Flute just rang. Jillie's back, popped in long enough for a chat and a change of clothes. Apparently, whoever she met in Paris was quite enlightening. She claims she's got proof Swinton was on to something and she's gone to see your friend Marty Harty-whatzits. Wants his help in tracking down a certain Arthur Dalton."

"Oh, my God."

"Oh, my God," Martin said, amazed. "It's fantastic! I don't know what to say!" He held the de Duffand letter gingerly by the edges.

"But do you think it's real?" Jillie asked anxiously.

"Oh, yes," Martin breathed. "It's quite real." He carefully set it on the slab glass table by the silver cellars, smiling and shaking his head. Then he stood up and paced across the room, once and back, running his fingers through his thick white hair. "I'll put the kettle on for tea, settle us both down," he said.

She didn't really want tea, but when he poured her a cup, she sipped enough to be polite, and set it back on the saucer.

"Won't you tell me just a little more about this friend of yours, Jillie?" he wheedled. "What an incredible source he'd be for my work, I'm dying of curiosity."

"I'm sorry to be so secretive. He's a very private person, with good reasons to keep it that way. But I'm hoping you can think of a way to find Anthony Dalton's son. He might be able to tell us a lot more about what Chris was working on."

"Do you have any idea who or where he might be?"

"All I know is that Anthony Dalton went to Oxford, but that he's probably dead. He wasn't sure but he thought the son's name was Arthur, and that the Dalton family might have been from Gloucester . . ."

Her ears ached, like going down too deep in a swimming pool. She tried to yawn discreetly, popping her eardrums to relieve the pressure. It worked, but Martin watched her curiously.

"It's been a tiring trip," she excused herself, and wondered if she were coming down with a cold.

"Caffeine should do you good," Martin suggested.

Obligingly, she finished her tea. "More?" When she shook her head, he asked, "Have you told anyone else about this?"

"Keen Dunliffe knows quite a bit, but not about . . ." She hesitated, puzzled, her skin vibrating strangely as her heart began beating fast and hard, down to the pit of her stomach.

"Are you all right?" Martin asked, concerned.

"Yes, I think so. I feel a little funny . . ."

"You were saying? Not about . . . what?"

When she looked at Martin, tiny fragments of light whirled around the edges of her vision. He had his head tilted, his white hair reflecting rainbow shimmers from the chandelier. She looked from his worried expression to the empty teacup, flecks of leaf spotting the porcelain, black on white, as readable as words printed on a page. Her muscles felt heavy and thickened.

He opened her purse and began to remove the contents. She tried to stop him, surprised when she simply watched, unmoving.

"Oh," she said, and felt more stupid than she'd ever felt in her life. Looking at him, she said again, "Oh," suddenly embarrassed.

"Oh," he said, confirming it. He scanned through her notebook with casual swiftness. "Tell me more about this friend. Where does he live? What's his name?"

"What was in the tea?"

"You wouldn't be any the wiser if I told you," he said, still leafing through her notebook.

"*You* killed Chris." Her hands and feet were inert, not numbed but detached, as if they belonged to someone else. Her lungs felt odd, as if she couldn't quite suck enough air into them to keep from hurting. "And you're going to kill me."

"Yes."

She wondered why she was more curious than afraid. "Why?"

"They all ask the same silly question. 'Why?' What difference does it make?

Do you think if I explained, you could talk me out of it, as if this is some sort of debating society? I haven't time for that, and neither do you. Now, who gave you this letter?"

"You won't tell me, I won't tell you," she retorted, her words starting to slur.

The rage on his face was fleeting but chilling. Then he smiled. He had such a warm, friendly, nice smile. "All right, we'll play your game. I tell you, then you tell me. I'm protecting the royal family. Hannah Lightfoot was an unfortunate glitch, a genetic defect passing down from one generation to the next. Breeding is essential in horses, dogs, and the aristocracy. Bad blood musn't be allowed to continue spreading disease, don't you agree? And no one has that right better than myself."

Knight errant, slayer of dragons and other noxious pests . . .

"But Chris . . . ?" She was having trouble formulating the idea.

"Chris figured out who I was."

"But . . . who *are* you?"

"Haven't you guessed yet?" She opened her mouth to say no, but heard an odd mouse squeak instead. She wondered if it was LSD, wondered if that's why she suddenly had forgotten how to *breathe.*

Breathe. Breathe. Her fear was an isolated, distant thing, like a lost child in a crowd crying for her mother. Breathe. Karen. Breathe.

"Now. Tell me about the letter, where did you get it?" Martin's voice echoed weirdly, as if he were speaking from Planet Pluto. He tapped her lightly on the nose with the de Duffand letter.

"Jillie . . ." Robert said in his so-cold voice.

It startled her, what was her husband doing here? Her sense of time had lurched off the railings. Like knowing she was asleep, her mind slipping between that twilight of dreams and logic.

"We had a deal, Jillie. I told you, now you tell me . . ." Robert, who she knew was really Martin, who wasn't Martin at all, said in his odd grating voice. "This letter from your friend, where is it from? Who is he?"

She was going to die. Martin was going to kill her. Like Chris. Bummer. She wanted to laugh. Her lungs wouldn't let her, she was drowning. Like Chris. *"Bummer, Mom. This is so grossville . . ."*

She smelled smoke, bright flickers prancing before her eyes. He was burning the letter. Mme. de Duffand's letter, which had survived the French Revolution and two world wars, braved decades of moths and beetles and floods and mildew, was going up in flames. The ink flared brighter than the paper, the old script sparkling briefly with a magic life of its own before it vanished.

"Jillie. *Jillie!*" He shook her hard enough to rattle her teeth, as if she'd been left in the cold. She felt seasick as the world bobbled around. "Tell me who gave you this letter . . ."

Fear punched through her in a surge of panic. "Duhno . . ." The wheezy eeriness of her own voice in her ears frightened her.

He struck her. "Lying bitch!" It didn't exactly hurt when he slapped her across the face, the pain distant. "Tell me!"

And something very weird happened. She knew she was losing control, terrifying her. More than being back in that horrible house, she was back in that horrible house, expecting Karen to appear on the stairs, sleepy-eyed and pigtailed, forever frozen as a little girl with her headless Raggedy Ann doll under her arm.

Mommy?

"No . . . no . . ." She was weeping, desperate not to lose control, keep it locked tight, buttoned up, clamped down. She had to, *had to,* there was no choice. But everything slithered from her grasp.

A doorbell rang, and she wanted to answer it, shocked when her body didn't move, paralyzed like a sleeper floating in a dream. She couldn't figure out how she had stood up until he let go of her and she folded up into a heap on the carpet. She couldn't move, couldn't breathe as he opened a sliding glass door.

Glass door. That horrible house never had glass doors. Then she felt him dragging her, a distant sensation. She heard rather than felt her head hit the hard cement, noticed how immaculately clean his shoes were as they walked away. He closed the glass door and the curtain, leaving her outside on the balcony to stare at the stitching in the heavy brocade.

Keen left Phil in the courtyard below to keep an eye out for Jillie. Before he could buzz Harding-Renwick's interphone, a leggy redhead in running togs came out the security door with a matching Irish setter on a leash. She smiled sweetly and held the door open for him before jogging away. Phil nodded in time to her gait.

Keen took the lift up and rang the doorbell. When Martin Harding-Renwick opened his door, he seemed out of breath, gusting breezily, "Mr. Dunliffe, how nice to see you again. Something I can do for you?" His face was flushed as he smoothed a hand over his white hair.

Behind him, the drapes were closed, likely to keep out the heat of the day. Empty teacups cluttered the glass table behind Harding-Renwick. Keen sniffed the air, the burnt smell sharp.

"I'm sorry to bother you, if you've got visitors . . ."

"Not at all, my secretary's just left for the day." He opened the door further. "Would you care for a cup of tea? There's some made I can warm up in a tick."

"No, thanks. Has Jillie Waltham come to see you? I was told she might be here."

"Jillie?" Harding-Renwick's eyebrows rose. "No, she hasn't, I'm afraid." He smiled warmly. "Seems everyone is looking for our lovely Jillie today."

Keen's cheeks prickled with dread. "What do you mean?"

"The two policemen here yesterday. You know them, don't you? Inspector Rudiger and his partner, I forget his name. They know *you*."

Coffee-and-Mint-Breath. "We've met," he said grimly. "Did they say why they were looking for Jillie?"

"Not specifically. They asked the same questions you did about Chris Swinton's appointment with me. I told them I'd referred you to Mrs. MacFalgan. All they said was they'd like to ask Jillie a few questions, follow-ups, I believe they called it." His tanned brow creased in concern. "Jillie's not in any trouble, is she?"

"No, she's not in any trouble." He handed Harding-Renwick a card with Phil's mobile number on it. "If she shows up, would you ring this number straightaway?"

Harding-Renwick took the card and studied it earnestly. "Of course, Sergeant. You can count on me."

Jillie's fingers curled like the legs of a dead spider, so detached from sensation she wasn't sure they belonged to her. She had an enormous rush of despair and triumph as they wriggled disjointedly.

Could he have shot her full of Novocain? No, she remembered, he'd shot the teacup full of Novocain, like the Mad Hatter and she the Dormouse. She wondered how he'd inserted a needle into hard porcelain. Can you shoot Novocain in the brain? In pain. Insane. Inane. A familiar voice muffled behind cloth and glass made her want to scream. She tried to inhale enough and failed.

"Sorry to bother you . . ." That wonderful accent she had learned to love so much went up and down like a child's music box. ". . . Jillie Waltham . . . I was told she might be here?"

Me! Her heart leapt with joy, not because he was there to rescue her, of course he was, but that he even remembered her name.

"Here I am!" It came out a snake's hiss.

Except he hated her now, she remembered in the random firing of drugged synapses. He had come to arrest her. She lay still, not wanting him to find her hiding. Hiding. Who was hiding? Wait, Robert was planning to kill her . . .

"No, she hasn't, I'm afraid . . ."

Not Robert. That other man, the one she'd liked, although he'd turned out to be a total shit, just like Robert and that other son of a bitch . . .

"No, she's not in any trouble . . ."

But I am in trouble! She was outside, the breeze blowing her hair over her eyes to obscure even her boring view of curtain. His voice shredded her heart into confetti.

And as she broke, as the restraint of twenty years was stolen from her, the rage swelled up and exploded like the cap of a volcano ripped off. Mount St.

Jillie, she thought, as the rage sang in her ears. Enough adrenaline pumped into her blood to allow her to raise her head, wobbling precariously as she tried to focus her eyes.

Her arm flopped bonelessly as she rolled onto her back. She stared up at a blue, blue sky with just a hint of clouds flying overhead, like gauze escaping from an angel's tutu. She thought of Karen, eight years old and crying in her lovely Halloween ballerina costume because she'd wanted to go as one of the A-Team, army fatigues and plastic machine gun. *Oh, baby.*

Her head twisted, and her eyes took far longer than they should have to register the neat and tidy balcony, square terra-cotta flowerpots, and a broom in one corner. She couldn't walk, that much was out of the question, but if she concentrated she could crawl, just barely. She let herself believe in the magic that was somehow responsible for rolling her onto her stomach. She began creeping toward the broom, keeping her eyes on it unblinkingly.

Distantly, she felt her panty hose rip as she clawed at the cement with both hands and dragged her deadened body along it. She focused every shred of awareness onto the broom, ignoring the soft voices commiserating with each other, conversation she couldn't quite make out through the rising and falling of a tide of blood whooshing in her ears.

She would get the broom and use the handle to poke that fucking pot right over the fucking edge and let it fall on top of his fucking head. She heard an odd sound before she realized she was giggling. Good girls never said "fuck." But since she wasn't a girl anymore, she could say "fuck" all she wanted.

"Fuck," she murmured, but it didn't quite sound right. She reached for the broom, the ends of her fingers barely touching the bristly end, just enough to make it teeter upright before it slowly, majestically fell and smacked her hard on the ear.

"Fuck." This time it sounded better, but still not clear.

Then she heard: "If she shows up, would you ring this number straightaway?"

Then she heard: the door closing and the click of a lock.

Then she heard: Martin-who-wasn't-Martin laughing softly.

Wait a second . . . A thrill of fresh fear shut down her overloaded synapses the few seconds necessary for logic to slink back in, bruised and battered as it was. Wait a minute . . . Wait . . . By the time she could wait for him to walk down the stairs or take the elevator so she could conk him on the head, the other one (who? She couldn't remember his name . . . Had she ever known his name . . . ?) would have been back and dragged her off. So much for that plan.

"Oh, fuck."

She'd have to stand up.

She couldn't. She *had to.*

You can do anything if there's no other choice.

She curled her legs under her, puzzled by the blood on her knees before she remembered her panty hose ripping. Except she hadn't been wearing panty hose. It was skin. Using the broom as a crutch, she pushed herself up into a half crouch, feet braced absurdly ducklike, and was admitting this was about as far as she was going to get when the glass doors slid open.

Martin's eyes widened with amazement and, she thought, a bit of admiration. "My, my. Having a good time out here, are we?"

It was the wrong thing to say. "*. . . have a good time,*" he'd said in that false, friendly voice, the knife blade cold against her throat. "*Come on, I'll show you how to have a good time . . .*"

The sun at his back, his face blanked in the shadow. But she didn't need to see it, that face permanently etched into her memory. She thought she heard Karen crying. *Oh, baby! Don't wake up!*

"Come on," said Martin who wasn't Martin anymore. "Let's get you back inside." He reached down for her.

"Not this time," she said, without knowing no one but herself could hear the words. "Never again . . ."

She used every ounce of strength she could summon to push off from the broom. All the self-defense courses, all the practiced choreography, did little now except give her the absolute faith that she'd rather die than to let it happen again. What she lacked in finesse, she made up for in determination.

Her shoulder punched him in the chest in a football player's tackle. It did little to hurt him, but, startled, he lost his balance and slammed back against the balcony railing. He grabbed her by one sleeve, seam popping, her own momentum sending them both staggering. They pirouetted like two dancers. She could see the courtyard below with abnormal clarity; neat rows in the green grass where the mower had trimmed, a large horse chestnut jutting white candlestick blossoms in the air, red flowers in the center where cobblestone walkways made an *X* marks the spot.

Her uncooperative feet tangled together, her hand grappled with empty air, swiping the geraniums. A shower of petals floated down to where a tiny man sat on a bench, legs stretched out, as another tiny man walked toward him.

Martin teetered on the edge of the railing, then slowly, slowly recovered his balance with a triumphant smile. His own foot stepped on the brush of the broom, the handle leaping into the air. He yelped as it struck him squarely in the face. She saw the two tiny men below turn and look up, little faces with little mouths open in surprise, just before she collapsed like a boneless doll. Her arms flailed around his thighs, knees buckling under her, and her forehead slammed into his crotch.

Martin made an odd little sound between a whine and a gasp, as if he couldn't decide which way his lungs wanted to go. Both of them tottered backward and tilted over the railing. She was distantly aware of Martin's hands clutching her like a lover, dragging her with him, but she couldn't find her own hands or feet, felt nothing but cool air against her cheek. Saw nothing except Martin's white, grim face so close to her own, a smear of blood on a split lip, and the blur of green beyond.

He clawed his way back from the edge, pulling on her like a lifeline. Her blouse ripped in his hands. With a faint, disappointed cry, he slithered past her and continued on his way.

She watched him fall, watched how he rolled over halfway down, his arms and legs reaching for her like a child begging for its mother. At that distance, he looked small and vulnerable, and she suddenly felt guilty. "I'm sorry," she said, trying to reach her own arms down to catch him. "I'm sorry . . ."

He hit the ground with a muffled thump, as dull as a sack of flour falling off a shelf. One of the two little men crouched beside him as the other ran toward the building, face upturned.

"Jillie!"

It sounded so far away, so faint. And besides, she was tired, so incredibly tired. All she wanted to do was to lie down, just go to sleep. Someone pounded against a wall somewhere. How annoying, she thought, such rude neighbors, and let her eyes close, so very tired . . .

"They've got her," Keen said angrily as he strode toward Phil. "Those bastards who threatened my kids. I've got one of their names now, Rudiger, I'll bloody *kill* him—"

Keen saw Phil's horrified look that had nothing to do with what he was saying. He followed Phil's gaze up to where a woman half slumped over a balcony, and a man was falling over the edge.

Harding-Renwick hit the ground the instant Keen recognized them both. "Jillie!"

Both men ran to where Harding-Renwick lay splayed on his back. For a moment, Keen hesitated as Phil crouched over the body.

"Go on, for chrissake!" Phil barked at him.

It was taking forever to kick in the security glass, when someone buzzed the lock. He jerked open the door, still intact but shattered into brilliant radiating cracks, and raced up the stairway. A face gaped from the birdcage lift on its way down.

Keen yanked a fire extinguisher from the wall to use as a battering ram against Harding-Renwick's locked door. He ignored several people peering around their own doors nervously. The lock splintered, and he nearly fell into the room. He dropped the fire extinguisher, white foam spurting out the hose to bubble on the plush carpet. Jillie was still on the balcony.

He crept toward her as carefully as if she'd been a timid doe ready to bolt at the slightest sudden move. Her ankle snagged around the handle of a push-broom jammed under the ledge, all that was keeping her from following the rest of her body over the balcony.

"*Don't . . . move . . .*" He breathed the prayer.

But of course, she did. She lifted her head, the movement enough to allow her ankle to slide free. He launched himself desperately and grabbed her legs.

She was slipping. He jerked back with all his strength and felt her chin strike the railing before she tumbled into his arms, as limp as a rag. With a rush of sheer relief, he embraced her tightly, shivering violently.

"Don't move." A voice interrupted her dream.

Her eyes tried to open, then someone punched her hard under the chin, rocking her head back. That annoyed her although it didn't hurt, not really. The world rolled onto its back and she looked up at a blob of moving colors she couldn't focus on. She heard weeping and wanted so badly to comfort whoever it was.

Hush, baby, don't cry. Please don't cry.

"You're safe, Jillie. I've got you . . ."

Keen carried her through the open door and collapsed. Kneeling on the floor, he rocked her in his arms like a child, one hand tenderly brushing the hair from her eyes. Her face was deathly pale, bluish, the skin hot and dry. She was weeping, tears flowing from eyes rolled up into nothing more than blind slits.

Her skirt was hiked over her hips, legs splayed awkwardly. White cotton knickers made her all the more defenseless. Blood oozed from scraped knees. Under her ripped blouse, her chest panted shallowly. Her fingers twitched with a frantic animal mindlessness. He tried to stop them, catch her cold hands in his own. He was still badly frightened, but she was alive. Safe.

"It's over, Jillie," he said. "It's all over."

She sighed, a tiny relieved smile at the corners of her mouth.

Then she stopped breathing.

Phil had seen the woman's arms and hair swaying like a flag, his heart in his throat until Keen's head appeared on the balcony, relief washing through him as she was dragged back safely out of sight. He'd already dialed 999 on his mobile phone.

He knelt beside Martin Harding-Renwick, and gave terse instructions for police support and an ambulance. It was a miracle the man was still alive, then, with a shock of recognition, Phil knew whose pulse he was feeling. The hair was completely white now, the lines around the face more pronounced, the moustache shaved off. But it was definitely Arthur Dalton.

A gathering of business suits and stylish skirts coalesced around them, chattering eagerly.

"Isn't that Harding-Renwick?"

"You think he jumped?"

"Is he still alive?"

"Broke his neck?"

"Suicide?"

"What?"

"Who?"

A few moments later, Phil heard Dunliffe's scream clearly from the court-yard green, making his hair stand on end. Even the crowd around him hushed, wide-eyed.

"Shit," Phil muttered into the phone.

"What's going on?" the woman on the control room line asked.

"Now!" he barked at her. "We need help now!" He grabbed the first business suit within arm's reach. "You. Watch him. Don't touch him. Don't let anyone move him, you got that?"

"Me?" the business suit protested, then shut it as he read the fury in Phil's eyes. "Okay, okay . . ."

He raced up the stairs, in a breathless sweat by the time he reached Harding-Renwick's splintered door. A fire extinguisher lay in a puddle of dissolving foam. Phil's shoe skidded as he stepped over it.

Jillie Waltham lay on the floor. His back to Phil, Keen Dunliffe was on his knees, his mouth against hers. One hand tilted her head back and Phil could see her chest rise and fall spasmodically as Keen forced air from his own lungs into hers.

"Jesus Christ," Phil said, "what happened?"

Keen didn't answer, too busy driving oxygen into the comatose woman. Phil groped for her carotid artery. He found her heartbeat, thready and faint, at the same time he felt a warm splash on the back of his hand. For a moment, he thought the woman was bleeding, until he realized Keen was weeping.

"You're going too fast there, pal, slow down," he said, trying to calm him. "Not so hard, just slow the fuck down . . ."

The woman's spine arched, arms flopping in a violent convulsion. Keen gagged as she vomited.

"Roll her on her side, Keen," Phil instructed, his voice steady. He dug his handkerchief from his pocket, paused, and decided it didn't matter if he'd blown his nose into it. He wiped the vomit out of her mouth.

It took agonizingly long minutes before they heard the wail of police and ambulance sirens. The flat suddenly filled with busy people and busy hands. Paramedics dropped their gear around Keen and the woman, pushing Phil out of their way.

"She's not breathing!" Keen shook the hands off but stepped back to give the medics room to work. The room milled with noise and people, most of them uniformed police.

The paramedic with a stethoscope in her ears pumped air into a pressure cuff around Jillie's arm while her colleague jammed a plastic mask over Jillie's face.

"Ninety over sixty," the paramedic said coolly, pressure cuff hissing. She flashed a penlight into Jillie's dilated pupils. "Anaphylactic shock, looks like. Let's get her intubated." Her partner grunted impassively as he slid an ugly, L-shaped blade expertly down Jillie Waltham's throat to insert a plastic tube.

The paramedic glared at Keen, her disgust naked. "We need to know what kind of drugs you were using. What was it, cocaine? Ecstasy?"

Phil had never seen rage like that on a human face. Alarmed, he hauled Keen around to face him. "We're police," he snapped at the paramedic, although he kept his eyes on Keen.

The paramedic's hostility diminished, her expression puzzled. "Her pressure's dropping. Get an IV established," her partner said quietly. "One unit of Ringer's lactate, stat."

The plainclothes officer said to Phil, "Everything's under control here. Why don't you and your friend go get some air?"

"No," Dunliffe said hoarsely, "I'm not leaving her."

"Wait outside," the paramedic said testily. "Right now, the best thing you can do for her is to get the hell out of our way." She glared at the officer. "You, too."

The large man simply grinned at the paramedic and didn't move. Phil managed to propel Keen out the door and shoved him against the corridor wall, holding him there. Dunliffe stared back, still trembling.

"Just calm down," Phil insisted. "She's not dead, take it easy. That's it, better. You okay now?"

Dunliffe nodded. "What about Har—" His voice cracked.

"Dalton. He's Arthur Dalton." Phil wondered if Keen even heard him. "Still alive, last I knew. Come on, let's have a look round . . ."

It didn't take long. Two uniformed bobbies had found enough drugs in the drinks cabinet to stock a small clinic. One examined the label on a bottle that read:

For Use By Veterinary Professionals Only

A&D Pharmaceuticals, Bleisner, South Africa

A plainclothes officer with a beefy neck and shoulders picked up an empty teacup, not bothering with latex gloves, and sniffed, fragile porcelain ludicrous in his huge hand. Two uniformed bobbies exchanged glances. His partner stirred the ash in a bowl with his finger, obliterating any chance of salvaging anything from the charred paper. Phil locked eyes with him. The plainclothes officer slowly smiled. Phil didn't.

Keen pushed his way to the woman medic holding a clear bag of solution dripping into an IV tube in Jillie's arm as they wheeled her out of the room. She seemed frail and lifeless.

"She's breathing on her own now, but she's not conscious," the paramedic said, more kindly.

By the time they got Jillie down in the lift, Martin Harding-Renwick had his own coterie of paramedics clotted around him, his neck and back braced before they dared move him. The car park flickered with police lights, dozens of various uniforms jostling through the crowd of plainclothes officers and curious spectators.

Phil followed Keen as they trailed the gurney to the ambulance, but stopped as Keen climbed into the back with Jillie. Phil didn't bother with any optimistic encouragement, and Keen didn't even look back before the driver slammed the doors shut. Standing alone with his hands in his pockets, Phil watched the ambulance drive away, lights flashing and sirens nee-nawing.

Keen shared the small waiting room with two noisy children gleefully ripping magazines into shreds. Their exhausted mother cupped her forehead in one hand, spiky bangs jutted between her fingers. A cigarette smoldered in her other hand, her eyes closed. They all looked up expectantly when the door was opened by an equally tired looking doctor, rumpled white coat over a green gown.

"Mr. Dunliffe?"

The mother scowled. "Aye! We was 'ere afore 'im! Wha' about me old man?" She stabbed the cigarette into an ashtray overflowing with her previous butts. "'Ow long do we 'after sit 'ere waitin', aye?"

"It'll be a bit longer, Mrs. Kane, we're doing the best we can."

"Fookin' NHS, we bin waiting fer *'ours,* me bum's gonter sleep! Wha' about these kids' da, wha' about *'im?*"

"How is she?" Keen asked once they'd escaped.

"She's doing very well. Would you follow me, please?" The doctor gestured toward the lift. "She's ingested a mix of anticholinergic alkaloids, including scopolamine which is a belladona compound. The anaphylactic shock is what caused her respiratory failure and convulsions." Keen wasn't sure he understood it all, but didn't much care. "Luckily she's responded well to treatment. She's awake, and we'll keep her overnight but I'm sure she'll have recovered by tomorrow afternoon." She smiled. "You're a hero, you know. If you hadn't administered artificial respiration when you did, there's every chance she wouldn't be alive to thank you."

He didn't want to be a hero. "What about Harding-Renwick?"

"Not so good, I'm afraid."

Keen kept his expression neutral. "Will he live?"

"He's in stable condition," she assured him. "All things considered, he's lucky to be alive. There are some internal injuries which still concern us," she continued as the lift began to rise. "He's fractured several thoracic vertebrae, and there's evidence of severe spinal cord injury. He is able to breathe on his own, and has some response in his hands. But the prognosis for his ever walking again isn't hopeful."

The lift doors hissed open onto a busy nurse's station. The doctor sorted clipboards before Keen followed her down the hospital corridor, green walls, gray tiles, the smell of antiseptic in the chill air. She pushed open a door with the names "Waltham" and "Miller" posted on it.

Miller turned out to be a tortoiselike old woman, papery skin hanging from the thin arm with which she held the remote control, as she flipped from BBC One to BBC Two to ITN and back to One, over and over again. She muttered in a monotone grumble, indistinct without her teeth.

Jillie lay in the bed by the window, with only a curtain between her and her roommate. The white pillow framed a face nearly as pale. Her closed eyelids seemed blue, opaque. She reminded him of his sons, peacefully asleep, sweetly vulnerable.

"Mrs. Waltham?" The doctor touched her arm.

"Mmmm?" Jillie blinked awake, groggy and confused.

"Mrs. Waltham, there's a visitor for you."

Keen found it difficult to smile, as he sat on the edge of her bed and took her free hand in his. Her fingers were like ice. "Hello. Feeling any better?"

"Tired," she whispered. They waited as the doctor listened to her chest with a stethoscope, took her pulse. "My throat hurts."

"That's from the intubation tube. It should stop hurting in a while." The doctor turned to her roommate. "Mrs. Miller, let's turn the telly off for now."

Mrs. Miller glared with pure hatred in her rheumy eyes as the remote was pried from her bony hand. As soon as the doctor had left, the old woman immediately threw back the bedclothes and, using her IV stand for support, hobbled to retrieve the remote. She shot Keen a hostile glance before shuffling back behind the curtain. The television once more began its methodic flip through the meager selection of stations.

"What happened to Martin?" Jillie asked, her voice hoarse.

"We've got him in custody." He didn't want to tell her what condition he was in, however. "That's not his real name—"

"I know." She surprised him. "It's Dalton."

"Arthur Dalton. How did you know?"

"I didn't until he burned the letter and tried to kill me."

"What letter?"

"Madame de Duffand's letter. Proof Hannah Lightfoot was married to George and had two sons who survived. Not that it matters anymore. I was asked to find Anthony Dalton's son and return it, since it belonged to him. Looks like I did. Ironic, isn't it?" She rubbed her eyes. "God, I must look awful."

"You look fine."

"I don't feel fine. I feel like an idiot." Her hand fell back onto the bed. "How did you find me?"

"Mrs. Flute told me where you'd gone."

"I asked her not to," Jillie said, then shrugged. "How did you know he was Arthur Dalton?"

"I didn't. Phil talked with his ex-wife, and recognized him from a photograph. She thought he were still in South Africa."

Jillie closed her eyes. "I'll bet if you talk to the police there, they've probably got a few unsolved murders he's responsible for."

Keen was surprised. "Why?"

"I just *know*, okay?"

He lowered his head. "Jillie, I'm sorry. I should have trusted you more, I know that." He felt rather than saw her suspicion. "But I *did* trust you as far as my job would allow me to. You should have trusted me."

Her chin trembled. "You lied to me."

"You lied to me." It was said gently, but she flinched and turned away.

After a long silence, she said, "The man I went to see in Paris, who gave me the letter, is another Lightfoot descendant. Martin never found him, which is one reason he's still alive. But he doesn't want to be involved, and I'm not going to tell you who he is. So, are you still going to arrest me?"

It was said with a hint of a smile. He shook his head.

"All I can say is one of his ancestors immigrated to South Africa." She looked puzzled. "But how did you find Dalton's wife?"

"Ex-wife. Traced her through his drug company. That's what he used on you, scopolamine. It's an animal tranquillizer." For some reason, she found that amusing. "Jillie . . . I'll have to have that book back. The Dalton book. It was stolen from Harewood House."

"Chris?"

"I don't know. Maybe."

"Then how do you know it's stolen?"

"Richard Atherton." He hesitated. "He's had a heart attack."

"Poor man. I'm not surprised, considering what Chris did to him."

"How do you mean?"

She rolled her head on the pillow to give him a bemused smile. "That videotape. I honestly didn't know about it until you told me, but I knew she was blackmailing him with something."

"You're wrong," he said firmly. "Chris wasn't blackmailing him."

Jillie looked doubtful. "So what about all that stuff from the archives he was giving her . . . ?"

"All fakes Arthur Dalton made up for him. It was the only way Atherton could keep her interested in him."

"But that videotape . . . ?"

"Was Atherton's idea, not hers. Atherton was desperate. He went to Leeds to blackmail *her* with the tape, get back the forgeries before his ruse was discovered."

"But it was Dalton who killed her."

"Yes."

"Was Atherton in on it? Did he help kill her?"

It was a question he'd already asked himself. "I don't know."

"Keen . . ." She took an unsteady breath. "Was she raped?"

"I don't know that, either." At her look of incredulity, he said, "Forensics are not perfect. It can't tell you everything. She were in the water too long for anyone to be able to tell. So unless someone decides to confess, we'll never know."

She absorbed this quietly. "Oh, Chris."

"Jillie, it needn't have come out this way. We could have worked together rather than against each other, maybe we'd have found out Harding-Renwick and Dalton were the same person, before you got hurt."

She said nothing for a moment. "They want to keep me here for a while," she said tonelessly.

"Only overnight for observation."

She gazed out the window, although there was nothing to see but blank sky. "My plane leaves at eleven-forty Saturday morning."

"I can change it for you, if you want a few more days to recover."

"That's . . ." She looked back at him, her expression unreadable. "No. I just want to go home." Her eyes closed, bruised and exhausted.

"I understand," he said softly. "I'll take you back to Mrs. Flute's tomorrow. In the morning, I'll drive you to the airport, give you a hand with your baggage . . ."

He waited for her answer before realizing she had fallen asleep, her eyes moving under the thin-veined lids. Lowering his head as if in prayer, he looked at his own hand so close to hers, fingers almost touching. He wanted to hold it, but was reluctant to risk waking her. He left as the old woman switched channels and grumbled past atrophied gums.

Waiting at the empty nurse's station, he opened a door marked STAFF. Three nurses chatting around a coffee machine looked none too pleased at the interruption. "Excuse me, but can anyone tell me which room Martin Harding-Renwick is in?"

"Sorry," one of them said curtly. "That wouldn't be our floor."

"He's the man who fell from a building, broke his back?"

"I'm *sorry*," she repeated in exasperation, "but he's not—"

"Hold on," one of the others interrupted. "That's the casualty came in with five twenty-seven." Five twenty-seven was Jillie's room number. Was that how they thought of her, as just another number?

"Then he's probably still down in Acute Care."

"Thank you very much."

Through the glass door, Harding-Renwick appeared like the subject of some bizarre scientific experiment, the steel-and-wire apparatus holding him prisoner in the bed. A nurse hovered around the bank of machinery hooked up to him and ignored the attentions of a brawny man sitting with a magazine on his lap. Coffee-and-Mint-Breath. They both looked up as Keen pushed open the door. Only the eyes of the man in the bed moved, staring at him.

"I'm sorry, sir," the nurse said quickly, "no visitors." Coffee-and-Mint-Breath stood up, his stance menacing enough for her to glance at him in surprise.

"I'm a police officer," Keen said quietly. "If Mr. Harding-Renwick can manage it, I'd like to ask him a few questions."

"Mr. Harding-Renwick is in no condition to be answering any questions." Coffee-and-Mint-Breath took a single ominous step toward Keen. "You may leave now, Sergeant Dunliffe."

The nurse looked alarmed. "I should call the doctor."

"Why don't you do that, sweetheart? You run along."

"If you try physically ejecting me, Mr. Rudiger," Keen said, "I think you'll find yourself with far more trouble than you really want to deal with."

Rudiger laughed. "I don't think you're going to be any trouble to anyone. Not anymore. Now, would you care to leave while you still can under your own power?"

The nurse fled in openmouthed astonishment.

"Wait." The man imprisoned in the medical apparatus barely looked recognizable, face swollen, eyes bruised. The effort to speak obviously drained him. His breath came in a horrible tortured rasp. "Tell Jillie. Walpole . . . letter . . . forgery."

And Keen knew he was lying. "Then why burn it?"

Martin Harding-Renwick closed his eyes, unquestionably a dismissal. Rudiger propelled Keen out the door. "It's *over,* Dunliffe."

Keen stared at him evenly. "It's not over between you and me."

Rudiger sighed. "Yes it is. Take my advice. You're in enough shit. Best thing you can do now is go home and forget all about it."

Keen walked away. There was nothing further he could do, but the frustration burrowed in his gut like a slow heavy burn. In the car park, he stopped, car keys in hand.

McCraig leaned against the Vauxhall. "Have it all figured out, Mr. Dunliffe?"

Another puzzle piece fell into place with a sickening thud. "Well enough. If a little too late." He opened the door, but stood without getting in. "Why me?" he demanded without looking around.

"Because I'm a chief superintendent of the London Metropolitan Police and you're an insignificant sergeant from a small northern nick." It was said without scorn, without sarcasm. "Because I needed someone clean and expendable to do the muck work, and you very kindly offered."

"You didn't need me. If Phil Reaves hadn't stumbled across those videotapes, I'd never have found a thing."

McCraig chortled. "Thank God for sheer blind bloody luck. That and disgruntled informants are the real backbone of police detective work. But don't sell yourself short, Sergeant."

Keen watched McCraig tamp tobacco into a pipe before sucking the flame off a match into the bowl. A halo of smoke rose as McCraig shook the match to death.

"Who has the tapes now?"

"That doesn't concern you. There will be a few early retirements in the next few months, and believe me, the rest of our house is being cleaned up"—he nodded in acknowledgment—"in no small part due to your efforts. We won't be able to get them all, I'm afraid. We won't need to. Time will do it for us."

"Harding-Renwick killed Christine Swinton."

"Yes."

"And Guiscoigne and Wortley, all the rest of them."

McCraig nodded.

"There's no way he could have pulled that off on his own. He had to have had help and protection, from the inside." Still he got no response. "You covered up for him and you wouldn't have lifted a finger to stop him from killing Jillie Waltham. You bastards." His voice was quiet, almost impersonal, but Keen had never before in his life wanted so much to kill someone.

At that, McCraig finally did react. "I didn't cover up for Harding-Renwick. I used you to *find* him. And stop the people behind him."

"Who were 'they' then?"

"You don't need to know names. You know more than you should as it is." Taking his pipe from his mouth, McCraig said, "Think of it as a foxhunt. Your job was to run him to ground. Now it's our job to dig out the rest of the den."

"Never cared much for foxhunts," Keen said quietly. "Seems a pointless and cruel sport for pointless and cruel people."

" 'The unspeakable in full pursuit of the uneatable,' " McCraig quoted wryly. "But even the hounds are entitled to some of the kill. Harding-Renwick, or Dalton, whatever his name is, might never have been caught if he hadn't killed Christine Swinton. Classic 'Brides in the Bath,' all he had to do was take her by the feet and pull her legs up. Even a healthy woman and a strong swimmer like Swinton would find it impossible to defend herself. As drunk and full of drugs as she was, she never had a chance."

He contemplated the ashes in the bowl, aromatic smoke trickling from his mouth. "Although I don't believe he intended to kill her quite so quickly. I think he was attempting to torture information out of her, but with no time to even hold her breath, she sucked in a lungful of water and drowned almost immediately."

"Then why didn't he simply leave her there? A woman found drunk and dead in a hotel bath wouldn't have aroused half so much suspicion, or been as risky as carrying her body to Harewood lake."

"Because he had to make a statement. Send a message to the royals that their enemies were being disposed of by a loyal servant. Not that anyone understood the message, not at first, but then you're dealing with a psychotic sort of logic."

"Christine Swinton was never any dangerous political agitator."

"Political agitator, yes. Dangerous, no. All she wanted was to write a book which would have, at the very most, caused a small tempest in a Royal Doulton teacup." McCraig's smile was genuine, but his eyes were cold.

"And Harding-Renwick?"

"Crazy as a bedbug. There was never any conspiracy to topple the monarchy, except in his own mind."

"Then why cover up half a dozen murders?"

"Because his usefulness outweighed his liabilities." McCraig raised an eyebrow at Keen's narrowed look. "A and D Pharmaceuticals has been a valuable conduit for certain covert activities over the years, particularly in South Africa."

"What sort of activities?"

McCraig smiled without explaining. "As Harding-Renwick, Dalton had the perfect cover to get back into Britain. He even went to his own drug company's charity dinners raising money for medical programs in South Africa, where no one but an old university mate recognized him."

"Timothy Sutton."

"Who unwittingly put him into contact with Schaefer, who just happened to be a dirty trickster with the government's Attack Unit. They both were on the Fabian Society commission, the government's think tank examining the retention of the ancient rights of a monarch on lawmaking. Harding-Renwick fit right in. But while everyone was busily hatching their clever plots and counterplots, nobody noticed their new friend was a complete raving loony."

"None of it was real, then? George the Third and Hannah Lightfoot?"

"Oh, strangely enough, that was all very real. He used Christine Swinton to track down the Lightfoot heirs. Then he killed them. But the way he went about it alerted his handlers. It became an unseemly scramble for damage control."

"You mean cover-up."

McCraig shrugged. "Semantics, Sergeant."

"What I don't understand is why. If Dalton's a Lightfoot descendant himself, it don't make sense."

"Dalton is a sick man. When his son was born with Down syndrome, he saw it as a sign his blood was corrupt, the legacy of Hannah Lightfoot. The only way to put things to right was to remove the stain. He sees himself as a sort of latter-day Sir Lancelot, fighting the impurity in himself to serve his monarch."

Another piece clicked into place, the rough white stones Harding-Renwick kept in the silver cellars, Jillie's cryptic remark. "Barrow was born in Cape Town. Some of the Lightfoots immigrated to South Africa."

McCraig raised an eyebrow, grasping the implication. "Thank you, Mr. Dunliffe. We'll look into it." His dry smile evaporated. "In any case, when the Lightfoot heirs started popping up dead in awkward places, it also alarmed other parties charged with the duty of observing and analyzing activities which may threaten the stability of the state. They felt it necessary to step in."

"I'd have thought covering up the cold-blooded murder of innocent civilians goes a bit beyond protecting our national security."

"Oh, so would I. But then, no one bothered to ask my opinion." McCraig's irony was too heavy. "If it hadn't been for Mr. Scudder's little faux pas, I'd never have been aware of anything in the first place. A left-handed honor, I suppose. There are a few of us with scruples still sticking to the bottom of our tarnished souls, and I was considered too honest to risk being let in on the scheme."

"So how does Schaefer fit into this?"

McCraig laughed sourly. "Schaefer is the perfect lawyer. He'll always be on the side that's winning. He was quite happy to lend a hand in discrediting Christine Swinton as a mentally unstable lesbian nymphomaniac waving forged papers about who talked to the ghost of Hannah Lightfoot via clairvoyants. No one, not even the *Daily Mail,* would take the Lightfoot story seriously after that."

"Why wasn't Dalton stopped, then? Why let him keep on killing?"

"Those few who knew Dalton was Harding-Renwick weren't about to expose him; he could compromise too many people who thought they could manipulate him while keeping their own hands clean. But I doubt he'd have been allowed to continue on much longer before he would have been gotten rid of, as well."

"Dalton also murdered Reece Wycombe," Keen said. McCraig gazed back calmly. "The only way Dalton could have known it had been Wycombe who broke into Chris Swinton's room in Leeds, looking for his stolen book, was from police reports. My tracing the shoemark. He was fed information from the inside."

McCraig nodded.

"So who was it warned off Marge Beecher? You?"

"You don't expect me to answer that, do you?"

Keen ignored him. "Inspector Rudiger, then?"

"Inspector Rudiger was only doing his job, just as you were."

Keen's anger flared, fists clenching. "Since when is threatening small children part of the job?"

"I took care of that. Your boys were never in any danger—"

"How the hell was I to know that?" McCraig's detached calm poured fuel on the rage in Keen's gut. "How can I believe anything you tell me now?"

"You can't." The pipe smoke scented the air like incense in a church. "You'll just have to trust me, won't you?"

Keen tasted acid in his throat. "Fuck you," he said quietly, small satisfaction in seeing McCraig's jaw tighten. "You're right. I'm just a thick Yorkshire plod, and all these grand and lofty intrigues are a bit beyond my ken. I don't give a toss about your bloody politics when innocent people end up murdered for them."

McCraig's lecturing pose vanished. "Believe what you like, Dunliffe, but there was nothing I could have done to prevent Christine Swinton's death. Nor Reece Wycombe's. I didn't even know who Harding-Renwick was at the time. I took a calculated risk using you and your American friend to flush out those behind him. I was going after dangerous people who don't have to play by the same rules as the rest of us. If I'd stepped in too soon, the people I was after would have twigged and we'd have lost them. As it is, a few slipped through the net. They're still out there, and it's going to be all the harder next time to catch them. All that can be done now is to make sure that when Humpty Dumpty has his great fall, we're not the ones to end up with egg on our faces."

Keen wasn't sure he understood all of McCraig's allusions, but the anger in the man's voice convinced him of his honesty, blemished and warped as it might be. McCraig stopped, mouth working as if realizing he'd said far more than he'd meant to.

"Except for me," Keen said bitterly. "I'm finished in the job now."

"Not at all." Keen tried unsuccessfully to hide his surprise. "Oh, you'll find yourself suspended from duty for a while, an unfortunate but necessary formality. But I can't afford to have you outside the tent pissing in, bearing a grudge with nothing to lose. People with nothing to lose are dangerous, indeed. You're safer to me on the inside."

The old anger growled, chained now but still alive. "I'll quit, then. I won't be used any further."

McCraig shook his head knowingly. "Don't be a fool. You won't quit. I know *you've* invested too much of your life into the job to throw it all away. And I've invested too much in you to allow it."

His narrow smile disappeared, his eyes hardened. "Like it or not, Mr. Dunliffe, I'm your guardian angel."

He stuck the pipe back into his mouth and walked away.

X V

SATURDAY

Keen's warrant card got him through passport control as he carried Jillie's carry-on bag to the terminal. They sat in the waiting area; the plane that would carry her home gleamed outside the huge plate-glass windows. She looked tired.

"I got your ticket upgraded to business. Sorry it's not first."

"I've never flown business class before. Should be fun."

Silence.

"Would you like a coffee? Or tea?"

"No, thank you," she said. "Have one if you like."

"I'm fine."

Silence.

Their conversation had been restricted to such innocuous exchanges ever since he had picked her up from Mrs. Flute's and driven in near total silence to Heathrow. If he didn't say something soon, it would be too late.

"Jillie . . ." She looked at him, her eyes so impassive he faltered. "This weren't how I wanted it to turn out."

"I got what I wanted," she said bluntly. "The truth."

The waiting area slowly filled with other passengers. A young mother ignored her two boisterous children and the glares of other passengers they were disturbing. Businessmen in carbon-copy business suits rattled their pages of the *Wall Street Journal* and the *Economist* self-importantly. The flight crew strolled past with their matching wheeled luggage, punching in a code to allow them onto the plane.

"Lies," she said, her voice sad. "So many lies."

"I'm sorry—"

"Don't be. I lied to you, you lied to me. Everybody lied to everybody." She smiled at him, but there was little emotion behind it. "And all with the best of intentions. Even Martin, in his crazy way." She looked away. "I've been thinking about why people tell lies. They aren't usually trying to hurt anyone; it's to protect what you love; your friends, your family. Your country, the principles you believe in, all good reasons. I'm not sure what the lesson is, except that maybe truth is overrated. '*Et ars arte deludatur.*' Deceive the deceivers. Saint Bernard."

Baffled, he said, "The one with the dogs and the brandy kegs?"

This time when she smiled at him, there was a definite warmth that gave him a shimmer of hope. "That came later. No, Bernard of Clairvaux is more my field, twelfth century. Pope maker and king breaker. He hated women, excommunicated anybody who disagreed with him, preached killing anyone who wasn't Christian. He was so convinced he was right that he would do anything to get his own way, lie, cheat, steal, bully, kill. The ends justified the means." She laughed, a barely audible exhalation. "They made him a saint."

"Don't sound all that saintly to me."

"Funny how fashions in morality change, isn't it?"

Or don't, Keen thought. He sat with his elbows on his knees, staring at his feet. "What will you do when you get home?"

"I don't know. Classes don't start for another month. Read some books, go out for pizza and a movie with Karen before she goes back to Denver. Tell her lies," she said bitterly. Bright sunlight gleamed off the plane and streaked the windows white. The light shimmered on the downy curve of her cheek like gold fire. "Tell her Chris drowned by accident in a pond. Because the truth doesn't matter, does it?"

There didn't seem much to say to this, either, and after a moment, he bowed his head again over his clasped hands.

"Good afternoon, British Air would like to welcome all passengers flying to Los Angeles today on our nonstop flight three fifty." The desk steward's practiced voice echoed around the lounge. "First class and business passengers and those traveling with small children are invited to board the aircraft at this time . . ."

"This is it," she said as they stood. She shouldered her carry-on and fumbled with her ticket. As they faced each other, he was tempted to kiss her. Instead, he took her arm and walked with her, waiting in the queue until she could hand the attendant her boarding pass. She walked through the barrier to follow the long corridor to the plane. His stomach fluttered as he realized this was his last chance.

"Jillie . . ."

She paused, looking back expectantly.

He wanted to say, *Don't go. Don't leave.*

He wanted to say, *I love you, stay with me.*

He said, "Have a safe journey home."

She smiled, nodded, and was gone.

He didn't stay to watch her plane take off.

PART THREE

Winter

EPILOGUE

His suspension lasted longer than he'd anticipated, although he continued to draw his full pay. He'd gone into his disciplinary hearing and waived the offer of legal counsel against the advice of an annoyed Police Federation representative. If they wanted him, they'd have him; that's just the way the system worked. He stood before the stone-faced tribunal and answered with brutal honesty every question put to him for each charge of offenses under the discipline code made against him. Then he'd gone home to wait for their decision.

The moors blazed brilliant amethyst before the icy breath of winter killed the heather. Chill winds rattled the windows of his house. He read all the books he'd meant to read for years. He repaired the little things he'd left wanting done round the house, cleared out all the rubbish from the barn. When he ran out of make-work, he took long walks in the hills, shoulders hunched against the cold, hands deep in the pockets of his thick anorak. He took the train to London once a month to see his boys, but he never rang Phil and never talked about much with Laura. She must have noted the difference in him, the silence that had nothing to do with serenity, but she never brought it up.

Sometimes he watched the news: A DS with seventeen years of exemplary service gets the sack and nine months in prison for stealing two hundred pounds. The Marquess of Bristol gets two years' probation for possession of heroin. A WPC gets the Queen's Commendation for Bravery after being stabbed dead through the heart during a burglary arrest.

A LibDem candidate forced to pull out of a by-election after being discredited by smear stories planted by the Attack Unit is cleared of all fraud allegations. One of their own moles is caught stealing the Attack Unit's Excaliber dirty-tricks files. Felix Schaefer, newly appointed QC, is to defend council officers in a vote-rigging scandal. Crassfield & Robyns goes into receivership, the company millions of pounds in debt.

A cat named Fudge survives six weeks trapped inside a metal pipe in a paint factory. A rare Siberian Blythe's pipit flies seven thousand miles to Suffolk where it is promptly eaten by a local kestrel.

He wasn't there; it wasn't real. Mostly he dozed as the television muttered its endless nonsense at him.

Once or twice, he had dinner with Derek and Joan, discussed the disturbing reccurence of scrapie disease, and new EU regulations on compulsory dipping for sheep scab. But mostly he ate alone, cooking dull meals and drinking exactly one tin of lager with it. When sleet began falling like needles of ice, he built roaring wood fires and stared into the flames, Thomas a ball of fur warming his lap. Sometimes, he even thought about his life. But not often. He tried hard not to think too much.

Every evening, very late, he brought the phone in and set it beside him in the lounge. He could calculate the time zone difference in seconds. Occasionally his hand settled on the handset, lingering long enough to warm it. Two or three times he picked it up to listen to the hum of an empty line. Once, he punched the first three numbers he knew by heart. He had listened curiously to the tones before hanging up.

He never rang her.

Finally, word came for him to return to work.

Early on a brittlely cold Monday, Keen drove down to the village of Gildersome where a construction crew was starting up the day's work on a half-built duplex. He pulled the Vauxhall up to the curb, shut off the motor, and simply sat there, watching. Men in safety hats and dirty jeans roughhoused with their mates shivering in down vests over work overalls. Other men strapped on leather belts laden with tools and climbed about on the framing of what would eventually become another neat brick home like all the others along the curved street. Hammers banged out an uneven rhythm and the squeal of an electric saw disturbed the raw morning air.

A few glanced in his direction, but he was a stranger, a subject of only momentary curiosity. Then one of them, a tall, lanky man with a shaggy ponytail, walked to the edge of the concrete slab, a pronounced limp in his right leg. He set down a large tool chest and squinted uncertainly in the morning sunlight.

Keen looked down at his knuckles clenched on the steering wheel. He still had time to start the engine and pull away. He was shaking, his mouth dry. His heart thumped high in his chest, the interior of the car too warm. He got out, closed the door, and stood by the car to face the astonished man staring back at him.

"Hello, Clive."

Leaves turned from green to brown and fell within a week, almost no blaze of the autumn color Jillie longed for. Wind hurtling down the Columbia Gorge rudely stripped away the remaining dead leaves, leaving the trees stark naked. The weatherman warned of a cold front moving in from the coast that would likely bring in another typical Pacific Northwest storm, which meant more traffic accidents from cars skidding on black ice and the inevitable power outages as electrical lines sagged and snapped under the weight of the freezing rain.

Great way to start the week.

Inside the lecture hall, the furnace pumped out stultifying heat until the fifty or so students lounged half-asleep in front of her. To make it worse, the lights were dimmed to make her lecture notes visible on the overhead projector behind her.

"But by the turn of the eleventh century," Jillie was saying, "we find the concept of law itself undergoing drastic revisions. In a culture based on an agricultural economy, and largely controlled by nobles over their serfs, judicial proof too often was a matter of unreliable luck in deciding trials. Compurgations—"

Next to a capital *A,* she wrote the word with a wax pencil onto the heated top of her projector. Melting wax duplicated it on the screen behind her in two-foot high letters. Fifty pens scribbled it into fifty notebooks.

"—the clearing of an accused person by the oaths of others risking God's wrath if they lied as proof of innocence . . ." The light hurt her eyes as she printed a capital *B* and wrote: "trial by ordeal." "The clearing of an accused person by either the accused or someone else championing his or her innocence in an armed battle—"

Fifty pens scrabbled like the claws of fifty little mice. Peering out into the darkened room, she tried to make out the faces of her students. With their heads bent over open notebooks, she could see only shadows.

"—were legal methods too rigid and too easily abused when being applied to an economy based on commerce rather than agriculture." She cranked the roll of plastic to give herself more room to write. "New sets of laws had to be created to manage this changing economy. The *ius mercatorum"*—scribble, scribble—"regulating commercial rights at fairs and markets can be seen already forming by the beginning of the eleventh century. Legal proof now had to be provided by eyewitnesses before a magistrate's court. Fines and sentences, usually of corporal punishment rather than by imprisonment, were being codified not only for civil offenses such as murder and theft, but for an entire business law regulating debts, liens, property rights, and mortgages . . ."

What the hell was she doing here?

The question hit her so abruptly it took her breath away. She gazed openmouthed at the shadows in the dark scribbling, scribbling, scribbling. She swallowed hard, and groped through her notes.

"The . . . ah . . . the system of enforcement of these laws was likewise undergoing radical change. There was no . . . no police system for law enforcement as such, not as we know it in the modern sense. Within the home, the husband exercised the *ius corrigendi"*—scribble, scribble—"while outside the home, law was regulated by either secular and ecclesiastical courts"—scribble, scribble—"often coming into conflict with each other, the most spectacular example of which was, of course, Henry the Second's conflict with the Archbishop of Canterbury, Thomas à Becket . . ."

Memorize those names, eat those dates, choke down those bits and pieces of arcane Latin, then barf it up on next week's test and forget it all the week after. She was useless, teaching useless things to useless people. The sheer absurdity of what she did for a living made her want to laugh.

She became distantly aware of staring blindly out over the darkened auditorium. Then, jolted by the silence, she focused on incurious faces in the gloom looking up at her patiently. What the hell are you all doing here? Blinking rapidly, she glanced at her notes in panic. She couldn't find her place.

Silence gave way to whispers. She had another half hour to go and for the life of her couldn't imagine what she would say to any of these dull, indifferent students who didn't want to be here. She didn't want to be here, either, year after year of endless scribbles.

"Chapters five and six by Wednesday." She stacked her books on her notes and carried them out into the cold wind rolling shriveled brown leaves along the abandoned campus commons. Her toes ached in her thin-soled shoes by the time she'd reached her office, a tiny cubicle so small the only window was the pane of glass in the door. She sat at her desk, staring at the charts of classes and time schedules and notes in her own useless scribbles which had seemed so important when she'd made them. Picking up her phone, she dialed Lena's extension.

"Hi, it's Jillie. You busy?"

Lena's office was three times the size of her own, still cramped with bookshelves and filing cabinets. They sat together as Lena poured two cups of mint tea out of her huge chrome thermos.

"Lena, am I going to make tenure this year?"

Lena harrumphed her laugh. "You'll quit if you don't?"

"Yes. I think I will."

It was her seriousness that surprised her boss. They sipped their tea in silence.

"Probably not," Lena admitted. "It's nothing personal. Your work is excellent and you certainly deserve tenure. But with student enrollment down, the college having to economize . . ." She shrugged her regret. "Jillie, don't you think this might be an overreaction? It's been a rough year for you. Don't do anything rash; give yourself a little more time and I'm sure things will work out . . ."

"Lena . . ." She didn't know how to explain. "I'm suffocating."

A discerning smile turned the older woman's face soft. "Ah-hah. You're having a midlife career crisis."

"I honestly don't know. I just can't stay here."

"Without tenure, there's no guarantee you'll have a job when you decide to come back, you understand."

"I'm aware of that."

Lena digested this before she nodded. "What will you do?"

Go back to England, she wanted to say. Go stark raving out of my mind. Go anywhere but here. "I don't know."

"Will you at least finish out the semester?"

Jillie nodded, although she didn't think she would.

Lena sighed. "You're a good teacher, and I'll hate to lose you."

By the time she got back to her own office, a weight had lifted from her shoulders. She stripped the corkboard over her desk, crumpling all those useless scribbles and dropping them one by one into the trash can. As she gathered her research books to return to the library, she uncovered *The Life and Works of Alexander de Sancto Albano* and stared at it for a long moment.

It didn't take much. A bit of red fingernail polish painting in false numbers on the spine, a bit of tape over it once the polish had dried, despoiling the edges of the pages with her own rubber stamp—CASCADE PACIFIC UNIVERSITY—and she had created yet another ordinary library book. Only this one would have no Dewey decimal entry in the computer catalogue reference.

Jillie knew it might be decades before anyone even realized it was there. Maybe it would show up in an inventory, and someone would wonder how it slipped through the cracks. Then they'd shrug, give it a proper entry, and put it back on the shelf where it could linger, forgotten and anonymous, forever.

Before she left for the day, she carried it into the restricted access stacks of the research library, walking along the tall shelves until she found the right spot. Gently pushing books aside to make room, she slid Alexander Nequam onto the shelf. Her fingers caressed the title in a silent, final goodbye to so much she couldn't have even begun to explain. Then she walked away, letting it vanish into obscurity.

Tom Flaxton slumped over his desk, phone jammed between his head and shoulder in a twisted position that made Keen's neck ache just to look at it. "That is correct, madam," he was repeating in a weary voice. "The lollipop ladies are supposed to be there only for the schoolchildren. However, we— That's true, but—" Even from this distance, Keen could hear the shrill, tinny voice leaking from the receiver. Flaxton sighed.

Keen sorted through the stack of memos and letters that had been fruitful and multiplied during his absence, tossing most of them into the dustbin with no more than a cursory glance. Then he stopped at a postcard of a pretty hotel on the coast of Dieppe, drenched in flowers and sunshine. He turned it over and read:

Four days in France, poured down buckets nonstop, worst weather in a decade, we never once left this lousy hotel. Just stayed in bed all day and all night. Absolute paradise! Cheers, Phil.

He smiled and propped it against his in-basket. He picked up a small envelope with the address handwritten and used the barrel of his mechanical pencil to rip open the flap. The card inside had an embossed drawing of lilies on the front.

Flaxton had finished a file and tossed it into his out-bin. He rolled his eyes ruefully at Keen and changed ears. "I do believe that even when the light is green, it is still illegal to run down old dears with Zimmer frames . . ."

Darryl Guiscoigne had died.

It somehow touched him that, for whatever reason, someone had made sure he had been notified. The date of his death and the cremation had been printed on the card, along with a request that donations be sent to GLASS. On a hunch, he compared their address with where the envelope had been franked.

Flaxton had another file open, sorting through his Filofax for a telephone number. He found it, jotting that down on the file. "What I'm trying to explain," he was saying patiently at the same time, "is that supervision of the lollipop people is no longer overseen by the police. I suggest you call your local council . . . Madam, they are supposed to tell us what to do, we don't tell them what to do."

By the way Flaxton suddenly straightened in his chair, his smile slowly broadening, Keen knew he was being thoroughly abused. It must have been quite a string of invective for it was several seconds before Flaxton said cheerfully, "And a very good day to you, too, madam!" His eyes twinkled as he let the handset drop from a height of several inches into the cradle.

"Good Lord," he said with a laugh, "what sorry little lives some people must lead. I'm looking for a twelve-year-old runaway drug addict who's the only witness to her mother's getting her throat slashed, and this woman's in a tizzy because a couple of geriatric pensioners can't get out of the way of her friggin' BMW quick enough!"

"Such is life in the fast lane," Terry Dales said.

"And just what the hell does 'contumelious' mean, anyway?"

"It's a fancy word for 'bloody cheek,'" Keen said, smiling, as he wrote out a check for twenty pounds to the Gay and Lesbian AIDS Support Society.

"Huh." Flaxton jotted it down. "Con . . . tum . . . elious. That's good, have to remember it. Love to be able to work that into a report, I would."

Keen was still smiling when Daheny came looking for him. "Davis would like a word, when you have a moment."

The chief inspector was gazing out the window, his back to Keen as he knocked on the open door. "You were wanting to see me, sir?"

Graeme turned, unsmiling, a bad sign. "Come in, Keen, and shut the door." That confirmed it, and Keen's heart sank. He sat in the plastic chair in front of Graeme's desk while the CIO sat down and frowned at his clasped hands. "Having any trouble getting back into the job?"

Four months' suspension had been trouble enough, Keen didn't want to be asking for any more. "No, sir, no trouble at all."

"I thought it best if you heard it first before the word got round," Graeme said to his hands. "Roger Osborne is retiring end of this year." He looked up. "The job goes to Mullard."

Passed over again. That he wasn't to make inspector was hardly unexpected, but that it was Nigel who would, made the news all the more wrenching. "Thank you for telling me." He exhaled against his disappointment, tried to smile and failed.

"I'm sorry, Keen." Graeme leaned back in his chair. "The fact is, I wanted you but I couldn't justify it. Not this time." He slapped his desk with open-palmed frustration. "What were you thinking, going off on an inquiry on your own? The end result: several complaints for criminal damage, another for assault, a wrongly accused suspect paralyzed, and a nonnational injured, while compromising another officer with his own nick."

Keen felt the muscle in his jaw twitching. It wouldn't do any good to correct Davis, or to protest. The truth didn't matter.

"You've embarrassed too many people in Home Office who can do you harm. It doesn't matter whether what you were trying to do was right or wrong, no one is ever going to thank you for grassing up your own, you do understand that?"

"Yes, sir." *The system isn't kind on idealistic policemen,* McCraig had said. "If that would be all?"

Graeme twisted in his chair to stare out the window of his office, springs squeaking. "No, that is not all."

Keen's anger flared, and he decided that if there were going to be any disciplinary reaction, he would pack in the job and to hell with it. For a brief, almost happy moment, he tried to envision what life might be like, in faraway Oregon . . .

Then Graeme said, "You've made enemies, Keen, but it seems you've also made a few friends. The chief constable's taken a personal interest in you. You're being transferred to CID, starting next Monday."

Under Nigel Mullard? "Should be interesting."

Davis understood what he meant. "I don't want 'interesting,' " he warned. "I want you to do the job the way you're supposed to, good and proper, and I'll expect the same from Nigel. I want no horseshit from either one of you."

McCraig had been right. As much as he might hate the job, hate what it had become, four months of waiting out a seemingly eternal suspension had taught him well; he had nothing else, had invested too much of his life to walk away from it all now. And, if he was honest, doing the job the way he was supposed to, good and proper, was all he had ever wanted to do in the first place.

"Understood, sir."

"Good. That's all."

On his way to lunch, he ran into Jasmine Farrell. She gave him a look more appropriate if someone in his family had just died. "I'm so sorry, Keen. You made sergeant long before he did, it should've gone to you by rights."

Word had gotten round damned fast.

"Nigel deserves that promotion just as much."

"No he don't—"

"Yes," he insisted. "He does. And we're all going to do our best to work together. Right?"

She frowned, unconvinced. "If you say so. Anyway, I am glad you're back. In CID, I mean."

"Thanks." He hesitated, then said quietly, "There's something else I did want to ask you about . . ."

"Sure." She waited with a puzzled half-smile as he struggled to find the right way to put the question.

"How do you do it, you and Stan? With him always off on a plane?"

And because everyone in the station knew everybody else's business, which was sometimes uncomfortable and sometimes useful but always an occupational hazard, she understood the unspoken and unspeakable ramifications, knew exactly what he was asking.

"It isn't easy, love," she said with more compassion than he'd expected. "I could hand you all that rubbish about true love conquering all, abstinence makes the heart grow fonder, and that's not what you're wanting to know, now, is it?"

"Not really, no."

"The truth is, we just do it. We don't waste time moaning about how impossible all the obstacles are. And we take risks other people don't think about, work around screwed-up plans because there's not enough time as it is not to. We have something a lot of people don't, and he's worth all the bother."

He was listening with his head bowed like an obstinate schoolboy trying his best to learn a particularly difficult lesson.

"Listen, Keen," she said, her voice lowered confidentially. "The only thing I am sure of is that we all need more in life than this sorry job. So if you love the lady, hell, even if you aren't sure, no one will shoot you for making a telephone call."

He looked up at her sharply. She patted him on the arm consolingly, but her wink was mischievous. "Go on. Make a bloody fool of yourself. Some women find that irresistibly charming."

The telephone woke Jillie out of a dreamless sleep, the first decent night's rest she'd had in a long time. Her eyes flew open in the dark, disoriented. Outside, freezing rain had encrusted the earth, dampening any normal sounds. In the hush, ice-coated spikes of dead grass crackled oddly like the sound of frying bacon.

The phone rang again. She glanced at the alarm clock on the bedside table, glowing red numerals: 4:27 A.M. Jesus Christ, who in the hell could be calling at this ungodly hour? She didn't notice her reaction was one of annoyance rather than fear.

Throwing back the covers, she gasped at the shock of cold air. She grabbed her thin bathrobe from the end of the bed as her bare feet searched for her slippers in the dark, the floor glacial. She gave up, the phone in the living room still ringing insistently, and scrambled for it in the dark, not bothering to turn on the lights. She snatched up the receiver, shivering, her teeth chattering uncontrollably. Outside, droplets of supercold rain hammered against the window, crusting instantly to ice. Streetlights wavered through its fairy twinkling.

"Hello?" she demanded irritably. Then both hands cradled the phone as she sank onto the sofa, suddenly feeling very warm after all.

"Oh, it's you . . ."

Keen slogged through his files with an odd sense of dislocation. As if he'd never been suspended, never gone to London. His half-empty mug made another brown ring on the stack of logbooks on his desk, the coffee tepid. He glanced up to see Glen still hunched over his elbows with his phone against one ear and a finger stabbed into the other, seemingly eternal. Nothing had worked out quite the way he might have wanted, but all in all, he felt at peace with himself. Oh, no doubt Mullard would be in to gloat soon, and Clive hadn't exactly welcomed him with open arms. But neither had he broken Keen's nose; their meeting had been cautiously amiable.

Then he'd only made a moderate fool of himself, his charm apparently less than irresistible as Jillie's reaction had been warm if indecisive. Maybe something would come of it, maybe not, but he was willing to give it a try. He had hope again.

And by next week, someone else would be sitting at this desk, swimming against the relentless tide of paper. Thank God, he thought as a PC dumped another armful of files on his desk.

Ben Felson punctured the afternoon calm, storming into the detectives' room dripping wet and incensed. "Bloody hell! Jesus, bloody hell! Look at me!"

Terry turned around, then screwed up his nose in surprise. *"Phwew!"* He clamped a hand over his face.

The stench hit Keen a few seconds later. "What happened?"

"Kellett picked this bloke up on a D and D, right? He's fucking legless, can't hardly stand upright, but he's been making a nuisance of himself throwing empty bottles at Barclay's Bank all morning. Kellett puts him in the car, no trouble, we get him into the charge room, searched and registered and all, and just before we pop him in a cell, he starts gobbin' off, sayin' he wants to make a bloody statement."

Keen had one hand over his nose and mouth as well now, trying vainly to breathe without inhaling as the luckless detective sergeant stripped off his tie and sodden shirt. Terry was doing his best to stand downwind without much success.

"He's in no condition to be interviewed, but I say, 'righto, love, what about?', and he starts in wanting to cough it for a multiple homicide. I know damned well he hasn't done no multiple homicide but he's getting stroppy, so I think, fine. We'll get him set down with a tape recorder, let him babble his DT fantasies before he passes out, and then we'll all be happy. We get it set up and him sat down, I'm on the other side of the table with the tape going, and I say . . ."

Ben paused, his shirt off and belt undone, his voice altered for theatrical effect, " 'The tape is now running, Mr. Alswick, sir. What exactly is it you wished to make a statement about?' And he goes, 'This,' and fucking throws up all over the tape recorder! It were like a bloody fire hydrant, he's sitting there laughing his head off and spewing like that fat bloke in the Monty Python film. I can't believe anybody could have that much puke in them!"

Kellett appeared in the doorway, trying unsuccessfully to keep the amusement off his face. "You got it in your hair, Sarge."

"I know I've got it in my hair, damn it!" Ben screamed at him. "And you weren't of no bloody use at all, were you!"

Unable to help himself, Keen started to laugh behind his hand still clamped to his face. Terry's shoulders were also shaking. "You should have washed up a bit in the gent's first, Ben," Keen said, speaking through his fingers.

The detective stopped, furious. "I *did*! You should've seen me before!" He looked down the front of his jeans in horror and wailed, "It's gone down me trousers!" He grabbed his gym sweats from his locker and glared at Keen. "These are brand-new Levi's 501s. The department damn well better pick up the bill for my dry cleaning."

He stormed off, still swearing, Kellett snorting back laughter in his wake. A door slammed, and the silence returned, the smell slowly fading. But not fast enough. Terry stood up languidly.

"You know," he said, "I might have seen a can of that flowery aerosol spray up in the personnel office. Think I might just go have a look-see."

"Excellent idea," Keen said.

Terry paused in the doorway, looking at Keen with a lopsided grin. "Never a dull moment round here, aye? Welcome back, Keen."

"It's lovely to be back."

He meant every word of it.